Peter Lovesey was born in Middlesex and studied at Hampton Grammar School and Reading University, where he met his wife Jax. He won a competition with his first crime fiction novel, *Wobble to Death*, and has never looked back, with his numerous books winning and being short-listed for nearly all the prizes in the international crime writing world. He was Chairman of the Crime Writers' Association and has been presented with Lifetime Achievement awards both in the UK and the US.

www.peterlovesey.com

There is only one Peter Lovesey

'Peter Lovesey has an extraordinary talent for picking up the conventions of the classic English detective novel and delivering them with an entirely contemporary twist'

Val McDermid

'A stunning tale of the macabre and the mundane'

Publishers Weekly

'Brilliant is the only word for veteran Peter Lovesey's latest venture into the macabre . . . A whip-crack pace, gasps all the way, and yet another winner for Lovesey'

Scotland on Sunday

'Absolutely riveting . . . I read *The False Inspector Dew* because I couldn't resist it and now I wish I'd saved it for the weekend. He's such a stylish, lucid writer, and wickedly clever as well, with a wonderful knack of springing really astonishing surprises . . . A masterpiece. I defy anyone to foresee the outcome'

Ruth Rendell

'Brilliant . . . stunning'

Evening Standard

'One of the best mysteries ever written, one that opens up new possibilities for the genre' *Dictionary of Literary Biography*

'Tremendously good. There are a fair number of good crime novels 'you can't put down'; but there are very few

Peter
LOVESEY

DIAMOND
SOLITAIRE

sphere

SPHERE

First published in Great Britain in 1992 by Little, Brown
Published in paperback in 1996 by Warner Futura
This edition published in 2014 by Sphere

A CIP catalogue record for this book
is available from the British Library.

ISBN 978-0-7515-5367-3

Typeset in ITC New Baskerville Std by Palimpsest Book Production Limited,
Falkirk, Stirlingshire
Printed and bound in Great Britain by Clays Ltd, St Ives plc

Papers used by Sphere are from well-managed forests
and other responsible sources.

MIX
Paper from
responsible sources
FSC® C104740

Sphere
An imprint of
Little, Brown Book Group
100 Victoria Embankment
London EC4Y 0DY

An Hachette UK Company
www.hachette.co.uk

www.littlebrown.co.uk

DIAMOND SOLITAIRE

1

An alert shattered the silence in Harrods, a piercing, continuous note. The guard on duty in the security control room, Lionel Kenton, drew himself up in his chair. His hands went to his neck and tightened the knot in his tie. On the control panel in front of him, one of the light-emitting diodes, a red one, was blinking. If the system was functioning properly, someone – or something – had triggered a sensor on the seventh floor. He pressed a control that triggered the video-surveillance for that floor. Nothing moved on the monitors.

Kenton was the senior security guard that night. He was so senior that he had a shelf above the radiator for his exclusive use. On it were framed photos of his wife, two daughters, the Pope and Catherine Deneuve; an ebony elephant; and a cassette rack of opera tapes. Puccini kept him alert through the night, he told anyone so philistine as to question opera in the control room. *None shall sleep.* Listening to music was more responsible than reading a paper or a paperback. His eyes were alert to anything on the panel and his ears to any sound that clashed with the music.

He silenced Pavarotti and touched the button that gave him a direct line to Knightsbridge Police Station. They must already have received the alert electronically.

He identified himself and said, 'Intruder alert. I'm getting a signal from the seventh floor. Furniture. Section nine. Nothing on screen.'

'Message received 2247 hours.'

'Someone *is* coming?'

'It's automatic.'

Of course it was. He was betraying some nervousness. He tried another survey of the seventh floor. Nothing untoward was visible, but then he hadn't much faith in video surveillance. Every terrorist knows to keep out of range of a camera.

And he had to assume this was a terrorist.

Twenty-two night security officers were posted in various parts of the store. He put out a general alert and asked for a second check that all the elevators were switched off. The security doors between sections were already in position and had been since the cleaners left. In the business of counter-terrorism nothing can be taken for granted, but really it wasn't feasible to break into Harrods. The intruder – if one was up there – must have hidden when the store closed and remained out of sight. If so, someone's job was on the line. Someone who should have checked section nine. You weren't allowed one mistake in this line of work.

His second-in-command that night, George Bullen, burst in. He'd been patrolling when the alert sounded.

'Where's it from?'

'Seventh.'

'It bloody would be.'

The furniture department was high risk: a brute to patrol. Wardrobes, cupboards, chests of drawers and units of every description. The nightly check for devices was a wearisome chore. It was conceivable – but in no way excusable – that the guard on duty had been so bogged down opening

2

cupboards and peering into drawers that he'd missed someone lurking out of sight behind the damned things.

Another light flashed on the console and one of the monitors showed headlights entering the delivery bay. The police response couldn't be faulted. Kenton told Bullen to take over and went down to meet them.

Three patrol cars and two vans already. Marksmen and dog-handlers climbing out. More cars arriving, their flashing alarms giving an eerie, blue luminosity to the delivery bay. Kenton felt a flutter in his bowels. The police weren't going to vote him security man of the year if this emergency had been triggered by a blip in the system.

A plain-clothes officer stepped out of a car and ran across to him. 'You're . . .?'

'Kenton.'

'Senior man?'

He nodded.

'You put out the call?'

He admitted it, and his stomach lurched.

'Seventh floor?'

'Furniture department.'

'Points of access?'

'Two sets of stairs.'

'Only two?'

'The section is sealed off by security doors.'

'No lifts?'

'Switched off.'

'Any of your lads on the stairs?'

'Yes. That's routine. They'll be guarding the stairways above and below level seven.'

'Lead the way, then.'

Thirty or more uniformed officers, dog-handlers and men in plain clothes, several carrying guns, came with him as he set off at a run through the ground floor to the first stairway. A squad of a dozen or so peeled off and raced up that staircase while he led the remainder to the next.

Mounting seven floors was a fitness test for Lionel Kenton. He was relieved to be told to stop after six and a half, and even more relieved to find four of his own security staff in position as he'd claimed they would be. Now he had a chance to recover normal breathing while radio contact was made with the party on the other stairs.

'What's the layout here?'

Essentially the police marksmen wanted to know how much cover they could rely on. One of Kenton's team, a burly ex-CID officer called Diamond, gave a rapid rundown of the furniture display positioned nearest to the stairs. Peter Diamond was the man responsible tonight for this section. You poor bugger, thought Kenton. You look more sick than I feel.

A team of three marksmen went up the final flight. Others took up positions on the stairs. The rest moved down to the landing below.

This was the worst – waiting for the unknown, while others went up to deal with it.

Someone offered Kenton some chewing-gum and he took it gratefully.

Perhaps six nerve-racking minutes went by before there was a crackle on the senior policeman's radio and a voice reported, 'Negative so far.'

Two dogs and their handlers were sent up to help.

Another long interval of silence.

Security Officer Diamond was just to the left of Kenton. He had his hands clasped, the fingers interlaced as if in prayer, except that the fingernails were white with pressure.

The last dregs of Kenton's confidence were draining away when someone announced over the scratchy intercom, 'We've got your intruder.'

'Got him under restraint?' said the man in charge.

'Come and see.'

'You're sure he's the only one?'

'Positive.'

The tone was reassuring. Strangely so, as if the tension had lifted altogether. Police and security staff dashed up the stairs.

The seventh floor lights were fully on. The marksmen had converged on a section where armchairs and settees were displayed. But they weren't in the attitude of gunmen. They were lounging about as if at a wine and cheese party. Two were seated on the arms of chairs. There was no sign of anyone under arrest.

Suddenly cold with his own sweat, Kenton went over with the others. 'But you said you found someone?'

One of them flicked his eyes downwards, towards a sofa.

It was the kind of vast, black corduroy thing that an advertising executive would have in his outer office. At one end was a heap of scatter cushions, brilliant in colour. The face looking out from under the cushions was that of a small girl, her hair black and fringed, her eyes oriental in shape. Nothing else of her was visible.

Kenton stared in bewilderment.

'Ah, so,' said the senior policeman.

2

'You're sacking me.' Peter Diamond, the guard responsible for section nine on the night the child was found, spoke without rancour. 'I know the score.'

The score was heavily against him. He wasn't young. Forty-eight, according to his file. Married. Living in West Ken. No kids. An ex-policeman. He'd got to the rank of detective superintendent and then resigned from Avon and Somerset over some dispute with the Assistant Chief Constable. A misunderstanding, someone said, someone who knew someone. Diamond had been too proud to ask for his job back. After quitting the police, he'd taken a series of part-time jobs and finally moved to London and joined the Harrods team.

'I shouldn't say this, Peter,' the security director told him, 'but you're bloody unlucky. Your record here has been exemplary apart from this. You could have looked forward to a more senior post.'

'Rules are rules.'

'Unfortunately, yes. We'll do the best we can in the way of a reference, but, er . . .'

'. . . security jobs are out, right?' said Diamond. He was inscrutable. Fat men – and he was fat – often have faces that seem on the point of turning angry or amused. The trick is to guess which.

The director didn't mind exhibiting his own unease. He shook his head and spread his hands in an attitude of helplessness. 'Believe me, Peter, I feel sick to the stomach about this.'

'Spare me that.'

'I mean it. I'm not confident I would have spotted the kid myself. She was practically invisible under the cushions.'

'I lifted the cushions,' Diamond admitted.

'Oh?'

'She wasn't on that sofa when I did my round. I definitely checked. I always do. It's an obvious place to plant a device. The kid must have been somewhere else and got under them later.'

'How could you have missed her?'

'I reckon I took her for one of the cleaners' kids. They bring them in sometimes. Some of them are Vietnamese.'

'She's Japanese, I think.'

Diamond snapped out of his defeated mood. 'You *think*? Hasn't she been claimed?'

'Not yet.'

'Doesn't she know her name?'

'Hasn't spoken a word since she was found. Over at the nick, they spent the whole of today with a string of interpreters trying to coax her to say something. Not a syllable.'

'She isn't dumb, is she?'

'Apparently not, but she says nothing intelligible. There's almost no reaction from the child.'

'Deaf?'

'No. She reacts to sound. It's a mystery.'

'They'll have to go on TV with her. Someone will know her. A kid found in Harrods at night – it's just the sort of story the media pick up on.'

'No doubt.'

'You don't sound convinced.'

'I'm convinced, Peter, all too easily convinced. But there are other considerations, not least our reputation. I don't particularly want it broadcast that a little girl penetrated our security. If the press get on to you, I'd appreciate your not making any statements.'

'About security? I wouldn't.'

'Thank you.'

'But you can't muzzle the police. They have no interest in keeping the story confidential. It's going to break somewhere, and soon.'

A sigh from the director, followed by an uncomfortable silence.

'So when do I clear my locker?' Diamond asked. 'Right away?'

3

The priest looked into the widow's trusting eyes and rashly told her, 'It's not as if it's the end of the world.'

The words of comfort were spoken on a fine summer evening in the sitting-room of a country villa in Lombardy, between Milan and Cremona. Pastoral care, Father Faustini termed it. Ministering to the bereaved, the sacred obligation of a priest. True, the ministering in this instance had continued longer than was customary, actually into a second year. But Claudia Coppi, cruelly widowed at twenty-eight, was an exceptional case.

Giovanni, the husband, had been killed freakishly, struck by lightning on a football field. 'Why did it have to be my husband when twenty-one other players, the referee and two linesmen were out there?' Claudia demanded of the priest each time he came on a visit. 'Is that the Lord's will? My Giovanni, of all those men?'

Father Faustini always reminded Claudia that the Lord works in mysterious ways. She always gazed at him trustingly with her large, dark, expressive eyes (she had worked as a fashion model) and he always told her that it was a mistake to dwell on the past.

The priest and the young widow were seated on a padded cushion that extended around the perimeter of the sunken floor. As usual, Claudia had hospitably uncorked a Barolo, a plummy vintage from Mascarello, and there were cheese biscuits to nibble. The sun had just about sunk out of sight, but to have switched on electric lights on such an evening would have been churlish. The scent of stocks, heavy on the cooler air, reached them through the open patio doors. The villa had a fine garden, watered by a sprinkler system. Giovanni, not short of money – he'd made it to the top as a fashion photographer – had called in a landscape architect when the place was built. For Father Faustini, the remote location of the villa meant a three-mile trip on his moped, but he never complained. He was forty and in good health. A rugged man with tight, black curls and a thick moustache.

'You're doing so much better, now,' he remarked to the widow Coppi.

'It's window dressing, Father. Inside, I'm still very tense.'

'Really?' He frowned, and only partly out of concern for the tension she was under. It was a good thing the room had become so shadowy that his disquietude wouldn't be obvious to her.

'My usual problem,' she explained. 'Stress. It shows up in the muscles. I feel it in my shoulders, right across the top.'

'As before?'

'As before.'

There was a silence. Father Faustini was experiencing some tension, also.

Claudia said, 'Last week you really succeeded in loosening the muscles.'

'Really?' he said abstractedly.

'It was miraculous.'

He cleared his throat, unhappy with the choice of word.

She amended it to, 'Marvellous, then. Oh, the relief! I can't tell you how much better I felt.'

'Did it last?'

'For days, Father.' While he was absorbing that, she added plaintively, 'There's no one else I can ask.'

She made it sound like a plea for charity. Father Faustini sometimes fetched shopping for elderly members of his flock. He often collected medicine for their ailments. He'd been known to chop wood and cook soup for poor souls in trouble, so what was the difference in massaging Claudia Coppi's aching shoulders? Only that it set up conflicts within himself. Was it right to deny her Christian help because of his moral and spiritual frailty?

On the last two Friday evenings he had performed this service for her. Willingly he would have chopped wood instead, but the villa's central heating was oil-fired. He would have fetched shopping with alacrity, but she had a twice-weekly delivery from the best supermarket in Cremona. She had a gardener, a cook and a cleaner. What it came down to in practice was that the only assistance Father Faustini could render to Claudia Coppi was what she was suggesting. The poor young woman couldn't massage her own shoulders. Not well enough to remove muscular tension.

There was another factor that made him hesitate. Once a week in church he heard Claudia Coppi's confession, and lately – he wasn't certain how many times this had occurred, and didn't intend to make a calculation – she had admitted to impure thoughts, or carnal desires, or some such form of words. It wasn't his custom to ask for more details in the confessional once the commission of a sin was established, so he couldn't know for sure that there was a connection with his visits to the villa.

'I found something you could rub in, if you would,' she said.

He coughed nervously and crossed his legs. This was new in the routine. 'Embrocation?' he queried, striving to limit his thoughts to muscular treatment, remembering the over-powering reek of a certain brand favoured by footballers. The stuff brought tears to the eyes.

'More of a moisturiser really. It's better for my skin. Really smooth. Try.' She reached out and smeared some on the back of his hand.

He wiped it off immediately. 'It's scented.'

'There's a hint of musk,' she admitted. 'If you'd like to hold the pot, I'll just slip my blouse off.'

'That won't be necessary,' he quickly said.

'Father, it's silk. I don't want it marked.'

'No, no, *signora*, cover yourself up.'

'But I haven't unbuttoned yet.' She laughed and added, 'Is it as dark as all that?'

'I wasn't looking,' he said.

'That's all right. I've got my back to you anyway.'

As she was speaking he heard the blouse being slipped off her shoulders. Now he was in a real dilemma. She sounded so matter-of-fact, so nonchalant. By protesting, he was liable to inflate this into a moral crisis. It could appear as if he were letting himself be influenced by things she had said in the confessional.

'Not too much at once,' she cautioned. 'It goes a long way.'

He suppressed his misgivings, dipped in a finger and spread some over his palm.

Claudia's back was towards him, as she had claimed. He reached out and applied some of the moisturiser to the back of her neck.

She said, 'Oh dear, the straps are going to get in your way.'

'Not at all,' protested Father Faustini, but the brassière straps were tugged aside, regardless.

On the previous visits, he'd been persuaded to massage Claudia without using a liniment, through her T-shirt. This was a new experience. The contact with her flesh unsettled him more than he cared to admit. He traced the slope of her shoulders, feeling the warmth under his fingers. The smoothness was a revelation. When his hands cupped the round extremities of her shoulders he was compelled to pause.

She sighed and said, 'Bliss.'

In a moment he felt sufficiently in control to resume, spreading the moisturiser liberally across the shoulder-blades and up the spine to her neck. She had her head bowed so that her long, dark brown hair hung in front of her. He gave some attention to the deltoid muscles, gently isolating them, probing their form. In spite of what Claudia had said about tension, everything felt reasonably flexible to him, but he was the first to admit that he was no physiotherapist.

'Let me know if I'm causing any discomfort,' he told her.

'Quite the reverse,' she murmured. 'You have the most incredible hands.'

He continued to apply light pressure to the base of her neck until quite suddenly she raised her head and drew the hair back behind her shoulders.

'Enough?' he enquired. He hoped so. The movement of her hair across the backs of his hands had given him a physical sensation not to be encouraged in the priesthood.

But Claudia Coppi remained unsatisfied. She told him that there was still some tension at the tops of her arms.

'Here?'

'Yes. Oh, yes, just there. Do you mind if I lean back against you, Father? It's more comfortable.' She didn't wait for his answer.

The back of her head was on his chest, her hair against his cheek. In the same movement she placed her hands over his own and gripped them firmly. Then she pushed them downwards.

He hadn't discovered until now that she had altogether uncovered her breasts. She guided his hands over them. Exquisitely beautiful, utterly prohibited breasts offered for him to experience. For a few never-to-be-forgotten seconds of sin, Father Faustini accepted the offer. He held Claudia Coppi's forbidden fruits, passing his hands over and under and around them, thrilling to their fullness and their unmistakable state of arousal.

A monster of depravity.

With a supreme effort to banish fleshly thoughts, he blurted out the words, 'Lead us not into temptation,' and drew his hands away as if they were burned.

Tormented with shame, he stood up immediately and strode resolutely through the patio doors and around the side of the house without looking back. He didn't respond to Claudia Coppi's, 'Shall I see you next Saturday?' He knew he had to be out of that place and away.

He thought he heard her coming after him, probably still in her topless state. As swiftly as he could manage, he wheeled his moped out to the road, started it up and zoomed away.

'Fornicating fool,' he howled to himself above the engine's putt-putt. 'Weak-willed, degenerate, wanton, wicked, wretched, sex-crazed fellow. Miserable sinner.'

The little wheels bore him steadily along, his headlight

14

picking out the road, but he was barely conscious of the journey. His thoughts were all on the depravity of his conduct. A man of God, a priest behaving like some beast of the field, only worse, because he was blessed with a mind that was supposed to be capable of overcoming the baser instincts.

How will I answer for this on the Day of Judgement? he asked himself.

God be merciful unto me, a sinner.

Precisely at which stage of the journey he became aware of what was ahead of him is impossible to say. Certainly he must have travelled some distance before he was ready to submit to anything except the writhings of his tormented conscience. It had to be spectacular, and it was. Father Faustini stared ahead and saw a pillar of fire.

The night sky was alight above the Plain of Lombardy, fizzing with hundreds of brilliant fiery points. Their origin was a fiery column, perhaps three thousand metres away, and towering over the land. Emphatically this was not a natural fire, for it was more green than orange, bright emerald green, with flares of violet, blue and yellow leaping outwards. Father Faustini was seized with the conviction that the Day of Judgement was at hand. Otherwise he might have suspected that something had been added to the Barolo he had swallowed, because what he was seeing was psychedelic in its extraordinary combination of colours. He'd seen large fires before, and mammoth firework displays, but nothing remotely resembling this.

What else could a wretched sinner do in the hour of reckoning, but brake, dismount, go down on his knees and pray for forgiveness? He felt simultaneously panic-stricken and rocked with remorse, that this should happen on the very night he had transgressed, after a lifetime of blameless (or virtually blameless) service in the Church. He knelt on the turf at the roadside, his hands clasped in front of his anguished face, and cried, 'Forgive me, Father, for I have sinned.'

He couldn't discount the possibility that his lapse with Claudia Coppi was directly responsible for what was happening. By speculating that his few seconds' fondling of a pair of pretty breasts had hastened the end of the world, he may have been presumptuous, but he felt an ominous sense of cause and effect.

He sneaked another look around his clasped hands. The state of the sky remained just as awesome. Streaks of fire were leaping up like sky-rockets, leaving trails of sparks.

As yet there were no avenging angels to be seen, nor other apocalyptic phenomena. He heard no trumpets, but nothing would surprise him now.

Instead he saw two brilliant lights, so dazzling that they made his eyes ache. And immediately there came a low droning, becoming stronger. The source wasn't supernatural. A car, its headlights on full beam, was moving at high speed towards him along the road, from the direction of the pillar of fire. Father Faustini could understand people fleeing from the wrath to come, but he knew that they were deluding themselves. There could be no escape.

And so it proved.

The engine-note grew in volume and the lights intensified in brilliance. Ordinarily, Father Faustini would have waved to let the driver know that he was dazzled. But of course he wasn't mounted on his moped. He was on his knees at the side of the road. He'd abandoned the bike when he'd first seen the pillar of fire. Abandoned it where he had stopped, in the middle of the narrow road.

The car was racing towards it.

He clapped his hands to his head.

There simply wasn't time to drag the moped out of the way. He could only hope that the driver would spot the obstruction in time and steer to the side. It might be academic at this late stage in the history of the world whether an accident – even a fatal accident – mattered to anyone, but Father Faustini had always been safety-conscious and he couldn't bear the thought of being responsible for anyone's death.

In truth, the driver of the car would share some blame, for his speed was excessive.

What happened next was swift and devastating, yet Father Faustini saw it in the curious freeze-frame way that the brain has for coping with danger at high speed. The car bore down on the moped without any let-up in speed until the last split-second, when the driver must have seen what was in front of him. The rasp of tyre-rubber on the surface of the road as the brakes were applied made a sound like a siren's blare. The car veered left to avoid the moped, and succeeded. But it hit the curb, went out of control and ricocheted to the opposite side. Father Faustini registered that it was a large, powerful saloon. The white light from the headlamps swept out of his vision and was replaced by intense red as the car skidded past with its brake lights fully on. It mounted the curb and started up a bank of turf that bordered a field. The band of rear lights lifted and spun in an arc. The whole thing was turning over. It was thrown on its back not once, but three times, tons of metal bouncing like a toy, smashing through a fence and finally sliding on the roof across the ploughed earth.

One of the rear lights was still on. It went out in a spray of sparks. Smoke was rising from the wreck.

Father Faustini's legs felt about as capable of holding

him up as freshly cooked pasta, but he stumbled across to see if he could get anyone out before the entire thing caught fire.

The weight of the chassis had crushed the superstructure. The priest got on his knees beside the compressed slot that had once been the driver's window. There was a figure inside, the head skewed into an impossible angle. Too late for the last rites.

Round the other side was the passenger, another man, half on the turf. Literally. The other half, from the waist down, was still trapped inside. The halves were separated at the waist.

The priest crossed himself. A wave of nausea threatened, but it was vital to stay in control because the air reeked of raw petrol and the whole wreck was likely to turn into a fireball any second. Still troubled that someone might be alive and trapped inside, he lay on his stomach to try and get a sight of what had been the back seat. He needn't have troubled. There wasn't a centimetre of space between the torn upholstery and the impacted roof.

As he braced to get up, a sound like the rushing mighty wind of the Pentecost started somewhere to his right. The petrol had caught fire.

He sprang up and sprinted away. Behind him, there was a series of cracking sounds followed by an almighty bang that must have been the petrol tank exploding. By then, he was twenty metres away and flat to the earth.

He didn't move for a while. His nerves couldn't take any more. He actually sobbed a little. It was some time before he thought of saying a prayer. In his embattled mind, the car-crash had overtrumped the Day of Judgement.

Finally, he sat up. The wreckage was still on fire, but the worst of it was over. Filthy black smoke was taking over and the stench of burning rubber stung his throat and nostrils. He stared into the flames. The charred, mangled metal that remained barely resembled a vehicle.

Every muscle he possessed was trembling. With difficulty, he got to his feet and walked past the burning wreckage towards the moped, which still stood untouched in the centre of the road, a testimony to his stupidity and his responsibility for this tragedy.

Beyond, the night sky was still rent by the vast pillar of fire that had so distracted him. The colours were still unearthly in their brilliance and variety. Even so, Father Faustini was forced to reconsider whether it could really be Judgement Day. The shock of the car-crash had altered his perception. He couldn't explain the phenomenon. There had to be a reason for it, but he hadn't the energy left to supply one.

He got astride the moped, started up and rode off to report what had happened.

4

A Saturday evening performance in the Metropolitan Opera House, New York. Domingo and Freni in full voice, before a packed, enthralled house. The entombment scene was drawing to its climax. United in Verdi's tear-jerking *O terra addio*, the tragic lovers, Radames and Aida, embraced in the crypt, while the massive stone slabs that would bury them alive were lowered inch by agonizing inch. Off-stage, the priests and priestesses chanted their relentless chorus, and the unhappy Amneris prayed for Radames' eternal soul. There are moments in an opera when no one minds too much if people wriggle and sway in their seats, straining for a better view, or trying to bring relief to aching buttocks. But when *Aida* reaches its poignant finale, when the slave-girl is expiring in the arms of Radames, and the lights are slowly dimmed to signify the sealing of the tomb, the stillness in the auditorium is palpable, from the orchestra stalls right up to the sixth tier.

Or should be.

This evening in the Center Parterre, the most expensive seats in the Met, there was a disturbance. Of all things at this heart-rending moment, a series of electronic beeps shrilled above the singing, a call-signal considerably louder than the wristwatch alarms that are always going off in cinemas and theatres. Some philistine had brought his pager to the opera.

The most absorbed of the audience ignored the source of the sound, refusing to have their evening blighted. Not everyone was so forbearing.

'Jesus Christ – I don't believe this!' a man spoke up in the row immediately behind, regardless that he was adding to the disturbance. Others took up the protest with, 'Knock it off, will you?' and stronger advice.

In the third row, the source of the bleeps, a silver-haired man in black-framed bifocals, tugged aside his tuxedo, unhitched the pager from his belt and pressed a button that silenced it. The entire incident had lasted no more than six seconds, but it could not have been more unfortunately timed.

And now the curtain was down and the performers were taking applause, and in the Center Parterre as many eyes were on the man in the third row as on Domingo. Dagger thrusts of obloquy struck at the offender. Try as he did to ignore them by energetically applauding and focusing his eyes fixedly on the stage, he could expect no mercy from the offended patrons around him. New Yorkers are not noted for reticence.

'I know who I'd bury alive.'

'How do jerks like that get admitted?'

'I bought a ticket for a fucking opera, not a business conference.'

The jerk in question continued vigorously clapping through six or seven curtain calls, until the house lights were turned on. Then he turned to his companion, a stunning-looking, dark-haired woman at least twenty years younger than he, and attempted to engage her in such earnest conversation that the rest of New York was shut out.

She wasn't all that impressed. It was some consolation to those around as they got up and started to file out that the lady was unwilling to gloss over the lapse. In a short time, her voice was raised above his and snatches of the tongue-lashing she was giving him threatened to shake the chandeliers. '. . . never been so humiliated and if you think after this I'm going to tag along for dinner and a screw, forget it.'

Someone called out, 'Attagirl! Dump him!'

And that is what she did, flouncing off between the rows of seats, leaving her escort staring after her and shaking his head. He didn't attempt to follow. He remained seated, judiciously letting the people he'd upset get clear. And when everyone had filed out of his section of the auditorium, he took out the pager again and keyed in a set of numbers.

Having got something on the display, he delved into his breast pocket and, impervious to the surroundings, took out a cell-phone and pulled out a length of aerial.

'Sammy, were you trying to reach me, because if you were, you could have timed it better, my friend.' While listening, he settled deep in the seat and propped his feet over the row in front. 'The hell with that. I sure hope for your sake this item of news measures nine point nine on the Richter Scale.'

What he then heard was enough to cause visible disturbance in Manfred Flexner. He withdrew his feet from their perch. He crouched forward as if it might enable him to hear better. His free hand raked through his hair.

Six minutes later, shaking his head and trying to stay calm, he reeled out of the opera house into the plaza of the Lincoln Center and took some gulps of fresh air. At this time of night the esplanade was thick with sables and minks, the audiences from the ballet and the Philharmonic jostling the opera-goers in the scramble for taxis. Flexner had his chauffeur waiting across the street with the limousine, so he had no reason to rush, but he wasn't going home yet.

He stared into the floodlit fountain for a while. Inside the last half-hour he'd interrupted an opera, lost his companion and slipped forty points on the international stock markets. He needed a drink.

The world was not a happier place next morning. He watched the Alka-Seltzers fizzing in the glass on his desk and brooded on what might have been. Pharmaceuticals were Manny Flexner's business.

Pharmaceuticals.

And here he was relying on the product of a rival company. He'd worked all his life in the expectation one day of finding a market leader like Alka-Seltzer that would become a steady seller for the foreseeable future. His was the traditional story of a Lower East Side boy with a head for business who'd made some bucks driving taxis, lived frugally for a time and invested his earnings. Realizing, as all entrepreneurs do early in life, that you get nowhere using self-help and savings, he'd borrowed from the bank to buy a share in a small business supplying labels to pharmacies. When self-stick labels came in, he'd just about cornered the market, and made enough to borrow more cash and move into the supply side of pharmaceuticals. The sixties and seventies had been a prosperous time in the drugs industry. Manny Flexner had taken over a number of companies in the USA and expanded internationally, buying shrewdly into Europe and South America. One of the Manflex products, Kaprofix, a treatment for angina, had become a strong source of income, a steady seller throughout America and Europe.

23

The story had a downturn. The pharmaceuticals industry relies heavily on the development of new drugs; companies cannot survive without massive research programmes. In the early eighties, scientists working for Manflex had identified a new histamine antagonist with potential as a treatment for peptic ulcers. It was patented and given the proprietary name of Fidoxin. The potential market for anti-ulcer drugs is enormous. At that time, Smith Kline's Tagamet dominated the field with sales estimated at over a billion dollars. Glaxo were developing a rival product called Zantac that would eventually outsell every drug in the world. But Manny Flexner was in there and pitching.

The early research on Fidoxin was encouraging. Manflex invested hugely in studies and field trials designed to satisfy the federal panel that advised the Food and Drug Administration, for no drug can be marketed without the FDA seal of approval. By 1981, Manflex was set to beat its rivals in the race to a billion-dollar market. Then, at a late stage, long-term side-effects were discovered in patients taking Fidoxin. Almost every drug has unwanted effects, but the possibility of serious renal impairment is unacceptable. Reluctantly, Manny Flexner had cut his losses and abandoned the project.

Too much had been gambled on that one drug. Through the eighties Manny had been unwilling to sink so much into any research project. The recession in 1991 had hit Manflex harder than its rivals. Thanks mainly to the old standby, Kaprofix, the company still rated in the top ten in America, but had slipped from fourth to seventh. Or worse. Manny didn't care to check any more.

Today was the worst yet. He had the *Wall Street Journal* in front of him. Overnight, his stock had plummeted again in Tokyo and London. The reason?

'The biggest firework display in history is what they're calling it,' he told his Vice Chairman, Michael Leapman, throwing the paper to him. 'A twenty billion *lire* burn-up. The flames could be seen thirty kilometres south of Milan. How much is that, Michael?'

'About twenty miles.'

'The *lire*, for God's sake.'

'Not so bad as it sounds. Say seventeen million bucks.'

'Not so bad,' Manny repeated with irony. 'An entire plant goes up in smoke, a quarter of our Italian holding, and it's not so bad.'

'Insurance,' murmured Michael Leapman.

'Insurance takes care of plant and materials. There were research labs in that place. They were testing a drug for depression. Depression. I hope to God some of the stuff is left because I need some. Research is irreplaceable, and the market knows it. Do we have any news from Italy? Is it a total write-off?'

Leapman nodded. 'I spoke to Rico Villa an hour ago. The scene is a heap of white ash now.' He crossed the room to the drinks cabinet and took out the Scotch. 'Can I pour you one?'

Manny shook his head and indicated the Alka-Seltzer.

'Then you don't mind if I do?' Thirty-seven, six-foot two, and blond, Michael Leapman was less volatile than his boss. He was half Swedish. Supposedly the Swedish half kept him from throwing tantrums. He'd joined Manflex five years ago through no action of his own, when Flexner had bought the small company he managed in Detroit; Leapman had proved to be the only valuable acquisition from that take-over, a creative thinker with fine organisational skills. He'd developed a good rapport with his tough little boss. Within a year he'd been invited to join the board.

'Anyone died yet?' Manny enquired in a voice that expected nothing but bad news that day.

'Apparently not. Seven people were hospitalised, two of them firemen. They inhaled fumes. That's the size of it.'

'Environmental damage?'

Leapman raised an eyebrow. His boss wasn't known for his green sympathies.

'That could really put us in trouble,' Manny explained. 'Remember Seveso? The dioxin fumes? Wasn't that Italy? How many millions did the owners have to pay out in compensation?'

Leapman helped himself to a generous measure of Scotch. 'No poison fumes reported yet.'

The tension in Manny's face eased a little. He took off his glasses and wiped them with a tissue that he took from a Manflex dispenser.

'We can ride this,' Leapman said confidently. Providing reassurance was one of his most useful talents. 'Sure, it's going to bruise us. The markets will mark us down for a week or two, but we're big enough to absorb it. The Milan plant wasn't a huge moneymaker. Rico kept reminding us it was in need of modernisation.'

'I know, I know. We were going to inject some capital later in the year.'

'Now we can give priority to the two plants near Rome.'

Manny replaced his glasses and studied Leapman. 'You don't think we should rebuild in Milan?'

'In the present economic climate?' His tone said it all. Rebuilding was out.

'You're right. We should consolidate with what we have out there. We can sell the Milan site.' Having weighed the options, Manny seemed satisfied. 'What I want now is for someone to go to Italy and tidy up, sort out the staffing problems, salvage anything we can from this mess.' He hesitated, as if casting about for a name. 'Who do you think? Would you say David can handle it?'

'David?' The name wrongfooted Leapman. He was fully expecting this assignment for himself.

'My boy.'

'No question.' He knew better than to try and talk the boss out of handing the assignment to his son, whatever he privately thought. Young David Flexner – young, but by no stretch of imagination still a boy – conspicuously lacked his father's enthusiasm for the business world, yet Manny cherished the unlikely hope that he would make a contribution eventually. After four years in business school and three on the board of Manflex, David should have been ready for responsibility. In reality, all his energies went into amateur film-making.

Towards the end of the morning, the screens in the large office adjacent to Manny Flexner's were registering some improvement in the group's ratings. Taking its cue from Tokyo and London, Wall Street had over-reacted to the first news of the fire. Now the market was taking a more measured view. The Manflex group was showing a sharp fall, but it wasn't, after all, in dire trouble.

Manny exhibited his positiveness by treating his son to lunch in the four-star-listed Quilted Giraffe, in the arcade of the Sony Building on Madison and 55th Street. Freshness was a watchword there. Even the wine list came on a computer print-out to underline that it was updated each day. 'You know this place, Dave?'

'No.'

Manny was twice-divorced and lived alone. Technically alone, that is to say. In reality he had a string of women friends who took turns to join him for dinner in New York's top restaurants and afterwards passed the night in his house on the Upper East Side. So he knew where to eat well. And the diet had to be good to keep up his stamina. He was sixty-three.

But lunches were strictly for business.

'I recommend the salmon with sweet-hot mustard. Or the duck salad with sour cherries. No, try the salmon. It really is something. You heard about the burn-up in Milan?'

Clearly his son hadn't looked at the business section of whichever newspaper he read. David had gone past the stage of youthful rebellion. He was a grown-up rebel, with dyed blond hair that reached his shoulders. Blond hair looked wrong on a Jewish boy, in Manny's opinion. The dark green cord jacket David had put on was a concession to restaurant rules. He often attended Board meetings in a T-shirt.

Manny filled him in with the painful essentials and told him his plan for dealing with the Italian end of the problem.

'You want *me* to go there? That could be difficult, Pop,' David said at once. 'How soon?'

'Anything wrong with tonight?'

David smiled. His engaging smile was both an asset and a liability. 'You're not serious?'

'Totally serious. I have up to two hundred people without a job, unions to deal with— '

'Yes, but— '

'An insurance claim to file and for all I know, lawsuits pending. Things like this don't get sorted if you ignore them, David.'

'How about Rico Villa? He's there, and he speaks the language.'

Manny pulled a face and shrugged. 'Rico couldn't close a junior softball game.'

'You want me to fly out to Milan and wield the hatchet?'

'Just point out the facts to these people, that's all. Their workplace is a pile of ash now. There's no future in rebuilding it. If anyone is willing to transfer to Rome, fix it. Talk to the accountants about redundancy terms. We'll give the best deal we can. We're not ogres.'

David sighed. 'Pop, I can't just drop everything.'

Although Manny had expected this, he affected surprise. 'What are you saying, son?'

'I have commitments. I made promises to people. They depend on me.'

Manny gave him a penetrating stare. 'Do these commitments have anything remotely to do with Manflex?'

His son reddened. 'No, it's a film project. We have a schedule.'

'Uh huh.'

'I'm due on location in the Bronx Zoo.'

'Filming animals, huh? I thought you said you made promises to people.'

'I was talking about the crew.'

The waiter arrived a split-second before Manny was due to erupt. Father and son declared a truce while the gastronomic decisions were taken. David diplomatically elected to have the salmon his father had recommended. It would be no hardship. When they were alone again, Manny started on a different tack. 'Some of the best movies I ever saw were made in Italy.'

'Sure. The Italian cinema is up there among the best. Always was. *The Bicycle Thief. Death in Venice. The Garden of the Fitzi-Continis.*'

'*A Fistful of Dollars.*'

David gave a fair imitation of the sphinx. 'Ah – you mean spaghetti westerns.'

Manny nodded and said with largesse, 'You could get among those guys. Take a couple of weeks over this. Tidy up in Milan, my boy, and you have a free hand. Go to Venice. Is that a reasonable offer?'

Such altruism from a workaholic was worthy of a moment's breathless tribute, and got it.

Finally David confessed, 'I know you want me to step into your shoes some day, Pop, but I think I should tell you that the drugs industry bores the pants off me.'

'You're telling me nothing.'

'But you won't accept it.'

'Because you won't give the business a chance. Listen, Dave. It's the most challenging industry there is. You stay ahead of the game, or you die. It's all about new drugs and winning a major share of the market.'

'That much I understand,' David said flatly.

'One breakthrough, one new drug, can change your whole life. That's the buzz for me.'

'You mean it can change a sick person's life.'

'Naturally,' Manny said without hesitation. 'Only what's good for sick people is good for my balance sheet, too.'

He winked, and his son was forced to grin. The ethics may have been clouded, but the candour was irresistible.

'Research teams are like horses. You want to own as many as you can afford. Once in a while one of them comes in first. But you can never be complacent. When you *have* the drug, you still need government approval to market it.' Manny's eyes glittered at the challenge. He didn't smile much these days, but occasionally a look passed across his tired features, the look of a man who once picked winners, but seemed to have lost the knack. 'And in no time at all the patent runs out, so you have to find something new. I have teams working around the globe. Any moment they could find the cure for some life-threatening disease.'

David nodded. 'There was a strong R & D section in the Milan plant.'

Manny said with approval, 'You know more than you let on.'

'I guess you really believe I can handle this.'

'That's why I asked you, son.' He gestured to the wine waiter. When he'd chosen a good Bordeaux, he told his son, 'This trouble in Italy has gotten to me. I always believed that someone up there was on my side. You know what I mean? Maybe I should think of stepping down.'

'Pop, that's nuts, and you know it. Who else could run the show?' Then David's eyes locked with his father's penetrating gaze. 'Oh, no. It's not my scene at all. I keep telling you I'm not even sure that I believe in it. If it was just a matter of making drugs to help sick people, okay. But you and I know that it isn't. It's about public relations, keeping on the good side of politicians and bankers. Thinking of the bottom line.'

'Tell me a business that doesn't. This is the world we live in, David.'

'Yes, but the profits aren't in drugs that cure people. Take arthritis. If we found something to stop it, we'd lose a prime market, so we keep developing drugs to deaden the pain instead. They're not much different from aspirin, only fifty times more expensive. How many millions are being spent right now on me-too arthritis treatments?'

Manny didn't answer. However, he noted with approval his son's use of the trade jargon. A 'me-too' drug was an imitation, slightly reconstituted to get around the patent legislation. There were more than thirty me-toos for the treatment of arthritis.

31

David was becoming angry. 'Yet how much is invested in research into sickle-cell anaemia? It happens to be concentrated in Third World countries, so it won't yield much of a profit.'

'I was idealistic when I was your age,' said Manny.

'And now you're going to tell me you live in the real world, but you don't, Pop. Until something like AIDS forces itself on your attention, you don't want to know about the real world. I don't mean you personally. I'm talking about the industry.'

'Come on, the industry was quick enough in responding to AIDS. Wellcome had Retrovir licensed for use in record time.'

'Yes, and hyped their share price by two hundred and fifty per cent.'

Manny shrugged. 'Market forces. Wellcome came up first with the wonderdrug.'

David spread his hands to show that his point was proved.

The waiter approached and poured some wine for Manny to sample. After he'd given it the nod, Manny said slyly to his son, 'You know more than you sometimes let on. When you become chairman, you'll be God. You can try injecting some ethics into the drugs industry if you want.'

David smiled. All these years on, his father still had the *chutzpah* of a cab driver.

'So we'll get you a seat on tonight's Milan flight,' said Manny, taking out his portable phone.

5

Kensington library was built in 1960, yet the reference room upstairs has an ambience emphatically Victorian. The carpet is a dispiriting olive green and the chairs are upholstered in dark leather. Notices everywhere urge the readers to beware of pickpockets and to tell the staff immediately if they see anyone mutilating or taking newspapers. True, certain of the papers are heavily in demand. The *Evening Standard*, which arrives early in the afternoon, can be seen only on request – not because of anything unseemly in the contents, but because it would go from the open shelves and not be found again. The assistants at the desk get to recognise the beady-eyed men who hover from two p.m. onwards, each hopeful of being the first to spot a secondhand car bargain, a tip for the greyhound racing, or a job.

Peter Diamond – formerly of Harrods security staff – had become one of the job-seekers.

He got his turn with the *Standard* and ran his thumb down the columns. If he could imagine himself filling any of the posts on offer, he would hurry to the nearest phone. Most of the ads were couched in a friendly style – *Call Mandy* or *Ring Trish* – and you were encouraged to picture a sweet-natured personnel officer on the end of the line eager to talk you into a thirty-grand job with bonus and pension. Today, as usual, no Mandy or Trish in London seemed to have an opening for a forty-eight-year-old ex-detective who couldn't be relied upon to patrol a floor of Harrods.

He gave up. The *Standard* reported another rise in unemployment with the headline DESPAIR OF LONDON'S JOBLESS. The despair wasn't much in evidence in High Street Kensington, apart from the droop of Diamond's shoulders. Young women with laminated carrier bags stuffed with goodies from the department stores stood by the kerb waving for taxis. Middle-aged men in designer tracksuits jogged in the direction of Holland Park. The lunch crowd were still installed in Al Gallo D'Oro, the Italian restaurant across the street.

For the past seven months, Diamond and his wife Stephanie had subsisted in a basement in Addison Road, a one-way street where the traffic noise was almost unendurable without double-glazing and ear-plugs. The house was a stuccoed three-storey building with rotting window frames that never stopped shaking. Across the road was St Barnabas, a great smog-stained block with a turret at each corner, not by any stretch of imagination an attractive church, but one that might have been improved by exterior cleaning. Someone had tried to distract attention from the grime by painting the doors in bold Oxford blue, only it wasn't visible from the Diamonds' fox-hole. Apart from the towers of St Barnabas, all that they could see as they peered up were the topmost levels of multi-storey flats. It was a far cry from the view across Georgian Bath that they'd enjoyed until a year ago.

Not wishing to be idle, Diamond had refreshed the walls and ceilings of the flat with a coat of emulsion called primrose on the colour chart. He had turned out every drawer and cupboard, oiled every hinge, brushed the chimney, checked the electric plugs, changed the washers on the taps and fitted draught excluders to all the doors. The drawback to this admirable zeal was that he was no handy-man, so oil and paint got on the soles of his shoes and was transported everywhere; the taps dripped worse than ever; the doors stuck halfway; soot fell into the living-room whenever the wind blew; and the cat had moved into the airing cupboard for sanctuary.

Stephanie Diamond would have joined the cat if she could. She worked two mornings in the Save the Children shop and had lately upped this to four, just to be out of the house. To discourage the DIY, she'd started bringing home jigsaws people had donated, getting Peter to occupy himself assembling them to see if pieces were missing before they were sold in the shop. It was not the good idea it had first seemed. She woke up one night at four a.m. with something digging into her back.

'What on earth . . .?' She switched on the bedside lamp.

Diamond turned over to see. 'Well, what do you know! It's that corner piece I was missing.'

'For crying out loud, Peter.'

'Fancy a cuppa?'

She remembered the taste of the tea since he'd descaled the kettle. 'No, go back to sleep.'

'God knows how it turned up here, of all places.'

'Oh, forget it.'

After an interval he said, 'Are you awake, Steph?'

She sighed. 'I am now.'

'I was thinking about the kid.'

'Which kid?'

'The Japanese girl I got sacked over. Why would anyone abandon a kid like that? She was nicely dressed. Clean. In no way neglected.'

'Perhaps she ran away from home.'

'And turned up on the seventh floor of Harrods? I can't believe that.'

'Fretting over it won't help,' said Stephanie. 'She's not your responsibility.'

'True.'

He was silent for a while.

She was almost asleep when he said, 'There must be a way of keeping all the pieces in one place.'

'Mm?'

The jigsaws. I was thinking if I were to help in the shop—'

She sat upright. 'Don't you dare!'

'I was going to say I could do the jigsaws there, and if pieces went missing at least we'd know they were on the premises.'

'If you so much as set foot in that shop, you'll leave it on a stretcher when I've finished with you, Peter Diamond.' A bold claim, considering she was about seven stone and he eighteen, but she knew what havoc he would wreak – innocently, let it be said – in all that clutter. She'd known when she married him that he was accident-prone. He was badly co-ordinated. Some fat people are graceful movers. Her husband was not. He knocked things over. In the street he failed to notice kerbstones. Hazards like dog-mess seemed almost to seek him out.

'This getting old – I don't care for it,' he said at breakfast next morning.

'Fishing?' Stephanie said.

He gave a shrug.

'All right, I'll say it. You're not *that* old.'

'Too old for work, apparently.'

'Snap out of it, Pete.'

'You want to see them lining up for unemployment

36

benefit. Younger men than me. Much younger, some of them. Kids, straight out of school.'

She heaped streaky bacon on his plate. 'Things could be worse.'

'You mean one of those unemployed kids could be ours.'

She looked away, and he cursed himself for being so boorish. In her first marriage, to a shop manager, Steph had miscarried three times. She'd lost another baby when she married Diamond. That time she'd suffered complications that were finally resolved by a hysterectomy. Surgery had been the cure-all in the early seventies. She'd lost her womb, but not the maternal urge. Before he met her she'd taken on the role of Brown Owl to a pack of brownies. Did it for years, and did much more than Baden Powell had ever intended. Always willing to be a second mum to small girls whose parents neglected them. They were all young adults now and she still wrote to some of them.

He put his hand over hers and said, 'Sorry about last night, love.'

Her face creased into a bewildered look. 'Last night?'

'In bed.'

She stared at him with wide eyes.

'The jigsaw piece.'

'Oh!' She laughed. 'I'd forgotten *that*. I thought you were on about something entirely different. It didn't make sense at all.'

The day was fine after more than a week of overcast skies and rain, so instead of joining the queue in the library again, he called in at the newsagent's, treated himself to his own copy of the *Evening Standard* and took it into Holland Park to read. Finding that nothing in the jobs columns grabbed him, he put the paper aside and basked in the sun for a while on one of the wooden benches facing the pond beside the Orangery, watching people walk their dogs and push their prams along the length of the arched cloister. Everyone but he had some accessory, some visible reason for being in the park. A model aeroplane, a tennis racket, a camera, a spiked stick for picking up waste paper.

He got up decisively. Hell, he had no cause to be idle. He'd remembered an urgent job of work. Overnight a couple of air bubbles had appeared on the freshly emulsioned kitchen ceiling. Stephanie hadn't said anything, but he was sure she'd noticed them. He'd see if he could rub them out with sandpaper.

At home, trying to be tidy, he spread the sheets of the *Standard* across the kitchen floor below the bit of ceiling he was about to sand. Then he stood on a kitchen chair and examined the job. There were two bubbles the size of marshmallows. No question – they had to be removed. He picked at one with his fingernail. The paint was dry, so he gave it a tentative pull. It was pliant and springy, like plastic. He pulled harder and suddenly a sizeable piece of the coat of paint detached itself from the ceiling and flopped over his head and shoulders like a bridal veil.

He swore, stepped down from the chair, extricated himself, and examined the damage. This was no longer a simple sanding job. The entire ceiling would have to be stripped and repainted. Worse, it needed washing before he applied the paint. It was obvious even to an incompetent that the grease and grime from years of cooking should have been removed before the first coat was applied. The emulsion hadn't adhered. By seeking quick results, he'd wasted an entire can of paint. In a couple of hours, Stephanie was going to come back from the shop to find her kitchen under occupation again.

Resigned to the major redecoration, he tugged off the rest of the coat of emulsion. It came away in large pieces and spread like dust-sheets over the units, table and chairs. That done, he put on the kettle. He deserved a break before he washed that ceiling.

But it never did get washed, or repainted. Something more urgent came up.

When Stephanie got home, she found the kitchen a disaster area, the sheets of dried emulsion festooned over everything, the ceiling as gruesome as it had looked the day they moved in, newspapers and sandpaper scattered around the floor and a half-filled mug of cold tea on the table. Diamond wasn't there. He finally came home about seven, apologizing profusely.

'But I've had an interesting afternoon, Steph.'

'So it appears.'

He related the episode with the paint. 'So when it was all off the ceiling I made myself some tea, feeling gutted after what had happened, and while I was drinking it, I happened to pick up a section of the *Standard* that I'd spread on the floor to protect it, you see?'

'You could have fooled me.'

'I just wanted something for distraction, something to read and—'

'You found a job in the paper? Oh, Pete!' She turned to him, arms spread wide.

'A job? No.'

Her arms flopped down. 'What, then?'

'I was telling you. I picked up the paper and saw this.' He handed her a scrap of newspaper.

She read:

MYSTERY GIRL STILL UNCLAIMED
The small girl who was the cause of a bomb scare when she was found in Harrods five weeks ago has

still not been claimed or identified. The girl, believed to be about seven, and Japanese, is unable or unwilling to speak. A publicity campaign to find her parents has so far been unsuccessful despite extensive enquiries among the Japanese community. Meanwhile she is in the care of Kensington & Chelsea social services department. A spokesperson said, 'We're at a loss to understand why no one has come forward yet.'

'Poor mite,' said Stephanie, ever ready to brush aside her own concerns to take pity on a child. 'She must be terrified. First the police, and now the social workers. I'm not surprised she's silent.'

'Then you don't mind if I try and help?' said Diamond.

She gave him a wary look. 'If I did, would it make a jot of difference?'

'I found out where she's being kept.'

Stephanie frowned, stared and then allowed her face to soften. '*That's* why you dropped everything and went out? To see this little girl? Peter, you're a softie at heart.'

'Softie?' he said. 'You're calling an ex-cop a softie?'

'You always had time for kids,' she insisted. 'Who got a job as Father Christmas last year?'

'That was work. This abandoned kid is a challenge, Steph. A chance to do what I'm trained for instead of standing on a chair washing a ceiling – which I *will* do, I give you my word. Face it, I've got experience. I was a bloody good sleuth.'

'With a heart of gold.'

He rolled his eyes upwards in dissent – and found himself staring at the grease-marks. 'Anyway, I tried the town hall, and they weren't willing to release information. I don't blame them. I could have been a weirdo, or something.

They were perfectly entitled to show me the door. I went round to the police, told them I was ex-CID, and got an address. Some kind of assessment centre. Of course, when I got there, the kid had been moved on. I needed to be a bloody Sherlock Holmes to track her down. They put me onto some child psychiatrist, and he was no help, but his secretary took pity and handed me the address of a special school in Earls Court.'

'Special?' Stephanie said dubiously. 'You mean for kids with mental problems?'

He nodded.

'Is she retarded?' said Stephanie.

'No one actually said so, but that's where they've sent her.'

'They must think she is. What kind of place is it?'

'It's residential. I didn't get there this afternoon, but I'm going to try tomorrow. Apparently they haven't given up entirely. A Japanese teacher visits the school and tries to get her to speak. Up to now she's had no success.'

She was frowning. 'If everyone else has failed, what can you do about it? You don't speak Japanese.'

'I don't propose to try. It's just possible that everyone is too preoccupied with the speech problem. I'd like to try other lines of inquiry.'

'Such as?'

He wouldn't commit himself. 'I'd need to win the kid's confidence first. I've got the time to do it, Steph. For once in my life, I haven't got someone breathing down my neck.'

'Well . . .' said Stephanie, letting her eyes slide upwards.

'Don't say it. I'll scrub the damned ceiling tonight.'

6

One useful thing Diamond had learned in the police is that anyone with an air of authority can get admitted anywhere, with the possible exception of 10 Downing Street. The children's home was a detached Victorian house just behind the Earls Court exhibition building. The woodwork around the windows needed replacing and brickwork was visible here and there where weathering had invaded the layer of stucco. The local authority had more urgent priorities.

He rang the bell and a woman in an apron came to the door. Raising the 1940s trilby he still wore in private homage to the great detectives of past years, he said, 'Morning, madam. You must be Mrs . . .?'

'Straw.'

'Mrs Straw, Mrs Straw . . .' he said thoughtfully as if deciding whether she qualified for the holiday of a lifetime in the Caribbean.

She waited, intrigued.

He said, 'You're not the head of this school?'

'No,' she said, fingering her apron. 'I'm the general help.'

'A general! General Help.' He made a gesture towards a salute.

She didn't smile. 'You want Miss Musgrave.'

'Miss Musgrave. Of course!' He stepped forward, compelling her to stand aside. 'Peter Diamond, General Help, here to speak to Miss Musgrave.'

She succeeded in saying, 'You have an appointment.' If she meant it to sound like a question, as she probably did, the attempt was foiled by a huge, disarming grin from Diamond. The upshot was that Mrs Straw's utterance ended on a descending note and became a statement. She added, 'Miss Musgrave is very busy.'

'Don't I know it!' Diamond said.

'You know Miss Musgrave?' she said with relief.

He shrugged like a Frenchman in a way that could mean everything or nothing. 'She'll see me, I think.' He was in the hall now and Mrs Straw was closing the door. From the depths of the house came the cries of children. 'She's not in class, is she?'

'If you'd only wait, I'll tell her you're here.'

At that moment a face appeared around a door halfway up the hall. Diamond called out, 'There you are, Miss Musgrave.'

It wasn't a stab in the dark. The face was weighing him up with the look of a person in authority.

'Peter Diamond,' he told her, advancing with his hand extended. A man of his size in motion isn't easy to stop. 'Mrs Straw here was telling me how busy you are, but perhaps you can spare me a minute. I'm not selling anything.'

Miss Musgrave must have been in her thirties, tall and slim, with blonde hair drawn back to a small ponytail and tied with a black ribbon. She didn't immediately accept the handshake. She asked, 'What is this about, then?'

He beamed. 'It's about one of the children, the Japanese girl. I may be able to help.'

43

'You'd better come in.'

Her office evidently doubled as a classroom. There were three infants' chairs and tables. Her own desk had a line-up of painted masks made from egg boxes. The floor was spotted with paint. A menagerie of stuffed animals sat on the filing cabinet. Children's paintings ranging from competent to inept were taped to the walls. Diamond found it congenial. In the absence of a spare adult-sized chair, he perched himself on a wooden chest with a flat lid that he reckoned would take his weight.

Miss Musgrave asked if he wanted a coffee. She had a full cup on her desk.

'No, thanks. I really don't mean to be a nuisance.' At this stage he judged it wise to throw himself on her mercy. 'I used to be in the police as a detective superintendent. Used to be. I must make it plain that I'm here in a private capacity.' He explained about losing the Harrods job. 'I saw the little girl that night, and I'm appalled that after – what is it? Six weeks? – her people haven't been found.'

'I'm sure the police are doing their best,' Miss Musgrave said.

'No question of that.'

'Meanwhile we're making her as comfortable as we can. She does need specialised care. That's *my* province, Mr Diamond.' She sounded defensive, yet well in control. From the guarded looks she was still giving Diamond, she hadn't much cared for his steamroller tactics in gaining admittance.

'It's not easy, I imagine, when a child doesn't speak at all,' he ventured.

'We deal with a variety of problems here.'

'With limited resources, no doubt.'

'If you're hinting that Naomi isn't being given the

44

attention her predicament deserves, Mr Diamond, you're mistaken. She's been the subject of the most intensive tests and inquiries.'

'Naomi – you know her name?'

Miss Musgrave shook her head. 'We have to call her something. One of the staff from the Japanese Embassy suggested it as a name that their people and ours have in common.'

'Naomi. That's Japanese? I thought it was Old Testament.'

Hosanna! His early days as a choirboy paid off. Miss Musgrave's expression softened. A man who knew his Bible couldn't be wholly disreputable. 'What exactly are you here for, Mr Diamond?'

'To help the kid find her people.'

'Oh – and how will you succeed when everyone up to now has failed?'

'By being the Sherlock Holmes round here – except that I come free.'

'That's fine as far as it goes, but I don't know what the police would say about it.'

The police are up shit creek without a paddle, as Sherlock used to remark to Dr Watson.'

She put her fingers to her mouth, possibly, Diamond suspected, to hide a faint smile.

He pointed to the cup and saucer on her desk. 'Your coffee's getting cold.'

She lowered her hand and she was definitely smiling. 'It's Bovril. Is that an example of your detective skills?'

He made a pistol shape with his fingers and held them to the side of his head.

Miss Musgrave, serious again, said, 'Naomi can't answer questions, so I don't see what good you can do.'

'I can observe.'

'And make deductions?' She mocked him with her eyes. 'You've got to admit the kid needs help.'

This was a telling point with Miss Musgrave. She took a long sip of the Bovril. 'If you're serious, come back at two this afternoon. I'll be taking the autistic class. In this room. You can come in and see what happens. Then perhaps you'll understand the difficulty.'

An adult-sized chair had been installed just inside the door for Diamond. It wasn't possible for a man of his bulk to be unobtrusive in an office so small, but Miss Musgrave didn't mind and the children scarcely gave him a passing glance. They were shepherded in by Mrs Straw and another woman who looked mightily relieved to be handing them over.

One of them, a boy, was screaming, as if in rage rather than pain. On entering the room he broke away from Mrs Straw, ran to a bookcase, swept the bottom shelf clear of books and squeezed into the narrow space underneath, where he continued to scream.

'That's Clive,' Miss Musgrave told Diamond above the racket. She made no move to restore the books to their places or to calm Clive. 'And this is Rajinder.'

Rajinder moved erratically, with a springy step, both arms flexed and his wrists limp. He went to one of the infant chairs and sat there, rocking, it seemed, in time to Clive's screaming.

'Come on, you two,' the second teacher urged the rest of the class, who seemed reluctant, not without cause, to enter. 'Tabitha, Naomi, we can't wait all day for you.' She cupped her hand around the back of one child's head and drew her in, a pale, worried-looking girl of about seven with fine blonde hair, presumably Tabitha. She had thick plastic glasses fastened with a band around the back of her head like a tennis player's. She had scarcely taken a step into the room when Miss Musgrave remarked to the other teacher. 'She needs changing. Do you mind?'

Tabitha was recalled and Naomi was ushered forward in her place. Diamond had seen the child briefly that night in Harrods, and remembered how impassive she had looked, surrounded by security guards. This morning she had the same preoccupied expression, as if her eyes saw nobody. There was clearly a level at which her mind was functioning efficiently, because she moved normally, straight to a chair and sat down, composed, indifferent to Clive's screaming and Rajinder's rocking, or to the presence of the adults. Someone had fastened a white ribbon in her hair and she was in a red corduroy dress, black tights and trainers.

'She'll stay like that for as long as I let her,' said Miss Musgrave. 'I can get through to the others. Outwardly they appear more disturbed than Naomi, but she's inaccessible, and it isn't just the problem of language. It must be some form of autism.'

Diamond had seen television programmes about autistic children who appeared physically normal, but tantalisingly locked in their inner worlds. They exhibited a range of behaviour that could include tantrums, grimacing, avoidance of all human contact, inappropriate emotional reactions such as laughing when someone else was hurt and, in rare cases, strange feats of memory enabling them to play music they had heard only once before, or doing complex drawings of scenes and buildings only briefly visited. From what he remembered, there was controversy about how autism should be treated. He'd watched a disturbing film of mothers forcibly embracing

47

their struggling children until they stopped resisting, which could take hours. In some cases, the results had been encouraging.

Miss Musgrave closed the door and took a pencil and worksheet to the howling Clive. To Diamond's surprise the boy took it, went silent and started to write or draw, still in his cramped position under the bookshelves. Rajinder, also, was persuaded to take a worksheet and give it his attention, though he needed a patient explanation of what was required.

'Now see what happens with Naomi.' Miss Musgrave held out a pencil. Naomi stared ahead and didn't move. Gently, Miss Musgrave took the child's right hand and positioned the small fingers around the pencil.

Diamond said, 'It's not for me to interfere, but do the Japanese hold pencils like that?' He took a pen from his pocket and demonstrated. 'I thought they held them upright, like this.'

Miss Musgrave's first reaction was a cool stare. Then she accepted the validity of the information.

The child allowed her fingers to be repositioned. A clean sheet of paper was placed on the table in front of her. Miss Musgrave stood behind Naomi and guided the pencil, making a mark on the paper. 'Now prove me totally wrong, Naomi, and draw a picture.' But Naomi's eyes weren't on the paper, and as soon as Miss Musgrave stepped back, the hand was still.

'I've had mutes before,' Miss Musgrave said, 'and they can usually be persuaded to use a pencil.'

'She's mute?'

'Silent, anyway. Not dumb. She makes little sounds if she's surprised in any way.'

'That's something.'

48

'Some autistics never learn to speak.'

Rajinder seemed to take this as a challenge and started repeatedly saying, 'Miss,' until Miss Musgrave examined his drawing, praised it and provided him with more paper. From the bookshelves came a new sound. Clive, tiring of paperwork, had taken a toy car from his pocket and was spinning the wheels with his finger, watching them intently.

'He'll do that for the rest of the lesson if he's left. It becomes obsessive,' Miss Musgrave said. 'He fits the stereotype of the autistic child.'

'Meaning what?'

'He shuns the company of others. Doesn't use eye contact. Refuses to be cuddled. Throws these tantrums if he feels his privacy is being invaded.'

'And is Naomi like that?'

'She's the aloof type. The muteness is a symptom.'

'Have you tried cuddling her?'

'She's indifferent to it. Passive. That's another kind of abnormality in these kids.'

'The others, Rajinder and Tabitha – are they autistic?'

'Yes.'

'Does Clive speak?'

She nodded. 'But he tends to repeat things parrot-fashion.'

'Does he progress at all?'

'A little. Listen,' she said, 'if you want to try and get through to Naomi, please feel free.'

The invitation was tempting, but he knew better than to accept. On first acquaintance a man his size terrified any kid if he went close. 'At this stage,' he told Miss Musgrave candidly, 'I'd rather get through to you. That's my game-plan for today.'

She tensed. 'What exactly do you mean?'

49

'I want to convince you that I won't be a nuisance. I want to come here again. And again. I can sit here and observe, or I can make myself useful, but I want to be here. I don't kid myself that I can work a miracle for Naomi. I sense that if she's going to give me any clues at all, it's going to be slow progress. How would you feel about having me here on a regular basis?'

She didn't answer at once. She went over to attend to Clive, who started screaming again at her approach. For a moment she wrestled with him for the toy car. In the struggle he bit her hand and she cried out in pain. 'If I don't do this,' she told Diamond, 'the entire lesson is wasted. Now *will* you let go?' She snatched the toy from Clive and he set up a piercing wail. 'You'll have it back presently. Now do me a drawing of the car. A drawing.' The child subsided by stages and picked up the pencil.

Massaging her hand, Miss Musgrave returned to Diamond. 'Before I say anything about this suggestion of yours, would you tell me something about yourself?'

'Whatever you want to know.'

'All right, then. Why did you leave the police?'

He hesitated. 'I resigned. I blew my top in front of the Assistant Chief Constable.'

'What about?'

'A kid. A boy of twelve. I was accused of hitting his head against a wall.'

She stared. After an interval, she said, 'At least you're honest.'

'Okay,' he added, 'I'm hardly a suitable person to invite again. Forget it.' He picked up his hat.

'Sit down, Mr Diamond,' she told him firmly. 'Did you do it?'

'Do what?'

'Hit the boy?'

'No, but it's academic now. He came at me and I pushed him aside. He knocked his head on the wall. I wasn't believed, so I said some things I lived to regret.'

'Have you got kids of your own?'

He shook his head.

'You're married?'

'Yes.'

'But you like them?'

'Kids?' He nodded.

She held out a hand. 'My name is Julia.'

7

'Any idea how this happened?'

David Flexner gazed at two blackened pillars rising some ten feet above the rubble that had once been Manflex Italia's Milan plant. Immense heat had melted those pillars into stark, Dali-esque images in the ashen landscape. All this, and a perfect, cloudless sky. What a location for a film, he found himself thinking.

He had been driven there by Rico Villa, the plant manager, whose Zegna suit and D'Anzini shoes weren't the best choice for stepping through ashes. Rico always dressed the part of the business executive, but David, casual as usual in white denims, black T-shirt and faded red running shoes, regarded him as a kindred spirit, one of the few in his father's employ that he might actually have chosen to drink with.

'Some electrical fault, I guess,' Rico answered. 'Isn't that what usually starts a fire?'

'Or a lighted cigarette.'

'I don't allow smoking here.'

In that gutted ruin, Rico's use of the present tense amused David. He had to turn his face away in case Rico noticed. 'Smokers will always find somewhere.'

'That's true, but the Saturday shift had finished when the fire started. The plant was empty except for the two security guards.'

52

'A fire can take some time to get going,' David pointed out, adding with more tact, 'but I guess the fire service are making a report.'

'The fire team and the insurance investigators, too,' said Rico. 'The boys from Prima Roma Assurance came out here the next day to see what they could find.'

'Any theories yet?'

'Nothing anyone will say.'

'How about arson? Someone with a grudge against the company.'

'Arson?'

'Was anyone dismissed in the last six months?'

Rico was shocked. He pressed his hand to his mouth as if unwilling to admit the possibility. 'I guess five or six for absenteeism and petty theft. The personnel records went up in smoke with the rest. We won't have their addresses any more.'

'Then the computer wasn't linked to our offices in Rome?'

'Some files were. Not personnel. That's against the data protection legislation.'

'We'll have to rely on memory, then. How's yours, Rico?'

Rico made a negative gesture.

'Let's check with some of the people who worked in personnel. Draw up a list of everyone they can remember who was fired and anyone else with reason to dislike the company.'

'I'll see to it.'

'Fine.' David stared around at the devastation. 'Must have been one hell of a fire. Where was your office in this heap?'

'To your right, approximately sixty metres,' Rico answered bleakly. 'Nobody would know.'

'Lose anything personal?'

He shrugged. 'My certificates. I had them framed on the wall. Membership of the Institute of Pharmacists and so forth. They can be replaced. And some photos of my family. They can't.'

'What will you do? Do you want to move to Rome?'

'Not really. I'm fifty-three. My home is here. My father is in a retirement home. I have kids in school. I guess I'll look carefully at the redundancy terms.'

'Jesus, Rico, we can't afford to lose you,' David heard himself say, and it was a perfectly obvious thing to say, except that he surprised himself by so readily taking on the role of spokesman for Manflex. Until now, he'd never truly identified with the company. He only attended Board meetings out of loyalty to his father. 'We'll find some way of keeping the family together. For the present, you're wanted here in Milan, so no problem. We need a temporary office. Can you find one?'

'Michael, I'm dying.'

Michael Leapman jerked around to look at Manny Flexner. There was no hint of amusement in his features, but that wasn't necessarily significant. Manny was capable of the straightest face when stringing hapless people along. He was a shameless liar in the cause of fun. And Manny's style of humour frequently eluded Leapman.

At Manny's suggestion, they were walking through the Essex Street Market in the Lower East Side after lunching on blintzes and beer in Ratner's. This place, throbbing with life, filled with pungent aromas of breads and cheeses, hardly seemed right for such a morbid announcement, but you could never be sure what Manny was up to.

'Did I hear you correctly?'

'How would I know?'

'I thought you said you were dying.'

'Correct.'

'You really mean that?'

Manny nodded solemnly. 'I saw my physician this morning. He sent me for tests a while back. Now he has the results. It's inoperable. I have maybe six months, maybe nine.'

Leapman stared at him. There was still no indication that some kind of black humour was intended. 'But that's not possible.'

'Precisely what I said to the doc. I have my faculties. I can read the paper still, eat a good meal, take a woman to bed when I want, and I don't disappoint. I'm not the biggest in that department, but what I got is in working order. He said fine, some people aren't so lucky. They languish and droop. At least I was going out in style. I said I didn't believe him. He asked if I wanted a bet. I said okay, Doc, fifty bucks I'm still alive for Thanksgiving. I thought I was on a sure thing, but he suggested we put the money in a brown envelope and leave it with his receptionist because he didn't want to trouble my executors. That really brought it home to me, Michael. My executors. He meant it.' Manny exhaled, vibrating his lips. 'I called off the bet.'

'You should get a second opinion,' said Leapman, trying sincerely to be helpful while he assessed what this grim news would mean for his own prospects. He believed the story.

'More tests, more bad news.' Manny groaned at the prospect. 'No, thanks. I'd rather spend my last days on earth profitably, robbing banks while I have my strength left.' He turned to a woman behind a fruit and vegetable stall. She must have overheard the last statement, because she was goggle-eyed. 'Ignore me. I'm in shock. How much are your pineapples, ma'am?' He chose one and felt it for firmness. 'Do you buy many pineapples, Michael? They can look fine outside, like me, and when you put in the knife, they're rotten. No offence,' he told the woman. 'I'll take this one.'

They reached the end of the market and made their way back down Delancey Street. 'Still, this isn't all bad for Manflex,' Manny remarked altruistically. 'We can do with a change at the top.'

Leapman's flesh prickled.

Manny went on smoothly. 'My shares will pass to Davey. He'll have a controlling stake, and he'll be fine.'

'For Chairman, you mean? David?' Leapman tried to sound casual, but the shock couldn't be stifled.

'I can't put it better than Shakespeare: some guys are born managers, some achieve management and some, like my son, have it thrust upon them.'

'The market won't like it,' said Leapman, impervious to Shakespeare.

'Davey taking over, you mean?'

'Your going.' An answer more tactful than honest.

'What choice do I have?'

A pause. 'Fair point.'

'He'll need your support,' Manny said.

'He can depend on it.'

'And the know-how. You have a grasp of the business. He doesn't.'

'Of course I'll help any way I can.' Michael Leapman was functioning on autopilot. The news of Manny's illness was bad enough. The prospect of his son taking over the Chairmanship was beyond everything.

Manny shifted the pineapple to his left hand and rested his right on Leapman's shoulder. 'Thanks, Mike. You don't have to tell me the sharks will be circling, but I have confidence in the boy. I like the way he's shaping up. As a matter of fact, I called Rico last night. Davey's doing a great job in Milan, and that isn't easy, closing down a plant.'

It was a skill that might soon be required nearer home, Leapman thought cynically. 'Have you told him?'

'Told him what?'

'This terrible news your doctor gave you.'

'Not yet. It's not easy over the phone.'

'You'll wait, then?'

'Davey doesn't need to be told at this stage. Maybe not at all.'

Frowning, Leapman said, 'But you just told *me*. Surely you owe it to him. He needs time to adjust.'

'Weren't you listening just now?' said Manny. 'About management being thrust upon him? It's better he doesn't have time to think about it. Knowing Davey, he'd look for an out.'

Leapman didn't pursue the point. Maybe Manny was right from the company's point of view, given the staggering premise that David Flexner had to be installed as the next Chairman. What was the point in getting steamed up about David's sensibilities when his own had been ruthlessly trampled over?

And now the misguided old jerk was weighing the group's prospects without mentioning the obvious fact that Manflex might be vulnerable to a takeover. 'We're lower down the league than I'd like to be, but we're not in bad shape right now. We still have a good cash-flow.'

'Mainly from Kaprofix.'

'What's wrong with Kaprofix? It's helped millions of people with angina.'

'Nothing – except that it's a declining asset.'

'Since I put the lid on development costs, we boosted the operating margin by 2.6 points. You talk about Kaprofix as if it's all we've got. We have a wide base of steady-selling products. The surplus from the pension fund was over ten million last year. Sure, we could do with a big-selling new drug—'

'Soon,' said Leapman.

'What?'

'Soon – we could do with it soon.'

'I wouldn't argue with that.'

Leapman wasn't letting it pass so lightly. 'We missed out on beta-blockers, salbutamol for asthma, L-dopa for Parkinsonism, H2-antagonists—'

'Okay, okay,' said Manny irritably. 'I get the point. We staked too much on Fidoxin. That was the biggest fuckup of my career. On the other hand, we've got a clean record. No one ever sued us. I can meet my Maker knowing I never damaged anyone through negligence.'

'Leaving aside environmental damage,' Leapman couldn't stop himself saying.

'What do you mean?'

'We did get fined for polluting French and Italian rivers.'

'Piss off, Michael.'

They walked on in silence for a bit, each feeling the strain of the changed situation.

'Will you say anything to the Board while Davey's away?' Leapman eventually asked.

'About my condition? There's no need. I'll step down and then they'll find out.'

'So you want me to regard it as confidential?'

'For the time being. How did I come to confide in an obstinate schmuck like you? What a mess.' He turned and looked at Leapman. There was just a glimmer of amusement in the look, yet the rest of the face was sad, undeniably sad. This time, Manny Flexner wasn't kidding.

8

Three black limousines cruised along the stretch of Eighth Avenue opposite the lake in Central Park and presently halted and disgorged a number of large men in a motley collection of tracksuits. Enough for a football team, except that footballers would never have looked so ill at ease. They were peeking over their shoulders as if someone they knew might be spying on this freak show. The last to climb out of the front car was Massimo Gatti, a man of influence in the Italian-American community – or at least that section of it that requires round-the-clock bodyguards. Unlike his minders, Gatti was short and over-weight, with high blood pressure, which was why he had taken up jogging.

As a preliminary, he went through a token exercise to limber up, flinging his arms outwards like a cheerleader and simultaneously running on the spot. Some of the others in the party attempted sheepishly to do the same. Then Gatti moved off at a sedate jog, and with his henchmen in tow he could easily have been taken for a shorter, fatter embodiment of a recent President of the United States. The limousines inched forward, staying parallel with the joggers.

As usual in the park, New York's fitness freaks were out in force. This morning Michael Leapman was among them.

He'd asked for an urgent audience with Gatti, and this was the arrangement, a refreshing variation on the working breakfast. Having spotted the group, he raised his pace and strode across to meet them. He was one of those envied beings who rarely take exercise, but succeed in keeping in shape.

'Hi, Mr Gatti.'

They had met before, through a chain of intermediaries too tedious to list. Leapman's inside knowledge of the drugs industry – the legitimate drugs industry – had appealed to Gatti. In the depressed world of finance, pharmaceuticals were one of the few commodities that promised good returns. Medical supplies were necessities, and as nearly recession-proof as anything could be. A stake in the industry was what Leapman had offered, and Gatti had found it irresistible.

Gatti may have nodded in response to the greeting, or the dip of the head may have been part of his running action. It wasn't in his nature to greet people, even in less demanding circumstances. After just a few minutes of slow jogging, he was moving with a spastic jerkiness and taking noisy gulps of air.

A long exchange was clearly out of the question, so Leapman drew alongside and came quickly to the point. 'There's a hitch in our arrangement, I'm sorry to say.'

Gatti stopped jogging and turned away from Leapman, flapping his hands at his entourage to step back and give him some privacy. They reversed several paces. The procession set off again with a decent gap in the ranks.

'What are you trying to tell me?'

Leapman resumed, 'Manny Flexner saw his doctor for a check-up and found that he has only a few months to live.'

'So?'

'So that's the problem.'

'His problem, not mine,' Gatti wheezed.

'With respect, it isn't so simple as that. He says he's going to step down.'

'Resign?'

'Yes.'

'What's wrong with that?'

'He wants to nominate his son to replace him.'

'He has a son?'

'Yes.'

'You didn't tell me.'

'I'm sorry, Mr Gatti. I know I should have mentioned it before now. I didn't rate David Flexner at all. He takes no interest in the business.'

'Is he on the Board?'

'Yes, but—'

'You didn't rate him, huh?'

'Well, no.'

'Flexner's own son? You didn't rate him?'

The questions appeared to indict Leapman and he was becoming alarmed. 'He sits through the Board meetings and says nothing,' he said in his own defence.

Massimo Gatti stopped running again. The pursuers stopped, too far off to overhear anything. Across the band of grass separating the park from the roadway, the three limousines also came to a halt. Leapman stood tamely, waiting for Gatti to recover his breath. 'We made an agreement, Mr Leapman,' the little man eventually succeeded in saying. 'You needed funds. You came to me with a proposition. Fine. My people were impressed with your scheme. So we backed you. We did as you suggested. We took out the factory in Milano. And two good men were killed.'

Horrified, Leapman was quick to say, 'That wasn't my suggestion, Mr Gatti. You wanted to buy in at the lowest price. I wouldn't have recommended arson.'

'Good men killed,' Gatti reiterated. 'For nothing.'

'Not for nothing. Let's be frank – the fire achieved what you wanted. Manflex shares plunged on the news. The price recovered a little after you started buying. It *was* you, wasn't it? You and your associates, buying at rockbottom prices?'

There was no response.

'The shareholders are losing confidence,' Leapman insisted. 'Manny Flexner's position as Chairman is untenable. I'm certain I could have achieved a boardroom coup. Manny has no rescue plan. The cupboard is bare.'

'So what's different?'

'He's dying, and it's altered the equation. People who would have supported me are going to back his son out of sympathy or loyalty. Manny's dying wish and all that crap. There's no way I can pull this off right now.'

Gatti stared at him. 'Mr Leapman, I don't give a shit who is Chairman. You enter a billion dollar agreement with me, you deliver. You know what happens when an agreement breaks down.'

Just three days after his arrival in Italy, David Flexner was installed in a temporary office suite in Milan with telephone system, fax machine, photocopier, word-processor, computer and PA – whose name, fittingly, was Pia. She had short, Titian-red hair and garnet-coloured eyes. Pia was so watchable that David had instantly decided she would get the female lead if he ever actually got to make a film in Italy, never mind whether she could act. The fact that she also spoke English like a BBC newscaster and could use all the hardware seemed of trifling importance when she first walked in. She was not, he hazarded from the swing of her hips, a diehard feminist. Nor, for that matter, was he.

Diverting as the gorgeous Pia was, in the crisis resulting from the fire there wasn't time to observe her. Rico Villa had set up appointments with the insurers, the union representatives, the employment office and the main city newspapers, who would be the chief means of getting information to the staff. A meeting of all the Manflex Italia employees had been set for the following Saturday morning. They were to gather in a cinema south-west of the city. By then David would have something positive to offer in the way of redundancy terms. He'd spent yesterday with the accountants. Reluctant as he was to devote his life to the pharmaceuticals industry, what had happened in Italy was a problem he could handle with energy and sensitivity. Hundreds of people had lost their livelihood, and he would do his damnedest to treat them decently and fairly.

Towards the end of Thursday afternoon, Pia swanned in with two men who were definitely not on the roll. They were far too brash to be employees. They studied David with long, level looks as if mentally measuring him for his coffin. Unwilling to be intimidated, he made it obvious that he was assessing them, their off-the-peg suits and their uninteresting striped ties. One, in his forties, had his hair trimmed to about half an inch. 'These gentlemen are from the police,' Pia said superfluously. She turned to check on their names. They spoke no English, apparently. The short-haired one was a Commissioner, which sounded pretty senior. His name was Dordoni. The other must have been too low in rank to merit an introduction.

'Do you have any information about the fire yet?' David asked, getting in first.

Pia translated, listened and then gave the response, which was not an answer. 'The Commissioner is asking for a list of all the staff employed at the plant.'

'No problem. We can provide that.'

'He wants a check on everybody.'

'A check?'

'To know if they are still alive.'

'That isn't so simple. Would you explain to him that we're not in contact with everyone. We're having this meeting Saturday and we'll take names there. What is this about? My understanding is that no one was killed in the fire.'

The translation process began again. Commissioner Dordoni spoke rapidly, as if irritated by the delays, looking directly at David with moist, black eyes that reminded him of fresh sheep-droppings.

'He says a car . . .' Pia stopped and checked something with Dordoni. '. . . an Alfa Romeo Veloce saloon, crashed on a country road three thousand metres – that's about two miles – from Manflex Italia on the evening of the fire. The petrol tank ruptured and the wreck was badly burned.' She turned back to Dordoni for more of the story in Italian, and presently added, 'The remains of two men were found. Badly burned. Very badly. They have not been identified.'

'And he's trying to connect this with the fire at the plant?'

'He says the Alfa Romeo was coming from the direction of the Manflex plant. They can tell by the skid-marks that the car was travelling at high speed when it left the road. Apparently it turned over a couple of times. Inside the trunk they found five empty gasoline containers.'

David hesitated, frowning.

Pia said helpfully, 'I think he's implying that these men may have started the fire at the plant, but he hasn't exactly said so yet.'

'What does he want from me?'

She had another brief exchange with Dordoni before turning back to David. 'He says the fire service investigators haven't ruled out the possibility of arson. He's asking if you know of anyone who might have wished to destroy the plant.'

'The answer is no.'

Commissioner Dordoni didn't require a translation. He countered with a frenetic outpouring of Italian.

Pia, caught in the middle and handling her role with admirable cool, lifted her eyebrows a fraction and explained, 'He wants me to tell you it's unwise to refuse to co-operate with the police.'

'If that's a threat, Pia, you can tell this arrogant jerk that I resent it. I spoke the truth. I've no reason to suspect anyone we employ, or have employed.' Having let rip, David had second thoughts. 'No. Hold it. Tell him this. The possibility is very disturbing indeed, and he'll have our full co-operation.'

This undertaking lowered the temperature a little. Dordoni and his assistant got down to facts – the names of the two security men, the times of shifts, the number of employees and so on, all of which David supplied. They also demanded a list of the staff, with addresses, but he couldn't supply one, not before Saturday's meeting.

'If he'd describe these two men, we can make some enquiries and find out if anyone recognises them,' he told Pia.

Dordoni gave a sinister laugh when this was translated,

and made a rubbing motion with his finger and thumb while speaking his reply.

Pia impassively translated, 'The men were incinerated beyond recognition. It's possible that the forensic pathologists will give some information, but that is likely to take weeks or months.'

'What about the car?'

Dordoni revealed that the registration plates had been removed from the Alfa Romeo. Very little that would be useful was left.

David turned to Pia. 'Would you ask him a question from me? If these men haven't been identified, is there any evidence at all that connects them with our company?'

She conferred with Dordoni. 'He says no.'

'It's circumstantial, then.'

'Is that a question?'

'Don't trouble,' he told her. He wasn't scoring points. 'Ask him how this crash happened.'

Pia sounded reluctant to put the question. 'He already told us. The car was going too fast. It turned over.'

'Yes, but why? Was it being chased?'

She turned back to Dordoni and succeeded in getting the unhelpful answer, 'Nobody knows.'

Dordoni nodded to his assistant, preparing to leave. He wasn't waiting for any more idiot questions.

'Was another vehicle involved?' David pressed him.

Pia translated quickly.

Dordoni shrugged. At the door, he appeared to decide, after all, that he would volunteer something else. He turned and delivered a couple of sentences.

Now Pia gave a shrug. 'The car was travelling on a perfectly straight stretch of road. It went out of control, but they don't understand why. They can see from the tyre-marks that it didn't have a blow-out. It's an extra-ordinary thing to happen. They are calling it – I think you have the expression in England – an act of God.'

Later in the afternoon there was an opportunity to get Rico Villa's views on the mysterious car crash. He was dismissive, scornful of the suggestion that arsonists had started the fire. 'Why won't they admit that coincidences happen? Typical of the police, always looking for the first solution that suggests itself. Two serious incidents on one evening and they have to connect them.'

'Only a couple of miles from each other,' commented David, slipping into Dordoni's role.

'A couple of drunks turn their car over. What's so sinister about that?'

'How do you know they were drunk?'

'You're in Lombardy now, my friend. Have you tried the *Oltrepo Pavese*?'

'They did have those empty petrol cans in their trunk.'

'They were probably farmers. If you have farm vehicles to keep on the move, you collect extra petrol to take back with you.'

'But he said the registration plates were missing.'

'Kids. Souvenir-hunters. They'll help themselves to anything.'

David wasn't overly impressed, and said so.

'Okay,' Rico lobbed one back, 'in a couple of days we can take a roll-call. Then we'll know if anyone from Manflex Italia is missing. Want a bet?'

'The guys in the car don't have to be Manflex employees,' David said. 'Like Dordoni said, they could have been sacked. Or they could simply be troublemakers from outside.'

'Let it go, Dave,' Rico advised, putting a hand on his

shoulder. 'We have more important things to do right now. The police are going to take months over this. Years, probably. And then it's quite likely they'll file it as unsolved.'

For the first time in their friendship, David Flexner had a stirring of unease about Rico.

9

'What exactly do you *do* in that school?' Stephanie asked one evening as they waited to eat. A chicken casserole in the oven was sending out a rich aroma, but the vegetables still required their seven minutes in the microwave.

'A lot of sitting around.'

'Can't you make yourself useful in some way?'

'Occasionally. Today I was doing the job I do best – putting a jigsaw together. An eight-piece jigsaw.' Diamond offered the statement blandly, knowing Stephanie would pounce on it. Sometimes he took a wry pleasure in being the prey to his wife's sharp remarks.

'How many pieces went missing?'

'Unkind! Not a single one. They're the size of your hand.'

'This is for the children's benefit, I take it?'

'Naturally.'

'So you work with them, fitting the pieces together?'

He smiled. 'Some hope! I fit them together and they pull them apart.'

'Does Naomi join in?'

His voice altered, the by-play over. 'Naomi? No.'

'Why not? Jigsaws are pretty basic, when all's said and done. Language isn't involved.'

'She doesn't join in anything. She's completely passive.'

'Maybe she's terrified of the others.'

'She was like this before she was brought to the school.'

'Terrified?'

Diamond nodded. She was almost certainly right.

'But they insist she's autistic?' Stephanie asked.

'The diagnosis isn't carved in stone,' he said. 'Anyway, as far as I can tell it's a convenient label for a pretty broad spectrum of maladjusted kids. Clive, for instance, has these tantrums and has to find some corner of the room he considers the safest from invasion. Naomi's not like that. She'll sit where she's told. She's silent. Totally switched off. Her behaviour is nothing like Clive's, but they're both thought to be autistic. Is that ready?'

He'd been interrupted by five electronic bleeps. The microwave oven was a symbol of more affluent times. He'd bought it on the day he resigned from the police, but it looked older than that, copiously speckled during the redecoration of the kitchen. Some of the marks had been impossible to remove.

'Standing time,' Stephanie reminded him. 'The veggies need their standing time. I don't know if you remember Maxine Beckington, one of the brownies. She didn't last very long with us, but she was a bright little thing.'

'That was probably why,' said Diamond.

'Why what?'

'Why she didn't last. If she was as bright as you say, she probably objected to dancing around the toadstool on the grounds that it was a phallic symbol.'

She gave him a glare. The brownie movement wasn't a topic for levity. 'I was about to tell you that Maxine's mother had another child, a boy, and he was the envy of all the other mothers because he was such a contented baby, willing to lie in his pram for as long as they left him. I saw him myself – a beautiful child with gorgeous big blue eyes. He never cried. They never missed a night's sleep. But after a time, this angelic baby started to make them uneasy. They realized he didn't cry even when he was hungry. If they hadn't fed him as a matter of routine, he would have starved, still without complaining. It was uncanny. What started out as a blessing turned out to be deeply worrying, and with good reason. He was eventually found to be autistic. Your Naomi sounds similar.'

Diamond pondered the suggestion. 'Yes, I can imagine her as a baby acting like that, but we shouldn't make these comparisons.'

'Why not?'

'It's unscientific, that's why. One thing I've learned from Julia Musgrave is that autism has to be diagnosed by an expert. You can't pick out a single symptom as typical. Any characteristic you name – the aloofness, the odd movements some of them make, the difficulties with speech – could be the result of some other condition. You recognize autism by a whole range of things. And they vary. Not all autistic babies behave like the kid you just described. Some of them fight and scream from Day One and refuse to be comforted.'

'Dreadful for the mothers,' Stephanie concurred. 'And they look like normal children.'

'Prettier, sometimes. You used a word to describe that baby: angelic. Autistic kids tend to have large eyes and remarkably symmetrical features. They really seem to be other-worldly.'

'Is Naomi like that?'

'Well, yes.'

'Does she scream and fight?'

'Never.'

'What if she's provoked?'

Diamond frowned at the idea. 'No one wants to give the kid a hard time. She's had enough shocks already.'

'Don't the other children sometimes bother her?'

'They don't fight each other. They're too enclosed in their own worlds.'

Stephanie picked up the oven gloves and took out the casserole. Together they served up the meal. When they had savoured a few mouthfuls, Diamond said, 'I'd like to know how the geniuses at the Police Training College would cope with young Naomi. She'd test their information-gathering techniques all right.'

'It sounds to me as if you're warming to the challenge.'

'Me?' He raised his eyebrows in mock surprise.

Stephanie said, 'You and this kid remind me of something my science teacher told us at school, about when an irresistible force meets an immovable object. How do you resolve it, then?'

*

Julia Musgrave was more amenable to his proposal than he felt entitled to expect. The ten days he'd spent observing the class and occasionally assisting had disposed of any fears she may have had that he was a potential nuisance. After classes and in the staffroom he'd shown by his questions that he was quick to appreciate the difficulties of teaching handicapped children.

The staff, as one would hope in a special school, were strongly committed. They amounted to four full-time and three part-time helpers, plus the redoubtable Mrs Straw, who besides guarding the front door had a list of duties that included playtime supervision, first aid, general filing and heating up the lunches supplied by the meals-on-wheels service.

Diamond had persuaded Julia Musgrave to release Naomi from class for the last hour of Friday afternoon. In a one-to-one situation, he would try patiently to dismantle the child's wall of indifference. They would have the staffroom to themselves. This small room at the back of the house doubled as a work and rest area. Desks were ranged along the walls and there was a table with coffee-making facilities under the window at one end. Three armchairs were grouped around a low table on which were scattered magazines and newspapers. Diamond had brought in one of the small chairs and spent some time deciding where to place it. Eventually he settled for a position facing one of the armchairs. He poured hot water onto instant coffee and sat in the armchair.

Mrs Straw appeared in the doorway. 'Miss Musgrave asked me to bring Naomi here.' She made it obvious from her tone that she thought the headmistress must have flipped. She still harboured some resentment at the way Diamond had bluffed his way into the school. However, she produced Naomi from behind her skirt and ushered the child to the chair.

Composed as usual, Naomi sat facing Diamond. She was wearing the red corduroy dress and black tights.

'She'll be all right with me,' he assured Mrs Straw. 'You don't have to stay.' When she continued to linger he added, 'Would you mind closing the door as you go?'

Left alone with Naomi, he tried what he thought was a reassuring smile. The small girl didn't alter her expression or her gaze, which seemed to be focused on the far end of the room, regardless that Diamond's substantial form blocked the view.

A number of times in his police career he'd interviewed shy or disaffected children. None had succeeded so successfully as Naomi in making him feel not merely small, but imperceptible. She sat demurely, hands together on her lap, feet crossed at the ankles, showing no interest whatsoever in the unfamiliar surroundings.

Diamond reached for his coffee and was taking a sip when it occurred to him that Naomi might appreciate a drink. Orangeade and other soft drinks were banned in the school for the effect certain additives were supposed to have on children, but milk was permitted. He got up and half-filled a paper cup from the carton beside the kettle. He handed it to Naomi and she took it with both hands and put it to her mouth.

It wasn't a breakthrough, he knew. She must have been eating and drinking these past weeks to have stayed alive. But at least it was a positive action. He watched her drain the cup.

'More?' he enquired, pointing to the carton. 'Naomi.' No response.

He held out his hand for the cup. She ignored it.

'All right,' he said evenly. 'Hang on to it if you want.' He topped up his own cup with coffee and returned to the armchair. Faced with such indifference from one so small, he felt more than usually gross. Partly to restore some self-esteem, he privately declared time out while he finished drinking.

Under the fringe of black hair, Naomi's almond eyes gazed steadily ahead, rarely blinking. If she saw anything of Diamond, it was the area where his tie met the lapel of his jacket, but in fact her eyes weren't focused there. Even if he contrived to slide down in the armchair to get on a level with the child, he still wouldn't achieve genuine eye contact.

The absence of eye contact was, he knew, a characteristic of the autistic behaviour pattern. Taken together with Naomi's refusal to speak and her indifference to what was happening around her, it made a diagnosis of autism more likely than any other. Diamond knew from conversations with Julia Musgrave and from his reading that parents, and sometimes teachers, had the greatest difficulty in accepting the reality of the condition, still less its inflexibility. Tantalised by evidence that these children were unimpaired in many respects and normal in appearance, the people who cared about them tried unavailingly to unlock the personalities imprisoned by the illness. Quite possibly he was engaged in the same futile exercise.

The coffee finished, he sat forward in the armchair and extended his right hand towards the child until his forefinger lightly touched her chest.

'Naomi.'

She didn't react in any way.

He brought the hand back and reversed the finger to indicate his own chest. 'Diamond.'

This establishing of identities was the first step in understanding. A baby learned to say 'Mama', 'Dada' and 'Baba' before anything else. Once the concept of meaning was grasped, the world of language opened up.

Still no response.

He repeated the actions and the words several times without result.

If she wouldn't respond verbally, perhaps he could coax her to make a significant gesture. He reached out and removed the empty paper cup from her hand. Then he took her fingers in his hand, feeling their warmth. Leaning towards her, he pressed her hand against his chest and spoke his name.

Not a flicker of comprehension. He let go of her hand. It dropped limply in her lap.

Without much confidence that she would get the idea and point to his chest, he said, 'Diamond.'

Nothing.

If only he could elicit some response, it would be a platform to build on. He squirmed to the edge of the armchair and leaned so close that all she had to do was lift her hand to touch him. He repeated, 'Diamond?'

Naomi dipped forward and for a moment he thought she had twigged what to do. Her eyes were on him. Then she sank her teeth into his nose. She bit hard.

'Jesus Christ!'

The pain was severe. Diamond yelled and pulled away. He clapped his hand to his nose. She'd drawn blood. It started dripping steadily.

He got up and looked around for something to staunch the flow. Finding nothing, he went to the door, leaving Naomi self-possessed again, still on the chair, her hands resting in her lap.

Mrs Straw, in the kitchen, didn't disguise her amusement. 'What's she done – bashed you on the nose – a scrap like her?'

He ran the cold tap and dipped his face under it.

Presently Mrs Straw produced cotton wool and liquid antiseptic from the first-aid cabinet. Diamond asked her to take Naomi back to Miss Musgrave. The one-to-one was over for today. First blood to Naomi.

*

What was it about noses, that nobody took them seriously? If the point of his chin had been covered with Elastoplast, people wouldn't have grinned at the sight of him. He knew he looked ridiculous, but the plaster was necessary. The bleeding had persisted, in spite of the smallness of the cut. Naomi's sharp front teeth had opened a flap of skin at the tip and it was most reluctant to dry up.

At least Julia Musgrave's smile was accompanied by sympathy. 'It's one of the hazards of the job, I'm afraid. I've been bitten in most places, but my nose has escaped up to now. How did she do it?'

When he'd explained, she said, 'You invaded her space. They have a pathological fear of anyone getting too dose. You've seen how Clive runs to the bookcase the minute he comes into my office.'

'When you say "they", you mean autistic kids?'

'Well, yes.'

'Naomi isn't like that,' Diamond insisted. 'She sits where she's told. She doesn't run off.'

'Didn't I warn you that their behaviour isn't all the same? It's a mental condition, Peter, not a physical thing like mumps which always produces the same symptoms. With some of them it takes an aggressive form, while others are passive.'

'You explained this to me the other day.'

'Well, then.'

'So why did she bite me? Hasn't anyone invaded her space before?'

Julia Musgrave nodded. 'I see what you mean. This is the first time she's bitten anyone, or shown any tendency to fight.'

'Is it possible she learned it from Clive?'

'The biting? I suppose it is, but they don't imitate each other much. They're too independent.'

'You keep saying "they",' Diamond objected testily. The bite, and the amusement it had created, had made him irritable. Some of his old colleagues in the police would have said his true character was beginning to emerge. 'Let's suppose Naomi isn't autistic. Suppose she has some other problem that stops her from speaking. Mightn't she be influenced by what the other kids do?'

Julia Musgrave sighed. 'I can't help thinking you're heading straight up a cul-de-sac. People find it so hard to accept that their kid is autistic.'

'Naomi isn't mine.'

She gave him a long look, not without sympathy, but accompanied by the slight smile that hadn't left her lips since she'd seen the injury. 'Let's say that you're taking a special interest. That's the agony with these children. They look bright. They can show glimmers of intelligence, even of brilliance in some cases. The textbooks call such children idiot savants.'

'Cruel,' Diamond commented.

'It's a cruel condition.'

'For the parents, I mean.'

'Oh, yes. It's harder to accept than having a child who is moronic. Some autistic children can sing quite intricate tunes before they're a year old. I've known a four-year-old who remembers every bar of a Beethoven symphony. They can do incredible things with numbers. They can hide some favourite toy and then weeks, months later, go straight to it. People marvel at such things and persuade themselves that there's a genius trying to get free, that it's simply a matter of finding the miracle cure. It isn't so, Peter. These kids are impaired for life. The memory may be functioning with super-efficiency, but the rest of the brain isn't. They can't reason as you or I can. They can't interpret the facts they know to any purpose. It's incredibly frustrating, but you have to accept it if you work with them.'

'Of course.'

'You're not discouraged?'

'I'm not a quitter, Julia. I'm ready for the next round.'

She regarded him with a kind of pity. 'It isn't a boxing match, in spite of the evidence to the contrary.'

He peeled off the Elastoplast on the way home in the tube, not wishing Stephanie to see it. The small cut had dried, but the area still felt sore. It was too much to hope that Steph wouldn't notice the minute he stepped through the door.

She said, 'Lunchtime drinks today?'

'Naomi.'

'I thought you told me she was only this high.'

'Yes, but I was sitting in an armchair.'

'With the child on your lap?' She paused. 'Have you *got* a lap these days, my love?'

'Not on my lap, for God's sake. I don't want child-molesting added to my record. No, I was leaning forward in the chair, trying to get her to touch me.'

'Pete, that sounds even more deplorable.'

'To identify me. To show that she understood my name.'

'She's Japanese, my love.'

He switched on the TV.

Later she said, 'Maybe you ought to try a different approach.'

'Such as?' He spoke sharply. He was still feeling frayed.

'You seem to be trying to get through to her on the basis that she isn't autistic. Have you thought of doing the other thing? In other words, testing whether she *is*?'

'How do I do that?'
'Better ask.'

After two more arid sessions in the staffroom with Naomi (keeping his distance) he was close to being persuaded that no progress was possible, and he admitted as much to Julia Musgrave. They were in the school garden during what was wishfully described in the timetable as playtime. Rajinder and Naomi were seated on swings of the kind that had side supports and safety-bars, being kept in motion by Mrs Straw. Not one of the trio seemed to be taking any pleasure in the exercise. Tabitha, sucking her thumb, was watching dolefully and Clive was hiding behind a sack of grass-seed in the gardener's shed.

'I've got to admire your persistence, Peter,' Julia Musgrave told him, 'but I have to say that I think you're right. You're up against a brick wall. Have you talked to the police? They took away the clothes Naomi was found in. I wonder if they found any clues.'

'You can stop wondering,' he told her. 'I know one of the inspectors there. The kid's things were sent off to the lab, and after a couple of weeks a five-page report came back, saying – in a nutshell – that they appeared to have been worn by a dark-haired female child. Oh, and they had the Marks and Spencer label. That cuts it down to five million, I should guess.' He picked a sprig of lavender and rolled it between his finger and thumb, watching the bits drop on the path. The scent was a favourite of Steph's. 'My wife thinks I'm going at this the wrong way round.'

'How do you mean?'

'She says instead of looking for signs that Naomi isn't autistic, I ought to be examining all the evidence that she *is*. Normality is impossible to prove.'

'It's a questionable concept anyway. She sounds like a bright lady, your wife.'

'Brighter than me, for sure.'

'Why don't you talk to Dr Ettlinger? He's coming in to look at Naomi this afternoon.'

Ettlinger was a child psychiatrist attached in some unspecified way to the school, a short, troll-like man with a prodigious crop of wiry black hair. It wasn't clear whether he'd been appointed by the local health authority or was a freelance who had persuaded Julia Musgrave that there might be something in it for the children. As Peter Diamond was only there himself by courtesy of Julia, he was in no position to object, but his private assessment was that Ettlinger ought not to have been let within a mile of young kids. The man was abrasive, opinionated and humourless. In spite of that, he seemed to have convinced everyone at the school that he was an international authority on autism, and presumably it was true.

'You'd better not waste my time,' he told Diamond waspishly when approached in the staffroom. 'I'm Teutonic. I have no interest whatsoever in the weather, or cricket, or cars.' From anyone else, the remark might have been meant to amuse. Not from Ettlinger.

'It's a professional matter, Doctor,' Diamond assured him, uncomfortably kowtowing. The days when he could pull rank on smart-mouthed forensic experts were just a memory now. 'I'm interested in Naomi, the Japanese girl. She's here because they believe she's autistic.'

'Correct.'

'So you agree that she is?'

'I didn't say that. I was merely confirming your statement.'

'But have you formed an opinion yet?'

'No.'

'Is that because you have doubts?'

'Certainly not,' Ettlinger snapped. 'Dubiety is unscientific. I am open-minded. Do you understand the difference? *You* may harbour doubts. I am open-minded.'

Diamond was tempted to remark that the state of Ettlinger's mind interested him less than Naomi's, but he checked himself.

Ettlinger added, 'I would need to study the child in a more systematic way than I can on occasional visits. She is not my patient.'

'I understand she shows some of the classical symptoms of autism.'

'*Classical?*' Ettlinger almost choked on the word, he was so indignant. '*Classical?* The condition wasn't given a name until 1943, and it wasn't studied in a serious way until the 1960s. How can you speak of symptoms as classical?'

'Typical, then.'

'I could object to that as well.'

Diamond didn't give him the opportunity. 'She doesn't speak. She avoids eye contact. Is that the profile of an autistic child? Because if it is, Naomi fits it perfectly.'

'What you have just described, Mr Diamond, may be indicative of autism; it is also the appropriate behaviour of well-brought-up young women throughout much of Asia. Have you thought of that? One cannot discount the possibility that her behaviour is governed, to some degree at least, by her culture.'

A persuasive point that Diamond accepted. He supposed he had borne it in mind up to now without articulating it. 'But not to speak at all, not even to the woman from the Japanese Embassy?'

'That, I grant you, is exceptional.'

'How do you recognize autism, then?'

Ettlinger sighed and glanced up at the staffroom clock. 'All right, how does anyone recognise it? Are there tests?'

'What do you mean?'

'X-rays, blood-tests, scans. I'm no expert.'

'There are no objective tests of that kind,' said Ettlinger with disdain. 'One looks at the behaviour. What I will say is that every child who fits this syndrome suffers from some degree of speech impairment, ranging from mutism to aphasia – which is confusion over the proper sequence of letters and words. Every child, Mr Diamond.'

Diamond placed a mental tick against Naomi's mutism.

'It is also true by definition that the autistic child is manifestly indifferent to other people, especially other children. Autism comes from the Greek, as you probably know. *Autos*. Self. Right?'

Another tick.

'However, one would expect to observe other impairments, such as problems of motor control.'

'Odd ways of walking, you mean, like Rajinder?'

'Yes.'

'Naomi isn't like that. She seems well co-ordinated.'

Ettlinger nodded. 'Some of them are. Curiously, they sometimes have the ability to keep their balance better than other children. They climb on furniture and leap around in a sure-footed manner. They could probably perform prodigious feats on a tightrope.'

Which wouldn't be easy to test, Diamond thought.

'And they won't get dizzy if they spin around.'

'That's something I didn't know.'

'It's commonly observed.'

'Anything else?'

Ettlinger spread his hands. 'Much else, Mr Diamond.

84

Repetitive behaviour, such as head-banging, or rocking, or staring into a mirror, or spinning things. The wheels of a toy, for instance. You must have watched Clive do that.'

'Of course. I don't think Naomi does it.'

Ettlinger was already onto other symptoms of autism. 'Abnormal reactions to sensory experiences, such as pain, or cold or heat. Hostility to being touched lightly.' There was the hint of a smile.

'You heard what happened to me?'

'I can see.'

'Was that to be expected of an autistic child?'

'They bite, yes.'

'I mean does it make the diagnosis more likely?'

'It's a small indication. Next time you should try being more boisterous, and see if she responds to it. They often enjoy a good romp.' The moral objection to a strange man 'romping' with a small girl seemed not to have occurred to Dr Ettlinger.

'Is anything known about the cause of the condition?'

A laugh came from deep in Ettlinger's throat. 'The cause, you say? Nobody knows. No known cause and no cure. There are theories. More theories than I have time to list, my friend. Personally, I am inclined to believe that the problem is organic, rather than emotional. It has nothing to do with the way the children are reared, as was once suspected. It goes back, in my opinion, to pre-, prior post-natal injury or illness affecting the brain. And don't ask me what can be done. Every week, practically, I read of some Svengali claiming spectacular success. Cures, even. You can hug these children, reward them, punish them, isolate them, put them on diets. They can be trained to some extent. I don't deny it. But so can chimpanzees. Personally I would rather train a chimpanzee. They're capable of affection, you know. Autistic children give none. They are tyrants.'

Diamond had heard all this with mounting distaste. 'That's hardly a scientific word, is it? Tyrants?'

The little doctor glared. 'Think of a better one. Spend as long as you like observing Naomi and think of a better one – if you can.' He turned his back on Diamond and went over to talk to someone else.

10

This morning Diamond was equipped with a pad of drawing paper and a marker. If this intractable little girl wouldn't respond to sounds, he'd decided, maybe it *was* a problem of language. He was going to see whether symbols would do the trick. He moved his chair next to hers and placed the pad on a low table in front of them. Then he drew a large circle and added a smaller one on top. A body and a head, evoking childish memories of beetle drives on wet afternoons in English holiday camps. Except that this was meant to represent his body and his head. He added stick legs and arms, followed by the facial features, with a scribble of hair above each ear to establish the margins of his bald dome. He held it up for Naomi, beamed encouragingly and said, 'Diamond.' He pointed to his chest.

Possibly, he persuaded himself, her eyes gave his artwork the credit of a glance. They certainly didn't linger on it. And she remained silent.

He touched the drawing and then tapped himself on the head.

'See? Diamond.'

Not a muscle twitched.

Refusing to be discouraged, he folded the picture over and drew a smaller figure on the next sheet, with the suggestion of a skirt and a passable attempt at fringed hair.

'Naomi.'

He pointed to her. Indicated her hair. Then added a flourish to the drawing, a small bow poised on top of the head. 'Like it?' He chuckled a little, and was conscious how forced it sounded. 'It's you.'

Not only was she unamused, she hadn't even looked.

Determined not to be thwarted, he turned back to the first drawing, tore it from the pad and set it on the table beside the second one, to make clear the contrast in size. 'Big Diamond. And little Naomi. Diamond. Naomi. Me and you.'

She seemed frozen.

Several more attempts to establish the significance of the drawings came to nothing.

'Would *you* like to draw?' He slid the pad across the table in front of her. Once on television he'd seen a boy suffering from autism who could do remarkable drawings of buildings from memory, precise in detail and perfect in perspective. After a visit to London the boy had made sketches of St Paul's and other buildings equally ornate. Two books of his drawings had been published.

Diamond wasn't expecting fine art from Naomi. He was willing to settle for a mark on the paper, of any sort. He took hold of her left hand and carefully inserted the marker between her fingers. He'd noticed that she used the left when she held a paper cup. Plenty of thought was going into this.

Naomi declined to grip the marker and let it flop out of her hand.

'I think you could do this,' he said, more for his own morale than the child's. 'I really think you could.' He replaced her fingers around the marker and guided her hand to produce a shaky circle on the drawing pad. 'There!'

The accomplishment was lost on Naomi.

'Suit yourself, miss.' More disappointed than he cared to show, he turned his back on the child and stepped over to the table where the coffee things were. He might as well switch the kettle on now so that the teachers didn't have to wait when they came in at lunchtime. That would be the sum of his achievements for this lesson. He checked the water level, pressed the switch and stared out of the window, listening to the kettle begin the moaning note that was sometimes mistaken for a child crying.

Then he was conscious of a light touch on his right hand. Unbidden, Naomi had got up from her chair and reached up to place her palm against his.

He stared down, amazed. Elated. Did he dare feel elated? She didn't return his glance, but what she had done was enough. It was the first positive gesture she had made towards him, or towards anyone in the school, so far as he knew. He let his fingers gently enclose the small hand. He and Naomi stood together in front of the window in silence, in some sort of harmony, the irresistible force and the immovable object.

The kettle was coming to the boil and it had some fault in the mechanism that stopped it from switching off. He let it steam for a time and then leaned forward and with his left hand switched off the wall-socket. Naomi took it as the signal to remove her hand from his and go back to her chair. He turned, smiling to let her see that it wasn't meant as a rejection. She didn't respond.

His eyes were misting. For pity's sake, he thought, I'm not going soft, am I? Peter Diamond, ex-CID?

At lunchtime, he told Julia Musgrave about the drawing session. They sat together on a bench under a sycamore tree in the school garden eating sandwiches. By then he was able to be more objective, admitting that it might be a mistake to place too much significance on the incident.

'No, we need all the encouragement that's going in this work,' she said. 'Some kids never make a spontaneous gesture of friendship like that to another person. Never. It's terrific news, Peter. Let's face it, no one else has made any progress with her. I think the woman from the embassy has despaired of ever getting through. She didn't come at all this week. She phoned instead. They're talking about sending Naomi to a school in Boston that specialises in autism. It's run by Japanese teachers.'

'Boston?' Diamond said, aghast. 'Send her to America? That's going to confuse the kid even more.'

'They're getting remarkable results. Several children from this country have been taken there. It may be the best solution for her. We're making no progress here – well, not until this morning.' She paused, looking at him earnestly. 'They call it the Boston Hagashi School. Apparently *hagashi* means hope in Japanese. Don't you think that's a beautiful idea?'

If it was, he wasn't receptive to it. 'Look, I know you mean to do right by Naomi, but suppose she isn't autistic?'

'It's not really my decision, Peter. She's in the care of the local authority.'

'Who'd be very relieved to have her taken off their hands, no doubt.'

'Now you're being cynical.'

'Tell me something, then. What precisely is being done to find her parents?'

She sighed. 'The police are making enquiries. No one has given any worthwhile information, so far as I can gather. No one has reported her missing. Where are the parents? Somebody definitely looked after her up to the time she was found. She was clean and decently dressed. She's been abandoned, Peter, and I don't think the parents are going to change their minds. Young mothers sometimes come forward to reclaim newborn babies left on doorsteps, but this is something else.'

'Agreed.'

'I often meet parents who feel they can't cope any longer with disturbed children – only they don't just leave them in Harrods and walk away.'

'What is it, six weeks now?' Diamond asked, making a point rather than seeking the answer, which he knew.

'Almost.'

'In the first week, her picture was in the papers.'

'And on television. Nothing came of it.'

He said thoughtfully, 'The picture was only a still, and it was only on the regional news. I'd like to get her on to a national TV programme, like *Crimewatch*.'

Julia Musgrave frowned. 'We don't know that a crime is involved.'

'Abandoning a child her age?'

She shook her head. 'It's not the best way to reach her parents. Somewhere out there is a very distressed mother.'

'All right, let's see if we can get Naomi on a chat show.'

'A *chat* show?'

'You'd do the chatting, but she'd be seen by millions.'

'Peter, I'm not sure that it's right to put a disturbed little girl in front of television cameras.'

He understood her reluctance without supporting it.

'I'd agree with you if she was a gibbering idiot, or scared of people, like Clive. But you and I know how she'll conduct herself on television. She'll stay as calm as ever. Self-possessed. She's in control. You can't deny that. And if she appears live, it's going to make a far bigger impact than a still picture. There's a very good chance that someone will recognise her.'

'I'm not at all happy about this.'

'And I'm far from happy about the kid being whisked off to America when her parents may still be here in England. Let me make some enquiries. This is just the kind of story they like to take up on TV. She's a very appealing child.'

'Exactly,' she said with passion. 'I don't want her used. We don't have the moral right to turn her into an object for people to goggle at. If she's on television, you can bet the papers will take it up. We'll have all sorts of well-meaning folk offering to adopt her, sending her toys—'

'Does she have any toys?'

'She isn't interested, Peter. We have a whole menagerie of stuffed animals.'

'How about toys with wheels?' he asked suddenly, recalling Dr Ettlinger's observation.

'She isn't a spinner, rest assured. Look, television is an entertainment medium. Naomi isn't entertainment, she's a vulnerable child with a serious impairment.'

'Julia, people aren't going to laugh at her, for God's sake.'

She regarded him steadily. 'If this had been Clive or Rajinder whose people we couldn't find, would you take them on television?'

'Probably not in a talk show,' he conceded.

'And why not?'

'Their behaviour wouldn't do them credit – but they're different. You and I know that Naomi would acquit herself impeccably.'

'Oh, yes?' A glint came to her eye. 'How do you know she wouldn't bite the cameraman?'

92

He had to smile at the prospect.

Julia's attention switched abruptly to Mrs Straw, who was bearing down on them from the direction of the house. From the manner of her approach, the carriage of her shoulders and the swing of her thighs, she had something awesome to announce, and she was going to make sure that it received its proper attention.

'What is it, Mrs Straw?' Julia asked.

'I think you should look in the staffroom, Miss Musgrave. Somebody stupidly left a marker pen lying about. The Japanese girl found it, and she's scribbled all over the walls, and they were only papered three months ago. You never saw anything like it!'

The vandalism in the staffroom provided Diamond with his first opportunity of detective work since leaving Bath. The perpetrator of the graffiti had done an effective job, for the walls were copiously covered in aimless scribble. Nor had the furniture escaped. The thick, black lines had turned the lower half of the room into what one of the teachers described as a Jackson Pollock. The reference went over Diamond's head, although it sounded apt.

Nobody, he learned by questioning Mrs Straw, had actually seen Naomi at work with the marker. The child had been found with it later in the dining room. She had refused to give it up. 'I had to prise her fingers off one by one,' Mrs Straw asserted. 'She was all set to do it all over the school.'

This, it turned out, was a false accusation. Doubtful that Naomi was the culprit, Diamond was able to demonstrate her innocence. When he examined the staffroom walls, he found that the scribbles ran higher than she was capable of reaching. Thus it was that the real culprit was apprehended in his usual hiding place behind the grass-seed in the garden shed. Not only was Clive's reach four inches higher than that of any other child in the school, his hands and clothes were stained with black marks. It transpired that he'd wandered into the staff-room at a time when nobody was about and had done the deed, afterwards throwing the marker away in the garden. Later, Naomi had picked it up.

'I'm afraid Mrs Straw is a vengeful woman,' Julia Musgrave confided to Diamond. 'She does work hard for the school, though. I don't think we'd manage without her.'

'She was right about one thing,' he admitted. 'I was daft to leave the marker out.' In this confessional vein, he went on rashly to promise to redecorate the staffroom – a severe penance indeed. This little crisis had sidetracked them from the more vital issue of whether it was right to put Naomi on television; not for long, he was resolved.

As he was leaving, calculating how many cans of emulsion he'd need, Julia called his name and came after him into the corridor.

He stopped, uncertain what to expect.

'You can have your marker back,' she told him. 'Believe it or not, the ink isn't all used up yet.'

He pocketed it, slightly puzzled. The marker belonged to the school anyway. She must have known.

She said, 'You don't really have to go to all that trouble – over the staffroom, I mean.'

'It's no sweat for me,' he lied.

'I appreciate the offer, only I wouldn't want you to think it will change anything.'

'Except the colour of the staffroom,' he said, grinning.

When he turned, he almost fell over Naomi. She must have been standing extremely close behind him, apparently waiting, because she stretched up her hand towards him. Twice in a day, he thought. This is too amazing to be true.

He extended his hand towards hers, but immediately she pulled it away. She didn't, after all, wish to renew the contact.

'Have it your way,' he said, wryly reflecting that even at that tender age, women played fast and loose with decent men's affections.

Sure enough, she proffered the hand a second time, only now her palm was outstretched as if she were asking for money.

'What is it, Naomi?' he asked, bending lower. 'What are you trying to say?'

Her eyes had lost that habitual glazed look. She was focusing on him intently, her forehead creased in concern. She began jabbing her hand at him repeatedly like a beggar in a Cairo bazaar.

He asked, 'Are you hungry?'

Whatever the problem was, she was really trying to communicate – a huge advance after six passive weeks – and the least he could do in return was discover what she wanted.

'It can't be money.'

As he bent even closer to her upturned face, she reached for his jacket, pulled it open and dipped her free hand into the inner pocket.

'Young lady,' he said, 'you're sharper than anyone suspected.'

Only it wasn't his wallet she was after. It was the marker that he'd stowed away in there after seeing Julia. Naomi whipped it out and clutched it to her chest with both hands, as if she wanted nothing so much in the world.

'God help us!' he said to her. 'What do I do now?'

It was quite a dilemma. If he let her keep the thing, someone – Mrs Straw, knowing his luck – was certain to see it and inform the rest of the school that they had a fifth columnist in their midst. Julia Musgrave would feel betrayed. If, on the other hand, he insisted on taking the marker back, the first shoots of affection he'd cultivated would be trampled upon, destroyed for ever. He remembered Mrs Straw's saying how she'd needed to prise Naomi's fingers away one by one. Clearly, that pen was a treasure to the child.

He decided to let her keep it, and run the risk that Clive might snatch it away and go on a graffiti-spree again. He was pretty confident Naomi wouldn't lightly give up her prize.

Gently, he put a hand on her shoulder and steered her in the direction of the staffroom. She was as compliant as ever now that he'd made it plain that he wasn't going to take back the marker. Coming into the staffroom without thinking about Clive's handiwork, he was freshly shocked at the extent of the scribbling. No one was sitting in there, and he could understand why. He escorted Naomi to the wall where the scrawl was thickest.

'You see what happened?' he said, hoping she would share his outrage, even if the words meant nothing to her. 'Clive did it. You wouldn't, would you?' He swept the air with his hands to reinforce the message.

She stood solemnly facing the vandalised wall. Troubled that he might have been too heavy-handed, he reached out impulsively to stroke her hair, then decided he shouldn't. An action like that could be misinterpreted, by others, if not the child. But his hand was already on her head, so he ruffled the dark hair instead – and still felt it was a liberty he shouldn't have taken.

The drawing pad he'd used earlier remained on the table, open at the picture he'd done of Naomi. He folded the pad and handed it to her. 'This is for drawing. You can have it. It's yours. Yours. All right?'

She appeared to understand. Her eyes briefly met his and she tucked the pad under her arm.

'Now let's find where you should be at this hour of the day.'

He found the class in a lesson that was down on the time-table as music, and consisted of indiscriminate tambourine-banging while the teacher, a cool young girl wearing a black fedora, strummed something on the guitar. Naomi settled cross-legged on the floor away from the others, continuing to hold the drawing pad and marker. She declined to take the tambourine Diamond found for her. He nodded to the teacher and left.

Now Julia Musgrave had to be told of his decision to entrust the marker to Naomi. He didn't want the news to be passed on by Mrs Straw, or anyone else for that matter. He believed he could make a persuasive case.

Julia wasn't alone in her office, but she called him in. Her visitor was a bearded, balding man in a brown corduroy jacket with patched elbows. An envelope file rested across his thighs and from his neck a thick pencil hung on a cord, all of which suggested to Diamond that this was a social worker. He was mistaken.

'Dr Dickinson is a child psychiatrist,' Julia explained. 'He's here to make an assessment of Naomi.'

'Another assessment?' said Diamond, mildly enough considering the warning bells that were sounding in his head.

'On behalf of the Japanese Embassy,' Dr Dickinson put in, using the kind of we-all-understand-how-the-world-goes-round tone that expects no disagreement. 'They want my opinion as to whether the child is autistic. The general idea is that she'll be sent to the Hagashi School in Boston if it appears that she'd benefit. She's a fortunate child.'

'Why is that?'

Dickinson frowned. 'The fees are out of most people's reach – about thirty thousand pounds a year.'

'I'm not impressed by money.'

Dickinson said cuttingly, 'Well, I'm extremely impressed by everything I've read about the school. As Naomi, I gather, is Japanese, this must be a happy arrangement.'

'You think so?'

'Mr Diamond has some reservations,' Julia Musgrave quickly added.

'Oh, and what's your specialism?' Dickinson asked witheringly.

'Testing the truth,' said Diamond. 'I'm a detective, or was until recently.'

Dickinson caught his breath and turned to Julia Musgrave. 'Really, I can't begin to understand why a detective . . .'

Julia Musgrave briefly explained the reason for Diamond's presence in the school and finished by remarking that only that morning his perseverance had paid a wonderful dividend.

'Oh, and what was that?'

'Naomi got up from her chair and held my hand,' Diamond informed him. 'It may not sound much, but it's a real advance.'

'Let us hope so,' the psychiatrist commented in a tone that suggested the reverse. 'Unfortunately the condition of autism is full of false dawns – not that I question the accuracy of what you experienced. It's so tempting with these children to draw unscientific assumptions from their behaviour. You assumed when she took your hand that she wished to express some trust, or affection. On the contrary—'

'But I didn't say that,' Diamond interrupted him. 'All I said was that she got up from the chair and held my hand. And speaking of unscientific assumptions, I'm surprised to hear you talking about autism in relation to Naomi before you've actually seen her.'

'I specialize in autism,' Dickinson said icily. 'I wouldn't have been invited here unless the child had exhibited autistic tendencies.'

Julia Musgrave judged it right to interrupt the exchange. 'Peter, what was it you came in about? Something urgent?'

'Something I'd like you to hear from me before you get it from anyone else,' he answered, and went on to tell her how it was that Naomi was back in possession of the marker. 'You don't mind?' he said finally, encouraged that she'd nodded more than once as he was relating the episode.

'It's a risk I'm willing to take,' Julia answered. 'Anything is preferable to that passive state she's been in for so long. Yes, I'm really heartened. She's being positive at last.'

Without much tact, Dr Dickinson offered his interpretation. 'This is very characteristic. Autistic children frequently become possessive about objects, to an exceptional degree, I mean. Mirrors, wheels, bits of crumpled paper. They refuse to be parted from them. It's compulsive.' He took a writing-pad from his folder and made a note.

'Oh, is that a pencil?' Diamond remarked. 'I thought it was a necklace.' Afterwards he regretted saying such a bitchy thing, not because he cared a sparrow's fart about Dickinson, but because it wasn't clever to fuel the man's evident dislike of him, which could easily prejudice his assessment of Naomi. Talking first and thinking after was a failing that had got Diamond into trouble in the past, and would again. He had the sense to leave Julia's office after that.

He slumped into an armchair in the staffroom, bemoaning his lowly status in the school. In his days in the police, he would have overruled Dickinson or any other headshrinker if a child's interests were under threat. He wouldn't have taken that horseshit about compulsive behaviour. Well, he thought, I didn't take it. But I'd have shown him the bloody door.

He couldn't be sure which way Julia Musgrave would jump. Her calm personality was a tremendous asset in a school like this. She was approachable and open to suggestions; which meant inconveniently that people like Dickinson got a hearing. Under pressure from the shrinks, the Japanese Embassy and the borough council, she was going to find it difficult, if not impossible, to hold on to Naomi. She was massively outgunned. One failed policeman convinced that everyone else was mistaken wasn't exactly the US Cavalry riding to the rescue.

His thoughts were interrupted by the jingle of tambourines being carried along the corridor, and the music teacher tottered in with the instruments stacked in her arms and the guitar slung across her back, and still wearing her fedora. She dumped everything onto a chair and went to the kettle. 'Want a coffee?'

'I wouldn't say no.'

'Thanks for bringing Naomi in. I didn't know where she was.'

He nodded. 'Does she take to the music?'

'Not that I've noticed. Would you prefer tea?'

'Whatever you're having.'

They waited for the kettle. The girl, an Australian from her accent, said, 'Your name is Diamond, right?'

'Yep.'

'Hold on, then. I've got something to show you. I won't be long.' She left him to make the coffee.

Presently she was back, with a large sheet of paper. 'Did you know you have a secret admirer?' She held the paper up.

He stared, disbelieving. 'Naomi did this?'

'Who else?' she said. 'And in my lesson. The little hussy won't bash a tambourine for me while you're on her mind.'

The mark on the paper was bold and unmistakable:

11

A narrow blue rectangle was visible between the World Trade Center and the New York Telephone Company. It was the Hudson River. Viewed from Manny Flexner's office on the twenty-first floor of the Manflex Building on West Broadway, it glittered brilliantly in the morning sun. Manny's office had windows from floor to ceiling, divided at the centre, which was about head height. The upper sections slid open, a feature Manny had insisted on. He liked his air-conditioning natural when he could get it. Today was one of those blissful days when the wind was minimal and the temperature ideal.

While his eyes were on the river he was speaking on the phone to his son David in Milan, and the things he was hearing pleased him immensely. Why couldn't every Monday morning be like this?

'The meeting went more smoothly than I had a right to expect,' David was saying. 'Okay, we had a few tough questions about the decision to close the plant, but most of them understood the problems and appreciated the trouble we were taking to relocate them. It was all incredibly civilized.'

'Thanks to the hard work you put in last week,' Manny said with approval. 'You did your homework. People appreciate that. How many want to transfer to Rome?'

'Fifteen to twenty. Another twenty or so want more time to reach a decision.'

'How many of those are researchers?'

'Eight, at the latest count.'

'Not bad. You want to keep the ratio of research high. The norm in the industry is one-third research, two-thirds development. I always tried to better that. How did the buy-out offer do?'

'The union is asking for more, but that's a union's job. My feeling is that they're willing to settle.'

Manny let out a long, contented breath. 'Dave, you did a fine job. Is there any more news how the fire started?'

'No, the police haven't been back. I sent them a list of everyone at the meeting. I figure that won't please them much because we've accounted for every man jack on the books. The cops I saw here were pushing the theory that it was an inside job.'

'They still haven't identified the bodies in the Alfa Romeo?'

'Not so far as I know.'

'Are the insurers any wiser?'

'I doubt it. Everyone is resigned to long delays. Pop, if it's still okay with you, I thought I might take a couple of days off at the end of this week, go and see Venice, like you suggested. Rico can hold the fort.'

'Venice?' Manny brooded for a moment, then came to a decision. 'Sure, son, you've earned it. I'm proud of what you're doing. But don't wait. Go now. Today. And, Dave, don't tell Rico where you're staying. Make it a real vacation. You understand?'

'Pop, I'm in no hurry. I have a couple of appointments in the morning.'

Manny said earnestly. 'Cancel them. Do this for me. I

know what I'm saying. Get the hell out of there if you want to see Venice. And, Dave . . .'

'Yes?'

'I love you, son.'

'Love you, Pop,' David answered in a bemused tone.

'Take care.'

'Sure.'

Manny cradled the phone. On his desk were a number of letters he'd written by hand. He picked out the one addressed to his son and wrote on the envelope *Hope Venice was magic*. Then he got up and poured himself a large brandy at the drinks cabinet and swallowed it rapidly.

He removed his reading glasses and replaced them in the case on the desk. Then he took out his pocketbook containing credit cards and some paper money and positioned it beside the spectacle-case.

On the other side of the office was an oval mahogany table with four matching chairs. Manny collected one of the chairs, carried it to the window and used it to climb onto his teak filing cabinet. His movements were ordered, automatic, and, for a man with a malignant illness, remarkably spry. He could easily step up to one of the open windows from there, and that was what he did. He got both feet on the metal frame and balanced there momentarily supported by his hands. The space was tall, so there was no need to stoop.

Manny didn't look down. His gaze was on the glittering section of river way ahead. The Hudson. And beyond, New Jersey. To Manny, in his fatalistic state of mind, the river might as well have been the Jordan, and beyond that was the promised land – a comforting thought. He was still looking ahead when he jumped. He kept watching the far shore while he started to drop, kept watching for as long as he was able.

12

Before everyone except Mrs Straw arrived at the school next morning, Diamond was in the staffroom making an island of the desks and other furniture. He'd called early at a do-it-yourself shop in Hammersmith and purchased two three-litre cans of vinyl matt emulsion in a shade described as apricot. On the chart it had looked the sort of colour that would blend with the furnishings – or so he'd easily convinced himself on seeing that it was offered at a special never-to-be-repeated discount. With the money he'd saved he'd gone straight into a toyshop across the street and bought a toy car with a friction motor. Later, he would give it to Clive; he had a place in his heart for the school vandal in spite of the extra work he had created.

So he was in his overalls applying the roller to the wall behind the door by eight-fifty, when the first of the teaching staff put in an appearance.

'What's all this?' Sally Truman, who took the youngest children, asked.

'A cover-up.'

'Oh, it's you.'

He dipped the roller into the paint tray and applied another band of apricot. Now that people had started arriving he wasn't going to down tools, just when he was entitled to some credit for this public-spirited effort. 'And how are you this morning?' he asked Sally.

'Tired, until I looked in here. The colour's woken me up.'

'Do you like it?'

She evaded the question. 'I expect it fades as it dries. They generally do. What is it?'

'Apricot.'

'Looks more like tomato to me. Now would you mind if I lift the dust-sheet and find my desk?'

He was gratified by a spate of congratulations in the next half-hour, even though the consensus of the teaching staff seemed to be that he should have paid a pound or two more and got magnolia or some other insipid shade. He listened with good humour and carried on obliterating Clive's eye-swivelling murals. By ten he was ready for a coffee break, and that required a rearrangement of the desks to get at the kettle. He'd covered two walls. Now that he stood back, the effect did appear more red than apricot.

He was earning plenty of good will for trying, however, and no one had complained about the disruption. They rummaged under the dust-sheets for chairs and sat as usual with their coffee-cups, catching up on developments since they had last shared a break. The news from yesterday of Naomi's drawing was the main topic this morning. In this small school every child was known to the teachers.

'It's got to be good news, Peter,' the deputy head, John Taffler said. 'And by God, you deserve some encouragement after all the time you've put in with that kid.'

Diamond was less sanguine. He'd had a night to think it over. 'I'd be more encouraged if it was something I'd taught her.'

Taffler wagged a finger at him. 'Don't be so ungrateful, man. It's recognition. It's your name. She's registered that you exist.'

'I wouldn't bet on it.'

'Oh, come on – why else would she draw a diamond? She knows your name.'

He looked around him at the faces of the staff. 'How would she know the symbol for it? I didn't tell her, and nor did anyone else, so far as I can make out.'

'Maybe she plays poker,' someone said, and got a few laughs.

Sally Truman said, 'It proves that she speaks English. Surely that's apparent now?'

Diamond pointed out gloomily that she didn't speak anything.

'Understands it, then,' Sally insisted. 'She heard your name and related it to the shape. She's trying to communicate.'

Someone else, one of the part-time teachers, then voiced the uncertainty that Peter Diamond himself was feeling. 'Let's not read too much into this. The kid could have drawn the shape in a random way. She may never repeat it.'

'She may not have the opportunity,' Taffler commented in the arch tone of someone with inside information. 'Not in this place, at any rate. Did you hear that Olly Dickinson, the shrink who was here yesterday, confirmed her as autistic? She's off to America as soon as they can organise it.'

Diamond had feared he would hear something like this before much longer, but it still raised his blood pressure by many points. He slammed down his mug, slopping coffee over the table. 'So it's the tidiest outcome for everyone,' he said bitterly. 'This school unloads a kid it can't do

107

anything for, and so do the social services. The police stop making inquiries. Dickinson pockets a fat fee. The embassy stumps up and salves its collective conscience. Out in America they cash the cheque and add a new name to the roll. Bully for everyone – except one small girl who can't speak a word to prevent it.' He got up and marched out, straight to Julia Musgrave's office.

He swung the door open. 'When is she due to leave?' he demanded without preamble.

Julia looked up from some paperwork she had on her desk. Her eyes widened, no doubt at the sight of his over-alls. She hadn't been near the staffroom yet. 'Peter, why don't you sit down a moment?'

'I'm too bloody angry, that's why. Just tell me how long I've got. That's all I want to know.'

'What do you mean – how long you've got?'

'Isn't it obvious? To find her people.'

The colour had drained from her face. She said, 'Peter, I'm not ungrateful for all the efforts you made with Naomi, only I have to remind you that you volunteered. It gave you no stake in her future.'

He didn't exactly shake his fist at her, but he clenched it and pounded the space in front of him as he declared, 'You talk about her future. I'm still trying to reconstruct her past. You and your cronies are about to blow it away.'

She looked as if he'd struck her. Pitching her voice lower in the effort to control it, she said, 'I resent that remark. I resent it deeply. If you want to know, I argued, I pleaded, for Naomi to remain here until we'd exhausted every possibility. I was in a minority of one.'

There was a moment of strained silence.

'I'm sorry.' Completely deflated, he took a couple of steps towards her, raising his hands in a futile gesture of disavowal. 'Christ, that's me mouthing off again without getting a grip of the facts. Julia, I'm more sorry than I can say.'

She shook her head in a way that seemed to mean words of any sort could only distress her more. She simply said, 'Probably Sunday.'

Sunday.

Four days.

By the time he returned to the staffroom everyone else had left. Instead of picking up the roller, he dragged the phone and the Yellow Pages from under the dust-sheet and started calling television companies, trying the shows he'd targeted for a slot about Naomi and asking each time for the senior person on duty. If he found himself palmed off with a research assistant, he had no conscience about using his former police rank and asking for someone more senior. In the robust style of his days in the murder squad, he badgered his way steadily through the BBC, Thames TV and Sky, all the breakfast shows, the mid-morning studio debates, the women's interest programmes and the talk shows, early evening and night. He missed nothing out in selling the idea of an unsolved mystery involving a small girl who'd triggered the alarms in Harrods and still hadn't been identified two months later. From the majority came dusty answers. A few referred him elsewhere and some took his number and promised to call back if their editorial team (or whatever) expressed any interest.

After that, there was nothing for it but to pick up the roller again. By lunchtime the job was finished and no one had phoned back. His shoulders ached and his throat was dry. Mrs Straw came in, obdurately ignored the immaculate, gleaming walls and pointed out some paint marks on the floor. He assured her that the paint was water-based and easily removable. Feeling as he did, he didn't actually undertake to clear the offending spots immediately, so Mrs S. made a production number out of fetching a bucket and squeegee and soaking the entire floor just as the staff were arriving for their lunch-break.

But there was something to lift his spirits, and it wasn't a compliment on his decorating. John Taffler grabbed him by the arm and said, 'Come and look at this, mate.'

Diamond followed him out to the garden, where the children had already started their playtime. Seated on a low wall beside the vegetable garden was Naomi. She had the drawing pad on her knees and she was using the marker, entirely absorbed.

With stealth, Diamond approached close enough to get a sight over her shoulder of what she was doing. She had drawn a series of fifteen or so diamond shapes, roughly similar in size, each one in isolation.

'How about that?' Taffler said. 'Random, my arse. She's turning them out in batches.'

110

Pleasing as it was to Diamond, the drawing left him mystified.

Taffler was crouching on Naomi's level and talking to her. 'Nice work, my darling. Beautiful! Diamonds.' He tapped several of the shapes consecutively. 'Diamond, diamond, diamond.' Then he pointed upwards. 'Mr Diamond. That's what you're telling us, sweetie, right?'

The child paused in her work and actually glanced up for a moment at Diamond. Inconveniently there was nothing in her look to support John Taffler's assumption, nothing remotely indicating that Diamond was on her mind. She frowned and turned away.

'Let's be thankful for what we've got,' Diamond said, determined to be positive. 'She's using the pen, and that's progress.'

'Well, yes.' Taffler stood upright again. 'At least she's coming out of that totally passive state. On the other hand,' he added as they started back towards the house, 'it's a little worrying that she isn't drawing anything else. It could get obsessional.'

Diamond was in no frame of mind to face that particular scare. Nor was he overjoyed to find Dr Ettlinger in the staffroom when he returned there. The psychiatrist was holding forth to an audience of one – Mrs Straw – about colour in the working environment. Apparently apricot, or orange, as Ettlinger termed it, was a highly unsuitable choice for a common room, liable to stimulate aggression. Predictably, too, from a psychiatrist, there were sexual implications. Red and orange were the colours of heat and passion. Listening to all this, Diamond could hardly wait for the orgies over coffee and cheese sandwiches. Not content with putting suspicions of carnality into Mrs Straw's head, Ettlinger went on to speculate that whoever had chosen such an unsuitable colour must be in urgent need of therapy. There was a deep-seated and dangerous aggression in such a personality.

To which Diamond, dressed in his paint-spattered overalls, responded, 'Rest assured, Doc, if I find him, I'll strangle him with my bare hands.'

Hearing this, Mrs Straw quit the room without her squeegee and bucket.

Ettlinger, the dour Dr Ettlinger, actually raised a smile. He could appreciate a psychological quip, even if it was directed his way. 'I didn't know you had suicidal tendencies,' he said ponderously to Diamond. 'Self-strangulation is difficult to achieve, I hear.'

Curiously enough, this bizarre conversation got both men off on a better footing. Diamond admitted that he was feeling angry – not suicidal – about the decision over Naomi. This was the first Ettlinger had heard of it. He shared in the indignation. After all, he regarded himself as the school's pet shrink.

Diamond suggested a coffee and switched on the kettle.

'I shouldn't say this about a professional colleague, but I will,' Ettlinger declared. 'Oliver Dickinson ought to be ashamed of himself. I defy any psychiatrist to diagnose autism in one session, particularly in the case of a child like Naomi, whose behaviour is predominantly passive.'

'He could be wrong?'

'I keep an open mind.'

'I remember,' said Diamond, sensing a way to prise more information from his new chum. 'But without committing yourself, is there any other explanation for the fact that she refuses to speak?'

Ettlinger's eyes twinkled in triplicate through his thick lenses. 'You want to muddy the waters a little?'

'I wouldn't say that, but I'm fishing.'

'Well, it's not impossible that this is a case of elective mutism.'

'Say that again.'

Ettlinger obliged. 'It's a psychological disorder that affects some children of three years and upwards. Something inhibits them from speaking. In certain cases this manifests itself at school and they talk normally at home. The most serious cases go totally silent, and keep it up for months and even years.'

'Can it be treated?'

'There is no cure, as such. They grow out of it, and some of them are given help, but it's hard to say whether they would have recovered regardless. The best results are achieved one-to-one. Putting such children into a class with others is not always advisable, particularly if those others are disturbed in other ways. The child may imitate them, consciously or unconsciously.'

'And ape their behaviour?'

Ettlinger nodded.

'Such as biting?'

This drew a sly smile. 'Why not?'

Diamond was finding elective mutism increasingly plausible as a theory. 'Would this also explain the avoidance of eye-contact?'

'I wouldn't regard that as the sort of behaviour a child would notice in another,' Ettlinger said. 'However, if she is anxious to avoid speech, she will very likely shun situations requiring responses. So for that reason she may look away from people.'

'You say nobody knows the cause of this, em, what did you call it? . . . Elective, er . . .?'

'Mutism.' Ettlinger shrugged. 'One can't generalize.

Sometimes school phobia is thought to trigger it. You move the child to a new school, or a new class, and the speech returns. But in most cases the onset comes earlier in the child's life and the problem isn't so clear, or so easily resolved. It may result from some emotional disturbance of which adults are unaware.'

Diamond made the coffee and handed over a steaming mug. 'In Naomi's case, she's been parted from her parents. Abandoned, possibly. Is that the kind of disturbance you mean?'

'Yes, an experience as shocking as that could amount to a trauma.'

'Trauma? That's a different ball-game.'

Ettlinger pulled a face at the analogy, making it plain that matiness had its limitations. 'I would define trauma as a deep emotional wound, an injury to the psyche.'

'Can it make a child mute?'

'Certainly.'

'And is it curable?'

'Let's say that the condition is usually of limited duration.'

'So she will recover her speech?'

'I wasn't discussing a particular case.'

Diamond conceded with a nod. 'That's another possible explanation, then. So far we have autism, elective mutism, and now, trauma.'

Ettlinger beamed. 'Have we muddied the water sufficiently?'

Diamond nodded. Confusion wasn't the object, of course; quite the contrary. He'd enlisted the support of an expert in questioning the assumption that Naomi was autistic. He hadn't enough clout to prevent her being put on that flight to Boston on Sunday, but he felt more clear in his own mind that he was right to protest.

Late that afternoon there was another boost. A call from the BBC. A generous-minded producer who had given him not a glimmer of hope that morning had since talked to someone's PA over lunch at the Television Centre, and she'd passed on the word about Naomi to her producer, who was now on the line. A new programme Diamond had never heard of called *What About the Kids?* had been running on BBC2 for two weeks, a Friday afternoon show featuring children and presented by children. It consisted mainly of two- or three-minute items such as song and dance, circus acts, animal training, a word game, demonstrations of toys, interviews with kids who'd been in the news and with adults like writers and artists who produced work for children.

The whole thing sounded like a dog's breakfast, but Diamond was careful not to say so. 'I bet the kids love it.'

'Surprisingly, the audience figures aren't all that encouraging,' the producer, who revelled in the name of Cedric Athelhampton, admitted, 'but we are back-to-back with Tin-Tin and Jackanory. The controllers are willing to live with moderate figures as long as we have some educational content, social issues and so forth. We're trying to include some items with more weight.'

Try me for size, Diamond thought frivolously. In fact, he felt lighter than air at this minute. 'You're looking for serious issues?'

'Exactly – only they have to be conveyed simply and directly. And they must involve children, which is why I pricked up my ears when I heard about your Japanese girl. She *is* the child found in Harrods?'

'Yes.'

'And she still doesn't speak a word?'

'Not a syllable.'

'And nobody has identified her in all this time? I'll tell

115

you how I see this, Mr Diamond. I've had a rather creative idea. We'll present it as a challenge. Do you follow me?'

With admirable self-restraint, Diamond indicated that he was keeping up.

Cedric Athelhampton's voice thickened and swelled in anticipation. 'This will really engage our audience. Kids adore playing detective. See if they recognise her from school or the park or the street where they play. Tell me, Mr Diamond, what exactly is your connection with this girl?'

He was primed for this one. 'I just took an interest in her case. Speaking of detectives, I'm ex-CID myself.'

'How divine.'

It was the first time he'd heard it so described.

The only hitch in all this euphoria was that Cedric was thinking in terms of the programme a week on Friday.

'Sorry. No chance,' said Diamond. 'Can't you slot her in this week?'

'I wish I could, ducky, but we're in pink script for Friday.'

'Does that make a difference?' he enquired, trying manfully not to let the 'ducky' unsettle him.

'It's a live show, Mr Diamond. We can't take more risks than we have to.'

'A live show for children? Is that usual?'

'Nothing about our show is usual. That's why it's so riveting. Can you come in on Friday week?'

'No. She'll be in America by then.'

'America! Whatever for?'

Without hesitation, he said, 'Prime-time television. She's going to be a sensation over there, they tell me.' He could be creative too, when pushed.

13

David Flexner turned over the envelope for the umpteenth time and looked at the four hastily scribbled words *Hope Venice was magic*. Schmaltz, pure schmaltz, he told himself, as an all too genuine tear misted his vision. Pop, you always knew how to pluck the heart-strings; and you always succeeded.

No question, Venice had been magic. He'd acted on Manny's advice and driven there the same night. Dropped everything, or almost everything. Bullish from handling his first executive assignment so effectively, he'd invited the winsome Pia to accompany him. To his delight, she'd laughed, squeezed his hand and accepted. They'd stayed three days and two unforgettable nights in a palace – the Hotel Cipriani on the tip of Guidecca Island, facing the Lido. Venice had been magic and so had Pia.

All of which made the aftermath – the return to Milan – even more distressing. Rico's, 'Where were you? We had no way of contacting you,' may not have been meant as a recrimination, but sounded like it. On being informed what Manny had done, David had felt overwhelmed by guilt. Only afterwards, during the flight to New York, did he mentally run through the sequence of events and accept that his father had wished it this way, wished him to get away – actually to enjoy himself – before he learned the terrible news.

117

Manny had fallen twenty-one floors and died on impact with the parking lot. Cancer would have taken him in a matter of months. A double shock for David.

On arrival at JFK, he was met by Michael Leapman, who embraced him supportively and handed him the letter from his father. He didn't immediately open it. The message on the back was as much as he could take at this time. At David's own suggestion, they drove straight to the morgue and went through the necessary ordeal of identification. Amazingly Manny's face was unmarked. There was damage to the base of the skull, the mortician explained, but he had hit the ground feet first. For the viewing of the corpse, everything was covered except the face. Prepared for injuries so extreme that he would have difficulty in recognising his father, David was surprised and deeply moved to see the features he'd known and loved. He stooped to kiss Manny's forehead and whisper a farewell, and, as he did so, a curious thing happened. David's hair, fastened as usual in a ponytail, slipped off his shoulder and flopped over the pale face. Quickly he drew it aside and Manny's left eye opened. The dragging movement of the hair must have been responsible, but the effect was startling. It was almost as if his father winked at him. Straight away he stroked his hand over the face and closed the eyelid. The incident was over so rapidly that the others may not even have noticed. Certainly nothing was said.

Out in the daylight, Michael Leapman suggested a drink before returning to the office. They picked an Irish bar on the next block. 'You may wish to catch up on your letter,' Leapman suggested when they were seated. There was something else besides sympathy in his manner, and it was not unlike respect. In their previous encounters in the boardroom, more often than not he'd disregarded David – but then so had most of the other directors.

'Later.'

'Don't get me wrong. I don't want to be a drag, only I think you should look at it now, before we check in at the office. If it's anything like the letter I had, there are things to be done real soon.'

Leapman was right, David discovered. It was that sort of letter – Manny still calling the tune. Just one sentence to indicate that this was a suicide note: '*Sorry it had to happen like this, Davey, but you know me – couldn't ever wait for a darned thing.*' Then straight to business: '*I want you to take over as Chairman. My entire estate, including my holdings of shares, will come to you. I told Michael Leapman my wishes and he's promised his support. He'll propose you for Chairman at an Emergency Meeting I've asked him to convene. The Board will back you. It's essential there's no delay, no perceived reluctance from you, or the stock will drop and the predators will swallow us. Handle it as positively as you just handled the problem in Milan and we'll get through without damage, hell, no, we'll prosper. Take my word for it, Davey, when you're in charge, you'll be on a permanent high. Just remember you're the boss. You take the initiative, right? You need technical advice, take it, only don't let anyone railroad you. I don't mind admitting Manflex is short on new products that will pay off in the next decade. You have some major decisions to take. In this industry you can't play safe for ever. I could go on, but I figure I've said enough. You're going to make it, I know you are, kid.*' He'd signed it: '*Your loving Pop.*'

David sat rigidly in his chair and read the letter a second time. You can take so many shocks and then you enter a catatonic state. He felt close to that. *Chairman of Manflex* – it was bizarre. He'd never seriously contemplated such

119

an outcome. He'd always assumed that the family would retain a major stake in the business after Manny went, but that others would undertake the management. He'd be content to keep his nominal seat on the Board without ever burdening himself with policy decisions. He was into creative things, not pesky pills.

He leaned against the banquette and looked towards the ceiling.

'He surprised you?' Leapman queried.

'That's an understatement.'

'I urged him to speak to you, tell you his plans. He wouldn't have it. Said something about having management thrust upon you. Thought you'd function best if it came without warning.'

David's eyes switched to Leapman. 'Do you mean he told you he was planning to kill himself?'

'No. Well, not in a way that I understood.' Leapman nervously fingered his tie.

'He told you about the cancer?'

'Yes.'

'And what exactly did he say he would do about it?'

Leapman examined his beer intently, as if the answer to David's question might rise to the surface.

'Go on,' David insisted. 'I want to know.'

'He, em – this is embarrassing – he said he was going to . . . step down.'

David's lips softened slowly into a grin and the grin turned to a laugh, the first breach in the gloom since he'd heard that Manny was dead. 'And he stepped down twenty-one floors. That's typical of Pop. A bad-taste joke about his own suicide. Come on, Michael, I don't mind if you laugh. Pop certainly wouldn't. You bet he enjoyed saying it.'

Leapman mustered a smile from somewhere. He'd never been in tune with Manny's humour.

David found it comical, the more so when he imagined his father's secret enjoyment in seeding the idea to his solemn sidekick. 'So did he also tell you he wanted me to step up, so to speak?'

Leapman nodded.

'Did you think he was out of his mind? Be honest.'

'It was unexpected. But you can count on my total support,' Leapman added quickly.

'I'm going to need it.' A declaration of intent from David. Suddenly, intuitively, but irreversibly, he'd made the greatest decision in his life. He would give the job his best shot, in spite of his contempt for the business world. The mission to Milan had boosted his estimate of his own ability as an executive. Manny had been wise, as well as witty. He was right about the high to be had from being in control. 'The shareholders have to be reassured,' he said as if the matter had been utmost in his mind for weeks. 'What's been happening to our stock price? I saw in the plane it fell sharply when the news broke.'

'Down another six points this morning. Someone is going to stage a raid unless we buck the trend.'

'A takeover, you mean?'

'That's the danger. The bastards know that there's value there. It's all about loss of confidence. We go into decline and they wait for the moment to strike.'

'And then they break us up.'

'It could happen very soon.'

'Unless we act.'

'Right.' Leapman ran his right forefinger slowly around the rim of his glass. 'To restore confidence you need something positive to tell the market. Thanks to your father, we have the reputation of being rock-solid, or did, until the last couple of weeks. We have a good base of OTC products—'

'OTC?'

Over the counter. Consumer brands. And Kaprofix is still one of the top prescription drugs for angina.'

'But could be overtaken soon?'

'Already has been. Adalat-Procardia has raced ahead of us.'

'Whose is that?'

'It's jointly produced by Bayer and Pfizer. And Marion-M Dow are making inroads with their drug.'

'We must have plenty of things under development.'

Leapman shook his head. 'Not for the angina market. And the patents of Kaprofix start expiring in 1993.'

'That means our competitors can market me-too imitations?'

'Right.'

There was a bleak period of silence.

David resumed, 'It's becoming screamingly obvious that I need to bone up on our research and development programme. You're closer to it than I am, Michael. Is there anything at a promising stage? My father implied in his letter that decisions had to be taken soon.'

'That's a tough one,' Leapman hedged. 'Sure, I can run through the possibilities with you, only I'd rather do it in the office with some figures in front of me.'

'Good enough. Let's go.'

Leapman hesitated. 'Something I wanted to mention. There's a guy you really should meet. Professor Alaric Churchward, from Corydon University.'

'Corydon? Where in hell is that?'

'Indianapolis. They specialize in the biological sciences.

I think they were established during the Kennedy Administration, or soon after, about the time when the potential of genetics began to be appreciated.'

'After the DNA code was broken?'

He nodded. 'Churchward joined them from Yale about 1981, I believe. If you had to pick out a future Nobel Laureate, he'd be the obvious choice.'

'And you think he would be useful to us?'

'He already is. We have strong links with Corydon, thanks to your father. We're funding a good proportion of the research that goes on there.'

'In genetic engineering, you mean?' David's voice was pitched on a note of unease.

'You don't have to sound so dubious,' Leapman gently chided him. 'Genetically-engineered drugs are the future of our industry. The great advances in medical health from now on are going to be made by geneticists. They already provided us with safer and better insulin for diabetics. In the next twenty years, they're going to produce vaccines for every disease you care to name.' He paused and took more beer. 'But as it happens, the latest breakthrough owes nothing at all to biotechnology.'

'A breakthrough? You really mean that?'

Leapman actually summoned up a smile. 'From old-fashioned chemical compounds, David.'

'A drug?'

He nodded.

'What for – which disease?'

'The most prevalent killer of all.'

'Cancer?'

'Old age, David. Old age.'

14

Manny Flexner's funeral service took place in the ante-chapel of the Temple Emanu-El on Fifth Avenue, the world's largest synagogue. The attendance of over two hundred and fifty was a measure of his popularity; Jews, gentiles, a broad cross-section of New York society. 'He was a much-loved man,' the rabbi said in his address, admittedly something of a cliché in funeral orations, but in this case it was true on several counts, most obviously the high count of attractive women in the congregation.

Later the same afternoon, while most of the family were still crowded into the house on the Upper East Side eating sandwiches and trading stories about Manny's escapades in love and business, an Emergency Board Meeting was held at the Manflex headquarters. David Flexner was proposed as the new Chairman and elected unopposed. Michael Leapman, his proposer, made it clear that this had been Manny's wish. The seven executive and two non-executive members applauded politely and a bottle of champagne was opened. The price of Manflex stock, which had been falling all week, picked up a few points by the close of trading.

'Better news, then,' David remarked, when Leapman told him.

'Sorry, but it isn't. The price rose on a rumour that

someone is buying shares in significant numbers. The market senses a takeover bid.'

'So soon?'

'Sharks are fast movers. We've taken a hard knock and they scent blood.'

Vehemently, by his easy-going standard, David said, 'They can go to hell, Michael. No asset-stripper is going to tear Manflex apart. It was my father's life. Thousands of other lives are staked in it. I have a responsibility to the work-force.'

Leapman rested a hand on his shoulder. 'Don't let it get to you, David. This is the way the market works, unfortunately.'

'It's all about confidence, right?' said David. 'We have to demonstrate that Manflex has a future under my management.'

'Sure – and if we play it right—'

'I know what you're going to say, but it seems incredible to me that the survival of a great pharmaceuticals group like ours can hang on one blockbuster. Damn it, we sell hundreds of products.'

'So do our competitors. But where would Glaxo be without Zantac, or Smith Kline Beecham without Tagamet? In reality what you need is a steady flow of new products, but that requires an incredible outlay on research. Have you any idea how many drugs are patented and tested for every one that is successful? Five thousand, David. Five thousand to one. Those are the odds in this business. We're not equipped to compete on that scale, not any more.'

'Okay, I get the point. I must meet with Professor Churchward just as soon as possible. Does that mean a trip to Indianapolis?'

Leapman nodded. 'How soon do you want to go?'

'The next available flight, I guess. Really I should be back at the house with the family right now. They'll have to make allowances.'

'Can't you tell them it's important business?'

'You know what they'll say? "Isn't he just like his father?"'

They took the plane that evening and spent the night at the Hilton-at-the-Circle in Indianapolis. After breakfast, they took a taxi out to Corydon University, some fifteen minutes' drive west along Washington Street and beyond the airport. Leapman filled in some background on the man they were about to meet. 'He didn't discover PDM3, but he was the first to see its potential. He's been working on a treatment for Alzheimer's disease for at least ten years, originally for his PhD, I believe. About five years ago he started testing a compound that seemed to have some potential in combating the memory loss associated with Alzheimer's. We called it Prodermolate, or PDM3. The first results were promising, no more, but lately – and I mean just in the past few weeks – he's come up with some results that can only be described as sensational, David. They have implications not just for Alzheimer's, but for the mental capacities of the population at large.'

'You said my father knew about this project?' David enquired.

'Sure, Manny knew. He met Prof Churchward several times.'

'So what was his assessment?'

'Of Churchward?'

'Of PDM3.'

'He gave it his backing.'

'You mean he was willing to stake the future of Manflex on it?'

Leapman shook his head. 'He didn't have the information we have.'

'But it's only just over a week since he died. Has it all taken off since then?'

Leapman put his hand to his face and as if heralding a sensitive matter. 'Well, David, Manny was a terrific guy and we all loved him—'

'But?'

'But towards the end he had his mind on other things. I don't blame him for that. When he told me about his terminal illness, I saw problems for the business, so I did what anyone in my position would do – discreetly took the pulse of the company. I asked for an update on all the research that we were undertaking, right across the world. That was how I learned that Churchward was almost ready to publish these fantastic results with PDM3.'

'You didn't discuss it with Pop?'

'I left it too late.'

Corydon University campus was compact and unfussy. Not an ivy leaf in sight. Solid sixties pre-structured building with some computer-age additions. Security cameras at the entrance. A black-uniformed receptionist flanked by video screens and with a console in front of him. He keyed in their names and they watched them appear on one of the monitors. Then they had to go through the ritual of being photographed for identity tags. Finally, Professor Churchward's secretary arrived – a demure young woman with a tag that read *Bridget Walkswell* fixed on her shirtfront. She looked the sort who would suffer acute embarrassment if anyone made a joke of her name. With a walk so innocent of any suggestion of a wiggle that she must have worked on it in front of a mirror, she escorted them to an elevator.

They stepped out into a low-ceilinged laboratory bristling with equipment, huge transparent cylinders on stands and metal structures festooned with white tubing and electric flex. Buff-coloured notices were prominent everywhere warning of biohazards such as mouth-pipetting. The steady hum of computers from the far end drew their attention to a series of keyboards and screens ranged along a bench. Something very like a submarine periscope was mounted there. It was being used by a slight, dark-haired man in a white coat.

Bridget Walkswell announced them.

'One moment,' the professor said without moving from the eyepiece. He touched an adjustment control. Beside him on a video display there was a small movement in a pattern looking like a Chinese ideogram which David recognized as a configuration of DNA, the genetic blueprint. The professor continued with what he was doing for another half-minute or so. When he eventually drew back, he still didn't give his visitors a glance. His chair was on casters and he glided to his right and tapped something into the nearest computer.

Without exactly apologising for her boss, Ms Walkswell spread her hands in what amounted to a gesture of helplessness and then brought out two stools from under the bench. David and Leapman sat and waited.

Finally Professor Churchward swivelled around and said, 'So are we in business, gentlemen?' – at the same time snapping his fingers and gesturing towards the door. Ms Walkswell left the room.

Obviously the great man had more interesting things to do with his time than talk to a couple of business execs from New York. However, he offered them coffee, gesturing to a beaker of water simmering over a Bunsen burner.

Beside it were some chipped mugs and unwashed spoons. Speaking almost in unison, they said they'd only just finished breakfast.

Churchward looked like a marathon runner, without an ounce of spare flesh, but his metabolism didn't require athletics to keep him in shape. He was one of the type who burn up energy without getting out of a chair. His intense blue eyes, lodged in a small, bony face, flicked over David's casual attire, missing nothing. There was no clue as to what he thought. He wore a plain brown tie and his own hair was as short as a marine's.

'David took over as Chairman of Manflex yesterday,' Michael Leapman explained.

Churchward nodded as if he already knew. No words of regret about Manny's passing. 'And you want an update from me on Prodermolate. You know the background?'

'Let's assume I know nothing,' said David, who knew not very much.

'As you wish. The compound that we call PDM3 was discovered as long ago as 1975 by a team at Cornell. They were funded by Beaver River Chemicals, which is now a Manflex subsidiary, as I guess you know. The formula was registered along with a million others, but it wasn't considered to be of any commercial use until about five years back, when a decision was taken in this department to initiate research into protective agents. You know what I mean?'

David frowned. The question was addressed to him and he felt that he ought to make a stab. 'Contraceptives?'

The professor closed his eyes and took a deep, restorative breath before opening them again. 'Protective agents are drugs that appear to protect certain of the nerve cells in the brain from dying. Nobody understands why. Your

129

father, who kept up with developments, knew that some of his rivals in the industry were doing work in this field. The richest prize in the industry is a drug to treat Alzheimer's disease.'

'That much I do know,' said David.

Churchward nodded. 'Companies like Janssen and Miles had already started preclinical trials with drugs they had patented, so your father asked the people here to see if they had anything of potential use in the treatment of Alzheimer's.'

'And someone remembered PDM3?'

'Not at all.' Professor Churchward had no inhibitions about putting David down. 'Things don't happen like that. It was one of numerous compounds that were dusted off and tried. Targeted research is more rare than you would think in the discovery of medicines. We still rely heavily on blanket testing for biological activity. The first results were interesting, but not spectacular. PDM3 didn't promise anything remarkable in preclinical. Do you have any idea what I'm talking about? Do you know about the testing procedure?' he asked with intimidation.

This time David restricted himself to raising his eyebrows equivocally.

'I'm referring to the series of tests every drug is put through before it gets approval.'

'Ah – I'm with you,' David responded. 'In the preclinical stage, you're restricted to experiments on animals.'

Grudgingly, Churchward conceded, 'Correct. If that's satisfactory you go on to Phase One, which is merely testing for safety in a small sample of humans. In Phase Two you test for effectiveness, still using small numbers of humans. We've done all that. PDM3 has gone through Phase Two and now we're ready to undertake the third phase, the extensive clinical trials. Assuming they go well – and I've no reason to think they won't – we take it in front of the FDA.' He added, as if to a child, 'The Food and Drug Administration.'

'And when they recommend approval, we're in business?'

'And how!' murmured Leapman.

'You really believe this drug is something special?' David asked.

'Something special?' The professor hesitated, as if weighing his response. 'What we have, Mr Flexner, is the equivalent, in pharmacological terms, of the splitting of the atom.'

Goosebumps formed on the backs of David's arms. In his experience, scientists weren't given to such extravagant claims.

Professor Churchward said, 'PDM3 is not a protective agent. It is a regenerative agent. It enables dying nerve cells to grow and regenerate. No other substance in the pharmacopoeia is capable of that.'

'Brain cells *regenerate?*'

'Yes. Do you see the possibilities? This goes way beyond the treatment of Alzheimer's disease. We have the means of sustaining our mental ability indefinitely. There's no reason why we shouldn't make the drug available to healthy people. Young people. Men and women of forty can expect their brains to function just as efficiently when they are eighty. The drug will eliminate the process of ageing.'

'You mean mental ageing?'

Churchward reddened. 'Be reasonable. I wasn't suggesting we can make old men young again. That's a job for plastic surgery.'

'So it doesn't increase the expectation of life?'

He spread his hands in exasperation. 'What do you want from me, Mr Flexner?'

David told him coolly, 'I'm trying to get a grasp of this discovery, Professor. If you're looking for congratulations, fine. I salute you. I also want to make sure I fully understand you.'

'David, the potential is fantastic,' Leapman waded in fast. 'People will be capable of a longer working life if they want it. They won't be such a drain on the social budget. They can look after themselves for longer. Men and women of genius will be enabled to go on enriching the world for the rest of their lives instead of fading into senility.'

'And we're ahead of the field on this?'

'There are no other runners,' said Leapman.

'Some research is being done with nerve growth factor from naturally occurring brain substances,' Churchward thought fit to add, 'but it's at an early stage, and of course it's organic in origin.'

Leapman said, 'They can't compete with a drug.'

'You're quite sure we have it patented?'

'You bet we do.'

'What about ADRs?' David wasn't entirely ignorant of the jargon. An ADR was an adverse drug reaction, a side-effect.

'As you doubtless know,' said Churchward with unconcealed irony, 'every drug has ADRs. It's a matter of weighing them against the benefits. PDM3 has some temporary contra-indications. It produces mild headaches in some subjects, nausea and dizziness, but we also noted those effects in people receiving a placebo drug.'

'To the same degree?'

'Not quite the same,' he admitted. 'However, a high proportion of the subjects manifested no ADRs at all.'

'What proportion?'

'Up to sixty-eight per cent.'

The figure was meant to impress David, and it did. 'What about long-term effects? I suppose it's too soon to judge.'

The professor said, 'There is no evidence of any long-term ADRs.'

'There wouldn't be, would there? Did you detect any ADRs in the animal tests?'

'In a few cases, slight elevations in liver enzymes.'

'Isn't that a problem?'

'"A problem" would be putting it far too strongly. The liver has an excellent facility for regeneration, so if the dosage is monitored correctly, there is no danger.'

'How do you tell, Professor?'

'By taking blood samples.'

'If we want to market the drug, we can't expect people to subject themselves to blood tests,' said David, realising as he spoke that the remark was naive.

Churchward clicked his tongue and said nothing.

Leapman cleared his throat and said, 'I think there's a slight confusion here.'

'I'm confident that we can resolve the matter in the trials,' said Churchward. 'It comes down to an acceptable dosage, if that is a term we all understand.'

Almost everything the professor said was laced with contempt, and David couldn't understand why. He felt inept. He was sure his father would have handled this interview with less confrontation – in fact, with a mix of humour and cheek – yet Manny would still have managed to elicit the crucial facts. 'Don't get me wrong,' he said. 'I'm just trying to cover every angle. I understand about adverse reactions. I take your point that every drug has them to a greater or lesser degree. If you want to stop a cancer, you don't care so much if your hair falls out, right? The difference is that we wouldn't be treating a *disease* with PDM3.'

'We'd treat Alzheimer's,' said Leapman.

'Yes, but the professor is talking about offering this drug to fit people.'

'Hold on,' said Churchward. 'The first thing is that PDM3 is remarkably effective in the treatment of Alzheimer's, which was the subject of my research. We can safely go to Phase Three now.'

'But you're also confident that it improves the function of the healthy brain.'

'Improves, no,' Churchward corrected him. 'It can extend the time-scale of its efficiency.'

'Fine – but if we sell it to healthy people we're not balancing those ADRs, the nausea and the giddiness and the increase in liver enzymes, against a dangerous disease. We're asking them to accept risks.'

'I don't accept that. Let's not talk about risks. We would eliminate risks. There might be some inconvenience or discomfort,' said Churchward. 'That's up to them. Plenty of popular foods and drinks produce more disagreeable symptoms than PDM3. Health products, too. You take a multivitamin and there's a chance it will give you constipation.'

'So PDM3 is as safe as a vitamin tablet?'

'In the proper dosage, yes.'

'It's what Manny was looking for all his life,' said Leapman, spacing his words and speaking on a rising, evangelical note. 'A surefire product that will take the mass market by storm.'

David thought of his father. He remembered that bizarre wink in the morgue. The incident couldn't have meant anything, but it would never be erased from his memory. 'So when do we go public on this?'

'I'd say tomorrow if we want to keep Manflex afloat,' said Leapman. Quick to note David's startled reaction, he added, 'At this stage, we just have to announce tomorrow that we'll be hosting a conference soon to present the first studies of a new drug for Alzheimer's. That's enough to restore some confidence.'

The decision couldn't be put off. Now David felt his sweat go cold against his T-shirt. He looked towards Churchward.

'That's fine by me, gentlemen,' the professor said, positively fraternal. 'I'm ready to publish.'

'We're not going into production yet,' Leapman told David in reassurance.

'Yes, but once we've made this announcement, there's no drawing back, or it'll play hell with our rating on the stock market.'

'Agreed,' Leapman said cheerfully.

David was still troubled. 'The next step is going to require funding. Millions, probably. Clinical trials on a wide scale don't come cheap. And if we get FDA approval, we'll require massive new investment to launch this drug.'

'So we raise capital.'

'In a world recession?'

'We've got to be bold, David, or, frankly, Manflex is finished.' Leapman moved closer and said confidentially, 'Actually, I have some suggestions about additional finance that I can put to you later.'

15

With her drawing pad tucked under her arm and the marker pen in her fist, Naomi stepped into the waiting taxi as confidently as royalty. Just in case the little girl was more uneasy than she appeared, Diamond tried to enliven the short journey by pointing out the London buses they passed. After ten or so, he gave up. Naomi didn't need distracting.

Julia Musgrave had wanted to buy her a special dress with a lace collar until Diamond had reminded her of the reason why the child was going in front of the television cameras. So she was in clothes similar to those she had been found in – a brown and white check dress from Marks and Spencer, and white tights and trainers.

For a moment when the taxi circled the fountain in front of the Television Centre at Shepherd's Bush, a small hand reached for Diamond's and gripped it tightly. Nerves? He wasn't convinced. Maybe she thinks I'm looking jittery, he told himself.

In the course of his police career, he had notched up plenty of television appearances, so by rights he shouldn't have had any anxieties. But he was nagged by doubts whether an appeal for information on *Crimewatch* was any preparation for *What About the Kids?*

He had been asked to report to the reception desk with

Naomi by ten on Friday morning, and also to be patient, because Cedric was going to fit them in when an opportunity came; there was no way of predicting how soon it would be.

They were taken up to the hospitality suite. The purpose of such places is allegedly to put visitors at their ease. Diamond's confidence plunged as he stepped inside. He was a misfit here. The hospitality amounted to a stack of canned cola and plates of doughnuts and Penguin biscuits. Toys of various kinds were scattered invitingly around the leather and steel furniture. Naomi, for her part, appeared as indifferent to the food and the toys as Diamond was. She squatted on the carpeted floor and was soon completely absorbed in her drawing.

There are certain pivotal moments in any fanatical enterprise when you are compelled to pause, look around you and take stock. It wasn't the toys or the doughnuts that pulled Diamond up short, nor the arrival of three small girls in pink satin frocks, nor the boy with a punk haircut who came in on a skateboard. The critical factor was Sally, a deceptively docile-looking chimpanzee accompanied by a grey-haired woman wearing gauntlet gloves. Hardly had Sally been carried in and deposited at the far end of the settee where Diamond was seated before she started jumping and shrieking. The creature wasn't in distress, the woman assured them, nor was she nervous about appearing on TV. Sally, it seemed, was a regular, the mainstay of the programme. No, Sally was screaming out of sheer high spirits, because she was happy.

Moreover, she wanted to share her happiness with Diamond. Dressed in a red leather harness, but given a fair amount of play on the rein held by her trainer, she was allowed to venture within a yard or so of Diamond (it was a fine judgement on the trainer's part) and flail her arms in his direction. Then she bared her teeth and screamed.

Because she was happy.

That morning over breakfast, he'd told Stephanie where he would be spending the day, remarking bleakly that a kids' TV programme was a far cry from police work. Steph had pointed out that he was a free agent now. If he wanted to go through hoops for young Naomi, fine, but he'd better not forget that it was a self-imposed quest. 'What you mean,' he'd summed it up for her, 'is "stop griping".'

She hadn't disagreed.

So if Peter Diamond, notoriously short-fused, was willing to share a settee with a screaming ape, something fundamental must have happened in his life, and it had. The fate of one small, silent girl now governed him; and all she had done was place her hand in his a few times.

Not wanting to make waves, he endured a full fifteen seconds of Sally the chimp before moving to another chair. He even smiled good-naturedly at the trainer, acting on a shrewd suspicion that if it came to a show-down, he and Naomi would be out on the street, not Sally.

Not to be denied, the chimp continued to make screaming sorties in his direction.

'She likes you,' the woman declared in that evasion often used by owners of animals that terrorize other people. 'She's really taken a shine to you.'

Relief presently arrived in the person of a bright-eyed young woman who introduced herself as Justine and said she was Cedric's personal assistant. At her side was a black boy looking not much older than Naomi. 'This is Curtis

138

She stopped drawing and eased back on her thighs.

He studied the marks she had made on the paper. Some of them, at any rate, were joined at the corners. Maybe it was inevitable when she was drawing so many. He held out his hand and said, 'May I use the marker?'

She handed it to him. Not only did she understand, but she trusted him with the precious marker. A good sign.

He turned to a fresh sheet and started drawing diamonds linked at the corners. It would have been simpler to have drawn two sets of intersecting diagonal lines, but he reckoned Naomi's conception began with the basic shape, so he worked from that, gradually building a grid.

She watched him work, and he was encouraged, even though she remained passive. He completed the drawing by squaring it off with straight lines to represent a frame, and he had a passable lattice window. He handed it back to her. 'How about that?'

She gave his work serious attention, studying it as earnestly as if she were one of the Hanging Committee at the Royal Academy. She put out her hand and traced the grid with her fingertips. It seemed that something wasn't done to her satisfaction.

'You want curtains?' said Diamond. He reached for the drawing pad, but she refused to give it up. Instead, she held out her hand for the marker.

He passed it across.

Concentrating deeply, she leaned so far over the drawing pad that her hair flopped forward, exposing the narrow white nape of her neck. She was working on the area at the top of the sheet, above the window Diamond had drawn. He couldn't see it until she sat back.

This time she had baffled him completely by adding two rectangles and a small circle:

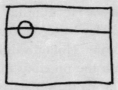

He was beginning to feel as if this were some kind of game for people with higher IQs than he possessed. He'd never mastered the Rubik Cube. He'd given up trying after one of Steph's brownies had demonstrated how to do the thing in a few rapid twists.

Curtis released him from further brain strain by coming back and saying they were wanted in the studio now. Naomi stood up immediately, not only appearing to understand, but seeming keen to get on with the real business of the day. The visit to the Television Centre had animated her; a pity Julia Musgrave hadn't been here to see it.

On the set, an adult-sized chair had been found for Diamond, the only drawback being that it was so low to the ground that he suspected six inches had been sawn off the legs. 'Just don't expect me to stand up while the cameras are rolling,' he warned Curtis, who was standing beside him for the interview.

Opposite them, Naomi perched serenely on a child-size upholstered bench. She appeared more interested in the model air-liner visible through the window than the cameras, and the floor manager had to snap his fingers to get her attention.

Then came the signal.

Smoothly, Curtis talked to the camera. Kids everywhere, he said, fancied themselves as detectives, and now they were getting the chance to solve a real-life mystery. In a few graphic sentences he gave the background, the terrorist alert in Harrods and the discovery of the small girl, his cue to introduce Diamond.

The interview went precisely as planned, with no trick questions and no stumbling answers. Afterwards, there was a chance to watch a recording, and Diamond was pleased to see how strongly the appeal to the viewers came over. Cedric Athelhampton emerged at last from the control room, a pencil-thin man dressed entirely in white, and shook Diamond's hand. 'Stunning, my love, simply stunning. You must have been hand-crafted for television, every chunky pound of you, did you know that? Such a substantial presence, a marvellous contrast with the little girl. My only problem now is that I didn't warn the BBC about the calls. I'm perfectly certain the switchboard's jammed already. I'm going to get it in the neck, but it was bloody good television, and I'll say so in my defence.'

'What about these calls?' Diamond asked, suddenly perturbed.

'What do you mean?'

'Who's taking them?'

'They're being put through to my office, to my assistant, Justine, at present. Between you, me and the BBC, ninety-nine per cent will be duff. The proverbial pisspot full of crab-apples. Kids get carried away when someone with

Curtis's charm and flair makes an appeal for information. Isn't he irresistible?'

Diamond was in no frame of mind for discussing anyone's charm and flair. He was furious with himself for failing to think ahead. He'd been far too preoccupied with the programme. 'Right now I'm interested in the calls, the one per cent. Is Justine capable of recognising the real thing?'

Cedric smiled roguishly. 'The real thing? How would I know?' Reacting fast to Diamond's glare, he added, 'She's bright, as bright as a guardsman's buttons. Don't fret.' He squeezed Diamond's arm. 'We'll let you know if we strike lucky.'

But Diamond wasn't satisfied. He insisted on being taken to the office where Justine was answering the phone.

She had a notepad open and a pencil in her hand, and was talking into a headset. 'Thank you, dear. Now give the phone to Mummy.' She glanced up at Diamond. 'Sodding little brats.' She pressed another switch and said wearily, '*Where Are the Kids?* . . . Where exactly did you see her? . . . *The King and I?* Do you mean the film with Yul Brynner? . . . Thank you, I've made a note of it . . .'

Maybe it wasn't opportune to ask if any of the calls seemed promising.

Justine said, 'The parents give them these ideas. They must do. They're dafter than the kids.' She told Diamond, 'I know why you're here. I've been doing this for over an hour and they're still coming in non-stop. Do me a favour and get me a sarnie and an orange juice from the canteen, would you? By then I might have got myself sorted.'

He didn't argue; he was going to have to rely on Justine.

She'd removed the headset when he returned. She bit hungrily into the sandwich. 'Thanks. What do I owe you?'

'Just a summing-up,' he told her. 'Have we struck gold, or not?'

'You're the judge of that. What it boils down to is at least twelve callers who swear they know her, at school, or in a dancing class, or something. I've got their numbers so you can call them back. And there was one spooky call.'

'What do you mean – spooky?'

'I didn't like the sound of it one bit. A Japanese woman. Well, I think she was Japanese. She sounded Japanese to me.'

'Did she give her name?'

'No. That's the point. She refused. And she didn't say anything about knowing who Naomi is, like all the other callers did. All she would say was that she was under instructions to send you a message. A taxi would be sent for you at seven.'

'Sent here?'

'Yes. If you really want to help Naomi, you're to get into the taxi, both of you.'

'Naomi as well?'

'Yes.'

'That was all? She didn't say where the taxi would take us?'

Justine shook her head. 'Will you do it?'

'Did you get the impression she was serious?'

'Mr Diamond, she was so serious that if I were you I'd think twice about going.'

'I'm not looking for a bunch of laughs,' said Diamond. 'What time is it now?'

147

16

Quick reactions can be vital to success; they can also get you into trouble. In the taxi, Diamond remembered he was no longer a senior policeman. He was doing the professional thing, following the only real lead to come out of the television programme. But as a detective acting on a tip-off he would have routinely radioed his movements to headquarters.

He asked the driver where they were going.

'My lips are sealed, mate.'

'Oh, come on!'

'The Albert Hall.'

'Get stuffed.'

He should have phoned the school, or at least got someone to pass a message to Julia Musgrave. For a middle-aged man to transport a small girl around London without informing her guardians wasn't just misguided, it deserved all the outrage it would trigger. The point wasn't that Julia would suspect him of abducting the child – she'd credited him with some responsibility up to now – but others would. Sexual abuse of children, an evil he was incapable of understanding, had come under the media spotlight in recent months and it wouldn't require much for a woman like Mrs Straw to brand him as a pervert. To be fair to Mrs Straw, any policeman would be duty-bound to treat such an allegation seriously. He resolved to get to a phone as soon as possible after they reached their destination.

And it was the Albert Hall.

The moment he and Naomi stepped out in Kensington Gore, opposite the north door, they were approached by a Japanese woman. Diamond cupped a hand around Naomi's head and steered her protectively towards him. He was taking no chances.

The woman gave a deep, ceremonious bow. She looked about sixty, far too old to be Naomi's mother. There was a wart at the left edge of her upper lip. 'Mr Diamond?'

'Yes.'

'Please come with me.'

'In a moment, madam.' He settled the fare. As his right hand returned to his side he felt Naomi clutch the ends of his fingers tightly. Clearly she didn't regard the woman as family. They followed her towards the building and he noticed Naomi's head go back, to take in the scale of the building's red-brick exterior. A casserole-dish for the gods, he always thought when he saw the Albert Hall. You could imagine a Divine hand lifting the roof, inserting an enormous ladle and giving the contents a stir during the singing of 'Land of Hope and Glory' on the last night of the Proms.

The woman moved briskly up a short flight of steps and through the arched entrance as if the Albert Hall were her home. She was dressed in expensive western clothes, a fawn silk jacket and finely tailored dark brown trousers. Her gold-framed glasses had a long retaining-chain that danced on her shoulders.

By the time they entered the building, Naomi's grip was threatening to stop the circulation in Diamond's hand. The woman turned right, leading them along the main passage that surrounds the auditorium. Others were moving about in there, young people for the most part, with the age and appearance of students. Yet Diamond didn't have the impression that the Hall was being used for a concert, whether pop or classical. Precisely what was being staged down here this week he didn't know. Slack thinking, he chided himself. He ought to have asked someone at the Television Centre.

Their guide stopped by a door marked 'Private' and tapped with her knuckles.

Diamond was uneasy about taking Naomi into an enclosed area. 'Do you mind telling me what this is about?' he asked.

The woman turned to face him. 'I am sorry. It is not for me to say.'

'Who are you? I don't even know your name.'

'I am nothing. Disregard me.'

'You speak good English.'

'That is the only reason I am here.'

The door was opened by a burly young Japanese man in a black tracksuit. The woman bowed. The young man dipped his head in a formal greeting directed more to Diamond than their guide and revealed that his hair was bunched and fastened in a topknot. Something was said in Japanese.

'Please enter,' the woman told them, standing aside to gesture them forward.

The sickly-sweet fumes of a floral perfume wafted over them. It was coming from the young man's hair, and the scent was camellia, Diamond registered, recalling a more subtle variety sometimes used by Steph. This was looking less and less like a homecoming for a lost child, but there didn't appear to be anything threatening about the invitation. He led Naomi through the door.

They were greeted by a spectacle that nothing had prepared them for: an enormous pair of buttocks, naked except for a strip of black silk squeezed into the cleft.

For reasons too complex to explore, the over-fleshed male bottom is not a feature much revered in modern Western society. It can be the object of mockery – literally, a butt – or, more positively, a source of extra poundage in the rugby scrum, or the tug-of-war team. This bottom manifestly aspired to higher planes of experience. It was monumental, as awesome in its way as the Albert Memorial across the road.

Motionless, pale gold in hue, smooth as traffic beacons, sturdy as two barrels stored side by side, it dominated the centre of the room and much of the sides as well. The rest of the owner's body was for the moment hidden, except for a partial view of stocky legs and bare feet. He was bending forward in a position that must have been painful to hold.

From Naomi's eye-level, the spectacle would have rivalled Mount Fujiyama.

Belatedly, Diamond recalled an item he had seen a couple of days before on a television newscast. A Japanese Festival had opened and one of the main attractions was a tournament for Japanese wrestlers. The sport had a devoted following here. He mouthed the word, 'Sumo?'

The man who had just admitted them nodded.

Although Diamond hadn't watched much sumo wrestling on television, he felt some sympathy with a sport for which the training amounted to gorging oneself with food and the action rarely lasted longer than fifteen seconds.

The buttocks flexed, shuddered and shifted position with astonishing rapidity as their owner, regardless of his guests,

151

went through a physical routine, raising his body level with his hips and lifting his right foot to shoulder height and then slapping it down heavily.

'The *shiko*,' murmured the woman from the doorway. 'To frighten evil spirits and the opponent.'

'Tell him the opponent isn't here,' Diamond muttered.

The *shiko* was repeated with the left leg. The great domes of flesh completed their movement, quivered, and were still. If anything, the reek of camellias had intensified. The wrestler, as well as his Jeeves, must have been pomaded with the stuff.

'I rather think someone has made a mistake inviting us here,' Diamond insisted.

Shocked that anyone should speak while the workout was in progress, the man in the tracksuit held up a restraining hand.

The wrestler treated them to the panorama of his backside again, bending so low that his head must have been between his knees. He was wearing the silk loincloth used in combat by the highest-ranking *sumotori*. The enforced intimacy with this mountainous rump was unsettling Diamond, and he didn't care to think what effect it could be having on the child. Actually, the room wasn't small. Indeed it must have been the star dressing-room. But when shared with a sumo wrestler and two heads coated in essence of camellia, it seemed minute. He turned to see if the woman was still present. She was standing just inside the door, trying to be unobtrusive.

Diamond asked her, 'Are you sure this is right?'

She nodded and signalled to him to be silent by pressing her fingers against her lips.

The wrestler grunted, raised himself from the jack-knife position and suddenly turned about to face them.

He was vast all over. His thighs looked as if they could have supported an overpass and in a sense they did, because his huge belly jutted so far over the belt of his loincloth that he appeared naked. A thick band of pectoral muscles lay over his torso, forming a deep, undulating crease. Above all that, almost extrinsic to the show, was his small, moon-shaped head. Its only real distinction was the hair tied at the back and folded forward in the traditional fan shape worn by the highest ranked *sumotori*. He exchanged the briefest of glances with the man in the tracksuit, who picked up a black jacket not unlike an undergraduate gown and wrapped it around the colossal shoulders.

Then the great man bowed in greeting and Diamond did the same. For once in his life, he was feeling physically diminished, skimpy, if not slender. A hand was extended for him to shake. Having seen the agility of Japanese wrestlers, he wouldn't have been surprised to have found himself on his back in the far corner. Instead he received nothing worse than a firm handshake. Something was said in Japanese, the voice high-pitched and husky.

The woman spoke up from behind Diamond. 'The *Ozeki* Yamagata wishes to introduce himself and welcome you to the Albert Hall, his temporary quarters.'

Diamond identified himself and Naomi. Chairs were produced for them. Yamagata squatted on a wooden bench and said something to his dresser, who spoke in turn to the woman interpreter.

She told Diamond, 'I have the honour to translate for Mr Yamagata. He instructs me to explain that *Ozeki* is the second highest rank in sumo. Mr Yamagata is a very important wrestler in Japan, and the most senior in this

153

tournament. You are welcome to be his honoured guests in the arena tonight if you wish.'

'We are honoured indeed,' said Diamond, fitting smoothly into the formal style of address, 'but I think the child is too young.'

When this was translated for Mr Yamagata he appeared to take it well, nodding sagely.

Naomi still had a tight grip on Diamond's fingertips. With some justification, she regarded these proceedings with the deepest suspicion.

Yamagata spoke again and the interpreter explained that by chance the Very Important Wrestler had watched the transmission of *What About the Kids?* A portable set had been brought in for him to see a Channel 4 programme about sumo, but it had concentrated too much on a rival sumo stable and he had switched channels. 'Mr Yamagata was deeply moved by the unhappy situation of this Japanese child who appears on British television and says nothing. He asked me to make enquiries, so I phoned the BBC,' she explained.

Diamond's hopes of a breakthrough were dashed. 'You mean he didn't recognise Naomi?'

She shook her head.

'He doesn't know who she is?'

'It was only a TV show.'

'For crying out loud!' Diamond jerked up from the chair, accidentally hoisting Naomi to her feet as well, because she still had hold of his fingertips. 'You brought us here for nothing, because this . . . this lump of lard happened to see the kid on the box? That's ludicrous. Who else have you dragged in – Arthur Daley?'

'Please! I cannot possibly say these things to Mr Yamagata.'

'Don't trouble. We're off. We've been conned by this heap of flab.' He turned to leave and found the way barred by the henchman in the tracksuit, hunched forward combatively, looking as if he wasn't messing. Naomi gave a whimper, dropped her precious drawing pad, and flung both arms around Diamond's waist, or as far around as she was able.

Not the ideal conditions for a first encounter with a sumo wrestler.

'Do you mind?' Diamond articulated in a straining-to-be-civil, British fashion. 'We would like to leave now.'

A volley of Japanese came from Yamagata, and the interpreter pushed herself between Diamond and the henchman. 'Mr Diamond, I implore you! Mr Yamagata has not finished speaking. You cannot leave yet.'

There's nothing else to say,' Diamond told her. The only reason we came was to find out who Naomi is. He doesn't know. He hasn't the faintest idea.'

'He wishes to help.'

'By questioning her in Japanese? The Embassy people tried. She doesn't respond. Now will you do me a favour and ask this buffoon to let us pass?'

'You should not turn your back on Mr Yamagata.'

She spoke this dictum like a universal truth. Probably it was well known and wisely heeded among the wrestling fraternity. Diamond heeded it and looked over his shoulder.

Thankfully, Yamagata hadn't moved from the bench. He was beckoning to Diamond to return to the chair.

Maybe, after all, Diamond rationalised, the guy has something constructive to suggest. I won't gain anything from an angry exit. I shouldn't let the frustration get to me. If I'd been questioning a witness in the nick, any old witness, I'd have heard him out in hope of eliciting something useful, wouldn't I?

'Okay,' he said, resting his hand on Naomi's shoulder. 'Two minutes.'

They sat down again.

'Mr Yamagata would like to hear from your own lips the story of this little girl.'

'I thought *he* had something to tell me.'

'Please, Mr Diamond.'

'As you wish.' Striving to be tolerant, he picked his way through the few known facts, starting with the bomb scare in Harrods and ending with Naomi's drawings, which she was willing to hand over for Yamagata's inspection.

The wrestler methodically turned the pages of the drawing pad, studying the diamond shapes and coming finally to the lattice window.

'That's my own work,' Diamond said, thinking how ridiculous he sounded, like some amateur artist looking for compliments. 'This drawing above is Naomi's. I wondered at one stage if she was writing in Japanese characters, but I was told not.'

When this was explained to Yamagata, he shook his head. He seemed as mystified about the significance of the drawings as everyone else. He closed the pad and handed it back to Naomi, graciously, with both hands, as if it were some precious item in the sumo ritual. He said something in Japanese to her, but she made no response. He then turned to Diamond and actually managed some halting words of English.

'Yamagata love little girl.'

Diamond had dreaded something like this. 'No. That's out. Definitely not possible,' he said, reinforcing it with a sweeping motion with his hand.

Yamagata frowned.

'I didn't bring her here to give her away,' Diamond tried

156

to explain. 'She doesn't belong to me, anyway. I'm taking her back to the school tonight, and that's how it is.' He turned to the interpreter. 'For God's sake tell him what I'm trying to say.'

There was a consultation in Japanese. The woman then told Diamond with another bow, 'Pardon me for mentioning this, but I think you misunderstood Mr Yamagata. He was beginning to tell you that he had a young daughter about Naomi's age. He loved her deeply, but she died of meningitis last year.'

Yamagata's eyes moistened noticeably while this was explained.

'I'm sorry to hear that,' Diamond said in sincerity. 'A child's death is the worst kind of grief to bear. But please get him to understand that Naomi belongs to someone else.'

'He understands that.'

Yamagata spoke again in Japanese, flattening his palm to his chest to reinforce his message.

'He says he wants to help this little girl.'

'Naomi? He wants to help Naomi?'

Yamagata was nodding.

'That's kind,' said Diamond. 'I appreciate the offer, but what could you do? Do you understand me? What could you do to help?'

She put this into Japanese and got a quick answer. 'He says you tell him.'

This exercised Diamond for some time. He didn't like to appear ungrateful. Finally, he answered, 'I suppose you could do what I've been trying to do – drum up some publicity.'

When this was conveyed, Yamagata curled his lip in a clear signal of distaste. He spoke again. The interpreter told Diamond, 'Mr Yamagata has heard your story and he

157

trusts you. You have been a police detective, so you are well qualified to find out the truth about the child. Mr Yamagata is a famous wrestler, not a detective. He is a rich man. He will pay all expenses. When you travel, fly to other places, stay in hotels, he will pay.'

A sponsor.

'I wasn't planning on flying anywhere.'

'Mr Yamagata thinks it will be necessary.'

Diamond shook his head. 'I doubt it.'

Another consultation, then she said, 'Mr Yamagata wishes to examine the drawing book again.'

'Again?' It was back on Naomi's lap. She allowed Diamond to take it from her and hand it across.

The wrestler turned the pages until he came to the drawing of the lattice window that Diamond himself had started. He traced a finger around the shapes Naomi had drawn and said, 'Aeroplane.' To reinforce the message he rested the drawing pad on his thighs and spread his arms wide.

'What?' By no stretch of imagination could the drawing represent an aircraft of any description.

Yamagata called his interpreter closer and spoke earnestly to her. She turned to Diamond. 'He says you should look closely at this drawing.'

On cue, Yamagata turned the drawing book in his hands and held it for Diamond to inspect.

'He believes this may be the child's view of inside an airliner.'

'Well, I wouldn't describe myself as a jet-setter, but I've flown a few times and not one of the planes had lattice windows.'

'Please study the drawings with Mr Yamagata.'

Yamagata held it higher.

As Yamagata spoke and traced the shapes with his fingers, the woman interpreted. 'This grid-shape that you have assumed to represent a window may be something else.'

'I drew it myself.'

'You drew it from the patterns the child was making. Mr Yamagata believes it may represent the document storage pocket that is fixed to the back of each seat.'

Diamond knew what was meant. 'That string thing that everything is stuffed into – the safety instructions and the airline magazine and so on? That's a thought. She *would* be on a level with it if she sat in a plane. And this other shape could be the flap that you rest your tray on. I believe he's right.' He snapped his fingers. 'That's brilliant. Bloody brilliant. She's letting us know that she was in an aircraft.'

'Or an Intercity train.'

An uneasy pause ensued.

'Did he say that?'

'I did,' said the woman. 'I live in England. Many train seats have these flaps. The aeroplanes I have travelled in generally have fabric pockets.'

She was right.

159

'Hang on a minute,' Diamond said. 'May I have the pad back?' He gestured with his fingers.

Yamagata handed it to him.

He turned to a fresh page, took a pen from his pocket and made two rapid drawings, very basic in shape, of an aircraft and a train. 'Now, let's see.' He held them up for Naomi's inspection and covered the train with his hand. 'This one?'

She made no reaction.

'Or this?' He revealed the train.

After a worrying delay, the child put out her hand and touched the drawing of the train.

'This one? This one, Naomi?'

She tapped it again.

'So you're right. He was only partly right. He worked out what the drawing represented,' Diamond told the woman, 'but she was telling us she travelled by train.'

'Japan Airlines,' said Yamagata, nodding.

'British Rail,' Diamond said, turning to speak to the woman. 'Fancy you working it out.'

She told him, 'The credit for interpreting the drawings belongs to Mr Yamagata.'

'You got it between you, then. Bloody brilliant!'

'Oriental people write their language in ideograms. We have a sharp eye for symbols.'

Yamagata spoke again in Japanese and his interpreter said firmly, 'Mr Yamagata must prepare for the *basho*. We should not delay him. He said he will pay whatever you need to find Naomi's parents.'

Diamond's eyes widened in surprise. 'He'll pay me?'

'That is so.'

'Let me get this right. He's offering to hire me?'

'Yes.'

'Does he really mean whatever I need?'

More consultation ensued. Then: 'Mr Yamagata possesses the Gold Card of American Express.'

'I'm impressed, but—'

'He will give you his Gold Card number. If you need to make expenditure, you quote the number. I will write this down for you.'

'He's giving me *carte blanche* to spend his money?'

'American Express,' said Yamagata himself, but with some difficulty over the letter 'r'.

'Mr Yamagata has satisfied himself that you are honourable.'

Encouraging as it was to have found unlimited sponsorship and been judged honourable, Diamond still had mixed feelings about the encounter. His expectation that these people had recognised Naomi had been dashed. He was pleased to have her drawing explained, but disappointed that it indicated nothing more than a journey on BR's Intercity.

After another bout of bowing and handshaking, he withdrew with Naomi to the blessedly unscented air outside.

The interpreter followed them out and handed him a card with Yamagata's Tokyo address. Below it she had written his credit card number. She said solemnly, 'And my phone number is on the back.'

The impulse to smile, or wink, or say something suggestive was hard to resist. But there are people you don't risk upsetting, and this oriental dowager was one. Actually the mention of the phone jerked Peter Diamond back to a matter of more urgency. He still hadn't called the school. He thanked her, pocketed the card and went to look for a callbox.

To his immense relief, Julia Musgrave answered. She

agreed that it had been right to follow up the summons from the sumo wrestler. She'd watched *What About the Kids?* Everyone in the school had watched it and there had been high excitement among the children when they had recognised Naomi. Julia was sorry that nothing of real substance had resulted from the programme, apart from Mr Yamagata's offer, because – she reminded Diamond, as if it wasn't paramount in his mind – Naomi's time in England was almost up. In less than forty-eight hours, she would be on that flight to Boston.

Miss Musgrave had gone home, Diamond learned when the school's front door was opened.

It was a good thing he'd phoned first. The worst Mrs Straw could find to complain of was that the child looked worn to a frazzle, poor mite. 'Look at her. She can hardly stand up, she's so done for.'

Naomi slipped her hand free from Diamond's and ran inside and up the stairs in quick, light steps, still holding her drawing pad.

He raised his trilby to Mrs Straw and went off to catch the tube.

17

Stephanie's advice across the breakfast table was eminently sensible, if totally unacceptable.

'Face up to it, Pete – you've run out of time. You can't solve that little girl's problem.'

'Which problem is that?'

She sighed. 'Oh, don't get pernickety, love. It's too early in the day.'

To demonstrate good will, he offered to put a slice of bread in the toaster for her. 'I was only asking you to explain what you're on about. Which of her problems am I incapable of solving?'

'The speech.'

'You mean the absence of it.'

She sighed, rested her chin on the bridge she had made of her hands and gave him a look that said he was being unreasonably reasonable.

He told her, 'I never expected to restore her speech. All I've been trying to do is find her people. I'm a policeman, not a speech therapist.'

'You're neither,' she reminded him mildly.

'An ex-policeman, then.'

'But you weren't dealing with abandoned kids.'

'I've been through the training. I know the procedures.

Look, Steph, you know me well enough. I'm not giving up now.'

She got up from the table and carried her plate to the sink. 'What can you do? It's Saturday morning. You told me they're flying her out to Boston tomorrow.'

'Correct.'

'Can't you see it may be the best possible thing, Pete? The school is run by the Japanese. They have a wonderful reputation.'

He had nothing against the school. 'You want to know what I can do?' he said. 'I can get her to draw things. She is definitely trying to communicate through the drawing. I'm getting her confidence now. She holds my hand.'

Stephanie looked down at the water she was running over the dishes. Unseen by Diamond, she was smiling. By the simple act of holding his hand, one small, silent girl had succeeded in taming the bear.

'Would you like to come with me?' he offered.

'To the school?'

'We could take her out together.'

She thought for a moment, pleased that he'd suggested it, and then shook her head. 'She doesn't know me. She's not going to open up if there's a stranger tagging along. She's seen too many well-meaning women already, social workers and embassy people and special teachers trying to coax something out of her – worthy, I'm sure, but not what the kid wants. Heaven knows how or why, but you seem to have reached an understanding with her. You go alone, love, only don't pin your hopes on it.'

Knowing the school routine on Saturdays, he timed his arrival for just before ten, after breakfast was finished, the rooms cleared and the kids dressed and playing. It was one

164

of those brilliant, cloudless London mornings that make urban pollution seem like a myth. He could hear the children outside in the garden at the rear, so he walked around the side of the house. Clive spotted him immediately and came running, holding the toy car Diamond had given him and making a convincing engine sound. Diamond stopped and spread his hands in welcome, but the boy veered off to the left, as if he had just remembered that he was autistic and didn't, after all, relate to adults.

Mrs Straw was on duty, seated on the bench under the sycamore, sedulously knitting something in a revolting shade of green.

He greeted her civilly and asked if Miss Musgrave was about. When speaking to Mrs Straw, everyone on the staff referred to everyone else as Miss, Mrs or Mr.

'She's busy.'

'In her study?'

'Busy, I said.'

'Yes, but where can I find her?'

'She doesn't want disturbing.'

'I understand that. I'm asking where she is.'

'On the phone.'

Some of Mrs Straw's statements, if taken literally, had a surreal quality. Diamond had a mental picture of Julia doing a balancing act on top of the phone. 'I didn't actually ask you what she was doing.'

Silence.

'The one in her office?' he asked. There were three phones that he knew about.

Still no word.

'I'll go in and see for myself, then. Where's young Naomi this morning?'

If anything, Mrs Straw pressed her lips more tightly shut.

165

This morning she was even more unobliging than usual. She continued to knit with tight, tense movements.

'Aren't you in charge?' Diamond asked, nettled by the dumb show. 'Shouldn't she be out here with the others?'

'She's gone.'

He tensed. 'What do you mean – "gone"?'

'It's plain English, isn't it?'

'Gone away?'

She gave a nod.

'Left altogether, do you mean?'

'Collected this morning.'

Mrs Straw hadn't even looked up from her knitting. She gave the information casually, as if it were common knowledge, and now she had started the next row.

Diamond was so astounded that he could only say an inane, 'What?'

'Are you deaf?'

He turned away and went to look for Julia Musgrave.

Just as Mrs Straw had said, Julia was on the phone. Seeing him in the doorway of her office, she said into the phone, 'It's all right. He's just walked in. I can tell him myself.' She put down the phone and said, 'I was talking to your wife.'

'My *wife?*'

'Trying to contact you. I didn't know you were coming in. I have some news that might upset you.'

'Mrs Straw just told me about Naomi.'

Her face tightened. 'That woman! She handed the child over without informing me or the social services or anyone else.'

'Weren't you here?'

'It all happened before I arrived. About eight this morning, when the children were having breakfast. The

166

only staff here were Mrs Straw and the Malaysian girl who cooks. I gather that this Japanese woman knocked at the door and announced that she was the mother and had come to collect her child. As proof of identity, she produced a passport and a photo of Naomi and Naomi definitely recognised her, according to Mrs Straw.'

He was trying to assimilate the information. 'A passport and a photo, or a passport containing a photo?'

Julia shook her head. 'The photo was separate. The passport belonged to the woman, but the child was mentioned in it.'

'Naomi?'

'Some other name. Naomi was the name we gave her, if you remember.'

'What was this woman like?'

She shook her head. 'You know what it's like trying to drag information out of Mrs Straw. I was so incensed when she told me that she'd handed Naomi over without reference to anyone that I lost my chance of a normal conversation with her.'

'We'd better have her in here immediately,' said Diamond. 'She's got to give a proper account of what happened.'

'All right. You'll stay?'

'You bet I will. I'll fetch her now.'

In the garden he got a glare fit to petrify, but Mrs Straw folded her knitting and went with him.

They sat stiffly among the children's toys and pictures in Julia's office, Diamond on the wooden trunk, Mrs Straw on a chair just inside the door, as if poised for a quick exit.

Julia explained that she wanted to go over the details of what had happened that morning.

Pointedly ignoring what was said to her, and thrusting

out her chin defiantly, Mrs Straw demanded, 'What's he doing here?'

Diamond drew breath to lambast her, but Julia got in first, and her rebuke was the more effective for being spoken in a soft, measured voice. 'Mr Diamond, as you very well know, takes a special interest in Naomi. He has worked for the police.'

'It's nothing to do with the police.'

'I didn't say it was, but I have to be sure about this woman who claims to be Naomi's mother. She could be an impostor.'

'Impossible,' said Mrs Straw.

'Not at all. It's quite possible that some childless woman could have seen Naomi on television and decided that she could pose as the mother.'

Mrs Straw was unimpressed. 'The woman had the photo of Naomi.'

Diamond intervened. 'Before we go into that, can we have it from the beginning, when the woman arrived?'

Without a glance in his direction, Mrs Straw said, 'I already told Miss Musgrave.'

'You gave me the essential facts,' said Julia. 'Now we need to know more.'

Mrs Straw sat back, exhaled noisily and folded her arms. 'There isn't any more.'

'Then tell me again, so that Mr Diamond can hear exactly what you recall.'

She rolled her eyes upward in protest. 'It's simple enough. I answered the door when the children were having breakfast.'

'What time?' Diamond asked.

'Round about eight. I don't have a watch. It was this Japanese woman. She asked if the little girl who was on

168

the television yesterday was here. She said, "I am the mother."'

'What was she like? Can you describe her?'

'She was Japanese.'

This, apparently, said it all, so far as Mrs Straw was concerned.

'And . . .?' Diamond prompted her.

'They all look the same to me.'

'What age would she have been?'

'I can't say. You can't tell.'

'Young enough to be the mother of Naomi?'

'I suppose so.'

'What was she wearing?'

'I'd have to think about that.'

'Please do. Now.'

After a pause, she said, 'A grey jacket of some kind and trousers to match.'

'Shoes?'

'Black, I think.'

'With heels?'

'I didn't notice.'

'Would you describe her as smartly dressed?'

'The clothes were Rohan, if that's what you mean.'

He hadn't meant it. He didn't know anything about Rohan clothes, or how you recognised them, but from Mrs Straw's tone, he took it that she was sure. 'How did she wear her hair?'

'Short.'

'Very short, do you mean? Cut close to the head?'

'No. It was permed.'

'In curls?'

'Waves.'

Little by little, he was getting a mental picture, though

not one that would distinguish the woman from a million other Japanese.

'What height would she have been?'

'Average.'

'Average for a Japanese?'

She responded once more with the unsatisfactory, 'I suppose so.'

After some more probing as to skin quality and colouring, and make-up (the woman had been well-groomed, it appeared), Diamond gave a nod to Julia, who said, 'Shall we continue, then? You invited the woman in.'

'Only after she showed me Naomi's photo and the passport.'

'Her own passport?'

'Her picture was in it.'

'A Japanese passport?'

'Any fool could see she wasn't from Timbuctu,' Mrs Straw said with contempt.

Diamond just about contained himself. 'She might have held an American passport, or Australian.'

'How would I know?'

'Couldn't you see the writing on the passport?'

'I can't read Japanese.'

'So you think it was Japanese script. We're getting somewhere. We're not trying to catch you out, Mrs Straw. We just want all the information you can give us.'

'It was in some foreign language. That's all I'm prepared to say.'

'And she also showed you this photo of Naomi?'

'Yes.'

'You're certain it was Naomi?'

'I said so.'

'You just implied that all Japanese people look alike to you.'

'If they're strangers. I've seen Naomi plenty of times.'

The point was fair.

'So was it a recent photo of Naomi?'

'Must have been.'

Julia asked. 'Did she have a name for Naomi?'

'Can't remember.'

'Come on,' Diamond urged her. 'Surely she gave a name?'

'I said I can't remember. It was double-Dutch to me. Anyway,' said Mrs Straw, willing to move on with her account to avoid further discussion of the child's name, 'I told her Miss Musgrave wasn't here and she said she wanted to see her little girl. She kept on saying it. She wouldn't be put off. So I let her come through to the dining-room.'

No one could doubt that any person who had talked her way past Mrs Straw was uncommonly persistent.

'The children were on their own,' she explained, to justify her capitulation. 'I was forced to leave them when I went to the door. I couldn't stand arguing on the doorstep.'

'Please go on.'

'There's nothing else. She came in and went straight to Naomi and anyone could see she was the mother.'

'How?' asked Diamond.

'You wouldn't understand,' Mrs Straw told him loftily. 'It takes a woman to understand.' She looked towards Julia for support.

Julia declined to conspire in this evasion. 'We want to know precisely what happened. Did Naomi get up and run to her?'

'Yes, of course.'

Diamond put up his hand too late to intervene, realising that he couldn't caution Julia for putting words into Mrs Straw's mouth, as he might if some raw police constable

171

were asking leading questions. The damage was done now. Mrs Straw was launched and away.

'They cuddled and kissed and wept a few tears and talked to each other in Japanese.'

'Talked? Naomi *talked*?'

'The mother, I mean. Then she said she was going to take Naomi home, so I said I didn't think she should until she'd seen Miss Musgrave. I tried my level best to keep her there, but you've got to remember I was on my own here apart from the girl in the kitchen. The other children had to be looked after.'

'Why wouldn't she stay?' Diamond asked. 'What was the hurry?'

'I can't say. You can't tell with foreigners.'

'What happened then?'

'I asked the cook to keep an eye on the children while we went upstairs and collected the clothes Naomi came in. I let them take the things she was wearing. I knew Miss Musgrave wouldn't mind.'

'Then what?'

'They left.'

'Without leaving a name or address?'

'I forgot to ask.'

'Brilliant.'

'She was in a hurry to go,' said Mrs Straw in her defence.

'And you couldn't wait to show her the door.'

'That isn't fair. And it isn't true, either.' Reacting to a convenient scream from the garden, Mrs Straw said, 'Lord knows what the children are getting up to. I'd better go.'

Diamond said firmly that he hadn't finished. He wanted to see the room where Naomi slept.

'Suit yourself. There's nothing to see,' Mrs Straw declared.

'Take us there now, if you please.'

She took a sharp, indignant breath and turned in protest to Julia Musgrave, who told her firmly to do as Mr Diamond instructed.

As if every step were on red-hot coals she led them upstairs and opened a door to a room containing three small beds. The quilts were thrown back.

'Which is Naomi's?'

Mrs Straw pointed to the one nearest the door. A light green pair of child's pyjamas lay over the pillow. Diamond picked them up.

'School property,' Mrs Straw informed him.

He tossed them back and opened the locker beside the bed. Nothing was inside. But before rising, he happened to notice the hard, straight edge of something squeezed between the bedstead and the mattress. He slipped his hand inside.

A remark of Julia Musgrave's came back to him: *They can hide a favourite toy and weeks, months later, go straight to it.* What he had found was Naomi's drawing pad. He withdrew it and flicked through the pages to be quite certain.

'She left this.'

'Must have forgotten it,' Mrs Straw said tersely.

'That isn't likely. She carried it everywhere, as you very well know.' He felt under the mattress again and this time found the marker pen. 'She kept the things here because they were so precious to her. She's unlikely to have left without them. Not freely.'

Ridges had formed at the edge of Mrs Straw's mouth.

'You were here,' Diamond pointed out. 'Did she have the opportunity of collecting her things?'

She gave no answer.

'Just now you gave the impression that this was a joyful reunion with her mother,' Diamond commented. 'Hugs

173

and kisses and a few tears into the bargain. Were they tears of joy, Mrs Straw, or distress? You see, this discovery has rocked my confidence. I'm beginning to wonder if the child was taken from here against her will. If that is the case, you'd better say so, fast.'

She shook her head vigorously, either in defiance or to contest his interpretation.

Confronted with the familiar challenge of the uncooperative witness, a trained interrogator like Diamond might have coaxed out the truth, but while Naomi was under threat, he wasn't wasting time on refinements.

'You lied.'

Mrs Straw arched her mouth and glared.

He shoved the drawing pad towards her, forcing her to sway back. 'She wouldn't have gone without this.'

'Get away from me,' she muttered.

He felt Julia Musgrave's hand on his arm, wanting to restrain him, without result. 'Admit it. That woman took Naomi off by force.' He portrayed the scene vividly. 'She dragged the kid out of here screaming and kicking.'

'No.'

He gave her a moment for a more considered answer.

She added, 'That isn't true – about the screaming. You can ask the cook.'

'I intend to.'

'She only struggled a bit.'

'We're coming to it,' said Diamond.

'There wasn't no screaming.'

'Crying?'

'No.'

'And there wasn't any kissing and cuddling, was there, Mrs Straw? You lied about that.'

'No.'

174

'But you just said the child struggled. Come on, what are we to believe – that after this touching reunion her so-called mother had to wrestle with her to get her out of the place?'

She emitted a sound between a gasp and a sob and clamped her teeth over her lower lip. The dragon who deterred visitors was a cornered creature now.

Julia, probably succumbing to the tension, said, 'No one is blaming you, Mrs Straw' – which wasn't strictly true, and Diamond didn't let it pass. He was angry. And, more vitally, he was conscious of the minutes passing.

'Blame is exactly what this is about,' he said without deflecting his eyes from Mrs Straw. 'You thought you could avoid more blame by telling this crap about kissing and cuddling. You don't want us to know what really took place this morning. And while you feed us horseshit, this woman is heading for God knows where with a child who was in your charge. You're in deep trouble, Mrs Straw. By Christ, you'd better speak up.'

The force of his speech had a dramatic result. Mrs Straw turned ashen. The rigid mouth softened and quivered. Her hand fumbled in a pocket of the apron she was wearing and extracted a large red handkerchief. She pressed it to her nose and, instead of blowing it, emitted a long, low moan of distress. Her eyes reddened and dampened. Huge sobs convulsed her. The outburst was the more disturbing because she had always seemed so implacable.

'Now, now,' said Julia in sympathy.

Unmoved, Diamond remarked, 'We don't have time for this, Mrs Straw.'

Dabbing her tears, she launched into a confession punctuated by frequent sobs. 'I was too frightened to tell you exactly what happened. Naomi didn't want to leave. She

175

put up a fight. What I said was true – about the picture and everything – and I'm positive they knew each other, only when it was obvious that the woman wanted to take Naomi with her, she went berserk – Naomi, I mean. She tried to run away and the woman grabbed hold of her arm and wouldn't let go. What could I do? I'm only supposed to be the help here. She kept on and on saying she was the mother and the passport was proof of it. In the end I went upstairs for Naomi's things. What I told you about the two of them coming up here wasn't true. Naomi was in no state to do anything, so I collected her things myself. I didn't think to look for the drawing book. I put the spare clothes in a carrier and handed them over. Naomi had to be pushed and dragged all the way to the taxi.'

'There was a taxi?'

'Yes, it must have been waiting. I noticed it when I first opened the door. And when they left, Naomi was struggling and kicking by the taxi door and only went in after her leg was slapped.'

'Oh, no!' said Julia, who wouldn't allow anyone to strike a child in her school.

'What sort of taxi?' asked Diamond, trying to exclude everything but the essential information, though, he, too, was disturbed at the treatment of Naomi.

'The usual. I won't lose my job, will I, Miss Musgrave?'

'Black?'

'What?'

'The taxi, Mrs Straw. Was it black?'

'Oh. Yes.'

'I suppose it's too much to hope that you took the number?'

She shook her head.

'Anything about it – adverts on the doors. Try and remember.'

'I can't. Anyway, I couldn't see it properly because of the hedge.'

'What time did they leave? How long were they here?'

'I don't know – about twenty minutes, I suppose. It might have been less. It seemed like twenty minutes.'

'Before eight-thirty, then?'

'I suppose so.'

He told Julia, 'I'm calling the police. We're going to need them.'

Mrs Straw covered her eyes and moaned.

18

The person who took the call at Kensington Police Station expressed doubt whether it would be possible to trace an unnamed Japanese woman and child who had stepped into a taxi in Earls Court at eight-thirty.

Diamond hadn't reprimanded a policeman for months, but he still had the knack. 'Who the hell do you think you are – God Almighty?' he boomed down the line. 'This is a bloody emergency. It isn't your job to look down from the clouds and say what's possible and what isn't. Action the call. I was in the police, son. I know what I'm talking about. The morning rush-hour is the busiest time of day for taxis.'

'That's just the point,' said the hapless officer.

'What are you, a civilian? Put me through to someone in uniform, will you? Who's the station sergeant?'

'I am.'

'God help us. Listen, I'm not telling you your job, sergeant, but there are ways of tracing taxis. Most of them work in fleets and radio their positions to the girl on the intercom, right? At the busiest times there's a large demand for cabs. If one was standing outside a school for twenty minutes, someone is going to remember – because it was unavailable for other work – follow me?'

'Yes, but—'

'And this cab driver, whoever he may be, is going to remember sitting there. He's also going to remember picking up a Japanese woman and a kid who was most unwilling to be with her. Now, you can't trace every taxi in London, agreed, but you can call the offices telling them to check with their controllers, or whatever they call themselves.'

'Have you any idea what you're asking, Mr—'

'Diamond. Ex-Superintendent Diamond. Yes, I know exactly what I'm asking, and it's the obvious course of action apart from questioning the neighbours round here, which goes without saying. If you want help—'

'That won't be needed.'

'Good. I'm glad you can handle that,' Diamond said and added before the sergeant had time to come in again, 'In that case I'll come straight down to the station. I can be more useful there.'

This had the desired effect, a definite infusion of urgency. 'Will you listen to me, sir? I want you to stay where you are. I'll be sending someone to take a statement from you.'

'Sod that. I've given you the facts. Do I have to repeat that this child was taken from the school against her will? Abducted, sergeant. We've got to know where she was taken, and we've got to know fast.'

He ended the call.

Julia Musgrave had overheard all this. She was pale, clearly disturbed by Diamond's bulldozing, without knowing that it was the sure way to get things done in the police. 'You said this is an emergency.'

His response was guarded. 'I know that sergeant's type. If you told him a bomb had been planted in Buckingham Palace, he'd want it in writing first.'

'Is Naomi in danger?'

179

'We've got to assume she is. Whoever this woman is – and she may be the mother, for all I know – she behaved suspiciously.'

'Maybe,' she commented. 'But you can't expect a mother deprived of her child to act rationally. She turned up here at breakfast time. Is that really to be interpreted as suspicious? If my child were missing, I wouldn't think twice about knocking on someone's door any time of the day or night.'

'In that case why didn't she come here yesterday, directly after the television programme?'

'We don't know where she was when she saw it. If she was in Manchester, for example, she'd have had to travel to London, wouldn't she?'

'She could have phoned.'

'Perhaps she tried. You told me yourself that the BBC switchboard was jammed.'

He wasn't going to get far with this line of reasoning and he hadn't started it anyway, so he mentioned another obvious cause for mistrusting the Japanese woman. 'I can't believe a genuine mother just reunited with her child would hit her.'

'Stress.'

He gave up. He knew really that his motives in treating the matter as an emergency were more instinctive than rational. Naomi had eventually come to trust him – at least to the extent of holding his hand. He wouldn't have admitted to Julia Musgrave or anyone else – bar Stephanie – that the child had captivated him. He'd felt the small hand in his own and now it was a self-imposed duty to find out whether she was safe. But he didn't want anyone running away with the idea that he – the veteran of a dozen murder inquiries – was a soft touch, literally a soft touch. He didn't particularly want to admit it to himself.

There was more to it, he insisted. He was deeply suspicious about the mother. How could she have allowed herself to be parted from her child for so long? Why hadn't she alerted the police, or at least her own embassy, when Naomi first went missing? Foreigners could be forgiven some confusion in a strange country, but anyone, of any nationality, ought to have reacted promptly to a crisis as basic as that.

So he wasn't giving up without satisfying himself that the 'mother' *was* the mother, and was capable of looking after her child.

Before carrying out his promise (or threat) to call at the police station, he decided to give the area car ten minutes to drive up. Someone may have seen the woman forcing Naomi into the taxi and it was worth making sure that the right questions were asked. Thus far, he wasn't over-impressed by the calibre of the Kensington plod.

Two PCs – male and female – arrived with a couple of minutes to spare, looking like extras in a TV soap opera. Why was it that no one in police uniform looked genuine any more? To do them justice, they went about their duties efficiently and agreed to divide forces, one knocking on doors while the other questioned Mrs Straw.

Diamond waited long enough to learn that not one of the neighbours had witnessed Naomi being bundled into the taxi. One man raised hopes by saying he had spotted the cab standing outside, and then could only add that the vehicle had been black and the driver white.

Down at the nick in Earls Court Road, someone must have issued a warning of imminent invasion. Two sergeants and a plainclothes CID officer – an inspector, as it turned out – were at the desk to repel Diamond. They didn't succeed, of course. He'd long ago checked the identity of the Deputy Assistant Commissioner for Six Area West and nothing opens a door better than naming the man in charge.

This being Saturday morning, the Big White Chief wasn't about, so Diamond had to settle for his surrogate, Chief Superintendent Sullins, another name usefully committed to memory from the police directory in Kensington Reference Library. For his part, Sullins, a foxy little character in white shirt and red braces, trying strenuously to look the part of the Kensington supremo, claimed to have heard of Diamond, though they had never met until this handshake on the stairs.

'Everything under control' was Sullins' text for the day, at least for Peter Diamond's consumption. He was giving this matter of the missing child high priority. The police already knew all about Naomi ('I wish I did,' Diamond commented in passing) from the night of the alarm in Harrods. They'd gone to extraordinary lengths to try and establish who she was. And now everything possible was being done to trace the taxi. Cab firms all over London were being contacted. So Diamond was free to leave in the sure confidence that nothing he could do would speed the process.

'Thank you, but I'd prefer to stay,' he said amiably.

'I'm afraid that won't be possible,' Sullins told him.

'Why?'

'We don't allow members of the public—'

'Ex-CID,' Diamond interjected.

'I appreciate the offer, Mr Diamond, but we have our procedures.'

He countered with: 'You mean you need to get the Chief's

consent? Understandable.' He smiled disarmingly. 'I'll fix it. What does he do Saturday mornings – play golf or go shopping with his good lady? I'm damned sure he carries a beeper, wherever he is. And if he has to trot back to his car for the phone, I dare say he won't mind. Do you want me to mention you asked me to get clearance, or should I leave your name out of it, Mr Sullins?'

No ambitious policeman was proof against that kind of blackmail. 'Ex-CID, you said,' Sullins remarked as if he had only just registered the information. 'I suppose it's possible you may be of use. It's highly irregular.'

Diamond nodded. 'Cheers. I'll keep myself inconspicuous.' Which was by some way the most unlikely assertion anyone had made that morning.

In the communications room, a WPC was keying something into the computer. Diamond squeezed around her to reach for the log of calls that the switchboard operator had beside her. 'Got anything back from the taxi firms – about the Japanese kid?'

'Zero so far,' she told him.

'How many are there?'

'Cab firms? Have you looked at the Yellow Pages?'

He picked a directory off her desk. What he saw depressed him. 'How many have you done?'

'About twelve.'

'Keep going.'

She gave him a withering stare. 'Who *are* you?'

'It is a young kid,' he said.

'Japanese, aged about five,' she chanted without looking at a note, 'red woollen dress, black tights, white trainers, accompanied by a Japanese woman about thirty, of smart appearance, with short, dark, wavy hair, grey jacket and matching trousers believed to be made by Rohan.'

He took the opportunity to ask how anyone would recognize Rohan garments and was told that the name was displayed on them.

So Mrs Straw was not, after all, a connoisseur of fashion, but her information was probably reliable.

They're not cheap,' the girl added, 'but they're smart. Kind of sporty. Rohans are really something else in trousers – all those pockets.'

He thanked her. 'Now can I help in any way, by calling over the numbers, perhaps?'

'Is that meant to be a hint, or something? I was going as fast as I could before you interrupted.'

'What if one of them calls back?'

'Harry over there will take it. He's had nothing up to now.'

Harry over there was wearing earphones. He looked up from a copy of *Viz* and raised his thumb in greeting.

'I'll let you get on, then,' Diamond told them tamely. 'Ta.'

He moved away. He fancied a cigarette now, and he hadn't smoked in years. Didn't even approve of it.

Feeling alien and ineffectual, a sensation he'd never have dreamed was possible in a police station, he went to look for the canteen. Five cigarettes and two black coffees later, he went back upstairs, only to be greeted with Harry's palms spread wide in a negative gesture.

In an hour he returned and the operator said that she'd contacted every taxi firm except three that had probably gone out of business. Most of them had said they'd need to check with their controllers or their drivers, some of whom had changed shift since eight in the morning. The standard arrangement was that they'd ring back if anyone could remember picking up the Japanese woman and child in Earls Court.

Harry was filling in a football pools coupon.

'Nothing yet?'

'Zilch.'

Diamond went in search of Superintendent Sullins. He found him in an office upstairs dictating a letter. 'About to leave, Mr Diamond?'

'We seem to have drawn a blank with the taxis.'

'*Nil desperandum.* One of the firms could ring back any time.'

'I know, but it's almost six hours since they were last seen.'

'Let's not be melodramatic,' Sullins unwisely commented. 'We're not dealing with a mine disaster.'

'*Melodramatic*? This is a missing child.'

'Possibly.'

'Have you alerted the airports and the mainline stations?'

'Alerted them to what? A mother slapping her child's leg? Let's keep this in proportion. And now you're going to tell me that we don't know if she's the mother.'

'We don't.'

'But she produced a photograph, Mr Diamond.'

An eruption was imminent. Only a buzz on the intercom prevented it.

Sullins touched a switch. 'Yes?'

The voice was female. 'Sir, we're taking a call from a taxi firm in Hammersmith called Instant Cabs.'

'Put it on,' Sullins ordered.

A man's voice was saying, '. . . went off duty at twelve, and we've only just been able to trace him. He's your driver, all right. He picked up a Japanese woman at seven-fifty this morning in Brook Green. She had a suitcase, dark blue. He drove her to Kempsford Gardens School in Earls Court – would that be right? – and waited until eight twenty-five,

185

or soon after, when she came out with a child, a small girl. Japanese, like the woman. She seemed to be playing up, he said. He drove them to the airport.'

'Heathrow?'

'Yes.'

'Which terminal?'

'Three. The inter-continental.'

Diamond didn't wait to hear any more. He was out and down the stairs and telling Harry to get Immigration on the line.

19

Wedged into seat 11B on Concorde, Diamond was about as comfortable as a stout person may expect to be on an aircraft noted for its slim contour. 11B was immediately behind the serving-bay, providing the dual advantage of increased leg-room and a tray arrangement that allowed him to stand his champagne glass on a level surface rather than having it on a slope created by his stomach.

Rapid decisions were responsible for his being on the flight. Around 5.30 p.m., he had learned from Immigration at Heathrow that someone remembered a Japanese woman and child passing through the departure gate about one p.m. More importantly, the woman had been wearing what was described as grey sportsgear and the child a red corduroy dress, black tights and trainers. Soon after this, British Airways check-in staff had confirmed that a Mrs Nakajima, accompanied by her daughter Aya, had boarded flight BA177 at 1415, due at John F. Kennedy Airport, New York, at 1705, local time.

New York. This wasn't a game for faint hearts, but Diamond was totally committed. By using his former police rank, he succeeded in extracting a promise from the Immigration Service at JFK that Mrs Nakajima and daughter would be detained for up to an hour. From

British Airways he had already learned that by taking the last Concorde flight of the day at 1900, he could be in New York fifty minutes after BA177 arrived – the sort of schedule that would have him looking at his watch all the way across. He'd booked a passage immediately, quoting Yamagata's Gold Card number. The thought crossed his mind that he ought to have called the Albert Hall to get his sponsor's approval, but he decided against it. 'Mr Yamagata is a rich man. He will pay,' the interpreter had promised when they had met, and presumably Mr Yamagata, a man of honour, wouldn't quibble over a mere five thousand and thirty pounds. Diamond preferred not to enquire at this stage.

Remembering just in time that he was a considerate husband, he did phone Stephanie to let her know that he was leaving the country. She wasn't quite as devastated as he'd expected. 'See if you can get me a pair of genuine New York sneakers while you're over there. White, of course. Remember I take a seven, but that's eight and a half in their size.' How did she know these things? he wondered.

He checked his watch again, thinking ahead. The US Immigration officials would be the first test. They were trained to spot con-men. He'd need to be sharp to convince them that he was on an official investigation. Then there was the Nakajima woman, who had thoroughly outfoxed the formidable Mrs Straw. She was a real challenge. Even if she folded under questioning and admitted to abducting the child, there was still the matter of what action could be taken, and where. Extradition law had never been his forte.

A stewardess came along the aisle and handed him a note that must have been transmitted to the cockpit.

To: Supt. Diamond
From: US Immigration
Time: 1721 NYT
Will meet you on arrival. Ms Nakajima and child detained.

A tingling sensation, a mixture of relief, anticipation and champagne, spread through Diamond's veins.

'Good news, sir?' the stewardess enquired.

He gave a dignified smile. 'Just confirming an appointment.' In truth, it deserved a fanfare. For one indulgent moment, he likened himself to Chief Inspector Dew, the man who had crossed the Atlantic in 1910 to arrest Dr Crippen and his mistress. A telegraph message, a dash across the ocean, and Crippen had been copped.

There the comparison ended. Crippen had been a murderer. Mrs Nakajima was guilty, at most, of abduction.

Concorde had already started its descent. The fasten seatbelts order came over the public address.

They touched down five minutes before schedule at 1750.

When the doors were opened, a woman immigration officer was waiting. Diamond introduced himself.

'May I see your ID?' she asked, taking stock of him. He didn't fit the stereotype of a British detective, judging by the way she eyed his waistline.

'Will my passport do?' Helpfully, it had been issued four years ago and still listed his profession as police officer.

'Would you come with me, sir?'

The 'sir' was encouraging. Stiff from the journey and slightly disorientated, but eager to see Naomi, he was taken through a roped barrier and along a corridor lined with filing cabinets. Another door, another corridor, and into an office looking like a scene out of a television police series with its sense of stage-managed activity as people

189

walked through, stopped, exchanged words, presumably to develop different plotlines in the story, and moved on. A black officer in tinted glasses carved a way around a couple of desks and said, 'You've got to be the guy from Scotland Yard.'

'Peter Diamond,' he said, offering his hand without going into the matter of where he was from. 'You still have these people detained, I hope?'

'Sure have.' The man didn't need to give his name. He had a tag hanging from his shirt that identified him as Arthur Wharton.

'Are they giving any trouble?'

'No, sir.'

'What have you told them?'

The usual. A small technical problem over their passport. They're yours.' Arthur Wharton nodded to the woman who'd brought Diamond this far and she beelined determinedly between two people crossing the office from different directions and into another corridor. Diamond realised that he was meant to go with her. Striving to go the same way, he found that he wasn't so adept at dodging people.

He caught up with her by an open doorway. A uniformed member of the airport police was sitting outside, drinking coffee from a paper cup.

Diamond looked into the room.

He stared.

A woman and child were in there, certainly, but the child wasn't Naomi.

She was at least two years younger. Seated on a steel-framed chair, swinging her legs, this little girl still had a baby face, tiny features and chubby cheeks. She wasn't even dressed like Naomi. She had a blue dress, white socks and black shoes made of some shiny material like patent leather. She was Japanese, admittedly, but there the resemblance ended.

The Japanese woman who looked up anxiously at Diamond didn't match the description he'd been given either. She was in a red skirt and jacket and she was wearing rimless glasses.

At a loss, he turned to his escort, but she'd already gone. He spoke to the man at the door. 'Those aren't the people. There's some mistake.'

The cop shrugged.

He found his way back to the hub of the Immigration Department, and vented his frustration on Officer Wharton. 'You detained the wrong people. I've never seen that kid before and they're wearing different clothes, for Christ's sake.'

'Hold on, Mac,' Wharton told him, pointing a finger. 'Don't give lip to me. We held the people you wanted. You gave us no description, just a name. That's Mrs Nakajima in there, no mistake. You want to see the passport?' He handed one across.

Diamond opened it. No question: these people were called Nakajima. 'But they don't match the description,' he said.

'You mean this passport belongs to some other woman?'

'No. What I mean is that the people who were seen at Heathrow were dressed differently from Mrs Nakajima and child.' Even as he spoke the words, the mistake he'd made dawned on him. 'Oh, no!'

Wharton eyed him dispassionately.

'I assumed because Mrs Nakajima and her daughter were Japanese and travelling alone that they had to be the woman and child seen going through the departure gate at

191

Heathrow. After BA came up with these people, I just didn't check the other airlines. They must have taken some other flight. They could have gone anywhere – any damned place in the world.' Mad with himself for being so obtuse, he ended by thumping his fist down so hard on Officer Wharton's desk that paperclips jumped.

Three thousand five hundred miles on Concorde chasing the wrong people. What a pea-brain! 'Listen,' he said to Wharton, 'it may be too late, but I want to contact Terminal Three at Heathrow. I want to fax every airline to check their passenger lists for a Japanese woman travelling alone with a child some time after one p.m. today. Could you arrange that for me?' Sensing that the request was too stark, he added, 'Arthur?'

'You want me to authorise these faxes?' Wharton's expression didn't look promising.

'You have the facilities here,' Diamond told him frankly.

'But you want me to handle this?'

'Exactly. If my name is given, there's so much to explain. If the request comes from US Immigration, they'll act on it promptly. No explanation needed. Speed is the key here.'

'Checking passenger lists? You've got to be joking, man.'

'They're computerised,' Diamond pointed out. He'd not often thought of modern technology as an ally, but he had no scruples in this emergency. 'It's just a matter of tapping a few keys.'

Wharton rubbed the side of his face.

'Listen,' Diamond steamed on, 'while you're doing this for me, I'll go back to Mrs Nakajima and make your apologies. Fair enough?'

It wasn't fair, and he knew it. Wharton knew it, too, but the urgency in the way it was put to him was compelling.

'You'd better write down the message you want me to send,' he said with a sigh.

*

The crucial reply from London came in forty minutes later. By that stage of the exercise, Officer Wharton had been thoroughly briefed about the quest to find Naomi and now he identified himself totally with the challenge. 'Hey, man, this is it.' He held up the fax he had just taken from the machine. 'You want some good news? She's here after all!'

Diamond was galvanised. 'Here? In New York, you mean?'

'Right. They flew in this afternoon on a Pan Am flight. A Japanese woman and a kid.'

'Brilliant! When did they land?'

'Seventeen-twenty. About an hour ago.'

'An *hour*?' Diamond's elation withered and died. 'By now they must have cleared customs and left the airport.'

But Wharton gave a reassuring grin. 'Not this airport. Takes a while to get through Immigration in JFK. The Pan Am flight?' He looked at his watch. 'I figure they *could* be as far as the customs hall by now, but I wouldn't bet on it.'

Diamond was on his feet. 'Which way?'

'Hold on, Peter,' Wharton told him. 'You're in serious danger of doing yourself an injury. We can check from here.' He pointed upwards to a set of eight television monitors mounted on the ceiling. 'Video-surveillance. See if you can spot your people. I'm going to see if I can raise the crew of that flight.'

Cameras were in positions where they could pan slowly over the entire queue snaking around the system of barriers towards the kiosks where their passports were

193

examined and stamped. Diamond studied each screen keenly, looking for a child. Some were tantalisingly half obscured by adults.

Wharton was busy on the phone. 'I've spoken to the chief steward on the Pan Am flight,' he presently informed Diamond. 'There's no question they were on board. He remembers Naomi in the red corduroy, and the woman in the grey Rohan jacket.'

'That's wonderful, but where are they now, I'd like to know,' said Diamond. 'I can't see them in the queue.'

'You won't. Seems the Pan Am flight has cleared Immigration. Take a look at the baggage claim hall – the monitors to your right. They should be in there somewhere. I'm trying to establish which of our officers dealt with them.'

He would rather have been in the baggage hall himself instead of staring at the grey screens. The figures grouped by the baggage carousel looked about as remote and un-focused as the pictures of the first moon landing. True, he could just about make out enough to distinguish one indi-vidual from another.

'If you think you spot them, we have a zoom facility,' Wharton explained, taking the phone away from his ear for a moment. 'We can take a closer look.'

'Thanks.' But he hadn't spotted them, and the possible explanations were depressingly simple to supply. They may have collected their luggage and gone. Or the woman may have owned a US passport, in which case they would have passed through at least half an hour ago. Or they'd carried everything as hand luggage.

Then Wharton started talking earnestly on the phone. He told Diamond, 'Okay, they just passed through Immigration. The woman's name is Tanaka – get that?

194

– Mrs Minori Tanaka, Japanese passport-holder. The kid is travelling on her passport, name of Emi.'

'Amy?'

Wharton spelt it. 'Mrs Tanaka put down the Sheraton, Park Avenue as her address. We can check with the hotel whether they have a reservation.'

Diamond's eyes hadn't left the monitors and a moment later he was rewarded by the image of two grainy figures of a woman and small girl approaching the carousel with a trolley. The child appeared to have Naomi's fringe and black hair.

He pointed. 'That one. Second from the end. The child.'

Wharton reached for a remote control and pressed a button to operate the zoom. The child's face increased in size until it filled the screen, placid in expression, gazing nowhere in particular, as if preoccupied in thought.

Naomi, without question.

'Let me see the woman with her,' Diamond requested.

'In close-up?'

The screen blurred momentarily, then he had his first sight of Minori Tanaka, a keen-eyed, intelligent face with prominent cheekbones and a small nose. The mouth, defined with an intense lipstick, was wider than usual in a Japanese, giving a suggestion of waywardness, or sexiness, according to interpretation. She was probably in her thirties.

'Attractive,' was Arthur Wharton's opinion.

Unexpectedly, the face slid out of shot.

'Can you pull back?' Diamond asked, and as the camera was being adjusted to give the longer view, even before it was complete, he saw that the woman was stooping over the carousel. 'Christ, she's collecting her suitcase! She'll be gone.'

Watching the screen, they had been lulled into a

near-disastrous passivity. In seconds, Mrs Tanaka could wheel her trolley through customs to the cab-rank and be driven away with Naomi.

'How do we get to them?' Diamond demanded.

'You need a stamp on your passport first,' Wharton told him.

'Oh, for crying out loud! That child has been abducted.'

'Passport.'

He handed it across. Wharton opened it, selected a rubber stamp from the drawer of his desk, adjusted the date and made the imprint in the passport. 'Now that you're legal we can go find them, Peter.'

Diamond was speechless. Speechless, then breathless, as Wharton led him at a jog along a moving walkway and down two sets of stairs. Through a door and they emerged into the main concourse of the air terminal, opposite the arrivals gate. It was busy with friends and relatives crowding the barrier for a first glimpse as the passengers wheeled their trolleys through.

They were in time to see Mrs Tanaka emerge, pushing one large blue suitcase on a trolley. At her side – and there could be no doubt any more – was Naomi.

The little girl appeared uninterested in the new scene unfolding in front of her, the mass of faces turned their way. She walked mechanically at Mrs Tanaka's side, one hand on the trolley. They passed the point where the drivers stood with notices displaying people's names.

'You gonna stop them?' asked Wharton, giving him a shove. 'You'd better go now, man.'

Diamond started forward, and it was brought home to him forcibly – for the second time – that he wasn't in shape for dodging and weaving. A man in a wheelchair skidded to a stop and yelled at him to watch where he was going.

He didn't have time to point out that he was doing exactly that – it was the stretch between that he'd ignored.

Just as he found a clear way through, he hesitated.

Someone had moved in to speak to Mrs Tanaka, a white man, tall, with cropped, dark hair and a distinctive nose that made Diamond think of Charlton Heston, though the resemblance ended there. He was in a black leather jacket and white jeans. He spoke to Mrs Tanaka and she nodded and frowned, apparently startled by the approach.

Naomi was looking past the man, straight at Diamond. But it was the stone-faced autistic stare that he knew so well. Nothing to suggest she recognised him, no reaction of surprise, or pleasure, or dislike, come to that. She simply let her eyes focus on him for a moment and then she was distracted by the electronic chime that signalled an announcement on the public address. She turned her face upwards towards the source of the sound.

A decision born of professional experience trailing suspects had made Diamond stop that split-second before going up to them. The man might be some predator muscling in to 'help' with the luggage for an exorbitant fee – easy bucks when the victims were women with children in tow. Yet his presence could be more significant. So the right move was to go straight past them, veering off to the left, and stand close to the queue at an information desk and keep tabs on what happened next.

Mrs Tanaka's body-language suggested she was agreeing to whatever the man was proposing, yet not without some reluctance. After some head-shaking and spreading of the arms, she twice took a step away from him. Finally she allowed him to take over the trolley and wheel it towards the nearest exit, so quickly that Naomi – still with her hand on the side – had to trot to keep up.

197

Diamond followed closely, secure in the knowledge that neither of the adults knew him and Naomi was unlikely to react. Allowing them to get this far without being challenged was something of a risk, yet he reckoned their movements were going to be limited by the trolley, whatever they did next.

They were heading towards the taxi-rank. If necessary, Diamond decided, he would let them get into a cab and drive off, and he'd follow in the next vehicle. If the man in the leather jacket travelled with Mrs Tanaka, one question would be answered: he'd be involved in this business.

Outside was the line of yellow cabs, superintended by a man with a whistle in his mouth. But Leather-jacket wheeled the trolley straight past and across the road. The air-shuttle buses, then? Apparently not. They were going into the short-stay parking lot, which was a possibility Diamond hadn't considered, and he clapped his hand to his face in self-rebuke. He wasn't thinking sharply at all since arriving here; he put it down to the flying.

He had to cross the road quickly, zigzagging through traffic, following them into the ground floor of the parking lot, where his problems increased. Leather-jacket and Mrs Tanaka weren't more than twenty-five yards ahead with Naomi when they turned right and entered the elevator. The doors had closed before he got to them.

What now?

There were stairs close by. He had no idea whether to go down to the basement or up to the decks above. There was no indicator to tell him which floor the elevator had reached.

He'd have to plump for one and hope they were still in sight when he got there. One direction was as likely as any other, so he went down, taking the stairs two at a time and bursting through the swing doors at the bottom.

No one was in sight among the ranks of cars.

Behind him, the elevator doors opened. Nobody was inside. He was certain now that he should have tried one of the upper levels. He got in and pressed the second-floor button, cursing the delay before the doors slid across.

He'd be fortunate if he hadn't lost them completely. The cage moved upwards, the doors opened and he stepped out and started running. No point in stalking the quarry now. If they stepped into a car and drove away, he hadn't the slightest chance of pursuing them. There were no taxis up here. But he *had* spotted them. They were three or four aisles to his right, about eighty yards ahead. So he ran, shouting to them.

'I say! Mrs Tanaka!'

She turned to look.

Leather-jacket also turned. He was in the act of unlocking a car door.

Diamond was still thirty yards from them.

Mrs Tanaka said something Diamond couldn't pick up and opened a door herself and bundled Naomi into the car.

'I'd like a word,' called Diamond.

But he didn't get a word. Instead, he got the trolley slammed into him as he advanced. Leather-jacket used it like a battering-ram, driving it at him viciously. It had the weight of the suitcase behind it and the full force of a large, young man.

Diamond's ankles could have suffered ugly damage if he hadn't reacted a split-second before the impact and jumped six inches off the ground – about as high as a man of his size could hope to achieve. He pitched forward, making

199

the suitcase take the main impact. His head crunched against the metal basket mounted at the top of the trolley. But for the cushioning caused by the suitcase, he might have ended with his head in the basket like a victim of the guillotine.

As it was, he rolled aside, tipping the trolley over and denting the wing of a car with his left shoulder. He was in no condition to spring up and fight.

Leather-jacket wasn't staying. He grabbed the suitcase (now split across the centre) from under the trolley, swung it into the back of the car, slammed the door, and got into the front with Mrs Tanaka.

A faceful of exhaust-fumes didn't help Diamond's condition one bit. The car – a large, white Buick with red strips along the side – roared. The tyres shrieked and it powered away.

20

Extensive bruising, definitely. Some torn skin on the shoulder and left arm, which was smarting. A rapidly developing headache. Really, though, there was no serious injury, except to his confidence. He'd blundered. Blown it. Gone down the tubes, as they would say in this city of fertile phrases. After flying thousands of bloody miles and actually catching up with Naomi, he'd allowed her to be snatched away again. She was being driven God knew where.

Hopeless.

He hauled himself painfully upright, more stricken with self-reproach than pain. Damn it, he'd ignored even the most basic procedures. Hadn't even got the car's number.

He could imagine the reception he'd get from the New York cops if he asked them to trace a white Buick with red trimmings and no number.

What now, then?

Was this really the end of the chase?

He glanced around, at the trolley, still lying on its side in the space the car had occupied. He supposed he ought to look over the side of the car lot in the hope of seeing the Buick making its getaway, but he was damned sure his eyesight wasn't good enough to read a licence plate from up here – even if he had the good fortune to spot the car.

And then it occurred to him that a vehicle making a

getaway from here still had to conform to the procedures. The designers of car lots made sure everyone was obliged to check out in an orderly way. There would be a barrier downstairs and a place where you paid. Maybe, in a busy car park like this, where you *lined up* to pay. Even if this place had automatic gates, you could only get out as fast as the machinery and the cars in front allowed you. Actually, he was quite sure Leather-jacket hadn't stopped at a pre-payment facility.

So they couldn't race out without paying. A car, however fast, took a little time to get out to the street.

He hobbled across to the lift at the best pace he could manage. The only point of exit from the car lot was on the basement level, and this was the quickest way down. By good fortune – and he was overdue for some – the lift door had remained open, so he stepped in and pressed the control. Each delay was mental agony – the pause before the door operated, the slow progress down – saying a silent prayer that the cage wouldn't stop at the floors between – and the hesitation before it opened. Then he was out and looking for the exit signs, trying to see the shortest way across the floor, because he didn't need to go by the same roundabout route as the cars.

He decided on a line to his left, through the ranks of cars, which meant some tight squeezes and several wing mirrors being knocked out of alignment, but it proved the quickest route.

Ahead five or six cars were curving out of sight up a ramp. He ran past four and was in time to see the barrier descend and the Buick – or at least a red and white car – on its way out.

He wasted no more time. The car now at the head of the queue was a pink Chevrolet. He dragged open the passenger door. The woman driver was in the act of paying her charge. She swung around. 'What is this?'

'Police.' With no credentials to show except a passport, he tugged it from his pocket and held it up like a warrant. 'Do you mind? Would you kindly follow the car in front?'

'Would you say that again?' She was young, in her thirties probably, with dark hair in a mass of loose curls that stirred as she spoke.

'I'm asking you to follow the Buick.'

'Are you from England?' she asked.

He groaned inwardly. 'This is an emergency.'

'You'd better jump in, then. I can take you into Manhattan, if that's what you want.'

He didn't prolong the conversation.

She moved off at a promising rate and soon got them out of the airport complex and on to the Van Wyck Expressway to Manhattan. There was no sign of the Buick.

'Can we go faster?'

'You said you're police?'

'I did.'

'You don't happen to have one of those portable sirens with you?'

He supposed she was being sarcastic.

'No.'

'Do I have police permission to break the limit?'

'It's a kid at risk, a small girl,' Diamond stressed.

She moved into the fast lane.

Two miles along, Diamond asked her to ease off a little. He could see the white Buick.

It was in a centre lane doing about seventy-five. He could see the outline of Mrs Tanaka's head above the front passenger seat.

'Not too close.'

'So you don't want me to force them off the road?'

'Not at this juncture. I'd prefer to stay inconspicuous.'

'I just love the way you say things.' She steered smoothly into a space three cars back from the Buick and they cruised in convoy. 'This kid – is she from England too?'

'Er, yes. What's your name?' he said to change the subject. Telling her the little he knew about Naomi would just confuse her. *He* was confused.

'Ken.'

'You said Ken?'

'Mm.'

'That's a girl's name here?'

'Short for Kennedy. I was born the week the President was killed. I get tired of explaining.'

'It's nice to have an unusual name. Mine is common enough. Peter.'

'Peter the Great.'

'Unfair.'

'What's wrong with that?' Ken asked.

He slapped the curve of his belly and she grinned. 'I didn't mean it that way.'

The line of cars was still cruising steadily in the same formation. The New York skyline was in view now. 'We're on Long Island here, am I right?' Diamond asked.

'This is the Long Island Expressway we just moved onto,' she confirmed. 'We're heading for Queens and the toll tunnel under the East River.'

'Is this the route you would have taken anyway?'

She shook her head. 'I live in the Bronx. It doesn't matter.' After a pause she added, 'You appeal to my curiosity. You're not really a policeman at all. I may look dumb, but I can tell the difference between a police ID and a passport. On the other hand, you don't have the look of

204

who'll be interviewing you,' Justine said, and explained as Diamond's eyebrows shot up, 'The programme is entirely presented by kids.' And with that, Justine smiled and left.

Curtis winked. He was wearing a red baseball cap and a black T-shirt with the programme's title across the front in white lettering. He extended a small hand to Diamond. 'Pete – you don't mind if I call you Pete? – I'm really sorry I can't tell you when we'll do our spot,' he said, sounding like someone five times his age, 'but I thought you and Naomi might like to see inside the studio while we have the chance.'

'We'd appreciate that,' Pete confirmed. About the only other person in the world who used the short form of his name was Stephanie. On a snap assessment, Curtis was worth making an exception for. No one else in the hospitality suite had been winkled out by their interviewer to become familiar with the studio.

Naomi had to be helped to her feet, she was so engrossed in her drawing.

'Is that Japanese writing?' Curtis asked.

'It's a nice idea, but I don't believe so,' Diamond answered after a glance at the sheet, which was decorated once again with diamond shapes. 'You know, of course, that she doesn't speak?'

'You bet I do, Pete,' came the answer. Curtis led them at a springy step through a couple of swing doors into the studio, a cavernous place, in semi-darkness except for the set of a pirate ship, where the technicians were setting up. With a caution to watch out for cables, Curtis made a beeline for an unlighted stage dressed up as an airport departure lounge, but scaled to child-size. Through a window, a model jumbo jet was visible on a realistic-looking runway.

'It's one of our permanent sets, no kidding. Isn't it the pits?' Curtis apologised. 'You're supposed to think this is where the action is. The jet-set, get it? It's where Cedric wants to shoot us.'

In view of the flight to Boston being planned for Naomi, the choice was not inappropriate and Diamond said as much to Curtis. 'The only problem is that I'm going to look like King Kong in a set that size,' he added.

'No sweat, Pete,' Curtis assured him. 'The cameraman can take care of that.' Whether such touching faith was justified was another question, but the boy couldn't have been more reassuring as he went on to outline the kind of interview he wanted to conduct. 'The way I see it, we need to get across the story of how Naomi was found. You were in Harrods that night, right?'

Diamond nodded.

'So we'll talk about how she caused a major alert, and then I'll ask you who she is and how she got there, and you'll say nobody knows, right? Then you'd better tell me she doesn't speak at all. Cedric says we should skip the reasons for that. Keep it simple.'

'Agreed,' said Diamond, warming to these people. He didn't want Naomi labelled as autistic, or in any way mentally impaired. Far better if her mutism was just presented as a fact.

'Okay, then,' said Curtis. 'The point I'll be making is that we need help with this mystery.' He paused, made quote signs with his fingers and spaced his words. 'Who . . . is . . . Naomi? Cut to a close-up of Naomi. We want people to look at her and say to themselves, "Jeez, where have I seen this chick before?"'

No question – the boy was a pro.

'And that's it?' said Diamond.

'Unless you have something else you want to throw in.'

'You've covered it.'

'Like to see the other sets?'

While this was going on, Naomi had remained at Diamond's side, her drawing pad held across her chest. Now that the conversation had entered a new, less earnest phase, she began shifting her feet as if she wanted to leave the studio.

Curtis shot her a glance and asked, 'Does she want the girls' room?'

'What?' Diamond was nonplussed.

'The girls' room. The loo. How do you know if she wants to go?'

This wasn't a contingency he'd foreseen. Being responsible for a small girl brought complications. 'You'd better show us where it is, Curtis.'

The toilets were next to the hospitality suite. As soon as Naomi sighted the doors she handed her drawing pad and marker to Diamond and ran ahead. Interestingly she understood the symbols, because she didn't falter over the choice.

Curtis looked up at the clock and promised to rejoin them after lunch, when they'd be wanted in make-up. He gave directions to the canteen. With a wink and a smile he left Diamond waiting uncertainly outside the toilets. There was no telling whether the little girl could manage unaided, and as luck would have it, no woman came by, or he'd have asked her to check.

Strewth, if the lads in the Avon and Somerset Police could see me now, Diamond mused.

Then she emerged composed and in good order. Together they went to explore the BBC canteen. The pace started to accelerate.

Lunch.

Make-up.

Back to the hospitality suite.

Curtis, by now dressed in a red shirt and black bow-tie, kept them up to date with the programme schedule. It seemed they might be included between the trio in pink satin and the skateboarder. Meanwhile Naomi continued with her drawing.

'She may be trying to tell you something. Have you thought of that?' Curtis commented.

'With the drawing, you mean? Certainly I have,' Diamond said, 'only I haven't cracked it yet.'

Curtis took another look over Naomi's shoulder. 'Is it a logo? You know, like you see in ads?'

'The diamond shape? Off the cuff I can't think of any business that uses it.'

'Have you noticed she doesn't shade them in? When most kids draw a shape like that, they fill it in.'

This was an observation he hadn't considered. For the moment he couldn't see its relevance, but Curtis was ahead of him.

'Could be something you see through, like those funny windows in old houses.'

Leaded windows.

'That's a fascinating suggestion, Curtis.'

'No fee,' said Curtis. 'I'd better get back to the control room now. Stay cool.' He strolled out, clicking his fingers to some tune pounding in his head.

Diamond weighed Curtis's idea. If Naomi had lived in a house with lattice windows, this could be a genuine clue. He levered his weight out of the chair and ponderously lowered himself to kneel beside her.

passenger door. The woman driver was in the act of paying her charge. She swung around. 'What is this?'

'Police.' With no credentials to show except a passport, he tugged it from his pocket and held it up like a warrant. 'Do you mind? Would you kindly follow the car in front?'

'Would you say that again?' She was young, in her thirties probably, with dark hair in a mass of loose curls that stirred as she spoke.

'I'm asking you to follow the Buick.'

'Are you from England?' she asked.

He groaned inwardly. 'This is an emergency.'

'You'd better jump in, then. I can take you into Manhattan, if that's what you want.'

He didn't prolong the conversation.

She moved off at a promising rate and soon got them out of the airport complex and on to the Van Wyck Expressway to Manhattan. There was no sign of the Buick.

'Can we go faster?'

'You said you're police?'

'I did.'

'You don't happen to have one of those portable sirens with you?'

He supposed she was being sarcastic.

'No.'

'Do I have police permission to break the limit?'

'It's a kid at risk, a small girl,' Diamond stressed.

She moved into the fast lane.

Two miles along, Diamond asked her to ease off a little. He could see the white Buick.

It was in a centre lane doing about seventy-five. He could see the outline of Mrs Tanaka's head above the front passenger seat.

'Not too close.'

203

'So you don't want me to force them off the road?'

'Not at this juncture. I'd prefer to stay inconspicuous.'

'I just love the way you say things.' She steered smoothly into a space three cars back from the Buick and they cruised in convoy. This kid – is she from England too?'

'Er, yes. What's your name?' he said to change the subject. Telling her the little he knew about Naomi would just confuse her. *He* was confused.

'Ken.'

'You said Ken?'

'Mm.'

'That's a girl's name here?'

'Short for Kennedy. I was born the week the President was killed. I get tired of explaining.'

'It's nice to have an unusual name. Mine is common enough. Peter.'

'Peter the Great.'

'Unfair.'

'What's wrong with that?' Ken asked.

He slapped the curve of his belly and she grinned. 'I didn't mean it that way.'

The line of cars was still cruising steadily in the same formation. The New York skyline was in view now. 'We're on Long Island here, am I right?' Diamond asked.

'This is the Long Island Expressway we just moved onto,' she confirmed. 'We're heading for Queens and the toll tunnel under the East River.'

'Is this the route you would have taken anyway?'

She shook her head. 'I live in the Bronx. It doesn't matter.' After a pause she added, 'You appeal to my curiosity. You're not really a policeman at all. I may look dumb, but I can tell the difference between a police ID and a passport. On the other hand, you don't have the look of a hitch-hiker. Or a rapist. Is it, like, a fight with your wife over custody of the child?'

He told her that Naomi wasn't his own child. He was almost persuaded, after all, to explain how the little Japanese girl had taken over his life. Then they entered the toll tunnel and he concentrated instead on the uncertainty of what would happen at the other end. 'Where exactly does this come out?' he asked, as if he had a map of Manhattan imprinted on his brain.

'East 34th,' Ken told him. 'It won't be so simple trailing them from now on.'

'Could you try and get closer, then?'

After they were out of the tunnel, she succeeded in passing one of the cars ahead and another turned off at the first traffic lights, leaving them with just a blue Volvo between their car and the Buick. But the tension grew as they crossed the city, negotiating lights, willing the Volvo not to hesitate. They passed the Empire State and Macy's before turning right, onto 8th Avenue, heading north.

The Buick picked up some speed.

'Can you pass the car in front?' Diamond asked.

When she moved into the next lane the driver of the Volvo took it as a challenge and blocked their way through. At the next lights he braked hard, forcing them to stop, while the Buick cruised on.

Diamond swore and turned to see if there was room to move out, but it was impossible.

'They won't get far,' Ken said in reassurance. 'The lights will hold them up.'

He wasn't so confident. He'd already watched them go through on the red at the next intersection. 'We've got to pass this clever dick.'

She did, on the next block, in front of the Port

Authority Bus Terminal, to a crescendo of car-horns. They had lost position badly. A glimpse of white some way ahead might just have been the Buick. They had to assume it was. Diamond strained forward with his face to the windscreen. 'Keep going straight ahead. If they turn I'll tell you.'

She overtook cars at each opportunity and sometimes when the opportunity scarcely existed. He couldn't fault her commitment to the chase. Occasionally he caught sight of the white car through the traffic about a block ahead and he just hoped to God it was still the Buick they were following. Central Park came up on their right.

'We keep going far enough, we'll get to the Bronx and I'll be home,' Ken told him.

But they didn't get that far. They had almost reached the northern limit of the Park when the white car ahead moved into the left lane and turned.

'Can you move over?'

'Sure.'

'That must be 109th.'

She handled the Chevrolet with confidence, accelerating into a space and taking the turn at a speed that made the wheels screech. But there was no white car ahead of them on West 109th Street.

'He could have doubled back down Manhattan Avenue,' Ken suggested.

'Try it, then.'

She turned left again. Mistakenly, for two blocks ahead there were only yellow taxis and grey saloons.

'Sorry. I'm really sorry,' she said, and her voice was desolate. 'Want me to turn?'

'Where do you think they were heading before we lost them?'

206

'Hard to say. We're not far from Columbia.'

'You mean the University?'

'Yes.'

'Can you work your way back in that direction? If we're lucky the car may be parked on the street somewhere.'

They turned right, onto Amsterdam Avenue. No sign of a white car. A vast church loomed up on their right. 'It's really popular with the students,' Ken remarked.

'The Cathedral of St John the Divine?' Diamond read from the board in a disbelieving voice.

'I mean the Hungarian Pastry Shop on this side.'

'Ah.' Neither of them felt like smiling. The confusion was indicative of their helplessness. Nothing is so hard to accept as the knowledge that you have failed. They were floundering, trying to buoy each other up with words, but the words gave no real support.

'The Columbia campus comes up on this side in a block or two,' she informed him.

'We ought to be checking these. Can you turn up the next one?'

It was 113th Street, and they drove as far as Broadway, then made two lefts onto 112th. Three white cars were parked there, not one a Buick. Almost ten minutes had passed since they had lost sight of the car; and ten grew to twenty while they continued to tour the streets without result.

'I can transfer to a taxi,' Diamond offered.

'I won't allow it,' Ken said. 'I'm as keen to find the damned car as you are.'

'It could have left the area by now.'

'We owe it to that little girl to keep looking.'

He didn't need telling.

It took them just under an hour to find the Buick. It

was parked near the Broadway end of 114th Street. They would have found it sooner if they hadn't chosen to start at 113th and work back as far as 108th, but the enormous relief at picking up the trail wiped out any regrets.

'What now?' Ken asked.

'I'm more grateful than I can say.'

She frowned, not understanding his English avoidance of the direct statement.

'I can manage,' he said.

'Hey, you don't think I'm quitting now? I want to see the kid for myself.' Her eyes dispelled any doubt that she meant what she said.

'In that case, I'll tell you what we do next. We go doorstepping.'

This section of the street was lined with apartment blocks and small hotels. They tried the hotels first. 'I'm hoping to find a couple with a small girl who may have registered here an hour ago,' was the disarming way he phrased his enquiry. 'The lady is Japanese and so is the child.' He was trying to project himself as the caring English gent, as if friends of his had left behind some lost property that he was anxious to reclaim for them.

After trying three hotels and getting suspicious looks and shakes of the head, but no verbal response, he changed his approach at the Firbank, a shabby brownstone with a sign in the window saying *Vacancies*. The window needed cleaning.

The door stood open and a man in a black singlet and jeans was behind a hinged table that passed for a reception desk.

'Is Mrs Tanaka staying here?'

'Who the fuck are you?'

It was, by certain lights, an improvement on silence.

208

Diamond said that he'd been sent by Immigration. 'And who the fuck are you?' he added.

'George De Wint.'

'Manager?'

'I have no illegals in my hotel,' De Wint said defensively. For a beefy, tattooed man with a Cagney profile, he suddenly sounded pathetic.

'But you have Mrs Tanaka, in this afternoon from England?'

'From England?'

'Japanese, with a male partner, and a small girl.'

'So what exactly is the problem?'

'Is she here, or not?'

'Sure, she's here. You want me to phone the room?'

Mentally, Diamond turned a backflip of triumph. 'Could I see the register?'

George De Wint leaned to his left, placed a hand on a dog-eared exercise book, and slid it along the counter.

Diamond opened it at the latest entry, which was *M. Tanaka*. 'There's only the one name here.'

'So what? Kids don't have to register.'

'How about the man?'

'The guy isn't staying here. He carried the suitcase.'

'Has he left yet?'

'Not to my knowledge. What exactly is this about, mister? I don't want trouble.'

'Which room?'

'Twelve.'

'Upstairs?'

'Third floor. She wanted a twin with bathroom, so I gave her my biggest.'

'Show us up.'

The Firbank reeked of some cheap scented spray. It

didn't run to a lift and the stairs creaked like rowlocks, so there was no point in trying to approach the room by stealth.

A DO NOT DISTURB notice was hanging from the handle of room twelve. Diamond knocked.

No one responded.

'Seems they went straight to bed,' De Wint suggested.

'With a child in the room?' said Ken in disbelief.

'To sleep. They could be jetlagged if they came from England.'

Diamond called out, 'Anyone there?'

Still silence.

He rattled the handle. The manager unhooked a bunch of keys from his belt.

When the door was unlocked, there was still no word from inside. And the room was not in darkness.

Diamond stepped in.

A moderate-sized, cheaply furnished room. Twin beds, one with the bedding pulled back. On the other, an open suitcase.

'They went out, then,' De Wint commented. 'People are so dumb, leaving notices on the door like that. When are my staff supposed to make up the rooms?'

'You said they were up here.'

'So I made a mistake. Mister, this is a hotel, not the city jail.'

Diamond crossed to the bathroom door, tapped once and opened it. The light was on. A saturated towel lay on the floor. There was water in the bath to the level of the overflow. He stepped closer.

'Someone is in after all,' he said.

The manager went closer. His reaction was less restrained. 'Jesus – why in my hotel, of all places?'

Lying along the base of the bath under several inches of water was a body, face down and dressed in a white blouse, grey trousers and shoes. The hair was short and dark.

Diamond warned Ken not to look.

Discovering a death is disturbing in any circumstances. What made this the more shocking was that the wrists were fastened behind the woman's back, bound with cord. Around the ankles a belt had been wound several times and fastened.

Diamond took off his jacket and handed it to De Wint, who was still carrying on about his misfortune. He rolled up his shirt-sleeves and stooped over the bath in an attempt to turn the body face upwards. The New York Police Department wouldn't be too thrilled at having the corpse disturbed; however, he needed to confirm the victim's identity at once. Taking a grip of the clothes, he tugged, but his figure wasn't shaped for turning over bodies in baths and he had to ask for the manager's assistance. 'Come on, man. I'm not talking to myself.'

De Wint was backing out of the bathroom. 'I can't touch it. No way.'

Fortunately, Ken was less inhibited. She came forward and said, 'Let me help. I'm not bothered.'

Splashing themselves liberally in the process, they managed the manoeuvre at the second attempt.

Without any doubt the body was that of the Japanese woman they'd followed from John F. Kennedy Airport, the woman who had brought Naomi from England.

He turned to De Wint, water dripping from his arms. 'Is she the woman who occupied this room? Come forward, man. Now, do you recognise the lady, or don't you?'

'Oh my God, yes. She's the one.'

Now the head could be lowered under the water again.

The question no one had spoken because it was so horrible to contemplate had to be faced, and quickly: where was Naomi?

Diamond felt some unsteadiness in his legs. He was literally shaking at the knees, and it wasn't brought on by what he had just discovered. He feared for what he might discover next. Without a word, he straightened, turned and moved back to the bedroom, leaving the manager bowed over the toilet bowl in the act of retching.

There weren't many places where a child's body could have been concealed. He could tell without pulling back the bedding that nothing was trapped beneath it. And the space under the divan beds was far too narrow. He opened the wardrobe. It contained only a woman's jacket, grey, with the name Rohan embroidered on the front in yellow.

There remained the window to check. In truth, he didn't expect to find Naomi dead inside the room. Some combination of intuition and experience told him she wasn't here. He felt less secure about looking out of the window.

It faced the rear of a building in the next street, and overlooked a narrow yard bounded by grime-stained brick.

He had to brace himself to look down.

Plastic bins. Some tired-looking geraniums in pots. A few dead leaves and scraps of paper shifting fitfully with the breeze. Nothing resembling a small body. A pigeon eyed him from a window ledge opposite.

He leaned out further. 'This fire escape on the left,' he called to De Wint. 'How do you reach it from inside?'

'The door at the end of the corridor.'

'And if I had to go down it, how would I get to the street?'

'There's a passage to 113th. You can't see from up here.'

'That's the way he left with the child, I reckon.' He withdrew from the window.

Time was precious. Faced with the dilemma of immediate pursuit, or trying to make sense of what was happening by going through the woman's things, he chose the latter and started a rapid search of the bedroom. No doubt he'd be hammered for disturbing the scene of a murder. Sod that: Naomi's safety came before anything else, and if there were clues here, they had to be found fast.

He went through the suitcase first, a blue fabric case with no manufacturer's name and no labels on the exterior.

The dresses and underwear folded neatly in layers were of fine quality. There were also some clothes for the child, bearing the Marks and Spencer label. He ran his hand several times through the contents of the case in the hope of locating documents or an address book. There was nothing more helpful than an A–Z Street Atlas of London and a copy of *The Times*, three days old. A toilet-bag contained wash-things, lipstick and other make-up and some Aspro Clear in tinfoil. A brush and comb. A portable hair-dryer. It was all very predictable.

He flicked over the pages of the A–Z and found a cross pencilled in against the location of the school. That, finally, made a categorical connection with Naomi.

With a face not markedly different from the pale green of the bathroom he was emerging from, the manager re–appeared in time for more questions from Diamond.

'This man who was with them, did he say anything when they registered?'

'Do you figure he could have done this thing?'

'Would you answer me? Did you hear him speak? Was he British?'

'No, the woman was doing all the talking, trying to shut the kid up.'

'The child was upset?'

'She was giving them hell.'

From across the room Ken's tough front suddenly gave way to the realisation of what that small girl must have been through. 'Oh, my God.'

Diamond, rigidly holding his imagination at bay, said to De Wint, 'Let's concentrate on the man for a minute. How was he behaving when they arrived?'

'He was smiling plenty.'

'While the child was giving them hell?'

'Yes, as if it embarrassed him.'

'Did he seem possessive towards the child?'

De Wint shook his head. 'He just grinned and left the woman to it. Don't know if this is any help, but there was a gold tooth somewhere. I noticed it when he smiled.'

"Somewhere", Diamond repeated without gratitude. 'The front? The sides? Upper jaw or lower? Come on.'

'Upper. This side.'

'The left.'

The mention of the tooth must have brought the rest of the face into focus in the manager's recall. 'His eyes were brown and he had a nose you wouldn't forget easy, kind of narrow and elegant, like some movie actor.'

'Charlton Heston?'

De Wint looked impressed. He didn't know Diamond had been charged down with a trolley by the man with a Charlton Heston nose.

Resuming the search, he found a handbag upended and left between the beds. The ejected contents – comb, another lipstick, pens, compact, some keys, two matches and a roll of peppermints – lay scattered over the carpet. A purse was left containing six hundred dollars and a handful of British coins. This was not a murder for money.

He picked up the handbag. Every section had been unzipped and emptied.

So what was missing?

The passport.

The photo of Naomi that the woman had shown to Mrs Straw.

Presumably a chequebook and credit cards.

The Pan Am flight tickets and boarding pass. She may have discarded these at JFK, but it was unlikely. People tended to dispose of them later.

In short, any documentary evidence that might have been used to identify the woman and child had gone.

He moved the beds and looked under them. Lifted the pillows and bedding. Went through the pockets of the jacket in the wardrobe.

Nothing.

Leather-jacket had taken what he wanted as efficiently as he had killed. With a terrified child looking on, he must have behaved with exceptional single-mindedness. Or callousness.

Diamond drew a hand across his bald crown, trying to decide if there was anything more to keep him here. The impulse to go in pursuit of the killer was almost irresistible. The man had Naomi. He might be taking her to some place to kill her too.

Yet where? It had to be faced that the trail was cold. Leather-jacket could have gone in any direction, anywhere in New York. Finding them wasn't a one-man assignment. It required the resources of the police.

He picked up the phone, got an outside line and dialled 911.

215

A patrol would be on its way directly, they promised. He was to stay where he was and touch nothing.

A bit bloody late for that, he thought.

He was racked with the helplessness of the situation. What a cock-up. Those cops were going to throw the book at him for handling the body and the dead woman's possessions, and so they should.

He'd defied the rules for Naomi's sake, and achieved precisely nothing.

He was so wound up that when Ken spoke from across the room there was a delay before her words got through. If the police were about to take over, she was telling him, she figured she didn't really want to stay, particularly as she couldn't do anything else to help.

He thanked her with as much warmth as he could muster, saying that she had come to his aid in a crisis and put up with him heroically. She said something about wishing the kid would be rescued real soon, and then she shook his hand and left.

This was no time for self-pity, but he was sorry she was leaving.

Alone in the room – De Wint having taken the opportunity to escort Ken downstairs – he found the wait unendurable. With nothing else to occupy him in the bedroom, he entered the bathroom again.

The corpse of Mrs Tanaka lay face upwards, submerged, the eyes closed, the mouth gaping. There was no point in turning her face down again, even if he could have managed it. He'd tell the patrolmen exactly what he had done since entering the room.

As he looked down at the body he recalled the rigidity of the thigh when he had gripped the clothes to turn her.

He'd handled the dead as a matter of necessity in his work on murder squads; for some reason the rigor mortis – experienced through the sensation of touch – always affected him more profoundly than the sight of the corpse. The loss of flexibility in the muscles, transforming the body into something like a plaster cast, was such a contrast with living flesh.

Then he thought, hold on, this is wrong. She was killed less than an hour ago. I know that. I saw her at the airport. I followed her here in the car. Rigor mortis takes effect after *hours*, not this short time.

He bent over the bath and put a hand on the upper arm. The flesh was soft to the touch. He placed his hand on the thigh again, where he had gripped it before. It still felt rigid.

A memory was triggered, and he had the explanation. He recalled something the switchboard operator at Earls Court Police Station had said. 'Rohans are really something else – all those pockets.'

The stiffness wasn't the result of rigor mortis at all. On each side of the trousers there were two front pockets fitted over each other, the inner one fastened with a zip. He pulled the tab. The cause of the rigor mortis effect was inside that inner pocket.

He drew it out: a substantial leather wallet. He opened it and found a Japanese passport, issued in December 1988. The water had seeped through, damaging the edges of the pages, but the entries inside were unimpaired. Everything was written in English as well as Japanese. The passport-holder was Mrs Minori Tanaka, aged thirty-six. The photo was clearly of the dead woman.

She had a Yokohama address. He took out a pen and pad and noted it.

There was an entry for her child Emi, date of birth 2 February 1984, sex female.

He sighed and shook his head. Emi . . . Naomi. Poor little kid.

Voices sounded downstairs and the tone was familiar to anyone who has worked in the police. They hadn't come to read the gas meter. There were solid footsteps on the stairs, and De Wint's voice came in at intervals, pitched high as he played the respectable hotelier who has never had trouble before.

Quickly Diamond examined the rest of the wallet. Those missing boarding-passes were there, and the flight-tickets. Also, tucked inside, a small batch of photographs. He glanced through them, picked one out and then stared at it in some surprise before slipping it into his pocket. On this occasion, he decided, he wouldn't declare everything to the police.

21

The two patrolmen first up the stairs had one thing, and one only, lodged in their brains: if this was murder, the scene had to be sealed until the Crime Scene Unit arrived. Having viewed the body, they didn't go so far as to take off their shoes and tiptoe from the room, but they were pretty fastidious about avoiding contact with anything except the carpet. Such discipline ought to have sounded a warning bell for Diamond, but his mind was on other things. He followed them out and told them that something else had to be done, and urgently. He gave them descriptions of Naomi and the man in the leather jacket, and the white Buick, including its licence number. The patrolmen seemed to take umbrage at this big, bluff Englishman issuing orders, so he changed to a more respectful approach. Patiently, more patiently than anyone who knew him would have credited, he repeated everything until one of them took the decision to transmit the message to Central that a murder suspect was at large with a seven-year-old Japanese girl believed to be autistic. He could do no more. The machine took over.

The scene of the killing became a honeypot for homicide detectives, the forensic team in white overalls, police photographers, the coroner's assistant and the medical examiner. Procedural activity compartmentalised the horror of violent death and made it manageable.

For the next three hours Peter Diamond was put through the grinder by detectives.

Violent deaths are commonplace in New York, but the case of Minori Tanaka had unusual features. More than one of the interrogators commented that it was a cruel killing. Even murders have their scale of acceptability and a bullet through the head rates several points above a drowning. The tying of the victim's hands was picked out as a particularly nasty feature. One officer commented that drowning may have been used because it was a relatively silent way to kill. It was true that the manager, De Wint, hadn't heard anything to alert him. If Diamond hadn't arrived and demanded to be let into the room, the body would have remained undiscovered until next day.

The workover he was given was outrageous, in his opinion, considering who he was, and he told them so. Homicide were unrepentant. As an ex-detective he'd conducted himself, in the words of one lieutenant, like Winnie the Pooh in a James Bond movie. While he didn't accept the comparison, he pretended to see it their way after a couple of hours of being shouted at.

He was driven to the 26th Precinct stationhouse to assemble a photofit of Leather-jacket; a task he'd often demanded of witnesses himself, without appreciating how difficult it was to arrive at a likeness. Afterwards, they got him to look through photos of known criminals. A fruitless exercise that had to be gone through.

By eleven that evening there was still no news of the Buick except that it was identified as a stolen car, taken from a street in Queens early that morning. If a car isn't stopped within the first two hours of a call going out, he was told, the chances of arresting anyone are slim. They abandon the car and take another if they're professional crooks, and who in New York would admit to being an amateur? He asked if the patrols were being reminded of the details. The transmitter was red-hot, he was told. When a kid is at risk, really at risk like this Japanese girl, the alert has top priority.

'So is there anything else I can do?'

He got the answer he expected.

'You're asking me to leave, then?'

'You got it. What's your address?'

'What?'

'Where are you staying, man?'

He hadn't even considered until this moment. 'I, em, haven't checked in yet.'

'Mister, it's a little late in the day.'

He settled for a room in the Firbank. Downstairs, without bath, at sixty dollars. Probably a sensible choice. While his sumo sponsor might conceivably have stumped up for a five-star hotel downtown, this was where the action was. And a five-star hotel downtown might have looked askance at a guest without any baggage at all.

The *action*? Why do I kid myself, he thought. I'm sidelined here. A killer is holding a child somewhere in this city. Even the police are getting no information.

Patience, self-discipline, confidence that something will turn up – these are the props a senior detective learns to support himself with when everything has been done and nothing seems to be happening. He'd been through it many times. The pressure was extreme, but you had to be strong.

In the privacy of the first-floor bathroom, he took from his pocket the photograph he'd found in Minori Tanaka's wallet, having suppressed his curiosity for hours. A curious picture to carry in a wallet. Not the kind of snap people hand out to friends when families are mentioned. It was a shot of a gravestone.

Most of the inscription was in Japanese, with the exception of some numerals showing the dates of birth and death of the deceased. He had to squint to read them: 2.2.1984-12.12.1988

He dipped into his pocket for the notes he'd made of the passport details and found that his memory wasn't at fault. The child named in the passport, Emi Tanaka, had been born on 2 February 1984, which was identical to the date of birth on the gravestone.

A coincidence?

No.

A twin?

Unlikely.

Most probably Emi Tanaka was dead.

If so, she had been dead four years. Yet Mrs Tanaka had brought Naomi through immigration at Heathrow and JFK by using this passport, suggesting that *she* was the child born on 2 February 1984. The age was about right. No other identification is required when children travel on their parents' passports. No photo. No birth certificate. Not even descriptive details.

He returned to his room and lay on the bed pondering the reason why a woman should take a child – an autistic child – all the way from Japan to England, pretending it was hers. The obvious assumption was that she had kidnapped Naomi. Maybe she was one of those unfortunate mothers who snatch somebody else's child because their own has died. He'd investigated a similar case in England, although both children had been much younger, just a few months old in fact. The distress had affected everyone, not least himself. He'd been relieved that the woman was treated with leniency by the court. Anyone who has suffered the loss of a young child, or the grief of a miscarriage, can understand the motive for such actions, criminal as they may be.

With the facts so far, he started putting together a scenario. Somewhere in Japan in 1988, Mrs Tanaka's child Emi had died, aged four years and ten months. The grief-stricken mother had been unable to come to terms with her loss. She had to endure the sight of her dead child's friends growing up and enjoying the world, as Emi should have done. Either by chance or intention she observed the children in a school for the handicapped. Naomi was one of them, and Mrs Tanaka noticed her particularly because she was about the age Emi would have been. She coveted her. Not understanding Naomi's autism, she persuaded herself that this beautiful and apparently normal child was merely unwanted and unhappy, and that she could be a good mother to her and give her the love she craved.

So she contrived some way of snatching her from the school.

Then she'd flown to England, using her own dead child's entry on the passport to get Naomi past the immigration checks.

In London (the scenario went on), in fact, on a shopping trip to Harrods, Naomi had succeeded in escaping from this woman who had kidnapped her. She had hidden in the furniture department, and there she had been found after the store closed.

Distraught, Mrs Tanaka had not known how to get the child back. Afraid of contacting the police or the Japanese

Embassy, she had waited for news of where Naomi was being looked after. Eventually, perhaps by recognising her on television, she had tracked her to the school. By calling there early in the morning, she had avoided meeting the teaching staff. Her strength of will had outmatched Mrs Straw's. Reunited with Naomi, she had made her escape to New York.

There the theory foundered. The events in America were inexplicable. Leather-jacket's involvement didn't fit any facts at all. Apparently he'd been waiting to meet Mrs Tanaka and the child – with murder in mind. If not, then he was a killer who picked up women randomly at airports and murdered them – but would a random killer approach a woman with a young child? Surely he'd have the sense to foresee the problems that would bring. Anyway, the nature of the killing didn't square with a casual pick-up. The usual motives of sex and theft just didn't apply.

Well into the night Diamond grappled with the inconsistencies, trying to develop the scenario and finding it impossible. Somewhere earlier in the chain of events there must have been an American connection he'd missed, he decided, but that was the limit of his speculation. At some stage he left the room and went upstairs to check whether anything new had emerged. He found a solitary cop slumped in a chair outside the murder room. No one was inside. Homicide had left, and the inquiry was now being conducted from Headquarters, wherever that was.

He returned to his room, stripped and got into bed. Back in England, it would be morning already. He didn't feel like sleep, but he was dog-tired.

22

The Crime Scene Unit were running the inquiry their own way, and the detective skills of Peter Diamond were not included in the plans. He was finding that being a bystander was more stressful than heading the murder squad.

Early in the morning, realising he hadn't eaten anything since the flight from London, he went looking for a coffee shop and found Hungry Mac's on Broadway and 114th. Number Seven on the menu, with just about everything in the kitchen included, carried the promise of what he regarded as a basic breakfast, and he ordered a double portion. He was on one of the stools at the counter – an uncomfortable perch for a big man – in order to get a view of the TV set. The Firbank wasn't the sort of hotel that provided television in the rooms, so he hadn't yet seen if there was any news coverage of the murder and Naomi's abduction. To add to his frustration, some kind of idiot game show was on the screen at present and two of the customers were watching as if it were the high point of their week.

He should have realised he'd get the information he wanted from the man who took his order.

'You think you can put away two breakfasts?'

'I'm certain I can.'

'You visiting?'

'Er, yes.'

'From England?'

'Yes.'

'Where you staying?'

He hesitated. He hadn't personally experienced rapid-fire interrogation by a New York waiter, though he'd seen others getting the treatment. 'The Firbank.'

'Where they found the dead woman?'

'Yes.' He tried to make light of it. 'Hot and cold in all rooms. Towels and corpse provided by the management.'

'You get some crazies these days,' the man remarked to the shop in general, and it wasn't entirely clear whether he meant Diamond. 'This guy slept in the Firbank last night.' Evidently he did mean Diamond.

The place was pretty full, but no one else seemed interested where Diamond had slept.

When the plateful of bacon, sausages, hash browns and four eggs, easy and over, was served with toast and coffee, there was an extra tidbit in the form of some hard information from the waiter. 'I hear they found the car the killer used.'

Diamond had the knife and fork poised over the plate. 'Where?'

'Some cop spotted it in Chinatown.'

'No one in it, I suppose?'

'No chance.'

He bolted his double breakfast at a rate that would be a talking point in Hungry Mac's for weeks to come and legged it rapidly down to the 26th Precinct stationhouse. There, his air of authority carried him through as far as Sergeant Stein of the Detective Bureau, a gangling, grizzled man in a faded pink shirt and black jeans, who – this morning – was the senior detective on the case.

'You're the British cop,' Stein said in a tone that suggested he'd been warned to look out for Diamond.

'I hear you found the car.'

'A patrolman did.'

'Chinatown. Is that somewhere near the Bowery?'

'You could say that.'

'Where exactly is it, then?'

'Chinatown?'

'The Buick.'

'They moved it,' said Sergeant Stein, and added, after a considerable pause, 'for forensic examination.'

'So what time was it found?'

'A statement will be issued later.'

'Come on,' said Diamond in a flush of annoyance. 'I'm not here out of morbid curiosity.'

'What *are* you here for?' Stein asked.

'For a missing child out there with a murderer. Isn't that a good enough reason for the New York Police Department?'

Stein was unrepentant. 'Mister, I should be asking you the questions.'

'Like what?'

'Like what is your special interest in this kid?'

Diamond tensed. 'What exactly are you driving at, Sergeant?'

'We take a good look at middle-aged guys who follow little girls.'

The sergeant came within an ace of being thumped, and he knew it, because Diamond advanced on him until they were almost nose to nose like boxers staring each other out. 'That is not only insulting, it's also provocation,' he said on a note from deep in his gut. 'If you want to hang onto your shield, don't ever give horseshit like that to a senior policeman.' The minor detail that he was no longer a senior policeman didn't arise. He'd reacted as if he was. In the heat of the moment, he'd have needed to think hard to remind himself that he was not. And Sergeant Stein wasn't to know.

Stein backed down, actually raising his right palm like an Indian making peace. 'Just overlook what I said, would you? It was a heavy night.'

'Tonight could be heavier,' Diamond told him. 'Well? What time did they find the car?'

'Around two a.m. on Mulberry Street.'

'Anyone see anything?'

'No witnesses yet.'

'Where was the car taken to be examined?'

'Forensic have a workshop on Amsterdam.'

'Is that a walking proposition?'

'You want to visit? You can ride with a patrol. Just wait here, Mr Diamond.' Nodding a number of times to demonstrate his new-found co-operativeness, Stein departed thankfully from Diamond's presence.

The ride to Amsterdam Avenue in the company of a laconic, gum-chewing officer allowed Diamond to weigh Stein's remark. Child-abuse had always been around, yet lately its notoriety had increased sharply. Whether the practice was on the increase was another question. As with rape and other sexual offences, the statistics needed to be put in the context of the greater opportunities for reporting and detecting the crimes. Whatever the truth, the public perception was that any man not actually a parent or a teacher had better not be seen alone with a young kid. He understood the need for vigilance, but he still regretted the fact that a few sexual deviants and sensation-seeking newspapers could make trust between man and child seem so unlikely as to be impossible any more.

Without a kid of his own, he couldn't truly view the question as a parent would, but were childless people who liked children fated to be treated as potential perverts?

The place where vehicles were taken for the forensic tests was hardly the squeaky-clean workshop-cum-laboratory Diamond had expected to walk into. It was a converted garage with a couple of ramps and inspection pits manned by young men in greasy overalls. The Buick was parked on the forecourt and was getting no attention at all.

He soon found an easy-going and friendly 'evidence technician' who appeared not to have been warned to watch out for a trouble-making British cop, and was quite willing to talk. 'The Buick? It'll take us at least a week. From what I can tell so far, half of New York seem to have driven that car and used it for sex and smoking. My guess is that it was owned by a syndicate of students.'

'You've done some preliminary work, then?'

'Had a look inside, removed most of the trash for examination.'

'What does it amount to?'

'The trash? Cigarette packets and butts, candy papers, sandwich wrappers, Kleenex, condom packets, gasoline receipts, Alka Seltzers, gum, ballpoints, parking tickets, panty-liners, takeaway containers – want me to go on?'

'Quite a heap, I should think,' Diamond commented. 'Or have you bagged it up already?'

'Give me a break, man. Four cars were brought in last night.'

'May I take a look at this collection? I am assigned to the case.'

'You're welcome.'

He was led to the back of the garage, through an office into a large room where the items he'd just heard listed were displayed on a long trestle table. The impression he'd first gained, of good-natured inefficiency, was given a sharp corrective. Every piece was already labelled and assigned a number, with the position where it was found in the car duly noted.

The Buick's interior hadn't been cleared of rubbish since February at least, judging by the date on a gasoline receipt. Someone had collected a stack and clipped them together. It would be the devil's own job to try and identify something discarded by Mrs Tanaka's killer.

'You checked the boot, I suppose?'

'Which boot was that?' his informant asked.

He could do without differences in the language adding to his problem. 'The storage place at the rear of the car.'

'The trunk. Yeah. We checked.'

'Just that I didn't see any mention of the boot on these labels. Now I understand why.'

'Right.'

He bent over to look at the ballpoint pens. 'I suppose you can tell if these were used recently. It's okay, I'm not going to touch.'

'How would we know that?'

'If a ballpoint hasn't been used for some time, it gets dry. When you write with it, you have to run the point over a surface for a moment to get some ink.'

His friend the evidence technician received this statement of the obvious more solemnly than it deserved. 'That may be true, but I know of no test that would tell you how long it is since a pen was used. It would depend on certain variables, such as the temperature where it was stored. Jesus, man, we can't even tell with accuracy how long a body has been left someplace, so I don't see us succeeding with ballpoints.'

'No, but if the pen delivers the ink straight away, the chances are it was used not long ago.' He was sounding like Sherlock Holmes, except that this wasn't impressing anyone, least of all himself. Better say no more about ballpoints. 'May I examine the receipts?'

'Sure. Just hold them by the clip and use this probe to separate them.'

'I can't imagine the killer stopped at a gas station anyway,' Diamond commented, picking up the sheaf of receipts. 'It's unlikely any of these would carry his prints.'

'We can check the date, no problem,' said the technician.

'I'm not looking for a date,' Diamond told him. He was acting mainly on impulse now, as he turned the receipts over and used the wooden probe to flick through the blank squares of paper. The pens had suggested a possibility, a long shot.

'You think there might be something written on the backs of those receipts?' the technician asked.

'Have you checked already?'

'Haven't had time. Why would anyone do that?'

'The little girl – the one who was kidnapped – was a dab hand at drawing.'

'And you figure that could give you a clue?'

'It might,' said Diamond. 'Unfortunately,' he added, replacing the receipts on the table, 'none of these are marked.'

He picked up the parking slips and inspected them in

the same way. Naomi had not used them for drawing either. He clicked his tongue in exasperation.

'Seen enough?'

'Am I holding you up?'

'It's okay.'

'Then I'd like to sift through the rest of this stuff. If you want to get back to your work, I can promise I won't leave my prints on anything.'

'That's okay by me.'

It was nice to be trusted.

The chance of finding anything significant was remote, but even sorting through a collection of rubbish was better than doing nothing at all. Using two probes like chopsticks, he examined the items systematically, looking for signs of recent use. There was a roll of peppermints, and it occurred to him that Naomi might have been offered one to pacify her, but the mint that was visible was so dusty that it must have been unwrapped months ago.

With his thoughts still on the possibility that Naomi might have been offered something edible to stop her from protesting, he turned to the takeaway containers – a stack of six of different shapes from various fast food places. Odours of sweet and sour – sweet *what* and sour *what* he preferred to pass over – lingered around them. Nor did he care to imagine what the interior of the Buick must have smelt like on a warm day when the windows had been closed for some time.

There were two containers apparently of fairly recent origin, so he extracted them from the stack. These weren't polystyrene like the others, but were boxes made from thin white card. Judged by the grease-stained, sugary interiors, they had probably contained doughnuts.

He turned one over to look at the underside. It would

have made a good surface for drawing. However, it was blank. Why was he so reluctant to drop this supposition that Naomi had left a drawing – a drawing, moreover, that provided information? He had a sense of being driven by some force akin to telepathy, as if the child were willing him to find what she had left. This wasn't entirely illogical, for occasionally in his life he'd experienced premonitions that had been fulfilled, such as the certainty that he would meet a particular old friend in a strange town.

So when he picked up the second box and saw pen-marks on the underside of the lid, his pulse may have quickened, but he did not punch the air with his fist or shout, 'Eureka!'

He explained with great patience to Sergeant Stein at the stationhouse how Naomi liked to make drawings, probably to compensate for the non-communication enforced by her muteness.

'And you think this is her work?' said Stein.

'Not this precisely. It's a copy I made of the drawing on the food-container. I left the box down at the workshop with all the other things found in the car. The ink matched one of the ballpoints found on the floor beside the front passenger seat. There's no way of proving Naomi did the drawing, but I could tell from the state of the box that it hadn't been lying in the car for long. I think the killer may have stopped at some point to feed her, or she may simply have found the box in the car and used it for the sketch.'

'You call that a sketch?' said Stein. 'Don't get me wrong, but it looks more like a doodle to me. What is it?'

'I'm not certain myself yet,' Diamond admitted. 'The original is about twice the size, or a little more,' he added, placing his notebook open on the desk.

Stein said after a pause, 'You really think this represents something?'

'If Naomi did it, yes. She has an individual way of looking at things, but her drawing is pretty accurate.'

'Is it a map?'

'I suppose it could be.'

'If it's going to be any help to us, it *has* to be,' said Stein. 'I mean, what have we got here? Is this some kind of overpass? Because they're not common in New York City.'

Diamond stared at the drawing. He saw what Stein had obviously seized on – the broad causeway stretching southeast to north-west, apparently crossing minor routes. 'If so, what's the rectangular object there?'

'Automobile, I guess.'

'A bird's eye view, you mean?'

'Could be.'

Then what is this elongated shape along the centre?'

Stein considered for a moment. 'You say this kid has an original way of seeing things. Maybe we're looking at the underside of the Buick. This could be the exhaust.'

The *underside*? Diamond doubted whether a child of that age had such technical know-how, and said so. He also doubted whether Naomi was capable of the conceptual ability necessary to draw a map. 'She draws from memory what she has actually seen. In England she was taken on a train, and later she made an accurate sketch of the back of the seat facing her.'

'Was that helpful to your investigation?'

'Not directly, no.'

Sergeant Stein lifted his eyebrows as if to question the value of more time spent deciphering Naomi's work.

Diamond said, 'This object that you think could be a car looks awfully like an old-fashioned razor-blade to me.'

'Uh huh,' said Stein without committing himself.

'Before they invented disposable razors.'

'I remember razor-blades,' said Stein, 'but if that's a blade, I have a problem understanding the rest of the drawing.'

'Me too.'

'I'll just attend to a couple other things that came up.'

Abandoned to ponder the mystery alone, Diamond tried turning his notebook to see if the picture made more sense orientated differently. There was no certainty that what he'd taken to be the top was actually so; you can turn a food container any way you like and draw on it. No new possibilities leapt out. The rectangular shape still looked like a razor-blade from every angle. Now that he'd lodged that idea in his brain, he couldn't visualise anything else.

Towards noon, Lieutenant Eastland, the officer in charge of the case – the man who had compared him to Winnie the Pooh – came in and said there was some progress in identifying the dead woman. The Japanese police had checked the Yokohama address in the passport. Mrs Tanaka was divorced and lived alone. Until the previous November she had been employed as a secretary at Yokohama University.

'A secretary? That begs a few questions,' Diamond commented. 'It could mean she was a high-powered administrator or simply a typist.'

'My information is that she worked in the faculty of science as one of a team of people operating word-processors,' Eastland told him. 'As for the kid—'

Diamond interrupted. 'Lieutenant, there's something I should tell you about the kid.' This would be embarrassing, but it had to be admitted. 'I'm pretty sure Naomi wasn't Mrs Tanaka's child. She had a daughter of her own who died. I, em, I found this picture of the grave. This was the child listed in the passport.' He produced the photo from his pocket and prepared to be sliced into small pieces. The withholding of evidence wasn't the way to win friends and influence people.

The inevitable question came: 'Where did you get this?'

He answered, explained and apologised.

'Why are you showing it to me now?' Eastland asked without otherwise reacting. He was a tight-lipped, gaunt-looking cop in his forties, with a measured style of speech.

'Because it may have a bearing on the case.'

'You knew that last night.'

'I only examined it after you'd finished with me.'

'Couldn't take more of the same, huh?'

'That wasn't the reason.'

'So what was?'

'Priorities. I wanted to keep it simple. The first thing was to get the machinery in place to find Naomi, never mind who she is.'

'Did you remove anything else from the wallet?'

'No.'

'Can I rely on that?'

'Absolutely.'

'You know what you are?'

'I know what you think I am.'

'So long as we both understand,' said Eastland flatly. 'Now would you be so gracious as to share with me the drawing you were discussing with Sergeant Stein?'

The sarcasm couldn't have been more blatant, but at least there was some recognition of Diamond's efforts at consultation.

He opened his notebook again. Not wishing to pre-empt any ideas the lieutenant might have, he said nothing about the razor-blade.

'You believe the kid drew this?'

Diamond explained that he had made a copy.

Eastland frowned at the drawing for some time. Finally, all he could find to say was, 'What's your opinion?'

'I think the small object is a razor-blade.'

'Could be. In that case, what is it standing on – a shelf? Are we in a bathroom here? This semi-circular section – does this represent a hand-basin?'

'I hadn't thought of that.'

'The bathroom attached to the murder room has a similar basin, only the shelf is at quite a different angle. No bathroom shelf I ever saw is suspended across the width of the basin. Mind you, kids draw things from strange angles.'

'She'd have needed to be taller than you or me to look down on the shelf in that bathroom,' Diamond commented.

'I'm saying kids get things out of line.'

'She's an accurate artist.'

'And you think this is significant?'

'With not much else to go on . . .' said Diamond, his voice trailing away as a new possibility dawned.

'Even if it is a drawing of the bathroom,' said Eastland.

'Even if there was a razor-blade in there – and I don't have any recollection of one – where does it lead us?'

Suddenly the marks made sense to Diamond. Everything clicked into mental focus. 'It's a tattoo.'

'*A what?*'

'The razor-blade is a tattoo. Take another look. This thing you thought was the shelf is obviously someone's arm against a steering wheel. She draws what she sees in front of her. I think that's the suspect's arm. It's the view Naomi must have had if she was strapped into the front seat beside him.'

Eastland stared at it for some time. 'You could be right.'

23

One of the older cops passing through the office had a memory of the razor-blade tattoo. It had been the emblem of a teenage street gang of the late seventies that had created a certain amount of mayhem in a rundown area of Brooklyn, inspired by the punk-rock movement. The membership had reached about forty at the peak around 1978. By the eighties new gangs had taken over.

'Presumably you keep records of tattoo-marks of known criminals?' Diamond asked.

'They'll be on computer, sure.'

They ran a check. Eleven males were listed as having a razor-blade tattoo on one arm or the other. Not all had been members of the Brooklyn gang. Several, it seemed, simply liked the razor-blade design; one extreme case had a chain of them running from the back of one hand, up his arm and over his shoulders down to the opposite hand.

The computer-operator accessed the details of each. Three of the Brooklyn gang had descriptions promisingly close to Diamond's memory of Leather-jacket. He asked for mugshots. This entailed a visit to Records, in another building on the same block. The files were spread on a table for inspection by the time he got there. His pulse quickened.

Naomi's picture had paid off.

One of them was Leather-jacket. No question. The mean, narrow face, the eyes and, in the profile shot, the Charlton Heston nose.

'That's him.'

'Lundin? He isn't nice.'

The name was Fredrik Anders Lundin. Aged thirty-two. A history of juvenile crime followed by two sentences for armed robbery. Sandwiched between them was one for murder, but he had been released on appeal. There was information that since coming out after serving three years of the second rap for armed robbery, Lundin was offering his services as a contract killer. He was currently under police surveillance (the file claimed), presumably in prospect of putting him away for a long term, rather than some token sentence for the charge of intent.

'It says you have tabs on him.'

Lieutenant Eastland said in his slow-speaking way, 'You're one hundred per cent certain this is the guy?'

'Absolutely.'

'You saw him meet with Mrs Tanaka and the kid in the airport car lot?'

'Lieutenant, I was as close to him as I am to you right now.'

'Okay, we'll pull him in.'

'How?'

Eastland gave a shrug that said English detectives were dense. 'That's what patrols are for.'

'Look, this isn't a simple arrest,' Diamond pointed out. 'This man is a killer. He's abducted a child. Her safety is paramount. You send two patrolmen in and people could start shooting.'

'What's your advice, then – a stake-out?'

'He's already under surveillance, according to this.'

'Don't believe everything you read in records,' Eastland cautioned. 'Surveillance could mean we have a guy who watches him play pool a couple of nights a week.'

Diamond couldn't be certain how much of this laid-back attitude was the New York detective's insulation against the dangers out there on the streets. He was in earnest, and he meant to leave nothing to chance. 'Lieutenant, you asked for my advice. I'm suggesting some subtlety is necessary. I don't think you should attempt to arrest him in the room where he's holding Naomi. That's putting her in real danger.'

'Mr Diamond, I'm deeply obliged to you,' said Eastland, affecting an English accent with about as much success as Dick Van Dyke in *Mary Poppins*. 'Let's take a jolly old spin out to Queens where the gentleman resides and be subtle. I assume you want to be on the team.'

Diamond wasn't amused by the sarcasm, but he accepted an offer from Sergeant Stein to ride in his car. When they emerged from the Mid-Town Tunnel, the afternoon was drawing on. Some of the streetlights were switched on.

'Do you carry a gun?' Stein asked at some point on the journey.

'No.'

'Is that right – that English cops go unarmed?'

'Generally, yes.'

'Didn't you ever need one?'

'Not up to now.' He could have added that he was notoriously cack-handed, that in his possession a gun would go off when it was least expected, like now, from the jolting he was getting. The seat had no springs at all that he could discern.

Stein commented, 'Me – I'd have been dead five times over without my automatic.'

The area they were driving into was neither the best of Queens, nor the worst. The turn-of-the-century tenements had probably been smart addresses when they were built. The fire escapes that fronted them were still festooned with evidence of the warm afternoon that had just come to an end: canvas chairs, pot-plants, bedding, beer cans, takeaway boxes.

A patrolman flagged them down on a street corner. 'You can't drive past here. The suspect has a view of the street.'

'Which side is his apartment?' Stein asked.

'The right.'

'Anyone sighted him yet?'

'No. But there's a light.'

'So we could get lucky.'

They got out and joined Lieutenant Eastland and two more detectives, who had pulled up behind. A third car of uniformed officers had arrived from another direction. Eastland used his mobile radio to make contact with people already in position closer to the apartment. Then he issued orders. He wasn't messing now, and Diamond formed a better opinion.

'We're getting good co-operation from the people in the adjoining apartments,' he told Diamond presently.

'Have they seen the child?'

'Sorry, but no.'

'Or heard her voice?'

'Nobody mentioned it yet.'

'Maybe the walls are too solid.'

'Could be.'

'So what's the plan?'

'We can afford to wait a while,' said Eastland. 'With luck, he may come out for food in the next hour, and then we grab him. You want to go closer?'

'Why not?'

Stein was told to accompany him. Like two local residents walking invisible dogs, they strolled along the sidewalk until they were level with number 224, where the lighted second-floor windows gave promise of Fredrik Lundin being at home. Any chance of a sighting was forestalled by venetian blinds. Even so, it wasn't wise to linger. A finger's-width gap between the slats could give a clear view of the street.

They walked almost to the end of the block before stopping. Stein offered his pack of cigarettes.

Tempted, Diamond remembered that he was supposed to be a non-smoker now.

Stein's personal radio crackled. Eastland's voice asked, 'See anything?'

Stein reported back, 'Light at the window. Blinds. First floor in darkness, apparently unoccupied. Front door looks easy. Want us to go in?'

'Not yet.'

'The problem with this,' Stein confided to Diamond when he'd switched off, 'is that if Lundin gets suspicious, we could have a siege on our hands.'

It was a risk Diamond was willing to take, in spite of the fact that darkness was setting in rapidly.

'Sieges can be heavy on man-power,' Stein explained. 'We don't let them happen.'

Three cigarettes later, the radio broke the silence. 'Okay, we can't wait all night for this jerk,' Eastland announced. 'You and Diamond can enter by the front and occupy the first-floor apartment. Be ready to go upstairs as soon as the suspect is flushed and separated from the kid. Check?'

'Check, Lieutenant,' said Stein.

Diamond had an impulse to wrench the radio from him and urge Eastland not to provoke a shoot-out, but cold reason told him it wouldn't alter anything. This was Eastland's operation, and with half his men looking on he wasn't going to take instructions from a limey detective. It was some reassurance that he'd expressed some intention of separating Lundin from Naomi.

He and Stein returned up the street towards 224. It was much darker by now and the front wasn't well-lit. They could barely see their way up the stoop to the door. Stein put a hand in his jacket, evidently feeling for the grip of the gun he wouldn't be without. He nodded to Diamond to try the door. It opened easily.

No sound came from upstairs. They were in a wide hallway with stairs facing them. Halfway along, on the right, was the door of the apartment where they were supposed to take up position. Diamond gripped the handle. Was it too much to hope that this door, also, would be unlocked? It was securely fastened. Probably a well-aimed kick would resolve the matter, but only at the risk of disturbing the entire house.

Fortunately Sergeant Stein had come prepared, with the strip of plastic known to housebreakers and policemen as the indispensable aid to easing latches aside. He used it confidently, the door opened inwards and they stepped inside. Warm air wafted over them, reeking of cheap perfume and body odour. Just like a knocking-shop, Diamond found himself thinking – a thought that lingered and lodged more firmly when he heard a female voice murmur sleepily but without alarm, 'Hi, who is this? What time is it?'

A sofa creaked and something stirred. The woman who had been lying there said, 'Is there one of you, or two?' She got up and moved unsteadily towards a table-lamp. 'I'm not taking two – not together. Sorry, guys. One of you has to wait.'

Her hand was on the lamp.

'Leave it,' said Stein in a stage whisper.

She started to say, 'What the fuck—' before Diamond moved fast towards her and clapped a hand over her mouth. She struggled, and he had to grab her round the back. She was wearing some kind of silk wrap that made her slippery to hold, because she was obviously naked under it. His terse, 'It's all right, we're police officers,' was not a message calculated to reassure a lady of her calling, but it was the first thing to come to mind.

Stein told her more bluntly, 'You make one sound and you're busted. We've come for the guy upstairs. Know him?'

Diamond relaxed his hold on her.

She said, too loudly for comfort. 'You mean Fredrik?'

They both made shushing sounds.

With less voice, she said, 'What's he done now?'

'Is there a kid with him?' Stein asked.

'A kid?'

'A girl.'

She hesitated. 'You mean, like, under-age?'

'A *small* kid, child, this high, Japanese.'

She seemed genuinely shocked. 'Fredrik? He never puts kids to work. I'm damned sure he never uses baby-pros. I wouldn't work for a guy who uses kids.'

Diamond remained quite still and said nothing, but a pulse was hammering in his head and his mouth had suddenly gone dry. Until this moment, child prostitution hadn't crossed his mind as a possible motive for Naomi's abduction. Now it had to be faced as a sickening possibility. Clearly Lundin had an income from pimping. Pray God the woman was right and he drew the line at selling children for sex.

'You heard any sounds from up there?' Stein asked her.

She shook her head.

245

'Nothing at all?'

'You can't hear anyone talk.'

'But you can hear them move about.'

'Well, yeah. I hear that sometimes.'

'Last evening?'

'I guess so.'

'More than one?'

'I can't tell.'

'Have you talked to Lundin since yesterday?'

'No.'

'You think he's home right now?'

'How would I know? I was asleep until you arrived. Did someone give you a key?'

'Why don't you go back to sleep?' suggested Stein without much generosity in his tone.

He radioed Eastland and updated him.

'Okay,' came their instruction, 'stay where you are. Send the pavement princess out to us. She can help us.'

'Did you hear that?' Stein asked the call-girl just as she was reclining on the sofa. 'Get dressed. Fast.'

'And, Stein . . .' the voice on the radio went on.

'Lieutenant?'

'When he comes out, leave him to us. You go right in and find the kid.'

Complaining bitterly, first that she wanted no part in the police operation and then that she couldn't see to get dressed, the woman stumbled about the apartment picking up clothes. Diamond scarcely noticed; he was still reeling from the suggestion he'd just heard. A minute ago, he'd been ready to urge the police to go easy on Lundin so that he'd be fit to give information; now, if this grotesque scenario was true, they'd have to restrain *him* from laying into the bastard.

'Jesus, what are you trying to find?' Stein demanded of the woman. He was standing at the open door.

'My face.'

'Your what?'

'The bag with my lipstick and things. It's here somewhere.'

'I don't believe this! Get your ass out of here.'

She went.

Eastland would use her as a lure. There was a better chance of Lundin opening his door to the woman who worked for him than to the New York Police.

Above their heads the floorboards creaked. Someone was definitely up there. Stein immediately radioed his lieutenant. Up to now, this operation couldn't be faulted. No doubt there were men at front and back, waiting for the swoop.

Diamond waited too, striving to apply concentration to the job he and Stein were about to do. He had to believe they would find Naomi unharmed in the apartment upstairs. He kept thinking how small her hand had felt in his. Usually he remembered the eyes of people. He could picture her eyes, but because of the nature of her disability, they weren't so eloquent. It was still the memory of a touch that moved him.

He and Stein took up position with the door fractionally ajar for a view of the hall. They knew this would take time to set up, and they waited at least twenty minutes before anything else happened.

Then there was the sound of the front door opening and footsteps across the tiled hallway. The call-girl passed her own door and started climbing the stairs, her leather-soled boots, tokens of her trade, clattering on the wooden treads.

Stein drew his gun.

Two shadowy figures crossed the hallway a short way behind the woman. They made no sound.

She turned on the landing and started to ascend the second flight. Her escorts followed.

Down in the hallway, more cops crept across the narrow bar of vision between the door-jamb and the edge of the door.

The woman was out of sight now, but the sound of Lundin's doorbell being pressed was loud and clear and so was her voice saying, 'Fredrik, it's only me, Dixie.'

Diamond heard footsteps cross the room above them, but he didn't hear Lundin's front door being opened. Presumably he was looking out through the peephole.

The bell sounded a second time.

By now the two gunmen would be flat to the wall on either side of the door.

'Fredrik, are you there?'

Something was being unfastened.

The woman's voice said, 'Hi, Fredrik, could you possibly step downstairs a minute?'

'What the fuck do you want?' Lundin's voice demanded.

'I have a small problem with a client. Please.'

'What kind of problem?'

'Em . . . he won't leave.'

'What do you mean?'

Come on, come on, Diamond mentally urged him. *Just step outside, will you.*

'Like I said. He's being difficult.'

'He won't leave the apartment? He had a trick and he won't leave?'

'I can't force him.'

'Who is he?'

'Some guy. I don't know him. I can't work if he won't leave.'

'Okay, okay, you go back. I'll see to it.'

The door closed.

Diamond clapped his hand to his head in frustration.

Dixie the call-girl came downstairs markedly faster than she'd gone up. She pushed her way in past Diamond and Stein. 'That's all I'm doing for you guys,' she told them. 'You'd better not mess up now, or I'll be dead meat.'

'Zip it up,' said Stein. There isn't much credit in helping the police.

The wait began again, and it seemed longer, even though it was under five minutes.

Then footsteps crossed the floor upstairs and Lundin could be heard unfastening the latch on his door. This time he definitely stepped out onto the landing, because there was a shout of, 'Freeze – police!'

Rashly, Lundin chose not to obey the order. He could be heard making a dash for the stairs. He must have got down two or three when a shot was fired, followed by two more almost immediately. A shriek of pain gave way to the sound of a body hitting the stairs and thumping down several steps.

'They got him,' said Sergeant Stein. He stared through the gap while shouts were being exchanged by the police in the hall, checking that it was safe to close in on the wounded man. 'Let's go.'

When they opened the door, a man in a white T-shirt and black jeans was lying near the bottom of the stairs and one of the cops was standing over him. Stein ran straight past, up the two flights, with Diamond close behind.

The door to Lundin's apartment stood open. The light from inside was dazzling after the long wait in darkness.

The place was lavishly furnished in brown leather furniture, cream-coloured units and a Chinese carpet. There were huge indoor plants and pieces of bronze abstract sculpture.

But there was no little girl.

Diamond checked the other rooms – bedroom, kitchen and bathroom. He tugged back the bedding, flung open cupboards, and – with grim apprehension – looked into the bath.

She was not there.

He went back into the living-room, looking around for some place he may have missed.

'Mr Diamond.' Stein had followed him into the bathroom and was still there.

Diamond found him kneeling by the toilet pedestal.

'Would this be the kid?'

A question that struck horror into Diamond.

'I always look in the john,' the sergeant explained. They panic and try and flush things away.' He was holding up some small torn pieces of a photo.

Diamond arranged them on the floor. There were seven altogether, and they made an incomplete, but recognisable picture.

'Yes,' he said. 'That's her.'

24

Diamond was being difficult again.

'Apart from anything else, I just don't think you're built for this,' Lieutenant Eastland told him. 'Stein can drive you to the hospital in comfort.'

'I'm going in the ambulance,' Diamond insisted. He had his foot on the step and it was just a matter of climbing inside. He would have appreciated a helping hand, because it was a high step for a heavy man.

'The paramedic has to travel in the back and so does one of our officers.'

'Let the officer ride in the front,' said Diamond. 'I'll keep an eye on the prisoner for you. Look, the man isn't going to run away with two bullets in his leg.'

'You can question him at the hospital.'

'I want the answers now, Lieutenant. You've wasted too much time already.'

This touched Eastland on a raw nerve. '*We* wasted time? You wanted to run this thing like a Thanksgiving party, not me. The subtle approach. You were bothered about the kid, remember?'

'Correct. And I'm still bothered about her.' With that, Diamond leaned into the ambulance and grabbed the end of the stretcher to hoist himself aboard, with near-disastrous consequences, because the stretcher was mounted on a trolley and started rolling towards him. He had just about enough momentum of his own to climb in and stop the thing from upending himself and the hapless Lundin in the street. Then he sank onto the spare seat beside the paramedic. For a man of his bulk, occupation was more persuasive than argument. 'See you later, Lieutenant.'

Eastland glared and delivered his parting shot. 'If you're typical of England, I'm not surprised it pisses with rain every day. It should crap as well.' He nodded to the driver to close the doors.

'How long will this take us?' Diamond asked the young man beside him as suavely as if nothing had been said.

'You mean to the hospital? Six – seven minutes.'

'Right.' He leaned forward to get a better view of the prisoner's face at the far end of the stretcher.

'Careful of his leg,' cautioned the paramedic.

'Careful of my leg,' said Lundin with even more concern. He'd been given a pain-killing injection, but a stray hand hovering over the wounded limb must have been painful in prospect.

'Never mind his leg,' said Diamond. 'Show me his arm. The right.'

The paramedic pulled aside the sheet from Lundin's torso. On the right arm was a razor-blade tattoo.

Lundin spoke up, 'You think I'm a needle freak, you're wrong.'

'You're not too far gone to talk, then,' said Diamond. 'I want to know about the child. Where is she?'

'I want a lawyer.'

That old gambit, thought Diamond. 'You know something, Lundin?' he remarked. 'Nobody likes weirdos like you who play around with little girls. Accidents keep happening to them in jail.'

'Little girls? What are you talking about?'

'Don't give me that. I saw you pick her up at JFK. With her mother.'

'So that's who you are,' said Lundin as realisation dawned.

Diamond was rather put out that he hadn't been recognised right off. Once seen, he was seldom forgotten. To be fair, Lundin had a difficult view from his stretcher. Anyway, they seemed to have got over the potential difficulty of requiring a lawyer in attendance. 'Right. So we know each other. I'm the fellow you knocked over and you're the child-molester.'

'That's a lie.'

'You definitely knocked me over with a trolley.'

'The other part – I'm no pervert.'

'You're acting for someone else who is – is that what you're telling me?'

'I'm telling you nothing.'

'That's even more despicable, supplying children to people like that.'

'You're talking horseshit.'

'Don't tempt me, Lundin.'

'What? Get away from my leg!'

'Where is the child? What did you do with her?'

'I don't have to talk to you. Who are you?' Lundin asked.

'A man with a weight problem,' said Diamond, folding his arms ostentatiously and inching closer to the wounded leg. 'Sometimes I need to prop myself up.'

'Bastard! Get away from me, will you?'

'Better not call me names, then. Where is she?'

'The kid?'

'Yes.'

'She's okay. It's nothing like you say.'

'Her mother isn't okay. Did you kill the child later?'

'No, I tell you. No!'

'She's alive?'

'Yes.'

'So where can I find her?'

Silence.

'Where can I find her, Lundin?'

'No, get off! I handed her over. The deal was that I would hand her over.'

'Who to?'

'I can't say – I don't know.'

'Do you care about the child?' Diamond asked.

'What do you mean?'

'Yes, I know it doesn't make sense to a hired killer to care about a child, but let me put it to you this way. You're going to stand trial for Mrs Tanaka's death. If the child is also killed, you're an accessory to a second murder.'

'She's okay.'

'You keep saying that, but how do you know? This person she's now with may already have killed her.'

'I don't think so.'

'They hired you to kill the mother. Why should they draw the line at the child?'

He hesitated and asked yet again, 'Mister, who are you?'

'My name is Diamond.'

'You a cop?'

'I am not.' Sometimes candour is rewarded with the truth. It was worth trying. 'I'm a private citizen. I came over from England because of the child. Naomi was taken illegally from a children's home, and I care very much what is happening to her.'

'You're not a cop?'

'That's what I said.'

'Are you taping this conversation?'

'No.'

After a pause, Lundin plucked up enough confidence to say, 'There was a contract on the woman, not the kid.'

'You were hired to kill the woman?'

This was a matter Diamond should have sidestepped, he realized the moment he'd spoken. It added nothing to his knowledge and it pulled Lundin up with a jolt. 'Forget it – I don't need to talk to you.'

'Who hired you?'

Silence.

Diamond adroitly switched to another question. 'You said you handed over the child. When was this?'

Grudgingly, Lundin muttered. 'Last evening.'

'By arrangement?'

Lundin started to say, 'I don't have to answer these damnfool—' and then interrupted himself when he noticed Diamond unfolding his arms. 'They told me to bring the kid to the Trump Tower and leave her at the top of the escalator on the second floor at nine p.m.'

'Hand her over to someone?'

'No, just leave her.'

'And you did?'

'I figured somebody was going to be waiting for her.'

'Did you see anyone?'

'Mister, in this game, you don't *want* to see anyone.'

'How did you get the instructions, then?'

'The phone.'

'Man or woman?'

'Man, I guess.'

All of this was leading nowhere. Fredrik Lundin didn't know where Naomi was, or who was holding her. He would be charged with Mrs Tanaka's murder, but the people who hired him had made damned sure he was incapable of putting the police onto them. The trail had gone cold.

'Let's go back to the first instructions you had. Who made the contact?'

'I don't know. I was phoned.'

And so it went on. Lundin had met nobody. A voice had told him what to do, where to pick up the money that was his down-payment for the elimination of Mrs Tanaka. He made it sound as commonplace as selling a house, with ninety per cent payable on completion, except that 'completion' had a more sinister interpretation.

Diamond didn't need the six or seven minutes the journey took. In four minutes flat he'd learned all he was likely to learn from Fredrik Lundin. The police would take up the questioning at the hospital and no doubt they'd extract enough information to put him behind bars for a long term, but they would find out nothing Diamond wanted to know, nothing of immediate use in tracing Naomi.

They got to the hospital and Lundin was wheeled away to have his wounds seen to. Diamond shared his disappointment with Lieutenant Eastland.

Eastland was still sore from the earlier exchange. 'What did you expect?' he commented when he'd heard how little had emerged about Lundin's paymasters. 'The guy is a functionary. Why keep a dog and bark yourself?'

'I hope you're not giving up on the child.'

'Did I say that? Did you hear me say that?'

'No, but—'

'Okay. What are your plans, Diamond?'

'Mine? I, em, I haven't decided.'

'Are you still staying at that two-bit hotel, the Firbank?'

Diamond had to think for a moment. 'I suppose I am.'

'You can ride back with me. I'm leaving soon. Stein will take over here.'

He saw, of course, that this wasn't an olive branch. Eastland wanted him away from the hospital while the questioning took place, and for once it seemed sensible to comply.

'Okay, I got a little above myself,' Diamond admitted when they were together in the back of the police car. 'I need your help more than you need mine.' It was the nearest he would come to an apology.

'I thought you would strangle the guy.'

'Lundin, do you mean? No, I was wrong about him. I really believed this was part of a vice racket. Now, I think the child was kidnapped for some other reason. Lundin happens to be a pimp, but that's not what he was involved in here.'

'He runs three or four girls in the street where he lives. He's small beer,' said Eastland. 'So what's behind this? What's the motive? Why would anyone pay to have a woman murdered and a kid handed over to them? What are we dealing with here – a custody dispute?'

'The tug of love?' said Diamond. 'Not the way I see it. Nobody has shown much affection for Naomi. She was abandoned in London until Mrs Tanaka came along – and she didn't treat the child with noticeable kindness.'

'She wasn't the mother.'

'Right. Where are the parents? They've been conspicuously silent. If they *were* in dispute for custody of the child, they'd have declared themselves by now. The people in these cases need publicity.'

'Do you have a theory, then?'

Diamond stifled a yawn. 'Lieutenant, I'm jetlagged. It's all I can do to stay awake. I'll say this much: whatever we're dealing with, it's high risk and there's big money behind it. But why a small, autistic girl should be mixed up in it is a mystery to me.'

'For a ransom?'

'The parents would have to be very rich.'

'Japanese industrialists?'

'Surely they'd have reported by now that their daughter is missing. You've been in touch with the Japanese police. Did they say anything about a tycoon whose child has been taken away?'

'No,' said Eastland. 'But you and I know that kidnappings don't get reported every time. The parents could be dealing with the kidnappers directly.'

'How does Mrs Tanaka fit into this theory?' Diamond asked in a tone that betrayed how unimpressed he was. 'Why was she killed?'

'She was caught in the middle somehow. Maybe she doublecrossed the people who hired her.'

'Do you really believe that?' Diamond asked.

'Can you think of anything better?'

He didn't answer, and for a time all that was heard was the car's suspension being tested by the uneven Manhattan street surfaces.

Finally, Eastland said, 'If we could positively identify the kid, we'd stand a better chance.'

'*We've* been trying to do that ever since she was found,' said Diamond.

They pulled up outside the hotel and he got out and thanked Eastland for the ride, adding that he might drop by in the morning.

He was deeply dispirited, and the prospect of another night in the Firbank did nothing to lift him. It occurred to him when he caught sight of the payphone in the front

258

hall that he hadn't spoken to Stephanie since leaving London. She wasn't the sort to panic, but she must have wondered why he hadn't been in touch before now. He felt in his pocket for some change, badly wanting to hear Steph's voice, even if she gave him some aggro.

Then he made a mental estimate of the time in London. About four in the morning.

Nothing was working for him.

25

In the morning when he tried phoning Stephanie, his timing was still wrong. After listening to the ringing tone until his ear ached, he worked out that it was noon in England and she would be at the Save the Children shop. He went out to breakfast convinced already that this would be another frustrating day.

But when he returned to the Firbank and tried again, she answered, and still the timing was wrong. Even five thousand miles and a time-zone away the disapproval in her tone was unmistakable. He was in the doghouse. He didn't make much impression explaining that he'd tried phoning earlier. The legendary Diamond charm was put to the test, and he had to dredge deep. 'The reason I'm calling you now – apart from wanting to hear your voice, my love – is to check something you mentioned just before I left, about shoe-sizes. Am I right? Is an English seven equal to an eight-and-a-half over here?'

There was time out for thought during which he could sense the reproach evaporating. Then they had a normal conversation. He didn't mention that Mrs Tanaka had been murdered, but he told her Naomi was still missing, and she sounded genuinely concerned.

He admitted, 'I may be forced to abandon this.'

'You wouldn't give up,' she said, shocked. 'Peter, you

couldn't leave the poor little soul a prisoner in New York. Besides, what would you tell that wrestler – the man who paid your fare?'

'I haven't even thought about that.'

'Listen, if it's me you're bothered about, I'll be perfectly all right for a few more days. Don't worry. Just do what you can for that child. There must be some way of tracing her.'

'I hope you're right.' And he added, meaning it, 'Love you.'

'Love you, too.'

'Thanks, Steph. You're very understanding.'

There was a distinct pause before she said, 'Sometimes I understand more than you give me credit for, pussycat.'

Outside, it had started to rain, so he borrowed an umbrella from the hotel before stepping out to the station-house, where pandemonium reigned. He learned rapidly that Naomi's abduction was yesterday's news. Overnight, there had been a triple killing in a shooting gallery in West Harlem. It took him rather longer to work out that a shooting gallery was the slang for an abandoned house frequented by drug-addicts and pushers. Some of them were having their prints taken while he waited to talk to anyone he knew.

Sergeant Stein came in and nodded. He would have walked straight through to another office if Diamond hadn't called across to him.

'Did you get any more out of Lundin?'

'Not much. He was sleepy.'

'Any clues about what happened to the child?'

'Zilch. Now, if you don't mind, I have the arrest report to type.'

'Nothing else has come through about her?'

Stein shook his head. 'Why don't you go sightseeing, look at the Empire State or something?'

'Is Lieutenant Eastland about?'

'This afternoon. Maybe.'

Biting back a sarcastic remark, Diamond walked out and hailed a cab, not to go sightseeing, but to drive out to Lundin's apartment at Queens. An idea had surfaced; when he was feeling fractious, his brain sometimes went into overdrive.

The van in the street indicated that a forensic team were at work in the house. Meeting one of them on the stairs, he explained who he was, which was received with a narrowing of the eyes, and then mentioned Eastland's name, which made more of an impression. 'When we were here yesterday, we found some torn pieces of a photogaph of the missing child.'

'In the toilet. Yeah, we have them. We found a couple of extra pieces trapped on the inside.'

'Could I examine them?'

'You'd better talk to my boss.'

The fragments of photograph were in a polythene bag in the van, and there was some reluctance to let Diamond see them until he explained his thinking to the senior man, giving it the sales pitch he'd noticed was obligatory when you wanted results in New York. 'The style of picture, from what I remember of it, full face with a pale blue background, strikes me as typical of a school photo. These commercial photographers are smart. They persuade a school to let them take shots of all the kids, one by one. The style is pretty much the same the world over. You see beaming kids in their school uniforms on businessmen's desks, the mantelpiece in the White House, everywhere. Are you a family man?'

'Yeah, we've got a grandchild.'

'So the photographer has to print dozens, maybe

hundreds of photos to order, right? And he has to have some way of identifying them. He can't get each kid to hold up a board with his name on it like a mugshot. So what does he do? He pencils some kind of serial number on the reverse. If we're lucky, one of those torn scraps may have the number that identifies the child.'

The senior man was sufficiently interested to send someone down to the van.

Diamond, pink with the effort, said casually, 'We may be unlucky, of course.'

Presently the pieces of the photo were tipped onto a table. No number was visible at once, but they started turning pieces over.

'How about that?'

It was not unlike a conjuring trick, except that this was no illusion. Just as Diamond had predicted, the number 212 was pencilled on a corner-piece. His luck seemed to have changed at last.

'That was just a hunch?'

'Yes.'

'Cool,' the senior man conceded.

'Thanks.'

'Now you have a number.'

'Yes.'

'So next you have to find the photographer, out of all the school photographers in all the world.'

'Right,' said Diamond without stopping to explain that there was a way of narrowing down the hunt. He was going to have inquiries made in Japan, and in particular, in Yokohama, where Mrs Tanaka had lived and worked. Of course there were plenty of schools in Yokohama, but fewer junior schools and even fewer children given the number 212.

Buoyant with his discovery, he returned to the station-house and told Sergeant Stein. In a matter of minutes they typed and faxed a memorandum to police headquarters in Yokohama. Unfortunately, it was already past midnight in Japan. Policemen might be on duty; school photographers probably not.

London, he knew, was awake. He asked Stein if he could make an international call connected with the case.

'You want to make a local call,' said Stein with a stage wink. 'No problem. We can make local calls whenever we want.' Evidently the NYPD, like the rest of the city, paid lip-service to economy measures.

Diamond tapped out the international code for Great Britain, took a card from his pocket and referred to the number hand-written on the reverse, realizing that he still didn't know the woman's name.

'Yes?' It was a man's voice.

'Could I speak to the lady who works as a Japanese interpreter?'

'One moment.'

She came on the line, still guarding her identity. 'Yes?'

'This is Peter Diamond, from New York.'

'I remember.'

'The sumo wrestler, Mr Yamagata, kindly agreed to under-write my expenses.'

'That is so.'

'I thought I should let him know what is happening. I'm working with the New York Police. The little girl is still, unfortunately—'

She interrupted. 'Mr Diamond, before you say any more, I should tell you that I am no longer employed by Mr Yamagata. The London *Basho* finished on Sunday. The entire party of wrestlers and officials has returned to Japan.'

'Oh.'

'If you remember, I handed you a card with his Tokyo address.'

'Yes, I have it right here in front of me.'

'Then I suggest you make contact with him in Tokyo later tonight.'

'With Yamagata himself?'

'He lives in the *heya*, the stable of wrestlers. They have someone who will interpret.'

'You think he'll stand by his promise? I'm running up some hefty expenses.'

'Of that there is no doubt.'

Without enquiring whether she was referring to the promise or the expenses, he thanked her and hung up.

The rest of the morning and the afternoon were notable only for the fact that he moved out of the Firbank to a better class of hotel, on Broadway, a place with phones in the rooms and a bar downstairs. It was still only a short walk from the stationhouse, where he returned at regular intervals, only to be told each time that no reports had come in of the missing child. Plenty of progress was being made on the shooting gallery murders.

'Has Lundin been put through the grinder to find out who hired him?' he asked Stein.

'Lundin knows nothing. The only thing he cared about was the money, and we think he was paid most of that in advance.'

'How much?'

'Probably twenty grand.'

About five, a fax arrived from Yokohama stating formally that inquiries would be pursued as requested. Further information would be dispatched if and when it became available.

'If and when. Doesn't sound too positive,' Stein commented.

'It sounds to me like computer-speak,' said Diamond, 'but I'm willing to wait around until late.'

'You can go back to your hotel. Well call you straight away if anything comes through.'

Diamond cast a glance around the office, still teeming with drug-addicts, detectives and patrolmen, and had more than a flicker of doubt. 'Thanks, but I'll stick around.'

Soon after nine p.m., he tried making a call to Yamagata in Tokyo. Over there it was eleven a.m. next day. Someone explained in English that the *sekitori* were at lunch, and could not be disturbed. He should call back in two hours. He was sympathetic. For these big fellows, lunch, he imagined, was more than a coffee and a quick sandwich.

He got through later, and talked to the same person, whose English was impeccable. Apparently Yamagata was somewhere close to the phone this time, because the interpreting was fast and to the point. Diamond reported on what had happened in the hunt for Naomi, ending by admitting that he was making some hefty use of the Gold Card number. This was not a problem, he was told. Yamagata wished to do everything in his power to assist the investigation. In fact, he would immediately contact the Yokohama Police Department to see what progress there was in checking with the school photographers.

The result was impressive. Just under twenty minutes later, a fax came through from Yokohama. All school photographers had been told to check their records. Another fax would be transmitted as soon as more information was supplied.

'I like that better than "if and when",' Diamond remarked to no one in particular. Sergeant Stein had long since gone off duty.

266

Just before two a.m., the first positive news came humming through the fax machine:

Police Headquarters, Yokohama
To: Detective Superintendent Diamond, NYPD

Reference your fax, PD/2, inquiries among Yokohama photographers reveal that thirty-five children, nineteen male, sixteen female, at nine different junior schools, were issued with school photographs, serial number 212, during the last two years. Kindly advise if further information is required.

'You bet it is,' he said, reaching for a pen.

26th Precinct, NYPD
To: Police Headquarters, Yokohama

Immensely grateful for your attention to my inquiry. It is vital to discover whether any of the female children is at present missing and has been absent from school for the past six weeks. Please include special schools for the mentally handicapped. Your urgent attention to this matter will be deeply appreciated.

A woman detective who had recently come on duty told him he was looking pooped, and he couldn't deny it. She offered to check the incoming faxes regularly while he caught up with some sleep on one of the cots used by officers forced to take off-duty spells in the stationhouse.

Police Headquarters, Yokohama
To: Detective Superintendent Diamond, NYPD

Further enquiries reveal that among the female children listed as 212 in photographers' records, none is reported as missing from school. Two were absent for periods of two weeks and ten days respectively with minor illnesses, but are now back at school. One left the city three months ago to live in Nagoya. All others accounted for.

He looked at his watch. 5.20 a.m. He ached in every muscle. 'Thanks.'

She said, 'You want coffee?'

'I must reply to this first.'

26th Precinct, NYPD
To: Police Headquarters, Yokohama

Many thanks. Kindly send details as soon as possible of the girl who moved to Nagoya. Could you double-check whether the family live there?

Maybe it was the time of day, but he was inclined to believe that the night had been wasted – a night he could have passed in a comfortable hotel instead of an iron and canvas cot. He decided to go for an early breakfast.

Police Headquarters, Yokohama
To: Detective Superintendent Diamond, NYPD

A search made of Nagoya school computer records has been unsuccessful in the case of the child you asked us to trace. We therefore transmit information from previous school records:

Noriko Masuda, aged 9, born 20 December 1983. Last known address: care of Dr Yuko Masuda, MSc, PhD, (mother), 4-7-9, Umeda-cho, Naka-ku, J227 Yokohama. Father, Jiro Masuda, occupational therapist, died in automobile accident, January 1985. Mother engaged in postgraduate research in Yokohama University Department of Biochemistry until 1985. Child attended Noge Special School, Yokohama; September 1987, until March of this year. Diagnosed autistic, 1987. School progress: slow, hampered by muteness. Above average skill in drawing. Temperament: good. Conduct: good. IQ rating (non verbal): 129.

He read it a second time, dazzled by this treasure hoard of information after the weeks of guesswork and despair. To have so much confirmed was beyond expectation, beyond anything he had dared to hope when the faxes had started coming. There were more than enough indications that the child was Naomi. Or, rather, that the child he knew as Naomi was actually Noriko. For her to be anyone else would be stretching coincidence to a ridiculous degree.

Noriko.

A simple name for a Westerner to get his tongue around. Personally, however, he was going to find it impossible not to continue to think of her as Naomi, so he'd have to stay with it. He justified the decision by telling himself it would avoid confusion in dealing with the police in New York. They weren't very adaptable.

The autism, then, was confirmed. As a corrective to the elation he was experiencing, he tightened inwardly upon seeing the word. Against all the evidence, he'd cherished the hope that something could be done to unlock the little girl's mind.

By fleshing out the report with a few reasonable assumptions, he pictured Yuko Masuda, the mother, a bright young woman who had given up her studies to marry, devastated by the death of her young husband, struggling to raise this difficult child who refused to respond in the way other women's children did. A problem she probably didn't understand until Naomi was three or four.

Was the poor mother under so much strain, Diamond pondered, that Mrs Tanaka, who worked in the university, had offered to take the child on a visit to Europe and America? A temporary reprieve for Dr Masuda from the stress of raising an autistic child?

How could such an act of kindness have led to murder and kidnap?

He shook his head, sighed and scribbled a note of thanks to Yokohama and, as a personal touch, added the one word of Japanese he knew: *Sayonara*. Then tore it up. Damn it, he wasn't functioning properly yet. This wasn't the time to sign off with Japan. It might be late over there, but the case had just opened up.

26th Precinct, NYPD
To: Police Headquarters, Yokohama

Your co-operation is appreciated. The details tally with the missing child. Request that you trace the mother, Dr Masuda, as a matter of urgency. We need to know the circumstances in which the child travelled to London prior to September this year. She was believed to be in the company of Mrs Minori Tanaka, 36, former secretary in Yokohama University. Request fullest possible information about these two women.

When he'd fed this into the machine, he left the station-house and walked to his new hotel to get a shower and a shave. He'd managed three hours' sleep at most, but this morning he felt like a billion yen.

26

The first person he spoke to in Columbia University Library said with a sense of discovery, 'You must be from England!'

He said tamely, 'How right you are!' Each time this happened – and here in New York it was commonplace – he felt that simply admitting his Englishness didn't come up to expectations. Something extra seemed to be expected of him: a burst of 'God Save the Queen', or a hitch of the trousers to reveal Union Jack socks. He couldn't manage either.

He introduced himself, claiming that he was a detective attached to the New York Police Department, a slight distortion of the facts, but he'd never had a conscience about embroidering the truth in the cause of justice.

The senior librarian he was addressing, a strange, thin man with the peculiar fixed smile seen usually on the faces of politicians and the earliest Greek statues, said that he just adored the British police, and was he at the library on official business, or personal?

Diamond explained that he hoped to consult an international databank of postgraduate research projects, if the library possessed one.

He already knew it did.

En route to the computer suite, the librarian confided

that his knowledge of Scotland Yard owed much to the British film industry. 'Did you know that the late Lord Olivier once played a lowly English bobby in a movie?'

Diamond undermined this promising conversation by saying, *'The Magic Box.'* It happened that he'd seen the film quite recently on TV one afternoon when it was too wet to go walking in Holland Park.

'Oh, you saw it. The story of the man who invented cinematography.'

'Friese-Greene.'

'You're so right!' the librarian said admiringly.

'But Friese-Greene wasn't the inventor of cinematography.'

'Wasn't he?' The smile began to look strained.

'My understanding is that several people in different countries, including yours, made the significant discoveries. Friese-Greene was a minor figure.'

'You're sure of this?'

'Check the facts, if you like. We're in the right place.'

'No need, Mr Diamond, I'll take your word for it, of course.'

'The film was a flag-waving exercise,' Diamond went on without much tact. 'Britain needed cheering up at the time. As a nation we're unequalled at making heroes out of nobodies.'

After a pause, the librarian said staunchly, 'This doesn't affect what I was about to say about the movie. The acting was superb. Do you recall the scene?' Without pausing for a response, he added, 'Just a cameo performance by Laurence Olivier as the bobby invited in to look at the images being projected, but one of his greatest, in my opinion. If he'd done nothing else, you'd have known from that scene that the man was a genius. Hardly a word spoken.'

273

Diamond nodded. 'Pity it wasn't true.'

'Ah, but remember the *Ode on a Grecian Urn:* "beauty is truth, truth beauty. That is all ye know on earth, and all ye need to know".'

'Not in my job,' said Diamond. He'd never believed in mixing poetry and police work.

They entered the computer suite, a place, he reflected, that a more cultured policeman might have observed had a hum like a hedge of lavender on an August morning. Ranks of display units stretched far back. The librarian showed Diamond to a vacant position and demonstrated how to access information. 'It was a directory of scientific research you required?'

'The International Directory of Research Projects in Biochemistry. I'd like to know what a certain Japanese graduate was working on a few years ago.'

'We should be able to locate it.' He tapped something into the controls. 'Maybe I should leave you to find your own way to the information. It's straightforward now. You just follow the instructions when they come up in highlighted text.'

'I'd rather you stayed,' Diamond admitted without shame. 'My brain goes dead when I sit in front of one of these things.'

'That's reassuring to hear. From some of the things you've been saying, I thought you were information-oriented, and nothing else. Do we have the researcher's name?'

'Yuko Masuda.'

The librarian keyed in an instruction. 'I hope you weren't serious – about not being able to appreciate the film because it wasn't strictly true.'

'Don't let it depress you,' Diamond told him. 'It's the way I was trained.'

'Too much left hemisphere.'

'Too much what?'

'Of the brain. The left side of the brain marshals facts. I've always thought the police would do well to recognise that they have a right hemisphere as well, with a capacity for intuition.'

'How, exactly?'

'Not "exactly" at all, Mr Diamond. I'm suggesting you clear your mind of all those facts you collect and allow it to be receptive to psychic forces.'

'You mean tea-leaves and Tarot cards?'

'No, no, I'm being serious. I think you detectives might benefit by tapping into your sixth sense occasionally.'

'Don't give me that. That's how the wrong people get stitched up,' said Diamond. 'A detective who thinks he knows the truth in advance of the evidence is a dangerous man. I've met a few in my time.'

'Isn't this a hunch – looking up a research student?'

'No, this is desperation. I know damn all about this woman. I've got to start somewhere.'

'And I think we've found her,' said the librarian, who had been scrolling the text as they talked.

Diamond stared at the screen and saw, midway down:

Masuda, Yuko. PhD. Yokohama Univ. 'An insult to the brain: coma and its characteristics.' 1979-81. S. Manflex. 'Narcosis and coma states.' (American Journal of Biochemistry, May 1981.) 'The treatment of alcoholic coma.' Paper presented to Japanese Pharmacological Conference, Tokyo, 1983. Drug and alcohol-induced comas, 1983. S. Manflex.

'Talk about an insult to the brain,' he said. 'My brain-cells turn their back and walk away when I'm faced with stuff like this. S. Manflex. Narcosis. Can you understand any of it?'

'That phrase "an insult to the brain" is faintly familiar,' the librarian said. 'Where have I heard it? Give me a moment.' Given a moment, he said suddenly, 'I've got it. That wonderful poet from your country, Dylan Thomas.'

'Not my country,' Diamond interjected. 'From Wales.'

'Isn't that the same thing? Anyway, they wrote "an insult to the brain" on Dylan Thomas's death certificate. Seemed appropriate – a kind of irony, considering he imbibed so much alcohol. I thought the doctor must have had poetic leanings himself. I didn't know it was a medical term.'

'I was talking about these other words,' Diamond said, becoming impatient with the frequent digressions.

'Hold on.' The librarian tapped some keys on the console and an insert appeared above the text explaining the abbreviations. 'S stands for sponsor, right? The research was sponsored by Manflex. I figure that must be the pharmaceuticals giant. You've heard of Manflex?'

'Vaguely.'

'If you buy something for a headache in this country, it's a fair bet it's made by Manflex.'

'And what's the other thing?'

'I have no idea. Science isn't my area at all.'

'Nor mine. Tell me about Manflex. Is it a Japanese company, by any chance?'

'You mean Japanese-owned? I doubt it.'

'It sponsors Japanese research.'

That doesn't make it a Japanese company.'

He accepted the correction. He'd been thinking aloud, trying to make connections that didn't exist, but should.

'You could be right,' the librarian conceded. 'They have

their base in America, certainly, but, who knows who owns it? The Japanese have taken over large slices of Manhattan. Even the Rockefeller Plaza. Would you like the address?'

This time it wasn't displayed on a screen. Diamond was handed the Manhattan telephone directory. In a few minutes he was phoning the Manflex Corporation on West Broadway, or trying to, because the number was busy. After ten minutes of dialling and swearing, he got through to a telephonist who, if anything, was in a more irritated state then he: 'Who is this?'

'Am I through to the Manflex Corporation?'

'Uh huh.'

'My name is Diamond and I'd like to speak to the managing director.'

'Sorry. No chance. Are you press?'

'No I am not.'

'Mr Flexner is unavailable.'

'When do you expect him to be available?'

'No comment.'

'Listen, I don't know who you think I am. I'd simply like to speak to somebody in authority. Is there anyone else?'

'You people are so persistent,' the voice said accusingly. 'A statement will be issued in due course.'

'About what? I just want to make an inquiry—'

'I'm sorry,' she said. 'I'm just too busy to prolong this.' And she cut the call.

He could tell that the rudeness wasn't personal. She was clearly under intense pressure.

'Can anyone tell me why a pharmaceuticals firm called Manflex should be under siege by the press?' he appealed to the librarians at the desk nearby.

There was some shrugging and head-shaking before one of them piped up, 'I heard something about Manflex. Their price is rocketing on the stock exchange, that's what's happening. They slumped badly and now they bounced back, only more so.'

If Manflex was currently reversing a fall on the New York stock market, people were making money. And if Manflex had been the sponsor of Naomi's mother's postgraduate research, then perhaps there was some reason why Naomi had been kidnapped just as the company's stock was soaring.

He tried phoning again, but the line was busy.

There was plenty to occupy him in the library. He located some reference books on medical science that were written in English he could follow, so he made a determined effort to interpret the gobbledygook he'd copied from the computer. Yuko Masuda's research papers were all concerned with the treatment of comas induced by alcohol and drugs. All comas were attributed to some kind of insult to the brain, as it was so evocatively expressed. Dr Masuda specialized in comas induced by poisoning of the brain, rather than by injury, pressure, infection or lack of sugar.

The half-hour's concentrated study may not have turned Peter Diamond into a neurological specialist, but he reckoned he was better equipped to talk to the people at Manflex.

He pressed out the number again. No one was answering. Instead, he left the library and went to look for a taxi.

The Manflex Building was one of the older landmarks on West Broadway, tall by most standards, yet dwarfed by the twin towers of the World Trade Center close by. When Diamond got close, he saw that the two sets of revolving doors to the entrance hall appeared to be locked. Armed security guards were preventing anyone from using the doors at the side. Two young women with the look of secretaries quite junior in the firm came out and were routinely approached by press people with microphones. They said with equal casualness that they were making no comment. It had the look of a ritual that had been going on for some while.

He ambled across to one of the reporters, a woman in an oversize suede coat and white boots. 'Excuse me, could you tell me what's going on here? Is someone famous in there?' He added in excuse for ignorance, 'I'm from England.'

She gave him a sympathetic look. 'This is the Manflex Building.'

'Should I have heard of it?'

'Pharmaceuticals.'

'Ah? Is that of interest to the press?'

Now she looked at him as if he were Rip Van Winkle. 'Manflex's rating on the stock market has been rocketing on rumours of a new wonder drug. They're due to make an announcement Tuesday and there's any amount of speculation.'

'Manflex – is that an all-American firm?'

She was obviously starting to think that she was stuck with a headcase. 'Haven't you heard of Manny Flexner? He was a legend in the pharmaceuticals business. Very dynamic. His son, David, just became chairman.'

'What's he like?'

'Nobody knows yet. He only took over a few weeks back. He's keeping his head down right now.'

'If this rumour is true, he's off to a good start.'

'He needs it. There was a big loss of confidence after Manny jumped.'

'Jumped?'

'Out of his office on the twenty-first floor.'

Diamond stared upwards.

'He fell the other side,' the reporter informed him. 'A small executive parking lot.'

Diamond thanked her and took a walk along Broadway, past City Hall, working out what to do next. He'd heard enough about the seesawing fortunes of Manflex to justify more inquiries, but he doubted whether he'd be able to convince Lieutenant Eastland that something should be done. For the present he preferred to pursue this tenuous line of inquiry independently. However, he wasn't going to be able to bluff his way past the security guards. Some different strategy was wanted.

He found a stationery store and went in to buy a notepad and envelope. Then he wrote a letter to David Flexner, the Chairman of Manflex, introducing himself as a detective from England conducting an inquiry involving murder and the abduction of a child. As a matter of extreme urgency, he went on, he needed an interview with the Manflex management to discuss the mother of the child, Dr Yuko Masuda, who had carried out research sponsored by Manflex at Yokohoma University in the early eighties. He gave the address and phone number of his hotel and added the words 'Detective Superintendent' below his signature. He addressed the envelope to Flexner, marking it 'Personal – Extremely Urgent'. Then he returned to the Manflex Building and handed the letter to one of the security guards, stressing that it was vital that it was delivered to the Chairman immediately. And once again his old police identity card came in useful; security staff are invariably ex-policemen themselves.

Before returning to the hotel he called at a bank and used his credit card to get more cash to patronize a deli he'd just passed. Later, he thought, he'd be able to tell

Steph that for lunch he'd restricted himself to a sandwich. She'd never seen the size of an American sandwich garnished with dill pickles.

It wasn't surprising that he took a post-prandial nap in his room.

The phone woke him.

'Hello.'

'Superintendent, er, Diamond?'

He sat up in bed. The digital clock beside it said 3.36. 'Yes.'

'David Flexner. You wanted to speak to me about this Japanese lady.'

'Correct.'

'There isn't much I can tell you at this point in time, and you'll understand that things are pretty busy here.'

'I appreciate that, but the child's life—'

'Sure.' There was a pause. 'I can meet you, but it would be easier some place else, not in this building. Let me think a moment. You know the Staten Island Ferry?'

'I can find it.'

'Battery Park. Anyone in New York will tell you. I'll see you in the ticket office around seven-fifteen. That's the earliest I can do. How will I know you?'

'I wear a fawn-coloured raincoat.'

'Like Columbo?'

'Like five Columbos. I'm well-fed. I'm also bald, but you won't be able to tell, because I wear a brown trilby.'

'A what?'

'I believe it's called a derby here.'

'Fine. Look out for a stringbean with long, blond hair and a red windbreaker. We shouldn't have much trouble, Super.'

He got up and took a shower. Super. No one had ever

281

called him that before. Flexner had sounded like a sixteen-year-old. If he had anything to be ashamed of, it hadn't come through in the voice. When this comes to nothing, Diamond thought, where do I go next? No messages had been left by the police, so they hadn't made any progress. These intervals of inactivity were the devil to endure. In his days on the force, he'd have spent this time chivvying the murder squad, or – as they would put it – making their lives a misery. Here, in this godforsaken hotel room, he had only himself to goad.

He went out and took a walk in Central Park that didn't deserve to be called a walk when compared with the gait of the exercise-minded fanatics who continuously strode past. When he rested on a bench he was immediately accosted by someone who wanted to compose a poem in his honour for five bucks. He said grouchily that he'd already heard enough poetry for one day and the poet spat on his shoe.

He tried some creative work of his own, devising scenarios in which Naomi's mother had given up her research as a result of getting disillusioned with the drugs industry; or that she had become a whistle-blower on malpractices in Manflex; or even a victim of some drugs experiment that had failed. He still couldn't work out why she had been parted from her child if she was still alive.

About six, no further on in his conclusions, he took the subway south and found his way to Battery Park. The Statue of Liberty was already a blue silhouette fading in the evening light. A ferry boat came in and he watched the procedure as the iron trellis snapped back and the passengers disembarked. With a strong breeze blowing, he was glad of his raincoat – which he'd never thought of as anything like Lieutenant Columbo's. It was a trenchcoat really, well-lined and with flaps that could button across the chest. With the hat, it was definitely more Bogart than Peter Falk.

He watched the ferry fill up and depart and then strolled across to the ticket office. Just after seven, too soon to be looking out for Flexner. The benches were fast filling up with passengers for the next ferry. Guessing that he might face a wait of twenty minutes or more, he claimed a seat.

Ten minutes passed. A mother brought her fractious toddler to the place beside Diamond and waged a noisy battle of wills over some chocolate that was certain, the mother said, to make the child very sick indeed after all he'd eaten. When junior had screamed enough to get his way, Diamond decided maybe the mother had not been bluffing. To safeguard the trenchcoat – which in his size wouldn't be easy to replace – he got up and moved away.

Nobody matching young Flexner's description was in sight.

'Are you Mr Peter Diamond, by any chance?'

He turned. Someone he must have seen and mentally dismissed had stepped over to talk to him, a pretty, dark-haired young woman in a cherry-coloured bomber jacket and jeans.

'That's my name.'

'Mr Flexner sends his apologies. He had a problem escaping from the press, so the meeting-place had to be changed. I'm Joan. I'm going to drive you there.'

'Drive me where, exactly?'

'I'm sorry but I can't tell you yet. There's a phone in the car. He's going to let us know.'

'You want me to come with you now?' What was being suggested sounded reasonable enough. He checked his watch and saw that it was already past the time Flexner had suggested that they meet.

'It must be such a burden for him, all this pressure from the media,' she remarked, leading Diamond across the park towards a place where several cars were parked.

'I appreciate that,' he said. 'Are you his PA or something?'

She smiled. 'Or something – I've no idea what you could possibly mean by that.'

'So you're on the payroll?'

'I drive a car. That's all.'

It was a smart car, a long, black limousine, the sort that would cause heads to turn in England but make no impression in New York. From some distance away, Joan used a remote control to disengage the security system. The indicator lights flashed briefly and the locks clicked. Just as automatically, Diamond went towards the left side.

She said quickly, 'I'm driving.'

He came to his senses. 'My mistake.'

Inside, she picked up the phone and pressed out a number. 'This won't take a minute,' she told him.

He sat back casually, trying to listen without appearing interested, but the voice on the end of the line was inaudible.

She said into the mouthpiece, 'We got here . . . Sure, he was . . . Yes, Mr Flexner, I know it. You want to speak to him? . . . Fine, we won't be long.' She replaced it between them and started up. 'Talk about cloak and dagger. You won't believe where we're going.'

Deviously, he suggested, 'The Trump Tower?'

It made no visible impression. 'No.'

'Where, then?'

'It's on the West Side.'

'You're being mysterious yourself. Is it anywhere I'm likely to know?'

'I shouldn't think so, but it's one of the "in" places.'

He had a depressing image of a trendy nightclub, the

sort of venue a wealthy young hotshot like David Flexner might frequent. 'Am I dressed all right?'

'Just fine.'

She would keep this going indefinitely, and he didn't know New York well enough to pin her down. He didn't like secrecy when he was the one being kept in ignorance. They were heading north, along the Hudson River waterfront. Occasionally they had glimpses of the lights of New Jersey. A diversion sent them away from the river, and they picked up their northward route on tenth Avenue. The Lincoln Tunnel was signposted, but they passed the approach roads and soon after slowed. Joan the driver was obviously counting streets, so Diamond helped.

'Forty-seventh.'

Thanks.'

'Which one are we looking for?'

'Forty-ninth will do.'

They turned left and tracked the street to its limit, under the girders of the highway. Soon they were back in a dockland area. Presently she turned onto a tarmac stretch between warehouses. Red hazard lights marked the tops of some cranes.

'He's *here?*' said Diamond in disbelief.

'I told you it was cloak and dagger,' she said. She flashed the headlights a couple of times.

A figure came from the shadows of one of the warehouses. 'Doesn't look like David Flexner,' Diamond commented as if he knew him well.

'This is one of his team,' she said, touching the control to let the window down on Diamond's side.

'I hope you'll be waiting,' Diamond remarked to Joan as he prepared to get out. 'I wouldn't want to walk back to my hotel from here.'

285

'I'm in no hurry,' she said.

The man stooped to look in. 'Mr Diamond?' The face was unshaven and smelt of liquor. As the face of an executive's personal aide, it wasn't convincing.

Diamond turned to look at the woman who called herself Joan. Even at this stage she returned a level look without a trace of perfidy. If this was a set-up – and he now believed that it was – she had played her part immaculately. She'd disarmed him with her poise.

The man outside reached for the door-handle. Diamond snapped down the lock.

Joan said, 'Why did you do that?' And before she'd got out the words she had released the lock from the central control at her side.

The man outside swung open the door. He was built like the stevedore he probably was.

Joan shrilled, 'Take him!'

Diamond jerked away from the door and made a grab for the steering wheel, whereupon Joan stabbed the sharp end of the keys into the back of his hand. The searing pain weakened his grip. She opened her door and leapt out on her side, yelling something across the quayside.

At the same time the thug leaned inside the car and put an arm-lock around Diamond's throat. It was painful and disabling, but it wasn't enough to eject him. He braced his legs to press his back against the seat and groped for the man's face, which was close to his own. He found a handful of hair, but he knew better than to work on that. You go for the eyes and ears.

He slid his hand across the surface of the face, got bitten badly in the fleshy area under his thumb, but succeeded in thrusting the same thumb hard into a fold of soft, moist flesh that could only be the man's eye-socket.

There was a scream and the arm-lock loosened.

But there were voices. Someone was shouting, 'Get out of my way!'

Something swung in a huge arc towards Diamond's skull. He couldn't duck. He put up an arm a fraction too late. The impact was terrific. His face hit the dashboard and smashed through glass. A second blow crunched into his shoulder. He was lucky to be registering anything.

'You got him,' someone was saying.

What now? he thought. Do I come quietly, or play dead?

Someone had two hands under his armpits and dragged him off the car seat. He went limp before hitting the ground.

'Bastard.'

Words, he guessed, wouldn't be enough for the man whose eye he had damaged. Two kicks in his kidneys followed. He couldn't stop himself crying out in pain. For this, he got another mighty crack on the head.

He was losing consciousness.

'Grab a leg, will ya?'

He didn't expect to survive. Joan had said this was the 'in place' and now he knew what she meant. They were going to dump him in the Hudson River.

27

He had swallowed a bellyful of foul-tasting liquid. His eyes were smarting and his nose was blocked. Repeatedly he spluttered and vomited and felt no better for it. Once or twice he opened his eyes and saw nothing. He was aware only of an occasional nudge against his right arm and shoulder. And that he was cold, indescribably cold. Parts of his body must have ached, but the cold subdued every other sensation.

He was face-up, most of him submerged.

He remembered nothing. For all he knew, he could be lying in a primeval swamp.

Waiting to die.

A stronger jolt forced his arm across his chest, turning him almost on his side. More of the liquid washed over his face, filling his mouth and nostrils again.

If this was drowning, he wouldn't recommend it as a way to go.

He turned his head and emptied his mouth.

Coughed.

Gasped for air.

Whimpered.

Your strength is going, Diamond. If you don't do something to help yourself, this is where you go under for ever.

He flung out his right arm. His hand slapped against a

surface slimy to the touch, but solid. He'd hardly begun to examine it when he felt the structure being moved out of reach. He groped for whatever it was and missed, realising as this occurred that the surface hadn't moved, but he had. As he was towed back to the right, he tried again, made contact and felt for the texture under the slime. Maddeningly, the action of the water rocked him away again.

His brain was beginning to function now. He realised that what he had taken to be nudging was the action of a current pressing him against some kind of obstruction. He pressed his hand hopefully towards it, grasped an object strange to the touch that he let go when he recognised its shape and texture as that of a large, dead bird. Then felt his knuckles come into contact with something smoother, some kind of container, a beer-can, perhaps. Mentally he was back in the twentieth century. He was part of the floating rubbish that collects along the banks and shores of waterways.

But there was some reason why the rubbish was trapped here. The current should have carried it downstream. Presumably he was caught against some obstruction.

As his thinking process sharpened, so did the cold – penetrating, demanding to be recognised, persuading him that it was futile to struggle. Feebly, he reached out again.

His fingers found something that didn't move, about the shape and thickness of a prison bar, only this was horizontal. He held on.

It was securely anchored. Without releasing his grip, he explored the shape, discovering a ninety-degree angle, a shorter length and then, coated with waterweed, the masonry from which it projected. He had found an iron rung attached to a stone structure.

He flexed his arm to draw closer. Then reached over and upwards with his left hand to see if a similar rung was located above the one he was holding.

The hand scrabbled against weed and stone.

Yes. His fingers curled around a second rung.

There was a ladder set into the wall.

But had he the strength to drag himself out of the water? Such an exercise would require an exceptional effort any time, and he was weak.

Try, or die, he told himself. One rung at a time.

He released his hold on the first and reached up with his right hand. Gripped and pulled. Found himself too feeble. Got both hands on the rung and slackened his body. His shoulders were out of the water, and now one of them was giving him pain he hadn't felt before. From the chest down he was submerged, and he just hung there, cursing his size, unable to achieve any more.

Then he was aware that his thighs were in contact with something. There was distinct pressure above his knees.

He'd found a lower rung. The ladder extended below the water-line. Not so far down as his feet, unfortunately, but if he could raise his legs high enough to get a foothold on this rung, he'd have a chance of making progress.

He raised his knees to the required level but found that, being pudgy, his knees wouldn't give him any purchase. The only way was to hoist himself up a couple of rungs by using his arms alone.

He breathed deeply and reached up. Got his fingers around the next rung and immediately felt such a searing pain in the shoulder that he let go. Now he knew he was injured. The right arm was virtually useless.

With the imminent prospect of sinking back into the filthy water, he braced himself for one more effort to go higher, reaching up with the left hand while holding on agonisingly with the right.

He made fingertip contact, got a grip and hauled himself higher one-handed, immediately releasing the right arm from its painful duty. The sense of achievement set the adrenalin flowing. Without pause, he forced the right hand into use again and held on, while jack-knifing his body in an attempt to get a foothold on the lowest rung.

He managed it.

Now it was a matter of leverage rather than brute strength and stoicism. With both feet securely positioned, he heaved himself upwards, raising his torso clear of the water. Clawing at the higher rungs, he began a steady ascent up the side of what he now perceived was a stone pier.

And as he climbed, his brain began to deal with his bizarre situation. Dimly at first, but with increasing clarity, he recalled where he was and why. He understood the reason for the pain that afflicted him, not just in the shoulder, but – as his circulation was restored – in his head and lower back. It had been a savage beating, and his attackers had assumed he would drown. Maybe the extra poundage that he was finding such a handicap while climbing the rungs had saved him. The body blows – apart from those to his skull – had been cushioned. In the water, his in-built insulation had kept him alive for longer.

But he still felt grim.

Not to say unsafe. He hesitated on the higher rungs, wondering whether anyone would spot him and throw him back again. A mere push in the chest would be enough. He wouldn't survive another ducking.

The darkness was an ally. He put his head above the wall, satisfied himself that no one was near and then climbed up the remaining rungs and flopped like a beached whale.

With no choice but to lie still, he waited for his pulse and breathing to reduce to rates he could cope with. He was getting messages from parts of his body that had suffered injuries he hadn't registered. Now his face was smarting. He put his hand to his left eye and felt a large swelling. There was a cut across the centre of his nose.

He couldn't tell how long he'd been in the water. There had certainly been an interval while he was unconscious. Presumably the shock of immersion had revived him.

In the open, darkness is never total. He rolled over and peered across the expanse of open ground between the pier and the warehouse from which his attackers must have come. The limousine had gone, maybe – he told himself optimistically – with the men as passengers. The instinct of killers is to leave the scene.

What now?

Clearly, he needed to get to the police. It was vital that they were informed what had happened, for the Manflex connection was no longer tenuous. Those people were revealed as willing to kill, and he wanted them interrogated as soon as possible. He wanted to hear David Flexner's explanation.

He just hoped he was capable of staying on his feet long enough.

Staying? He realised that he had yet to *get* on his feet, and now he was about to try. The effort required was immense. He achieved the standing position by a process of crouching for a while, then stooping, propped with hands on knees, and finally trying unsuccessfully to straighten and groaning at the effort. Movement was going to be a painful, shuffling process that made him think how useful a zimmer-frame would have been. Even the light shore breeze threatened to bowl him over.

Obviously he needed to find a way back to the streets, but getting there would be like finishing a marathon. To be positive, he still had both shoes on. All he seemed to have lost was his hat.

In the next twenty minues he made it across the waterfront, over a no-man's land cluttered with rubbish, and down a slope to where one of the West Side streets terminated. The nearest block of tenement buildings didn't really have the look of a haven for a half-drowned, badly-beaten Brit, but he staggered to the first door he could find, and looked for a doorbell – a facility the household lacked. He rapped the woodwork with his knuckles. Nobody came. He could hear nothing from inside.

He tried two more houses before anyone appeared, and this was a small, black boy who stared. Anyone would have stared.

'Hi,' said Diamond with an effort of the imagination.

The stare persisted.

'Are your parents about?'

A blink, and then a resumption of the stare.

'Your Mum and Dad? Sonny, I need help.'

The boy frowned and said, 'Where you from?'

He didn't want to go through that again, not in the state he was in, but the kid had broken his silence, so: 'From England.'

'England?' The kid raised a hand as if to strike him.

Just in time, Diamond saw what was intended and let his own right hand come in a sweeping movement to slap against the boy's in salute.

A short time after, wrapped in a blanket, he was seated in a wicker armchair in the living-room of the basement apartment, surrounded by a large Afro-Caribbean family.

293

They brought him coffee laced with rum and they put a Band-aid on his nose.

Twenty minutes or so of this treatment revived him remarkably. He was ready to move on. They wanted to know where he was going and he named the police at the 26th Precinct.

When the amusement had subsided, the boy's father offered to drive him there.

Thus it was that towards ten p.m., Sergeant Stein of the 26th, passing the 'front counter', was confronted by the disturbing spectacle of a grinning man, notorious across New York for the terms he'd served for armed robbery, carrying a heap of wet clothes, accompanied by Superintendent Diamond dressed in a blanket, a plaster on his nose, his left eye black and closed.

The explanation had to be given twice over, because Lieutenant Eastland, who was off duty, was called in to take decisions. He didn't go so far as to smile at Diamond's state, but he wasn't sympathetic. 'So what we have,' he summed up, 'is a link with Manflex through the child's mother. You set out to investigate, and you were beaten up and tipped in the river. Who by?'

'Come on,' said Diamond angrily. 'There were no lights out there except the car headlights. The girl who called herself Joan I'd know. But the point is that David Flexner himself must have given these people their instructions. Something I said must have really upset him.'

'You surprise me,' said Eastland.

'What *did* you say?' asked Stein.

'Just that I wanted information about the research Dr Masuda was doing some years ago in Yokohama on a grant from Manflex.'

'I wouldn't have said this was grounds for murder,' commented Eastland. 'Are we sure of this connection?'

'What do you mean?'

'I mean can we be certain that these people who jumped you were sent by Flexner?'

'It's inescapable. The girl told me she was working for him. She knew about the meeting. She knew where to find me, and when.'

'Okay, we'll pull him in and see what this is about.'

'One more thing,' said Diamond.

'You want to see a doctor?'

'I want to get my clothes to a laundry.'

'Okay. How you feeling now?'

'Impatient . . . to see Flexner.'

'You should rest.'

'Go to hell.'

In fact, he did get almost an hour on the cot he'd slept on the previous night. They had to wake him when Flexner was brought in, and then he felt worse than ever for the short sleep. Every part of him ached.

It was agreed that he should observe the first interview on closed-circuit TV. Lieutenant Eastland pointed out that Flexner had no reason to believe that Diamond had survived the attack. A first principle of interrogation was to give nothing away.

The young, long-haired man on the screen certainly looked uneasy, revealing in body language how agitated he was at being brought in for questioning. He flicked the tip of his tongue repeatedly around the edges of his mouth and worked his hands around his face like some actor over-playing Hamlet.

Eastland's voice started up, giving the routine information about the taping of interviews. 'You give your permission?'

Flexner nodded.

'Would you mind giving a verbal response?'

'I don't mind.'

'You agree to us taping the interview?'

'I agree.'

'Okay.'

While Eastland went through the preliminaries of establishing Flexner's identity and address, Diamond watched the young man keenly. For a business tycoon, he was pretty unconventional in style, dressed in T-shirt, jeans and windcheater with the mane of blond hair extending to his shoulders. It was pretty well the description he'd given of himself over the phone.

'You know a guy called Diamond – a British cop?' Eastland asked. He wasn't in shot. The camera was continuously on Flexner.

'I know the name, that's all. He called me this afternoon.'

'He called you? Is that an accurate answer, Mr Flexner?'

Flexner raked a hand nervously through his hair. 'What I mean is, he wrote me a note. I called him at his hotel.'

'Let's have the truth, huh?'

'I'm sorry. Was that important?'

'Everything's important. Do you still have the note?'

'Not here.'

'Can you tell me the contents, accurately?'

Flexner closed his eyes as he spoke, as if trying to visualise the note. 'He wrote that he was an English detective inquiring into a murder and an abduction, the abduction of a child. He wanted to meet me for information about the kid's mother who carried out research sponsored by my firm in Yokohama, Japan, in the eighties. Her name was Dr Yuko Masuda. He signed himself Peter Diamond, Detective Superintendent.'

'And he gave a number for you to call?'

'The Brightside Hotel on West 106th. I took it seriously.

I looked up the records on this woman. Then I called Mr Diamond and fixed a meeting at Battery Park, in the ticket office for the ferry.'

'Strange place for a meeting.'

Flexner gave a shrug. 'My circumstances are pretty unusual right now, for reasons unconnected with this. It was simplest to meet him someplace outside the office.'

'Battery Park? Why not his hotel?'

'Battery Park is a short cab ride from my office. It's also a place a stranger to New York could find easily.'

'So did you go there?'

'Sure, but I was delayed. He wasn't there.' Flexner leaned forward in his chair as if a sudden thought had come to him. 'What happened to this guy? Is he okay?'

'You tell me what happened to you,' said Eastland.

'I turned up at Battery Park—'

'No,' said Eastland, who was letting nothing by. 'You tell me what delayed you.'

'A smoke alarm.'

'What?'

'A smoke alarm went off in a storeroom on the twentieth floor.'

'What time?'

'Around six forty-five, just when I was ready to leave. Someone had dumped a cigarette in a trash-bin. It ignited some tissues.'

'In a storeroom?'

'That's where it was found. The result is I didn't get down to Battery Park until twenty-five after seven, and the guy wasn't around. I looked around, I asked—'

'Okay,' said Eastland. 'So let's have this very clear. Did you at any point instruct anyone else to meet Detective Diamond?'

'No. I just told you. I went myself.'

'Who else knew you made this appointment? Your secretary?'

Flexner shook his head. 'I handled it myself.'

'Is your phone system secure?'

'So far as I know.'

'You said that you consulted the records on this woman. Did somebody fetch them for you?'

'No, we have them on computer. We keep records of all our sponsorships and research programmes. I accessed them on the modem I have in my office.'

'Anyone see you?'

'I was alone in there. Look, would you mind telling me what happened?'

'Detective Diamond was met by a woman who said she was sent by you. You know about this?'

Flexner swayed back in his chair, frowning. 'Sent by me? No, I don't. I didn't speak to anyone.'

'Take your time, Mr Flexner. Think back. You're quite certain you mentioned this meeting to nobody?'

'Positive.'

'Maybe someone overheard you speaking on the phone. Is that possible?'

'I was alone in my office. The door was closed.'

'Yet this woman – who called herself Joan, by the way – found Detective Diamond in the ticket office, told him you were unable to get there and drove him in a black limousine to the waterfront area in the West Forties, where some goons were waiting to work him over good and sink him in the Hudson.'

'I can't believe this.' To his credit, Flexner was looking as if he meant what he said. He'd gone extremely pale.

'You'd better,' Eastland told him. 'And you'd better start

thinking who this woman is, and why it was necessary to do that to a guy you arranged to meet. You don't have to answer right off.'

'He's dead?' Flexner asked.

'Go over it in your mind, Mr Flexner. There may be something you forgot. I'll be back.'

Flexner was left staring. There was only the sound of the interview room door being closed.

Eastland came into the room where Stein and Diamond had been following the interview. 'Well?'

'I'd like to question him,' Diamond said. 'I still want the information he was going to give me.'

'You think he's speaking the truth?'

'He made a pretty good impression.'

'Yeah?' said Eastland with heavy irony. 'Maybe none of this happened. That's a phantom black eye you have.'

'I still want to question him.'

'Not yet.'

'This is urgent.'

'We can break this guy, no problem,' Eastland bragged. 'He claims he told nobody he was meeting you. That's got to be horseshit.'

Diamond contained himself, but with difficulty. There was a real danger that Naomi's plight would be overlooked in the eagerness to break David Flexner. Breaking him, as Eastland candidly put it, was not the way to get the crucial information. 'Listen, I think we should test the truth of what he's saying this way. He arranged to meet me. That's not in dispute. So he must have had something to pass on about Naomi's mother.'

'It was a blind, just to set you up.'

'Let's find out. Let's ask him what he can tell us. If he *is* telling the truth, it may lead us to Naomi.'

299

The lieutenant obviously wasn't impressed. He spread his hands as if his point had just been proved. 'Peter, my friend, you were asking about research the woman was doing seven, eight years back. That's not going to tell us who's holding the kid tonight.'

'It scared someone into wanting me killed. It can't be all that remote,' said Diamond. 'Let him talk while he still has an interest in co-operating. If you go in there and scare the shit out of him, we may get nothing.'

'Keep him sweet, you mean?'

'Play along with him. It won't take long, for God's sake.'

Eastland weighed the suggestion. 'You could be right.'

'I'll do it,' Diamond offered.

'You? No way. He thinks you're stashed away in the morgue, and we don't want to disillusion him. Okay, Diamond, we'll play it your way for a while. Just tell me what you would have asked him.'

Diamond outlined the strategy. Without going all the way to convincing Eastland, it seemed to mollify him somewhat.

In a few minutes, the questioning started up again. Eastland went straight to the point. 'Tell me about Yuko Masuda.'

'There isn't much. I haven't met her,' David Flexner replied. 'She's just one of thousands who have carried out postgraduate research funded by Manflex or one of its associate companies.'

'She's unimportant?'

'I didn't say that. According to our records, we've been sponsoring her researches for ten years or more. She's written some papers on the treatment of drug and alcoholic comas using sympathomimetic drugs.'

'Using *what?*'

'They imitate the effects of the sympathetic nerves. Adrenalin and ephedrine are examples.'

'I've heard of adrenalin.'

A sigh from Flexner betrayed some impatience.

'Alcoholic comas, you said?' Eastland continued. 'You mean these drugs pull the patients out? Restore them to their senses?'

'Inspector, all my information comes from a file entry on a computer. I am neither a biochemist nor a doctor.'

'Okay, okay. And what else does your computer tell you?'

'The usual stuff. Her age, address, qualifications. She isn't one of our employees, you understand, just a post-graduate research student.'

'Does the file show that she is married?'

'Yes. Masuda is her married name.'

'And is her child mentioned?'

'It wouldn't be. That's irrelevant to us.'

'She's based in Japan?'

'Yokohama.'

'And she's been doing research continuously since when?'

'1979.'

'Long time.'

'Research sometimes does take a long time.'

'Do you get updates on her work?'

'Not personally. The company keeps tabs on all our research programmes.'

'Did you know that she's been missing from her home for a couple of months?'

'No, I didn't know that. It wouldn't necessarily come to our attention for some time unless someone reported it.'

There was a pause in the questioning, as if Eastland was reluctant to move on, but couldn't think what else to ask.

Finally he said, 'Is there anything else on this woman's record that you planned to tell Detective Diamond?'

'No,' answered Flexner. 'Naturally, I wanted to be as helpful as I could, but that's all I could have told him. You've heard it all.'

'Forgive me, but it doesn't sound like the secret of the Sphinx,' Eastland commented. 'Why did you need to meet with Diamond like a couple of CIA agents? Why not simply call him on the phone and tell him what you had?'

Flexner shrugged again. 'I guess I wanted to be sure who I was dealing with. We don't give out information about people as a rule.'

'You didn't trust him?'

'I thought it right to meet him and make sure. I couldn't invite him to the office. He'd have had to run the gauntlet of the press. They're camped outside my building.'

'I've seen them. You're getting plenty of attention,' said Eastland. 'This is the wonder drug you're about to launch?'

Flexner shifted position in his chair. 'Look, this has no bearing on the matter of the Japanese woman.'

'How do you know?'

'It's unrelated.'

'We'll judge that for ourselves, Mr Flexner.'

'I'd rather not discuss the drug. If any of what I said leaked out prematurely, it could get us suspended on the stock market.'

'Everything you tell me stays within these walls,' Eastland assured him while the unseen watchers in the room across the corridor continued impassively to follow the interview.

David Flexner passed his hand agitatedly across his mouth. 'You're putting me in a difficult position.'

'The hot seat.'

'Excuse me?'

'I'm putting you in the hot seat.'

'Oh.' An unhappy smile flickered across the young man's lips. 'You appreciate that I only took over as Chairman quite recently, when my father died,' he explained. 'Frankly, the business hasn't gone too brilliantly for some while. We slipped badly in the pharmaceuticals league table. Our competitors like Merck and Lilly have developed new drugs and gotten away from us. And quite recently our stock market rating took a dive because of a fire at one of our major plants in Italy. The place was gutted.'

'And that hit confidence here?'

'Manflex Italia is our main European subsidiary. The investigation is still going on. We could be dealing with a case of arson.'

'But you hope to restore confidence with this new drug, is that it?' said Eastland.

David Flexner gave a nod. 'One mass-selling product can make one hell of a difference. Without saying more than I have to, I can tell you that Prodermolate—'

'Prodermolate?'

'PDM3. It's one of thousands of compounds that we patented over the years. The great majority never come to anything. Well, it happens that this drug – which was developed getting on for twenty years ago – is more effective than anyone suspected.'

'For what?'

'Forgive me, but I can't tell you that, Lieutenant. We're due to make an announcement in a couple of days and the future of Manflex rests on it. And thousands of jobs. We're under tremendous pressure to leak the information before Tuesday. I can't tell anyone, not even you, not even in this place.'

'You can't withhold information,' said Eastland in a voice more offended than threatening. 'I need to know.'

'I'm sorry, but—'

'You think I'm going to rush out tomorrow and buy shares in Manflex?'

'Well, no.'

'I have better things to do than gamble on the stock exchange, Mr Flexner. If I wanted to be a rich man, I wouldn't be in this job.'

'But I'm under an obligation.'

Eastland lifted his voice a fraction. *You're* under an obligation? What about me? I have to find a child, a handicapped child, as a matter of fact, who is in real danger of losing her life. This isn't hide and seek, it's child murder unless I find her.'

'Murder?'

After a sufficient pause, Eastland added, 'We've had one killing already.'

The quickness of Flexner's reaction, a spasm of shock that produced a rictus-like baring of the mouth, showed that he was primed for the bad news. Clearly he took the statement to mean that Diamond was the victim. This was the fear most on his mind. In a tone that showed he was about to capitulate, he said, 'I wish you'd told me right out.'

'You haven't been entirely open with me. Tell me about this drug,' said Eastland with the timing of a skilled interrogator.

Flexner had whitened noticeably. 'You give me your word it goes no further?'

'Secrets are my business.'

'Okay. I, em, I'm not the best-informed person to talk about the potential of the drug, but I gather it was patented back in 1975 at Cornell. The original research was carried out on a grant from Beaver River Chemicals, who became a subsidiary of ours when my father took them over about 1976. Nobody found much use for the stuff. That's the way things are. You discover thousands of compounds and register them without knowing if they're any use. Not many are chosen for development, which is extremely costly. It can run into millions. Professor Churchward has discovered that PDM3 is effective in regenerating the nerve-cells of the brain.'

'Is that special?'

He looked pained that such a question had to be asked. 'I said regenerating. It's unknown to science. It's a tremendous breakthrough. It means that we can arrest the process of mental ageing.'

'Alzheimer's?' said Eastland.

'Yes, but more than that, vastly more. PDM3 fosters the production of new cells. We can foresee its being used to sustain the brain at peak efficiency into advanced old age.'

'For anyone?'

'Exactly.'

'So it's a surefire money-spinner,' Eastland said in a swift descent to market economics. 'On Tuesday, you're launching this drug?'

Flexner raised his hands like a man looking into a gun barrel. 'No, no. That's still at least a year off. We're staging a conference to report on the work so far and announce that we're going into the third stage of testing, which is extensive pre-clinical trials.'

'But the mere fact that you are starting the trials will lead to massive investment in Manflex.'

'That is likely.'

'You mentioned a professor just now.'

'Churchward. He's at Corydon University, Indianapolis. I flew out there to see him last week. He's leading the teams at work on PDM3.'

'Did you form a good estimate?'

'What do you mean?'

'Did you like the guy?'

'I didn't have to.'

'Trust him, then?'

'My judgement is that he's a good scientist, or I wouldn't be putting our resources into the drug.'

'So you see a bright future, Mr Flexner.'

'For mankind, with an advance like this? Certainly.'

'For Manflex Pharmaceuticals.'

He looked faintly embarrassed. 'I expect so.'

'You can do without a murder inquiry on your doorstep right now.'

'Too damned true.'

'And you say you mentioned Detective Diamond to nobody?'

'Not a living soul.' Impulsively, Flexner said, 'Could we keep it out of the papers until after Tuesday?'

Eastland behaved as if the question hadn't been put. 'When you called him on the phone, did you dial the number yourself?'

'Yes.'

'You didn't ask the switchboard to get the number for you?'

'No.'

'Can they listen in to outside calls?'

'I'm pretty sure they can't.'

'Let's take another view of this,' suggested Eastland. 'Who else beside yourself knows what you intend to announce on Tuesday?'

'About PDM3?' He cast his eyes upwards, as if the names were written on the ceiling. 'My deputy, Michael Leapman, and Professor Churchward, of course. They'll both be at the conference.'

'The professor is in New York?'

'He flew in tonight. He's staying at the Waldorf Astoria.'

'No one else knows about PDM3?'

'I can't think of anyone. There are people working on various phases of the project, but only Michael and Professor Churchward know the whole picture.'

'Your wife?'

'I'm unmarried.'

'Girlfriend?'

Flexner shook his head.

'So who are the opposition?' Eastland asked. 'Who has an interest in screwing up your big announcement?'

'Competitors, you mean?'

'If you like. *Someone* took the child. Who do you suspect, Mr Flexner?'

'I've no idea. I'd rule out our competitors. They wouldn't get involved in anything criminal. Can't you find out from the mother if anyone has approached her?'

'I told you the mother is missing.'

Flexner let out a long breath. 'I can't explain any of this.'

'It's pretty obvious that someone in Manflex reacted quickly when Diamond got in touch with you. My guess is that your office is bugged. Have you thought about that?'

His eyes widened.

Eastland added, 'I can think of no other way they could have set this thing up, hired the team to take care of him and also set off the smoke alarm in your building. It was an inside job, Mr Flexner. No question.'

The young man shook his head, more as a way of coming to terms with the unthinkable than as a denial.

Eastland said, 'Where do I find Michael Leapman?'

'Michael? He has no reason to—'

'Was he in the building this afternoon?'

'Yes, but—'

'His address, please.'

'I don't know. He lives in New Jersey.'

'You have a phone number?'

'Somewhere.' He felt into the back pocket of his jeans. 'But Michael is the last man on earth to want to screw up our plans. PDM3 is his baby.'

28

I t couldn't have happened in England. Deep in New York's Chinatown at close to midnight a patrolman had acquired from a clothing emporium for outsize men called Chunky Chang a pair of white cotton trousers with a fifty-inch waist, an XL T-shirt, a loose-knit pink sweater, socks and white sneakers. Diamond was clothed again, if not remotely to his taste. And now he was being driven with Lieutenant Eastland and Sergeant Stein via the Holland Tunnel to New Jersey.

'So what have we got on this guy?' Eastland asked.

Stein had been assigned the problematic task of obtaining a profile of Michael Leapman by radio contact while they were driving to interview him. 'No record of arrests,' he said. 'Vice Chairman of Manflex for the past five years. Unmarried. Thirty-seven, originally out of Detroit. He worked there for a pharmaceuticals firm called Fredriksson and Lill. Worked his way up to executive director and then the firm got taken over by Manflex. You want to know the letters he can put after his name?'

'We get the picture,' said Eastland. 'Old man Flexner must have rated him to make him Vice Chairman.'

'David Flexner has a good opinion of Leapman, too,' Diamond chipped in, wanting to justify his presence in the party. 'And if we believe young Flexner – as I'm inclined to, having watched him under questioning – Leapman has a personal stake in the success of PDM3. He promoted it strongly inside the company. He arranged for Flexner to meet the professor in Indianapolis.'

The car moved on a couple of blocks before anyone followed up the remark, and then it was Stein who spoke. 'So why would a good company man like Leapman risk everything on the eve of their big announcement by putting out a contract on a British detective?'

'You mean what made me a threat?' said Diamond.

'No, I mean what made the little girl a threat? You're just a pawn in the game.'

Such offensive remarks were best treated with indifference, in Diamond's experience. 'I think it has to be connected with this drug, doesn't it?' he said without betraying the slightest resentment. 'PDM3 could be the jackpot of all time, as David Flexner made clear. Leapman is pushing like mad to get it licensed. We don't know yet how big his personal involvement is, but it's possible that he's seen this as a once-in-a-lifetime opportunity and invested his own capital in the company. He must have been shattered when the Chairmanship of Manflex was bequeathed to David Flexner. As I see it, he uses his inside knowledge to get a big payday as compensation.'

'Are you saying this could be a scam, this whole thing about the drug?' asked Stein.

'No, I think it would be difficult to fool so many people. There are all kinds of safeguards in the drugs industry. They must have had some very promising results from the pre-clinical trials. They couldn't fake them. But the timing is amazing, isn't it? They're ready to go public on the miraculous properties of this drug now, just when Manflex is nose-diving. The stuff has been around for twenty years.'

'He explained that,' Eastland pointed out. 'They didn't know it was useful until the professor started work on it.'

'But he's been working on it for some years.'

'You think they sat on it until now?'

'I'm just trying to account for Leapman's behaviour – if he really is the villain. Of course it may be that Manny Flexner knew about PDM3 and wasn't so convinced as his Vice Chairman. Manny may have put the brake on it.'

'If there is anything suspect about the drug, it won't stay secret for long,' said Eastland. 'Like you said, every drugs company in the world will want to know the formula and scrutinize the results, not to mention the analysts who advise the stock market.'

Diamond wouldn't be shaken from his conviction that the decision within Manflex to press ahead with PDM3 had triggered the crimes they were investigating. 'Yes, the results so far must be watertight, or they wouldn't risk publishing them. Let's accept that everything we've heard about the drug is true, and that it's the most exciting discovery since penicillin. Then isn't it certain – as sure as God made little green apples – that the criminal fraternity will have got to hear of the payday in prospect?'

'The mob?'

'The barons who run crime in this city of yours, from whatever community. They could be calling the shots.'

'Maybe,' said Eastland. 'Maybe.' After a moment he admitted, 'It's plausible.'

Sergeant Stein said wistfully, 'It's a terrific pay-off.'

Eastland then followed up his double 'maybe' by commenting insensitively, 'This is all very neat except that we're investigating a missing kid, not a killing on the stock exchange. The only link we have is that the kid's mother happens to be sponsored by Manflex.'

Of all people, Diamond didn't need reminding about Naomi, but he wasn't going to be shaken from the point he'd made. 'Come on, there's ample evidence that professional crooks are involved. Mrs Tanaka's was a contract killing. And the people who attacked me weren't amateurs.'

'So why was Mrs Tanaka killed?' asked Sergeant Stein.

'My guess is that she was given a job to do and she failed. They considered her untrustworthy.'

'She was expendable.'

'Just a pawn, like me.'

'How about the kid?' said Stein. 'Is she expendable, too?'

'No,' said Diamond, quick to dismiss the unthinkable. 'If they'd wanted to harm Naomi, they'd have done it long ago.'

'I may be dumb,' said Eastland, 'but nobody has explained to me yet how one small autistic girl is so important in this case.'

Diamond had no answer. He'd long since reached the conclusion that Lieutenant Eastland was anything but dumb.

Leapman's house was one of six in a cul-de-sac north of Hoboken, spacious two-storey wooden buildings with attached garages owned (Diamond guessed) by the kind of people who couldn't yet afford a prime position overlooking Manhattan, but had their hopes. They had plaster geese on their porches and flagpoles in their lawns.

No lights showed at the windows of the end house, but that wasn't remarkable considering that it was already 1.15 a.m. Two households were watching TV and the others were dark.

The police car glided to a stop in the street outside the Leapman address. Diamond reached for his door-handle and gasped with pain. His right arm still hurt.

312

'I don't think so,' Eastland told him. 'You've seen enough action for one night. We have our procedures. Ready to go, Stein?'

Submissive for a change, Diamond remained in the car and watched them approach the house, guns drawn, moving with stealth. At the front door, Stein stood well to one side when he pressed the bell, probably mindful of cops who had been shot through doors.

The chimes were audible from the street.

No lights went on.

Eastland moved around the side of the house, leaving Stein, who sounded the chimes several times more without response.

When a light did appear, it was only Eastland's flashlight bobbing around the other side, past the garage entrance. He pointed it through a front room window and beckoned to Stein to join him. They stood together staring inside for what became to Peter Diamond an unbearable interval.

Diamond told the driver, 'Blow this for a lark. They've spotted something. I'm going over.'

The action of removing himself from the car gave him another uncomfortable reminder of the strains he'd put on his physique that night. No catlike movement across the drive for him. He hobbled.

Lieutenant Eastland turned and came towards him.

'What have you found?' Diamond asked, but Eastland walked right past him and used the radio in the car.

'What is it?' He was addressing Stein now, but the question was superfluous.

Michael Leapman's front room looked as if it had stood in the path of stampeding buffaloes. The moving flashlight picked out a unit lying tilted across a sofa, with books and ornaments strewn across the floor. The television set was face-up, smashed. A chair lay across a table.

'Is he in there?'

'We can't see,' said Stein, still with his gun drawn. 'We don't know.'

'Shouldn't we go in?'

'The lieutenant wants a back-up.'

'I can provide that. Have you checked all the doors? The windows?'

'Don't get me wrong, but he wouldn't want back-up from you.'

'Why not?'

'Do you have a piece?'

'A piece of what?'

Stein gave a shrug that said he wouldn't want back-up, either, from a man without a piece and without knowledge of what a piece was.

'Any signs of a break-in?' Diamond asked.

'No.'

Eastland came back and reported that the Emergency Service Unit was on its way. 'The perps could still be inside. I'm taking no chances.'

Diamond awaited his opportunity to sidle closer to Sergeant Stein, from whom he learned that a perp was a perpetrator. The common language had its pitfalls.

A van was with them in six minutes, followed soon after by two cars. Armed men were sent around the side of the house. Lights were set up. There were dog-handlers and men in white overalls who spoke briefly with Eastland and then forced open the front door and went in.

Diamond stayed close to Eastland and followed the search of the interior as it came over the personal radios. The house was unoccupied, they learned, but there were more signs of violence, including blood spots on the wall in one corner of the living-room. There were bloody fingerprints on the phone, which was pulled from its socket and lying upside down on the floor. A bloodstained baseball bat was found beside it.

'Looks like someone used the phone after the victim was struck,' the voice reported.

'Or tried to,' said Eastland. 'Have you checked all the rooms now?'

'Yeah. No disturbance anywhere except the living-room. This don't look like robbery to me, Lieutenant. The drawers and cupboards are closed.'

Then a crackle of static was followed by the voice of the other searcher. 'I wouldn't bet on that. His car isn't in the garage.'

'They took the car,' said Eastland. He turned to Stein and asked him to get a computer check on Leapman's licence plate number.

Diamond groaned in frustration. 'Can we take a look for ourselves now?'

'Not yet. Crime Scene has to go through.'

'How long before they get here? Look, I'm not asking to tramp through the room where the assault took place. I'd like to see the rest of the house.'

'What exactly is your problem?' asked Eastland. 'Not satisfied with the search?'

'I'd like to take a look for myself, that's all.'

'There's no evidence that the perps went anywhere except the living-room.'

'In that case, there's no risk of disturbing anything.'

But they wouldn't permit Diamond to step inside until an hour and twenty minutes later, after the crime scene people had been through. The possibility that Eastland was exacting some kind of revenge for the liberties Diamond had taken at the murder scene in the Firbank Hotel did occur to him at the depth of his frustration while he was waiting, but probably he was wrong. They had their procedures and they observed them rigidly. Nevertheless he was hunched and resentful as he limped about the drive.

He was unsure what he might find, if anything. He just felt driven by some inner force. Maybe, he reflected, he'd taken to heart that advice from the librarian, to unlock his sixth sense, or right hemisphere, or whatever the man had been rabbiting on about. It wasn't easy to recall at two on a chilly morning.

Eventually, the Crime Scene Unit passed on the word that, apart from the living-room, the house was open to inspection. Leaving his new sneakers on the doorstep, he stepped inside with Eastland.

'You're looking for evidence that the kid was here, aren't you?' the lieutenant said.

'I'm keeping an open mind.'

'Yeah?'

The lights were on all over the house. It was very much the bachelor businessman establishment, with the feel of a furniture showroom rather than a home. Leapman seemed to be a man of tidy habits who favoured light oak and muted colours. The pieces of furniture had their functions, and there was little in the way of ornament, and certainly no clutter.

'Want to start upstairs?' Eastland suggested.

'The bedrooms.'

It wasn't entirely Diamond's sixth sense that was motivating him. If Naomi had been kept here for any appreciable time, it was likely that she would have been confined in a room out of sight of the neighbours.

At the top of the stairs, they glanced into a couple of rooms, getting their bearings. A guest bedroom attracted Diamond's attention. It was small and it faced the back of the house. However, there was nothing to suggest anyone had occupied it. The duvet was positioned four-square on the divan, the pillow plumped and tidy. Eastland went systematically through the chest of drawers and found only some spare bedding in the bottom drawer.

'Satisfied?' he enquired of Diamond.

'Almost.' Intuition was prompting him strongly now, spurred on by something Julia Musgrave had said. He told Eastland, 'Autistic kids quite like to hide things, toys and so on, objects that they value. If I'm right, it's just possible that she used a hiding-place she once favoured before, in another place.' He crouched by the bed. 'It was this side last time.' He slipped his hand between the mattress and the spring box of the divan with a sense of anticipation little less than Lord Caernarvon's at the opening of Tutenkhamen's tomb. His fingertips had touched something solid. He took it out in triumph: a ballpoint pen. 'I would say that it's ninety-nine per cent certain that Naomi was here.'

'You knew it would be in there?' said Eastland.

Elated, Diamond risked more strain on his battered body by pulling up the mattress. There may be something to intuition, but good luck is a deception. There was no drawing pad lying under the mattress. Not even a sheet of paper.

Cause for celebration: Naomi was alive – or had been at the time she hid the pen here. Cause for concern: the trail had gone cold again; there was no telling who was holding her now. The forensic tests might provide clues, but the men in white coats always take days to report their findings.

317

'Did Sergeant Stein get anything on the stolen car?' he asked Eastland.

'Leapman's car? It was a dark blue Chevy Citation. We have the licence plate number from Central. Every radio car in New York has it.'

There was nothing to detain them any longer. Knowing that he would keel over if he didn't get some sleep soon, Diamond asked for a lift to his hotel.

29

One can only guess at Lieutenant Eastland's thoughts next morning when he arrived at the stationhouse to find his office occupied by Peter Diamond wearing just an unbuttoned shirt and red jockey shorts. The fat Englishman was standing with the phone anchored between his shoulder and his fleshy jowl. The desk was heaped with clothes, some discarded, some obviously back from the cleaner. Judging by the clutter of phonebooks, notepads, pens and screwed-up Kleenex, he had been installed there for some time. 'Beef, for a start,' he was saying. 'Have you got beef? . . . Right. What else? Liver, I should think. Lamb, yes . . . Well, as much as you can manage at short notice . . . Excellent. How soon? . . . Oh, give me strength! I'm talking about lunchtime today. . . . Yes, *today* . . . Right, I know you will. I'll call you back around noon. . . . One o'clock, then. No later.' He put down the phone. 'Morning, Lieutenant. Did you oversleep?'

Eastland regarded him with glazed, red-lidded eyes.

Diamond told him, 'My clothes came back.'

'So I see.'

'There's just time to get down to the Sheraton Center.'

Eastland said, 'This used to be my office.'

Diamond announced in the same up-lads-and-at-'em tone, 'The conference opens at eleven.'

'Conference?'

'Manflex. Remember? This is the big one, when they unveil the wonder drug. David Flexner will be there and so will Professor Churchward. We've got to be there.'

'Who do you mean – *we*?'

'You and I. Sergeant Stein as well if you want.'

Eastland ran his fingertips down the side of his face as if to discover whether he'd shaved yet. 'The Sheraton Center, you said?'

'Seventh Avenue and Fifty-third.'

'I know where the Sheraton is,' Eastland said in a growl.

'Snap it up, then.'

'Diamond, you have all the finesse of a sawed-off shotgun.'

To be charitable to Eastland, he hadn't seen Diamond so animated before. The Englishman was unstoppable. Within three minutes they were in a sector car heading downtown.

'I've been turning things over in my mind,' Diamond said, as if to explain the transformation. 'Last night, the scene at Leapman's house seemed all wrong.'

'Wrong?'

'What we found.'

'The ballpoint?'

Diamond stared in surprise at the lieutenant. 'No. The ballpoint wasn't wrong. That was a genuine find. Just about everything else was wrong.'

'For instance?'

'The damage to the front room. It looked impressive at first, as if there'd been a fight, but what did it amount to in breakages? One smashed TV screen. The shelf unit had tipped across the sofa and some books and things were on the floor, a chair was overturned and lying across a table and that was it.'

'The phone was pulled from its socket,' Eastland added.

'True – but it wasn't damaged. To me, the scene looked as if it had been staged by a rather fastidious owner who didn't want to damage his living-room more than was necessary.'

'You think that was staged?'

'I think it's more than likely.'

'Aren't you forgetting the bloodstains?'

'No, I haven't forgotten them. First, consider the state of the bedroom where the child was held. Immaculate – apart from the ballpoint. There was no other evidence that Naomi had ever been there. Not so much as a hair on the pillow. Wouldn't you expect some sign that she'd been removed from there in a hurry?'

'Maybe she was already downstairs when the fight started,' said Eastland.

'Dressed in her coat and shoes and everything? They're not in the house.'

'Whoever took the kid must have taken her things.'

'Picked them up with his bloodstained hands and helped her into her coat? Does it sound likely?'

'Do you have a better explanation?' asked Eastland.

'Then there's the matter of the car,' Diamond continued as if the question hadn't been put. 'How did the assailant – what do you call him, the perp? – how did he travel to the house. On foot? If he came in a car, where is it, because he couldn't have driven *two* vehicles away from the house after the attack.'

'Two perps,' said Eastland doggedly. 'One drove their car, one drove Leapman's.'

'Taking Leapman with him?'

'Yeah.'

'All right – then why was it necessary to take Leapman as well as the child?'

'Maybe they killed him. There's enough blood, for sure. They got rid of the body.'

'To hinder your investigation, do you mean?'

'Sure,' said Eastland. 'They carried him to the integral garage, loaded him in the car and then opened the garage door and drove out with the body in the back. That way they avoided carrying him out into the street in the view of the neighbours.'

'And that's how you see it?'

'Do you have a better explanation?' Eastland asked for the second time.

'Let me take you back a bit,' said Diamond. 'Leapman definitely took the child to his house at some stage. We found the ballpoint where I said it would be. We agree on that, right?'

'Uh huh.'

'Look at this from Leapman's point of view. Yesterday when David Flexner arranged to meet me at the ferry, Leapman was listening. Either the office or the phone was bugged. He has links with organised crime and he alerted his criminal friends and asked them to meet me and dispose of me, while he created a smoke alarm diversion at Manflex Headquarters to delay David Flexner. Is that a reasonable inference from the facts as we know them?'

'It's conceivable.'

'Conceivable? I was dumped in the river. You won't question that?'

'No, I don't question that.'

'Leapman must have believed I was dead, but he still had a problem, because you – the cops – brought David Flexner in for questioning the same night. He couldn't understand how you made the connection, but he knew how dangerous it was. It was getting too close to home. And home was where he was holding Naomi.'

Eastland was waking up. 'He didn't want the cops calling. This is not a good time in his life to get arrested.'

'Right. If he's going to cash in on PDM3, it's essential that the conference goes ahead. Are you with me so far?'

Eastland only gave a shrug and said, 'Let's say I've been listening.'

'Now, Leapman isn't the spokesman for PDM3. He's just the Vice Chairman. It isn't absolutely necessary that he puts in an appearance at the conference. David Flexner and the professor can handle it. The only thing liable to ruin the day – and the big hike in his shares – is if he – Leapman – has a visit from the cops and is found to have the child in his possession. That would be a disaster.'

'So?'

'So he arranges to disappear. He will take the child with him, leaving no evidence that she was ever in the house. First he dresses the child and puts her in the car. Then he tidies her room so well that you wouldn't know she was ever there.'

'Unless you were smart enough to look under the mattress,' said Eastland in a bland tone that didn't amount to mockery, but wasn't respectful either.

Diamond's eyes narrowed, and one of them hurt. The black eye was still swollen. He sensed that he was being sent up, but he refused to be deflected. 'Then he fakes the attack. Tips over several items of furniture and smashes the TV screen.'

'How about the blood? You telling me it was ketchup?'

'No.'

'Self-inflicted?'

323

'I don't know.'

'That makes a change.'

There followed an interval when neither man spoke. Diamond needed to draw breath and Eastland was gathering himself to demolish the theory. 'It's one hell of a scenario to build on one ballpoint,' he said finally. 'In a nutshell, you believe Leapman arranged the scene himself, leaving us to deduce that he was beaten up and probably murdered?'

'Yes. I think you'll find that the only prints are his own. Probably he wore gloves to handle the baseball bat and the phone.'

Eastland supplied unexpected support here. 'It's true that whoever handled those objects wore gloves. That much we have established. And you think Leapman is alive and well? He drove off with the kid sometime before we arrived?'

'That's it.'

'Where to?'

'I've no idea, but at least we know who to look for. We can put out a description.'

'We circulated details last night,' Eastland said with a yawn.

'No response?'

'None.'

Diamond didn't have to be told about the problems tracing cars in New York.

'What's your reaction, then?'

'To what?' said Eastland.

'To what I've just been telling you.'

'I don't buy it.'

And that was that.

They arrived at the Sheraton Center and shared an elevator to the third floor with a throng of people wearing

324

name-tags marked with the Manflex logo. The conference was to be in the Georgian suite. Young women in red blazers and white skirts were handing out information packs. Diamond took one and saw with grim satisfaction that an amendment sheet was included: *Mr Michael Leapman, Vice Chairman, will not, after all, be chairing the session with Professor Churchward. His place will be taken by the Chairman, Mr David Flexner.*

Seated inconspicuously towards the back, Diamond and Eastland watched David Flexner enter, accompanied by the professor, a slim, brown-suited man with cropped hair who took a chair beside the podium. Flexner was the first to speak. He addressed his large audience confidently, unaffected, it seemed, by the alarms of the previous twenty-four hours. After welcoming everyone, he briefly outlined the history of Manflex under his father's management, listing the principal drugs for which the firm was known. This was a stage of the proceedings when a few latecomers were still finding seats and many of the audience were looking around them to see which faces they recognised.

To a scattering of polite applause, the man in the brown suit was introduced as Professor Alaric Churchward. Gaunt and pale, but well in control, Churchward surveyed the audience with pinpoint blue eyes for a few seconds before opening with an attention-grabbing statement. Some four million Americans, he said, could no longer remember the names of their friends and families. They couldn't put names to everyday objects, such as chairs and tables. They were sufferers from Alzheimer's disease and they included people who had held highly responsible and demanding jobs. The roll of victims of Alzheimer's was as impressive as it was distressing, including the actress Rita Hayworth, film director Otto Preminger, mystery writer Ross Macdonald and artist Norman Rockwell. The cause was unknown; it was likely that a number of different areas of the brain contributed to the symptoms. Research scientists the world over had been working intensively for the last fifteen years to find a successful treatment.

He summarised the main targets of the research in a way that signalled something new and revolutionary, describing how the bulk of the work had concentrated on finding ways of increasing supplies of the brain chemical acetylcholine, which has a vital and mysterious process in the functioning of the memory. The brain's supply of this chemical was known to diminish rapidly with the onset of Alzheimer's.

Churchward went on to say that his own approach (and now more pens came out in the audience and tape-recorders were switched on) was different because it was directed towards the nerve cells themselves. For twelve years, teams of scientists under his direction based in America, Europe and Asia had made animal studies to test the effectiveness of certain compounds as protective agents that could delay, or even prevent, nerve cell death. In the last eight years their work had been concentrated on a compound known as Prodermolate, or PDM3, that had proved to be something more than a protective agent.

Alaric Churchward was quite a showman. Having got to his product, he kept everyone in suspense by introducing film footage of some Alzheimer's patients he had tested five years previously, prior to the administration of PDM3.

The bemused people who were shown on the screen being asked which month it was and when they were born and who was the current President of the United States were not exclusively the elderly that Peter Diamond associated with the illness. There was a woman of forty-seven and a man of fifty-two, although the others were over sixty-five. The spectacle of people of intelligent appearance puzzling over quite basic facts was profoundly disturbing, particularly a couple of men who demanded angrily to be told who they were and where they came from.

'I guess this is the "before",' Eastland commented to Diamond.

'Is it? I don't think I . . . Oh – I see what you mean.' In his concentration on the film, he must himself have sounded mentally lacking. These pathetic people moved him more than he had expected. Progressive loss of memory was a deep-seated fear of his own, and he had no difficulty in identifying with their distress.

After the lights were turned up, the professor talked at length about PDM3, a technical briefing couched in scientific terminology that Diamond found increasingly difficult to follow. His attention drifted back to the poignant images of the Alzheimer's patients.

Then the room was darkened for another sequence of film, the 'after' interviews. Introducing them, Churchward explained that some of the volunteers (as he insisted on calling them, rather than patients, or subjects) had been administered with PDM3, and some, as a control, with a placebo.

The film was eloquent. The effects on those who had been given the drug were striking. Not only did they answer the questions they had found so baffling before, but they went on to give unsolicited accounts of the improvements in their lives. They could dress themselves, go for walks, use shops, write letters. In the standard word-test, they had averaged a seven-point improvement. The results contrasted cruelly with the steady deterioration of the group who had taken the placebo. For Diamond, cynical as he felt about the sales pitch, it was difficult to remain detached, difficult not to wish that every one of those sad, benighted people had been given the drug.

In a neat *coup de théâtre* when the lights went on, Churchward was seen to have been joined by a man and a woman, whom he introduced as people just seen in the film, volunteers whose lives had been transformed by PDM3. Each answered two or three questions lucidly and testified to the improvement in their memory and concentration. They left the platform to spontaneous applause.

David Flexner stepped up to play his part as Chairman. He invited questions.

A bearded man near the front made the point that certain drugs patented by other pharmaceutical companies had appeared to produce remarkable improvements in Alzheimer's patients, but the effects had proved only temporary. In two years, the deterioration had set in again. Was there any real possibility, he asked, that PDM3 could sustain the improvement?

Churchward answered the question so smoothly that it might have been seeded before the conference, and perhaps it had been. 'Of course I'm aware of the products you're referring to, sir, and I agree that they have disappointed as long-term remedies. There are six drugs to my knowledge that have been undergoing tests intended to give a boost to the cholenergic system that produces acetylcholine. It is beyond dispute that a certain amount of success has been achieved. Unfortunately, as you just implied, the duration is severely limited. The reason – and this is a personal opinion – would appear to be that the nerve cells that produce the acetylcholine continue to die. Our own approach, with PDM3, is quite different, for we are actually regenerating those cells. Our experiments in

328

Indiana and at our other centres in Tokyo and London have been running for seven years, and no significant deterioration has been observed. Clearly the patients get older – let's not forget that we are dealing mainly with geriatrics – but our tests and interviews are consistently encouraging. There is, of course, documentary back-up that some of my colleagues will present this afternoon. Next question.'

A woman to the right of Diamond asked if any adverse drug reactions to PDM3 had been reported.

'Remarkably few,' Churchward told her. 'Every drug produces some unwanted reactions, but in this case they are negligible. The majority of volunteers reported no untoward effects.'

'Maybe they forgot,' Diamond muttered to Eastland in a facetious aside. He was becoming irritated by the smoothness of Churchward's presentation.

'Fewer than twenty per cent of our volunteers reported mild dizziness, but this is notoriously difficult to assess, and was of short duration,' Churchward added. 'Five per cent of those taking the placebo also reported dizziness. It isn't perceived as a serious problem.'

Diamond leaned closer to Eastland and told him in a low voice that he was going out to make a phone call. It may have sounded remarkably like a smoker's excuse for a quick drag outside the room, but it was genuine. He was in the seat closest to the aisle, so he was able to move out without disturbing anyone.

When he returned ten minues later, the question and answer session was still in progress. Someone asked if PDM3 could be described as a 'smart drug'.

'That's not a term a serious biochemist would use, madam,' Churchward answered, 'but I know what you're

329

referring to, and you have touched on a matter of real significance. It's estimated that up to a hundred thousand healthy Americans take drugs daily in the expectation of increasing their mental capacity. Call them cognitive enhancers or smart drugs, the point is that their effects are as yet unproven. I read somewhere that as many as a hundred and sixty cognitive enhancers are under development, many of them being vasodilators. Do you know what I mean by that? A vasodilator has the effect of widening the blood vessels, thus increasing the supply of blood to the brain. However, if your blood supply is normal, there's no evidence that vasodilators will make you any smarter. I have yet to be convinced that any of the so-called smart drugs are effective. And yet . . .'

The professor paused, smiled slightly, and then leaned forward like a preacher, with one finger raised to focus the attention of his listeners. He need not have troubled, for they were totally attentive. '. . . PDM3 raises exciting possibilities. This afternoon, I shall give you details of a limited experiment that we undertook with a group of student volunteers. It's well known that certain highly intelligent people have poor memories. We administered PDM3 to twenty undergraduates from the University of Corydon in Indianapolis. Three of them were consistently below average scorers on memory tests and there is no question that the drug produced a marked improvement in their mental performance. We're not talking about forgetful elderly people here. This is something else. And now . . .' Churchward folded his arms and kept everyone in suspense for a moment. '. . . I want to take it a stage further. In Phase Three of our tests, I propose to examine in a wide-scale test the ability of this remarkable drug to regenerate and prolong the mental capacities of normal people. If our preliminary findings are right, the implications – for individuals, for society as a whole, for the economy, for the welfare of our nation, the progress of mankind, are truly—'

'Mind-blowing?' the questioner suggested.

Churchward smiled. 'I'm tempted to say that anyone taking PDM3 runs no risk of having his mind blown. But, yes, we can scarcely imagine the potential of such a discovery.'

It seemed a good note on which to end, or so David Flexner thought, because he reached for the microphone. 'Unless there are any other questions, ladies and gentlemen—'

'Yes, I have one more, if you don't mind.' Suddenly Peter Diamond was on his feet. He hadn't planned to intervene so publicly as this and he hadn't discussed it with Lieutenant Eastland (who muttered, 'Jesus!'). Only in the last few minutes had he come to a decision to fire a broadside across the bows of the two well-defended men at the front. A scare at this stage, when they thought they were fully in control, might panic them into revealing something really culpable – if they were implicated. 'This session was to have been chaired by Mr Michael Leapman. What is the significance of his absence?'

Flexner's right hand went straight to his long hair and raked through it. 'Mr Leapman is, em . . . Excuse me, sir, this is an organisational matter. I don't see that it has any relevance to what we have heard.'

'Ah, but it has,' Diamond insisted. 'It's well known that Mr Leapman is strongly identified with this drug. He promoted it actively within your company. He, more than any other individual, is responsible for this conference, for the decision to go into Phase Three of the testing. Yet he isn't here this morning. What are we to make of this, Mr Flexner? Does it mean that Michael Leapman has gone cold on the project?'

331

Flexner was staring. 'Sir, would you mind telling me who you represent?'

'My name is Diamond.'

This simple statement made a satisfying impact. Men don't return from the dead all that often, and David Flexner had not been informed that Diamond had survived his dip in the Hudson River. His hair didn't stand on end, but in every other respect he gave a fair impression of a man seeing a ghost.

To give him time to find his voice again, Diamond went on to say, 'I'd better identify myself properly. I'm a detective working with Lieutenant Eastland of the New York Police Department, with whom you are acquainted. He's sitting beside me, in case you can't see from there. But my question was about Mr Leapman. As you no doubt know, he has gone missing. I think your audience are entitled to know the circumstances.'

Flexner looked more bloodless than the spectre in front of him. 'It has no relevance,' he managed to say.

Churchward got up and spoke to Flexner and his remark was close enough to the mike to be heard all over the room. 'Let's wrap this up fast.'

No one else had any desire to leave. Diamond said, 'You may prefer to wrap it up fast, gentlemen, but the rest of us won't be impressed if you do. Mr Michael Leapman has disappeared from his house in suspicious circumstances. A certain amount of damage has been done inside his house in New Jersey. There are signs of a scuffle. Overturned furniture. Bloodstains. His car is missing. I believe you were informed of this when you tried to call him this morning.'

Flexner appeared to give a nod.

Seeing that his Chairman was bereft of words, Professor Churchward reached for the microphone and said, 'This is a scientific conference, not a police investigation. We're sorry to hear about the attack on Michael, but with all due respect it has no bearing on what we are discussing today.'

Diamond said at once, 'I believe you're mistaken there. You've assumed that Mr Leapman was the victim of an attack.'

'But you just described it,' said Churchward.

'No, Professor, I described the scene at the house. The evidence is that the attack was faked.'

There were gasps. Everyone had turned to hear what Diamond was saying.

'I was doubtful of the set-up anyway, so I asked the forensic lab to check the blood-spots found at the scene. I phoned to get the results a few minutes ago.' Savouring the moment, he found a wicked way of prolonging it. 'As there are so many scientists present, you may care to know that they test whether it's human by diluting it and bringing it into contact with animal serum. There should be a precipitin reaction between the human protein and the animal serum. A white line forms. No white line was found in this case. The forensic people have a good stock of anti-sera from a variety of animals.' He paused. He was as capable as Churchward of working an audience. 'The blood-spots in Michael Leapman's living-room were bovine in origin, probably from calf liver, which is as bloody as most things one keeps in a freezer.' Again he waited, allowing the facts to sink in. 'So I'm bound to ask whether either of you gentlemen has any idea why Mr Leapman should have gone missing in these suspicious circumstances at this crucial time.'

Churchward was careful to switch off the mike before conferring with Flexner, who had a glass of water to his lips.

Diamond remained standing.

Without getting up, Lieutenant Eastland muttered reproachfully, 'You could have told me first.'

'There wasn't time.'

'Was this what you were setting up this morning when I came in?'

'With the lab, yes. I called them back just now. The beef test was the first they tried.'

'I thought you were ordering a sandwich.'

David Flexner switched on again and did his best to sound composed: 'We are not aware of any reason for the incident that has just been described. Michael Leapman has served as our Vice Chairman with honour and distinction for many years. We regret what has just been reported, but we can't see that it has any connection with our business here today. The programme will resume after lunch. That is all I have to say at this time.'

The press closed in on Diamond.

'Satisfied?' Eastland asked, when Diamond had finally shaken off the last of them.

'I'm not here for satisfaction. I'm here to find out how much Flexner and the professor know about Leapman's activities.'

'So what did you learn?'

'Flexner, at least, was genuinely fazed. I'm less certain about the professor.'

Eastland appeared to concur. 'He's a different type. More mature as a personality. His mind was on damage limitation.'

'That was my impression, too. A cool customer. I suspend judgement on Professor Churchward.'

'His sort wouldn't be fazed if King Kong stepped into the conference.'

334

'But that doesn't make him a guilty man.'

'Want another look at him? He's taking the afternoon session.'

Diamond said he had other plans. While the big-shots were away, he was going to visit the Manflex Building. He meant to find out for himself whether Flexner had concealed anything of importance the evening before when he was being questioned about Yuko Masuda's file entry.

'You won't get in there without a warrant,' Eastland told him. 'They have security like a state pen.'

'Want a bet?'

'Sure.'

'I bet you the price of a meal, then,' Diamond suggested.

'One of *your* meals? Get out.'

Both men grinned. They worked better now they had the measure of each other.

Later, fortified by a sandwich (or two) he bought himself, Diamond stepped from a limousine and strutted confidently towards the front entrance of the Manflex Corporation. The security guard – happily one he hadn't met on the previous visit – asked for his pass.

Diamond admitted that he didn't possess a pass. He had something better.

'What's that?'

'A British passport.'

'Mister, are you trying to be funny?'

'No, I'm giving you the chance to verify my name. I'm Peter Diamond.'

'Am I supposed to have heard of you?' said the guard, a mite more cautiously.

'I'm glad you asked the question. You'd better give some thought to the answer.' Diamond peered at the man's identity disc. 'Officer William Pinkowitz.'

Anyone who has played the power game knows that you put a man on the defensive by using his name. 'Are you something in Safe Haven Security?'

Diamond repeated in a scandalized tone, 'Something in it?'

'Do you work for us?'

'I wouldn't put it that way, but you're getting there.' All this was an exercise in psyching out that he had used in various guises many times before.

'But you're not American.'

'Didn't I just make that clear?' He left the wretched man dangling a moment longer before saying, 'Safe Haven is just a subsidiary of Diamond Sharp International.'

'Diamond Sharp . . .'

'International. Do you want to check with your superior?'

There was a certain amount of hesitation before Officer William Pinkowitz apparently decided that to cast any more doubt on the word of Peter Diamond was a risk he'd rather not take. 'I'll just take a look at that passport, sir.'

'Certainly.'

After an interval came the inevitable, awed, 'You're a Detective Superintendent?'

'You're doing a good job, Pinkowitz. Keep it up.' He walked into the building. Behind him, he heard Pinkowitz's heels click in salute.

He got out of the elevator at the twenty-first floor, from which, he'd been told, Manny Flexner had jumped to his death. A woman was coming along the corridor and wasn't the sort to walk shyly past. Thirtyish, with dark hair, brilliant make-up and, of all things, a kiss-curl in the centre of her forehead, she couldn't wait to find out what he was doing there with his black eye and battered face. She called out when she was still fully fifteen yards away, 'Can I help you?'

'Personnel records?' he said.

'They're all on computer now.'

'Where could I, em . . .?'

'Are you Australian?'

'English.'

'Oh, you can't be!' she checked the position of her curl. 'I have some very dear friends in England. Which part of England?'

'London.'

'Really? My friends are in Welwyn Garden City. Is that near London?'

'Tolerably near.'

'Tolerably near – I love it! But what's happened to you? I hope you haven't had a bad experience in our country.'

'No, just a fall. I'm fine.'

'I wouldn't have said so! Are you here on a vacation?'

'Research,' he said, divining a way to get back on course. He wasn't sure how long he could rely on Officer Pinkowitz to keep his privileged knowledge to himself. 'Family history. Mr, er, Leapman suggested I consult the records for information about a distant member of the family.'

'Michael Leapman? He isn't here today. Isn't that just too bad?'

'It doesn't trouble me in the least. But if I could be shown how to use a computer . . .'

'I don't know if there's a spare desk. Hold on – I'll think of something.'

'Mr Leapman's desk?'

'Why, yes – of course!'

Neat and simple, satisfyingly simple. At least, he told himself, I'm functioning again.

She showed him into Leapman's office, a place with signs of long occupation. A comfortable reclining chair, worn at the arms. A desk with cup-stains apparently impervious to cleaning. Some far-from-new executive toys, including a Newton's cradle that Diamond couldn't resist disturbing. A poster of Stockholm, curling at the corners. Even the computer keyboard at a separate desk had the glaze chipped off some of the main keys.

He sat in front of it, and his latest help-mate pressed a switch. While the machine was booting up, she had a spasm of uncertainty. 'Are you quite sure Michael said you could inspect the personnel files? Only a few of us have the password to get into them.'

'That's all right,' he assured her. 'I'm not out to discover how much you people earn or what age you are. I just want to look up a research scientist, someone who is sponsored by Manflex.'

'That's no problem,' she said, with obvious relief. 'It's much easier to access researchers than permanent staff. What name are you hoping to find?'

'Masuda. Dr Yuko Masuda.'

'That doesn't sound English.'

'It isn't. I have a cousin who went to Japan.'

Let's try, then. Masuda. Would you spell that?'

When the name appeared on the screen, Diamond's hopes of new information were dashed. It was a thin account of twelve years of research.

Name: MASUDA, Dr Yuko (female) *Date of Birth:*—
Address: Care of Dept of Biochemistry, Univ. of Yokohama, Japan.
Qualifications: MSc, PhD
Dates of Sponsorship: From: September 1979.
　　　　　　　　　　To: Continues.

Subject of Research: Drug and alcohol-induced comas.
Drugs Under Research: Sympathomimetic.
Publications: 'An insult to the brain: coma and its
                characteristics.' Postgraduate thesis,
                1981. 'Narcosis and coma states.'
                American Journal of Biochemistry,
                May 1981.
                'The treatment of alcoholic coma.'
                Paper presented to Japanese
                Pharmacological Conference, Tokyo,
                1983.

'It isn't much,' he complained. 'Hasn't she published anything since 1983? I thought research scientists were constantly publishing.'

The woman gave a shrug. 'Maybe the file hasn't been updated.'

At least the file confirmed that David Flexner had been entirely frank about Yuko Masuda. This was all familiar stuff from the interview at the stationhouse.

'Is there any way of telling when this file was put together?'

'Oh, sure. There's a check-list of all the dates when entries or deletions were made.' She pressed two keys and a window was displayed on the right of the screen. 'Just two entries. As you see, the file was created on 10 September 1987, and the latest entry was only three months back.'

He hesitated. Something was wrong. 'But the last entry on file refers to a conference in 1983. Which piece of this data is new? What did anyone find to enter three months ago when all I can see here relates to work published up to 1983?'

'I'm sorry, I can't answer that. I have no idea.'

'The computer can't tell us?'

'No.'

He sighed. Three months ago would have been shortly before Naomi was brought to London. Possibly there was a connection. Apparently there was no way of finding out.

He had another thought. 'Can *anyone* make additions to these files?'

'If they can get into them, sure, but only a few of us have the password.'

'That would include the Chairman . . .?'

'The Vice Chairman, Personnel Director, Research Director, Senior Systems Analyst and some secretaries, including me.'

'Whose secretary are you?'

'Mr Hart's. He's Personnel.'

'And you are . . .?'

'Molly Docherty. I thought you were never going to ask.'

'I'm Peter Diamond. And who is the Research Director?'

'Mr Greenberg. Would you like to meet him?'

'How long has he been in the job?'

'About two years.'

'Then I don't think I want to meet him.' Diamond tapped the screen with his finger. 'Tell me, Molly, where was this information stored prior to September 1987?'

'It was all on a card index. Mr Flexner – Mr Manny Flexner, I mean – was a sweet man, but he was a little slow in catching up with the computer age. He didn't trust modern technology.'

Nor I, thought Diamond. 'And all the information on the card index was transferred to the computer?'

'Oh, yes. Everything. And triple-checked. I was one of the operators.'

Before asking the next question, he sent up a silent

prayer. He was agnostic in his thinking, but if help was to be had from any source he needed it now. 'Do those filing cards still exist?'

There was an agonising pause for thought before Molly Docherty said, 'I believe they were put into store somewhere.'

'Where?'

'Now you're really asking. The basement, I guess.'

'Would you mind escorting me?'

She laughed, he supposed at the way he'd expressed himself. 'I'll have to clear it with my boss.'

'You don't have to mention me.'

On the way down in the elevator, she said, 'You must be very devoted to your family.'

'Why?' He was thrown briefly, and then remembered his trumped-up reason for inspecting the files. 'It isn't just a matter of making a family tree. I want to get the background on these people.' Even to himself, he sounded pretty unconvincing.

The basement was a cold, echoing place stacked with outmoded office furniture: wooden desks with the veneers exposed, grey metal cupboards of the kind so popular in the sixties and a great variety of chairs with their covers ripped and frayed. The discarded personnel files were easy to locate, stored in five metal boxes – locked, but Molly had thoughtfully collected a set of keys from upstairs.

'These go back thirty years at least,' she told him. 'There must be a thousand in each box.'

'Let's open one.'

She stooped and found the appropriate box. As she tried the keys, she remarked, 'This is like treasure-hunting. I do hope it's worth your trouble.'

She flicked through the cards rapidly with a long,

lacquered fingernail, picked one out and handed it to Diamond. 'Voilà!'

He didn't need long. 'This doesn't match the computer entry.'

'It wouldn't,' she said. 'We're constantly updating.'

'Deleting information?'

'No, adding it.'

'What do you make of this, then?' He handed back the card.

Name: MASUDA, Dr Yuko
Address: c/o Dept of Biochemistry, Yokohama University
Qualifications: MSc, PhD.
Dates of Sponsorship: From: September 1979
                        To: July 1985
Subject of Research: Comas, drug-induced and alcoholic
Drugs Under Research: Jantac
Publications: 'An insult to the brain: coma and its
               characteristics.' Postgraduate thesis, 1981.
               'Narcosis and coma states.' American
               Journal of Biochemistry, May 1981.
               'The treatment of alcoholic coma.' Paper
               presented to Japanese Pharmacological
               Conference, Tokyo, 1983.

'What's the problem?'

Clearly the details weren't written so indelibly in Molly Docherty's memory. Diamond explained. 'It says here that the sponsorship terminated in July 1985. On your computer, that isn't mentioned. It states that the sponsorship continues. That's a big difference, surely?'

'I guess she resumed the research at a later date.'

'Wouldn't that be recorded upstairs?'

'The point is that she's back with us now. I guess whoever updated the entry did the simple thing, deleted the date she stopped and substituted "continues".'

He wasn't satisfied with that. 'It gives the impression she was continuously doing research. There must have been a gap.'

'For a short period.'

'Of about two years? The computer was installed in 1987, you said. And everything was triple-checked from these cards?'

As if resenting the implication that someone had erred, she said, 'I'll just see if there's an entry on another card. Maybe the data from two cards was collated.'

But there was no second card for Yuko Masuda.

'This drug – Jantac – isn't listed on the computer, either,' Diamond pointed out. 'There's something quite different and unpronounceable. Sympatho – something or other. What exactly is Jantac?'

'Sorry,' she said, 'but there are thousands of drugs. I can't tell you.'

'Is it a Manflex product?'

'It isn't familiar to me, but we can check the list upstairs.'

'And could we also make a photocopy of this card?'

She looked doubtful. 'Is this really for family history?'

'Only remotely, I'm afraid. I'm a policeman on the trail of a little girl who is missing from home. Dr Masuda is her mother.'

'And what did you find out about this drug?'

Eastland looked more at ease sitting at his own desk in the stationhouse.

'Jantac? Not much,' Diamond admitted. 'It was on the Manflex list of experimental drugs.'

'Was?'

343

'It isn't any longer. They pulled it in 1985.'

'The year your Japanese lady's research stopped.'

'Exactly.'

'Do we know why it was withdrawn?'

'No, but I intend to find out.'

'You think it could be important?'

'Someone wiped it from the computer record. I'm satisfied that it must have been transferred accurately from the cards. Molly – the woman who helped me – insisted that everything on those cards went on to the computer and was triple-checked. But listen to this – the computer entry was altered for the first and only time three months ago.'

'About the time you found Naomi in London?'

'Yes.'

Eastland leaned back in his chair. 'Where will you get this information – about Jantac?'

'Yokohama University, I reckon. That's where the work was done. I'll fax them.'

'Before you do that, there's something I should tell you. We found Leapman's car.'

'Where?'

'JFK.'

'The airport.'

'It was in the parking lot. Been there some time.'

'How do you know?'

'He flew out last night. Japan Airlines, direct to Tokyo. I've spent the afternoon checking passenger schedules.'

'Tokyo. Have you told them?'

'Too late. He's already landed and cleared. With Naomi.'

30

A Japan Airlines boeing 747 taxied down the runway at the International Airport at Narita, thirty-five miles east of Tokyo. From his window over the wing Peter Diamond could see watchtowers, water cannon and riot policemen in full battledress. He'd read somewhere about the mass riots here in the mid-eighties and the long-running dispute with the local farmers over landing rights. Even so, this degree of security was daunting. It led him to wonder how stringent the immigration arrangements would be. Narita was not the most auspicious airport at which to arrive if your luggage consisted of a carrier bag containing only a pink sweater, cotton trousers, disposable razor, face-cloth, toothpaste and toothbrush. His apprehension was borne out when he produced his passport and it was taken away. He was asked to step into an interview room, where he waited under video surveillance for twenty minutes while, presumably, they checked their lists of undesirable aliens.

Finally he had an opportunity to tell an immigration officer (who spoke faultless English) that he was a detective engaged in an investigation.

The young man eyed him dubiously. 'Scotland Yard Special Branch?'

'No.' He had the strong impression that anything he said was liable to be checked, so he kept to the truth. 'I've been working with the New York Police. Twenty-sixth Precinct.'

'You are with the NYPD?'

'In co-operation with them. I am a senior officer. My passport, if you examine it—'

'I already have. Is Detective Superintendent your present rank, Mr Diamond?'

He noted a distinct emphasis on the 'Mr'. 'Former, actually. I have retired from the regular police.'

'Retired? So you are a private agent?'

'Er, yes, in a sense.'

'And are the Japanese police aware of your present mission?'

'No – em, not yet. There wasn't time. They know about the case, but they didn't know I was flying here. Look, this is an emergency. I'm pursuing a suspect who has abducted a child. When I heard he had flown to Tokyo I took the next available flight.'

'The suspect is . . .?'

'An American by the name of Michael Leapman.'

'And the child?'

'The child is Japanese.'

'Japanese? You say the Japanese police have not been informed yet?'

This was sounding more reprehensible by the minute. He could see himself spending the rest of the day repeating his story to policemen – and not necessarily policemen with as good a command of English as this beacon of the immigration service. 'It's an extremely urgent matter. Obviously, I'll notify the police, but even as we're speaking, the trail is going cold, if you understand.'

'I understand, Mr Diamond. But I am not certain if you understand the difficulties you would face tracking a suspect in Tokyo. You don't speak Japanese?'

346

'No.'

'You don't know anybody in Tokyo?'

'Oh, I know someone.'

'Who is that?'

'A sumo wrestler by the name of Yamagata.'

'Yamagata?' The name had a remarkable effect on the immigration officer. He gripped the edge of the table, blinked several times and swayed back. 'You know the *Ozeki* Yamagata?'

'Yes.'

'You're quite sure of this?'

'I wouldn't have mentioned him if I wasn't.'

'You have actually met him?' It was if they were speaking of the God-Emperor.

This, Diamond thought, is an opportunity. Without trying too obviously to impress, he underlined his links with Yamagata. 'We met when he was in London. He's paying my fare. He hired me, in fact. He's taking a personal interest in the case.'

'You should have mentioned this.'

'I just have.'

'Yamagata-Zeki?' He repeated the name as if having difficulty in believing what Diamond was saying.

'He lives in Tokyo. I'm sure he'll vouch for me. Would you like to check with him?'

'I would.' The man's face lit up. 'I would indeed. Thank you.' This, it emerged, was an inspired suggestion, the bestowal of an honour. The immigration officer reached for a phone book. His face was flushed. The pages shook as he turned them.

He stood up to make the call, rigidly, like a soldier. Without understanding a word, Diamond watched fascinated as the stern face of the immigration department become coy, then ingratiating and finally elated.

347

After the conversation ended, the young man continued to hold the phone, gazing at it as if it were a thing of beauty.

'You got through all right?'

'Yes.' The voice was dreamy. 'I have just been speaking to Yamagata-Zeki.' He put down the phone and flopped into his chair.

'Is that all right, then?'

'I can't thank you enough.'

'May I have my passport?'

It was handed across. 'Now I must call a taxi for you. Yamagata-Zeki looks forward to greeting you in the *heya* where he lives.'

'There isn't time,' Diamond said flatly.

'You can't refuse.'

This was infuriating. How could he make a social call when he was chasing Leapman? But while thinking actively how to get out of the arrangement, he began to see that a detour to Yamagata's *heya* might actually be necessary. As the immigration officer had pointed out, a complete stranger to Tokyo faced problems. He couldn't begin to go in pursuit without some practical help from the locals, and that would be difficult if most of them spoke no English.

Not long after, still fretting over lost time, he was in a taxi being driven to the *heya*, which the immigration officer had informed him was one of thirty or more 'stables' for sumo wrestlers in Tokyo, most, like this one, in the district of Ryoguku, east of the Sumida River. His new friend for life ('forever in your debt, Superintendent') had assured him that no fare would be required. Diamond wasn't sure whether it would be settled by the Immigration Department or Mr Yamagata. He couldn't believe that the taxi-driver would make the trip for no other reward than the honour.

Yet undoubtedly the support of a famous sumo patron was going to be useful.

He wasn't really taking in his first sights of the real Japan. Instead he was trying once again to understand Leapman's motive in coming here. The necessity of escaping from New York was clear, but to escape to an alien country whose language the man didn't, presumably, speak was extraordinary unless he had something else planned. Something Leapman believed was vital to his survival.

On the plane, Diamond had been handed a *New York Times*. The conference at the Sheraton was reported in the business section under the heading MANFLEX DIRECTOR MYSTERY. Leapman's untimely disappearance was given a couple of paragraphs rich with innuendo, yet it appeared that the market had still been impressed by the claims Flexner and Churchward had made for PDM3. Manflex stock had soared by more than five dollars, offering large profits to insiders whose stake had been purchased cheaply. In all probability, Leapman was still set to make a fortune if he could keep clear of the law. He could take his profits simply by calling his stockbroker – from Tokyo, or anywhere else.

But why Japan?

Was it possible that the man had some humanity after all and had come here to return Naomi to her mother? Clearly, he didn't want to remain in charge of a small child. He knew she was being sought. To hold her for long was dangerous as well as impractical. He was a swindler, hand in glove with professional criminals, but maybe he drew the line at murdering a child because she was in the way. Could it be as simple as that?

Not likely.

The smoke-stacks of industrial Tokyo gradually gave way

to city streets crowded with purposeful people in sharp dark suits. The taxi-driver said something in Japanese with a man-to-man chuckle recognisable in any tongue and pointed to a lighted sign in English saying SOAPLAND.

'Massage parlour?' hazarded Diamond.

'You want?'

'No, no. Sumo.'

He was doing his best to get his bearings from the odd assortment of English words on signboards. They passed through an area thick with cinemas, theatres, and restaurants, and eventually came to the Kuramae subway station. Almost beside it was a sign for the Kuramae-Kokugikan Sumo Hall, of which all that was visible was a long stretch of white wall and a vast, pyramid-shaped roof.

'Is this it?'

It was not. They crossed a bridge over the Sumida River into a district signposted as Ryoguku. The *heya*, a building of much older design than the Sumo Hall, proved to be only a three-minute drive away.

The driver kindly left his cab and showed Diamond the door to use. He offered a five-dollar tip – not possessing any yen – but it was refused. This was certainly another civilization.

A bunch of teenage girls, evidently groupies – or whatever they called them in the sumo jargon – stood near the entrance and regarded him speculatively, but with reserve. He was big enough to join the ranks, but other factors ruled him out. The place he entered had a table just inside the door manned by a young fellow in a striped kimono with the oiled black topknot.

Diamond bowed self-consciously and said, 'Visiting Mr Yamagata.'

'You are?'

'Peter Diamond.'

'You wait, please.' He picked up a phone.

There was nowhere to sit, so he interested himself in a poster for a forthcoming *basho*, trying to decide whether the exorbitant rear of the figure in the foreground belonged to his patron.

The place was extremely clean, with strips of wood horizontally around the walls, not unlike the reception area of an upmarket health club. He looked down and noticed a rip in his bulging carrier bag; he wasn't adding much to the ambience.

Another hefty young lad in a kimono appeared from a door and approached Diamond. They exchanged the obligatory bow and he said in good English, 'Welcome to our stable, Mr Diamond. I am Nodo. I have the honour to escort you to Yamagata-Zeki.'

Nodo's thong-sandals scraped the wooden floor as he led Diamond through a place where wrestling practice was in progress in a rope-edged ring with a clay floor on which sand had been shovelled. Observed by a dozen wrestlers, two masses of living flesh shaped up to each other, encouraged by a silver-haired trainer with a bamboo stick that he wasn't hesitating to use on the exposed rumps. Nobody turned to look at the Occidental dressed in a suit who was being escorted past.

'These are lesser ranks,' Nodo explained with lordly confidence that none of the lesser ranks spoke English.

At the far end, on a shelf above a radiator, was a kind of altar-piece with candlesticks. Nodo clapped and bowed his head briefly as they passed it. Before opening the door, he confided, 'Shinto shrine. We call it *kamidana*.'

'Ah,' responded Diamond, doing his best to sound enlightened.

'Now you will meet the Yamagata-Zeki. He is printing the *tegata*. You will see.'

They entered another large room where Diamond immediately recognised his famous patron. If it were possible, Mr Yamagata looked mightier than he had in London, barrel-chested, with his broad face resting in folds of flesh indistinguishable as chin or neck. He was seated cross-legged between two acolytes. In front of him was a stack of large blank cards and he was making palm-prints by pressing his hand repeatedly onto a red ink-pad and then banging it down onto the stack, from which each print was adroitly removed by the man to his left. The great wrestler made eye-contact briefly and dipped his head in a perfunctory bow which Diamond returned. Some Japanese was spoken.

Nodo explained that Yamagata-Zeki had many fans and sponsors, who liked to receive *tegata*, or hand-prints, as personal souvenirs. They sent the cards to the *heya* with a small cash donation, and the *rikishi* obliged by printing up to a thousand in batches. With Diamond's indulgence, the printing would continue while they talked.

Nodo added, 'He invites you to be seated.'

Chairs aren't provided in sumo stables; they wouldn't last long if they were. Diamond wasn't equal to the cross-legged position, but he showed willing by lowering himself to the floor and sitting in front of Yamagata with his knees bent. Up to this minute he'd felt like a detached observer, but the feeling wasn't going to survive the pressure of the floorboards against his backside. He was now emphatically part of the scene.

The rhythmic thump of the palm-printing distracted him at first, but with perseverance and the help of Nodo he succeeded in bringing Yamagata up to date on the hunt for Naomi. He was thorough, treating it as the sort of briefing he would have given to the murder squad in the old days.

Another burst of Japanese was uttered without interruption to the printing.

Nodo translated, 'He says you should go to Yokohama as soon as possible. This is where the answers to these mysteries will be found.'

'I agree,' said Diamond, privately thinking that he hadn't needed to come here to be told that. 'How do I get there?'

'Better by train than taxi at this time of day.'

'The Bullet?' he asked, airing his fragmentary knowledge of Japanese life.

'No. The Yokosuka line is faster. I am to call a taxi to take you to the Central Station. Do you need money?'

He was answering when one of the apprentice wrestlers came in with a portable phone and handed it to Yamagata. Without hesitating, the wrestler grasped it with his inky right hand. Apparently a call was on the line. He listened, grunted some response, and handed a red-smeared instrument back to the unfortunate who had brought it in. Then he spoke to his helpers. It seemed that the printing session was over, because the blank cards were hastily taken aside. With a rocking motion, Yamagata prepared to get up. He pressed his clean hand against the floor, leaned on it and rose. Then he spoke to Nodo.

When translated, the news was ominous. 'That was a call from Immigration at Narita Airport. The officer who saw you has been checking to see if anyone has a recollection of the small girl and the American passing through yesterday. It seems they were noticed, and they were not alone. Two other Americans travelled with them, male, in their twenties, six foot plus, names Lanzi and Frizzoni.'

'I get the picture,' said Diamond gravely. 'He's got minders.'

'They were under surveillance by Customs and their luggage was inspected, but they were clean.'

'They can get guns here. They'll have contacts. I thought at one stage he was acting independently, but I was naive. The stakes are too big. This is bad.'

'Yamagata-Zeki agrees with you. He is going with you to Yokohama.'

This was hard to credit. 'He's planning to come with me?'

'He says you can't handle this alone.'

Diamond gave a low whistle as he tried to imagine it. 'I'm grateful, but doesn't he think he's rather conspicuous? I mean well-known,' he corrected himself.

'I don't think it would be wise to question his decision,' said Nodo.

'Are you coming too?'

'Oh, no.'

'Why not? We need a translator.'

'It isn't necessary. You are in Japan.'

Events moved on with the positiveness of a *basho*. In a matter of minutes, Yamagata, dressed only in a bright-patterned kimono and flip-flop sandals, was squeezing into the back of a taxi. There was no question of Diamond's sharing the seat, so he travelled with the driver. At intervals along the route to the station, whenever the taxi was forced to slow for lights, people reacted with double-takes to the sight of the passenger in the back. Whatever the benefits of having a famous sumo in support, secrecy could be forgotten.

The problem was worse at the station. A crowd gathered almost immediately and stayed with them all the way from the ticket booths to the train. Yamagata accepted the attention as his lot in life. He wore a frown that seemed calculated to keep people from actually asking for autographs or striking up a conversation. They chatted excitedly among themselves, but they didn't trouble him, apart from staring and generally obstructing the view. When he moved, no one was unwise enough to stand in the way for long.

The up-side of travel with a sumo hero was that seats were instantly offered on a crowded train, a double for each of them. Once settled, Yamagata closed his eyes as if to shut out the attention. Someone spoke something in Japanese to Diamond, so he followed Yamagata's example. There was no risk of falling asleep because the announcements over the public address system came every few moments with a staccato ferocity that would have woken the dead.

In thirty minutes they reached Yokohama station and changed trains. Yamagata led the way, still oblivious of all the attention he was getting. It was fast becoming apparent to Diamond that he would never have fathomed the intricacies of the railway system without help.

Two stations along, they got out again and went for a taxi. Other people were waiting for cabs, but the front of the queue melted away when Yamagata arrived with his entourage of the starstruck and the starers.

They climbed into the first one on the rank and Yamagata gave the driver his instruction.

Next stop, the University, unless I've been totally misled, thought Diamond.

31

Yokohama University was little different from Tokyo Central Station in the way people reacted to having a sumo celebrity among them. The administrative staff flocked into the reception hall to stare at the illustrious guest, who conducted himself in the same imperious manner, staring into the mid-distance as if to show disdain for an opponent. At the desk, however, he became animated and explained the purpose of the visit in fast, forceful Japanese. Confused and overcome, the young woman on duty didn't appear to take in what he was saying, so he repeated it. There was an embarrassing hiatus until one of the staff, a demure, blushing girl with wide, intelligent eyes and a tiny mouth exquisitely defined in brilliant lipstick, took Diamond aside and asked if he was American.

'English. Is there a problem?'

'We are not accustomed to visits from *sumotori*.'

'I can understand.'

'Of course we are honoured. We wish we could have made preparations, arranged a proper tour.'

'We don't want a tour, thanks. We just want to speak to someone in the Biochemistry Department – a research scientist. It's very urgent.'

'He said something about a missing child.'

'That's right. We want to speak to the mother, Dr Yuko

Masuda. Could you find out whether she's on the campus today?'

'I'll ask them.'

She came back without an answer, but with an instruction: 'Please, they say you should proceed to the science building and go to the Department of Biochemistry.'

'What's your name?'

She looked slightly dismayed to have been asked. 'Miss Yamamoto.'

Diamond tried repeating it exactly as she had spoken. He wasn't being familiar just because she was pretty. 'Can you come with us and translate for me?' She lowered her head decorously. 'That would be an honour, sir.'

'Excellent. And one more thing.'

'Yes?'

'It would not be wise to let Dr Masuda know who her visitors are. We don't want to alarm her.'

'I shall tell them.'

They were escorted through a labyrinth of cloisters to the science blocks, modern pre-cast structures several stories high. The news had travelled. Faces were at most of the windows and there was a gathering of interested students at the entrance, some taking photographs and some ready with pens and paper, but no one went so far as to ask for an autograph. Yamagata's look wasn't inviting.

Biochemistry was on the second floor. Diamond had doubts about sharing the elevator with so much poundage, but their guide didn't hesitate and the machinery survived the test.

As the doors parted, a silver-haired man in a white lab-coat stepped forward and greeted them in the traditional Japanese manner.

'This is Dr Hitomi, principal lecturer in postgraduate studies,' the indispensable Miss Yamamoto explained.

They were taken to the departmental office and offered seats. Yamagata looked dubiously at the plastic chair that was expected to support him and shook his head, so Diamond tactfully remained standing also. Anyway, he expected to meet Dr Masuda shortly, which would mean hoisting himself upright again.

A crushing disappointment followed. It emerged that Naomi's mother was not based at this campus after all. She had last worked here some seven years ago, researching into a drug for the treatment of comas.

'Jantac?' said Diamond when this had been translated.

Dr Hitomi nodded.

'But we heard that she is still carrying out research here, with a grant from Manflex Pharmaceuticals,' Diamond said.

This created some uncertainty.

'He repeats that Dr Masuda is not working here,' Miss Yamamoto told him. 'Her research here terminated in 1985.'

'Terminated? Definitely terminated?'

'Definitely.'

Dr Hitomi spoke some more.

'He says he knew Dr Masuda personally. She was a good scientist. Her work came to an end when Manflex took a decision to stop further experimentation with Jantac.'

'Why? Why was it stopped?'

When this was put to Dr Hitomi, he shrugged before giving his answer.

'He says Dr Masuda had worked with Jantac for more than two years and was getting good results in reversing coma symptoms, but about this time she detected side-effects from the drug.'

'Side-effects?' Diamond's antennae were out.

Dr Hitomi had taken a Japanese/English dictionary from the shelf behind him. He pointed out a word.

'Cirrhosis?' said Diamond. 'Liver disease?' His brain darted through the implications.

After another explanation, Miss Yamamoto translated, 'The side-effect of this drug was difficult to detect, because the coma patients were alcoholic and alcoholism is a major cause of what is that word?'

'Cirrhosis.'

'He says alcoholism causes cirrhosis anyway. However, Dr Masuda discovered that Jantac also caused an increase in liver enzymes, producing cirrhosis. A small side-effect is acceptable, but this was too much. When she reported her findings to Manflex, they terminated the programme.'

Dr Hitomi added something.

'He says Mr Manny Flexner, is that correct?'

'Manny Flexner, yes.'

'Manny Flexner himself took the decision to stop working with Jantac. Mr Flexner always put the safety of patients first.'

Diamond gave a nod while he wrestled with the implications. What he had just heard conflicted with the computer records he'd seen at Manflex headquarters in New York, yet confirmed and expanded on the information he'd seen on the record card in the basement. Jantac had proved to be a dangerous drug and as a result Yuko Masuda's research had been axed.

'Would you ask Dr Hitomi if the department has copies of any correspondence dealing with this matter?'

This, it seemed, was doubtful. Dr Hitomi picked up a phone.

It emerged that the correspondence had been returned to Manflex some months ago at their request.

Suspicious.

'This year?'

'Yes.'

Someone in New York had gone to unusual lengths in covering tracks. Diamond sighed and folded his arms. It was a strange situation, being surrounded by a group of people so willing to help and watching him intently, but without understanding the problem. It was down to him, and he was far from certain what to suggest next.

'Does the University possess copies of the papers Dr Masuda published?'

Almost certainly they did, in the library.

'In English as well as Japanese?'

It was likely.

The entire circus struck tents and removed to the library, where the by now predictable excitement and confusion prevented anything useful happening for several minutes. At length, Diamond was presented with a copy in English of Yuko Masuda's research paper on the treatment of alcoholic coma presented to the Japanese Pharmacological Conference in Tokyo in 1983. He sat down to see what he could discover in it, while everyone waited.

Inwardly he groaned. The text was way beyond his comprehension. He stared at the first page for some time before turning to see how many pages like this there were. Thirteen.

Then his attention focused on a paragraph towards the end of the last page:

The research continues. Present studies are concentrated on a compound patented by Manflex Pharmaceuticals and given the proprietary name Jantac, and early results are encouraging.

He looked for the footnote and found that it gave a chemical formula.

Ideas rarely come as inspirations. More usually they develop in levels of the brain just above the subconscious, over hours, days or years, and most of them never come to anything. He had kept a vague idea on hold ever since he had stood in the basement of the Manflex building with Molly Docherty and looked at Yuko Masuda's record card.

'May I use a phone? I want to call New York.'

They took him into the chief librarian's office. Fortunately he could remember the number he wanted.

'Police,' said a weary American voice.

'Is that the 26th Precinct? Lieutenant Eastland, please.'

'Who is this?'

'Peter Diamond. Superintendent Diamond, speaking from Yokohama.'

'Lieutenant Eastland isn't here just now, sir.'

'In that case, would you give me his home number. It's extremely urgent.'

'We can't disturb him right now, sir. Do you know what time it is here?'

Diamond erupted. He didn't care what the sodding time was in New York. A child's life was at stake and he needed to speak to Eastland right now.

She took the number and promised that she would ensure that the lieutenant called right back within the next few minutes.

The promise was kept.

The familiar voice, husky with sleep, protested angrily, 'Diamond? For Chrissake—'

'Listen. That conference at the Sheraton. Are you with me?'

'Yeah,' said Eastland, already capitulating. He *must* have been tired.

'Do you still have the literature?'

'Literature?'

'The press pack. The stuff about PDM3.'

'I don't know. I could have slung it out. It may be downstairs. Do you want me to look?'

'Oh, come on. Would I be phoning you?'

'Hold the line. I'll be right back.'

Through the door he could just see Yamagata doing an exercise that involved propping his left leg on a bookshelf. It looked liable to cause a disaster.

'Peter, you there?'

'Of course. Have you got it?'

'Yeah.'

'Good. Now, turn to the first page of that blue leaflet, the one that introduces PDM3. Somewhere, there's a chemical formula. Know what I mean?'

'Hold on. . . . Okay. You want me to read it out?'

'No, let me try. Listen carefully. Check every figure, would you? C_{18}.'

'Correct.'

'$H13$.'

'Check.'

Diamond's pulse beat more strongly. He was reading out the formula for Jantac. 'NO_3.'

'Yeah.'

It *had* to be the same now. His voice breaking up with tension, he completed the formula. It was precisely the same. Jantac, the drug dumped by Manny Flexner in 1985, had been resurrected as Prodermolate – the miraculous PDM3.

'Is that all you wanted?' said Eastland in a less than cordial tone.

'That's all I wanted – unless you can give me the form on a couple of hatchet men called Lanzi and Frizzoni.'

'Never heard of them. Can I go back to bed now?'

Diamond thanked him and put down the phone. He

gestured to Yamagata to come into the office and the big fellow thoughtfully grasped Miss Yamamoto's wrist and brought her in as well. Blushing as only a Japanese girl can, but not displeased – for his grip was gentle – she remained standing beside him when he released her.

It was vital that Yamagata understood the significance of this discovery. Others, including Dr Hitomi and a couple of librarians, had followed him in, but Diamond couched his explanation in terms meant for the wrestler. 'Do you see what I'm driving at?' he said when he'd given the gist of the phone call. 'Jantac was discredited here. It's dangerous, and shouldn't have been used again. We now know that another team of researchers, headed by Professor Churchward, worked independently with the same compound and came up with sensational results in the treatment of Alzheimer's disease. I'm not going to speculate whether Churchward knew that he was working with a dangerous drug, but someone at Manflex headquarters certainly knew, which is why all mention of Jantac was erased from Yuko Masuda's computer record.' He waited for this to be translated, and he had to repeat it more slowly. In his eagerness he'd strung too many sentences together. Also he suspected that Miss Yamamoto was distracted by Yamagata.

Yamagata said recognisably, 'Leapman.'

'Yes, it had to be Leapman. All his actions confirm that he's responsible. And something else was altered on the computer. Dr Masuda's project was stopped in 1985, but the computer record was falsified to make it appear that her research continues. Some other group of drugs is mentioned, but that's just a smoke-screen. On second thoughts,' he said quickly, 'don't try translating that last bit.'

After Miss Yamamoto had filled in, Diamond resumed, 'It isn't just a matter of falsifying the records. Leapman is in deep with organized criminals, who are set to make big profits out of PDM3. Manflex was on the slide at the beginning of this year.' He mimed the downward slope of a sales graph. 'Before Manny Flexner committed suicide, there was a big fire at one of their plants in Europe. Milan. Manflex dropped even lower on the stock markets. There's a police investigation still going on into a possible arson attack. To me, that suggests this plot was being hatched many months ago.'

He paused for the translation. Yamagata nodded gravely. He seemed to be following what was said.

'If they're capable of doing that, they're capable of murdering Yuko Masuda, who could have exposed them. I can't say for certain yet, but I very much fear that she is dead. I believe her little daughter – the child I know as Naomi – was given to Mrs Tanaka, a woman desperate to adopt. Maybe they drew the line at killing a child. Mrs Tanaka was ordered to get the child out of Japan, to Europe. She was horrified to discover that Naomi was autistic. She couldn't cope and she abandoned her. I'm sorry, I'm not giving you a chance,' he admitted to Miss Yamamoto.

'It's all right,' she said launching into a translation directly, looking up earnestly at the wrestler.

'As you know,' Diamond picked up his thread again, 'in England we did all we could to publicize Naomi's plight. After I went on television, Mrs Tanaka panicked and snatched Naomi back. She was in trouble now. She couldn't possibly stay in Britain, so she phoned her contact for orders. They told her to fly to New York, and she obeyed, a fatal move, if only she'd realised. Obviously the people behind this scam had decided Mrs Tanaka was unreliable and dispensable, and they hired a man to meet her and murder her.'

He stopped. He'd told most of it now. It all hung together so well. And yet . . .

Yamagata listened to the Japanese version and then spoke a few words that, translated into English, pinpointed the problem. 'If Dr Masuda is dead, why has Leapman come to Japan with Naomi and two American strongmen?'

Diamond was about to admit he was stunned for an explanation when someone interrupted in Japanese. It was Dr Hitomi, speaking in the modulated tone he had used before.

Modulated it may have been, yet it brought a swift, excited response from Yamagata.

The translation followed for Diamond's benefit. 'Dr Hitomi says he thinks you are mistaken in saying Dr Masuda is dead. He saw her here on the campus only last week.'

He made an effort to stay calm. 'Is he certain? When the police checked her last address, she was missing.'

Now one of the librarians chimed in, using imperfect, but perfectly comprehensible English. 'Is true. She alive. She sometimes use library. If you like I show you her name on computer.'

'No need,' said Diamond. 'I believe you, both of you.' He loosened his lips and blew out, making them vibrate. It eased his tension, somehow. 'And now we know the answer to Mr Yamagata's question. Leapman and his friends are in Japan to do the job properly this time and silence Dr Masuda for good.'

'With a child?' Miss Yamamoto said spontaneously.

'They'll use the child as bait. The point is, have they found her mother already?'

When this had been turned into Japanese, Yamagata spoke.

'He says the real point is, where to look for Dr Masuda.'

He was right. They did the obvious thing first, and checked the library records for an address. It proved to be the same place that Diamond had been informed by the Yokohama police was now let to someone else. A phone call confirmed this.

'So where in the whole of Japan do we turn now?' he said aloud, but speaking more to himself than anyone present, so that he was caught by surprise when Miss Yamamoto translated.

This time, no one had an answer.

And this was the nadir, the most depressing moment of the entire quest. To have come this far and be thwarted was hard enough, but to know for sure that every minute of inaction made it more likely that Naomi and her mother would die – that was intolerable.

He asked them to call the police. He was told that they had been notified hours before, apparently by the zealous young man in Immigration.

'Then we'll call and ask if they have any information yet.'

A call was made and the police had nothing to impart. Not even a sighting of the Americans.

Someone suggested coffee. Diamond wasn't interested.

'What else do they have on that library computer?' he asked Miss Yamamoto.

Only the titles of the books borrowed.

'What are they?' he asked, more to give an illusion of activity than anything else.

Yuko Masuda had one book out. On comas.

He wondered.

'Is there a hospital in this city, or in Tokyo, that specializes in treating alcoholics?'

Three.

'Would you phone each of them and ask whether Dr Masuda carries out research there?'

The second hospital they called said Dr Masuda was a regular visitor.

32

Diamond had been told that the hospital was south of the city, in the foreigners' quarter, Yamate-Machi, known as the Bluff. For about a mile the taxi-driver took a route along the north bank of the River Nakamura. He drove fast, with the horn blaring most of the time, on orders from Yamagata, who kept urging him to overtake more vehicles; you didn't need Japanese to understand. And there was no complaining from the driver. He was obviously a sumo worshipper having the trip of a lifetime. If he lived to tell the tale, he'd be the envy of every taxi-driver in Yokohama.

In the front passenger-seat, Diamond ground his teeth and braced himself for a collision. This kind of travelling, he reflected grimly, shouldn't be inflicted on the middle-aged. It was a bit much when the quickest you normally experienced was a bus up Kensington High Street. But he still hoped to God that he would get to Yuko Masuda before Leapman and his two gorillas.

They screeched right, the mudflaps rasping on the road, forced lower by the weight on the rear seat. They crossed a bridge, zigzagged along a busy stretch beside Ishikawacho Railway Station, and then onto the access road for a stretch of expressway. God help us, Diamond said to himself, he can really put his foot down now. But the taxi was close to its optimum speed anyway. They fast-laned under a tunnel and all the way to the next exit which took them into the Yamate-Machi area. Not a moment too soon, the hospital came up on the left, dominated by four high-rise blocks, a huge, modern site with its own system of roadways.

Yamagata had his door open well before they braked outside the main reception hall. Gesturing to Diamond to remain in the cab, he moved inside at impressive speed for a big man. It would have been interesting to see the reactions inside. When a *sumotori* charged in and demanded to know the way to the coma unit, you'd assume that he'd been rough with someone.

Yamagata emerged, running, shouting directions, and clambered in, causing the whole vehicle to rock, and they powered off again. The speed was even more reckless in hospital grounds with limit signs at every turn, but the driver wasn't slowing for ambulances, food trolleys or zimmer-frames; he could steer, couldn't he?

They rounded the out-patient block, swerving to avoid an unconscious patient being wheeled between two buildings, and raced through a narrow space between parked cars. Ahead was the building they wanted, if Yamagata's frenetic instructions meant anything. It was a one-storey, flat-roofed wooden structure that looked like an afterthought. The taxi screeched to a halt and the passengers leapt out and shoved open the door.

They were in a short corridor with doors along one side. A woman was walking towards them.

At this critical stage of the operation, with timing that can only be described as inopportune, Diamond had a deeply disturbing thought. He hadn't the faintest idea what Yuko Masuda looked like. If this woman were she, he wouldn't know. Nor, come to that, had he ever laid eyes on Michael Leapman.

He was looking for total strangers.

He told Yamagata, 'We need help,' and the big man seemed to understand because he spoke to the woman. When the name Masuda was mentioned, she didn't react as if it were her own. She came back with a question of her own that Yamagata answered. Then she pointed to a door just behind them.

Diamond opened it and walked into a ward about forty metres long, with five bays separated by glass-walled partitions. In the nearest they could see a patient surrounded by the apparatus necessary to monitor and sustain life in the unconscious state. Most of one wall was covered with photos and cards and there was a mobile of cardboard goldfish suspended above the bed. A nurse wearing a face-mask was attending to the drip-feed. She turned, her eyes widening in amazement.

Yamagata spoke.

The nurse pointed to the bay at the far end, nearest the window, and Diamond's heart-beat stepped up.

A small Japanese woman in a white coat was in conversation with two Caucasian men. They didn't have the look of hospital staff. One was tall and blond, wearing a dark, expensive-looking suit, white shirt and club tie and the other had reddish-brown hair with a flat-topped cut that might have been made with one sweep of a scythe. This second man was marginally shorter, but very large in the chest and shoulders, and was dressed more casually, in a suede jacket and black denims. Presumably he was one of the heavies seen arriving at the airport. If so, it was a fair bet that the blond man was Michael Leapman. Intent in their discussion, they hadn't yet noticed that anyone had come in.

Diamond approached to within a few yards without catching their attention.

'Mr Leapman?'

Both men wheeled around.

'Hold it! Who are you?' the blond man asked in an American accent.

'Someone you people thought you'd disposed of,' Diamond answered.

'You're that English cop.'

Confirmation, if it was required, that this had to be Michael Leapman. 'Drop it.'

The heavy had just whipped out a knife.

'You're joking.'

Diamond wanted no violence. But if necessary, he backed Yamagata – even against a hitman armed with a dagger. He beckoned to the woman with his right hand, inviting her to step away from the two Americans. 'Dr Masuda.'

Her face crinkled as if in pain and she pinched her lips together, but she made no move other than to shake her head and draw her arms across her chest.

Leapman said with confidence, 'We're walking right out of here with Dr Masuda and you can do shit-all about it. Let's move, Dino.'

Dr Masuda seemed petrified. She could have stepped away from them. It wasn't as if the knife was at her throat. She turned her head and glanced behind her.

There was a slight movement to Diamond's left and he saw that Yamagata had hunched into the position the *sumotori* adopt immediately before the charge. Then Dr Masuda cried something in Japanese.

Leapman said, 'Hey, tell blubbergut to take it easy, will you? This little lady has made up her mind.'

Whatever it was that Dr Masuda had just said, it appeared

to confirm Leapman's last statement, because Yamagata suddenly straightened and gripped Diamond's arm to restrain him.

A sumo champion backing down? It was difficult to credit.

Leapman gave the grin of a man who had won without so much as a scuffle. 'I won't say it's been good to meet you, gentlemen. Have a nice day, just the same.' He gestured to Dr Masuda to walk ahead and she obeyed. 'See what I mean?' He started to follow. The minder went, too, walking backwards to cover their exit, the knife held threateningly.

Yamagata's grip on Diamond's arm tightened. He would not allow Diamond to go in pursuit.

When they were out of arm's range, the reason why Masuda had gone so compliantly was made clear. Yamagata steered Diamond to the windows and pointed to where a figure was standing beside a red saloon car. Two figures, in fact. On first sight they had merged as one, for a man was holding a small Japanese child directly in front of him. She looked pale and passive, her hands limp at her sides, in spite of the cord around her throat.

It was Naomi.

Having anguished over her fate for so many days, having put so much into the search, this was a nightmare.

To do nothing now – while she was there in view, under threat of murder – would be unforgivable.

Leapman had reached the door. He told Diamond, 'She's coming with us because she wants her kid back. She hasn't seen her in months.'

'You'll kill them both.'

'Maybe, but she doesn't know that. She can't understand one word we say. And just in case you were thinking of following, I'm asking Dino to guard the door while we get clear.'

Dr Masuda had already gone through and Leapman followed. The henchman waited just inside, guarding the only exit with the knife held ready.

Although his heart was sick, Diamond knew in his head that Yamagata was right. To have made a move now would certainly have put Naomi at risk. It wouldn't require much for the thug out there to strangle her. Very likely he'd been hired to kill mother and child anyway. One unexpected move might precipitate the deed. But it must have required astonishing self-restraint on Yamagata's part to hold back when all his training, all his pride, was based on the the concept of the fight.

Even at this stage, he continued to hold Diamond's right arm in the iron grip.

'They're getting away, for God's sake!' The scene unfolding on the other side of the glass appeared as remote as television. In fact, the windows were about the size of portable TVs, much too narrow to have climbed through.

'Will you let go of me?' Diamond demanded.

Now he could see Yuko Masuda running towards her child, her hands oustretched.

The henchman released Naomi, probably on orders from Leapman, who was following closely. The child stood still, unaffected, and then was gathered into her mother's embrace.

'It's too bloody late now!'

Leapman had the car door open and bundled mother and child into the back seat and got in beside them. The other man got into the driver's seat.

Only at this point did Yamagata release Diamond, by now rigid with anger and frustration. 'Too bloody late!' he shouted.

Yamagata plainly didn't agree. Timing is fundamental to

sumo wrestling and for him the fight wasn't over yet. The huge man moved at astonishing speed before Diamond had even got the last words out. He went straight to the bed in the end bay. It was a good thing it was unoccupied, because Yamagata tucked his hands underneath, tipped it over, grabbed the underside and lifted the entire thing as if it were polystyrene. In the same forward movement he charged at the window frame and crushed the bed against it with tremendous force. Such was the impact that the entire casement and a section of wall collapsed at the first contact, leaving a gap framed by splintered wood and plaster. The rage, the humiliation of the last few minutes was being expelled in one eruption of action.

Yamagata almost fell across the bed when it landed upside down in a flower-border outside, but he just succeeded in stayng upright and clambering over it. His kimono was half off one shoulder, so he ripped it from his body without shifting his gaze from the focus of his anger.

The car was moving off, but it would have to pass Yamagata on the narrow road.

He stooped, legs astride, rubbing his hands, preparing to meet the car as if it were a rival in the wrestling ring. He actually indulged in some intimidatory action. He placed his left hand across his heart, stretched out his right, raised his right leg high in the *shiko* movement and slammed it down on the road.

There wasn't time to complete the ritual. The car was coming at him. Hunkering low again, he waited for the crunch. There was no question of giving way to two tons of automobile. Much more than his self-esteem was at stake.

With exquisite timing, he launched himself straight at the car at the moment it would have smashed into his legs. His huge body was visible rising over the bonnet in a movement that looked like a dive at the windscreen. The effect was made more spectacular by the car's acceleration, because all he needed to do was dip his torso and jump as the bonnet moved underneath him. His head shattered the windscreen and hit the driver with tremendous impact. The car veered off the road and smashed against a speed limit sign.

Peter Diamond was standing in a dust-cloud of plaster, mesmerised by what he had just witnessed. Whether Yamagata had survived, he couldn't tell. The wrestler's head and torso were entirely inside the car and the rest of him lay on the bonnet, ominously still.

Diamond shook himself out of the trancelike state and was preparing to clamber over the rubble to give help when there was a warning shout from behind, more of a scream than anything intelligible. Just in time he glanced behind and saw Leapman's other henchman charging towards him with the knife raised to strike.

Diamond was no sumo wrestler. Nor was he particularly fit. His right arm still ached from the beating he'd had in New York. But he still had quick reactions and his police training had given him some elementary judo. Until now he'd never been required to use the shoulder throw in a real fight. It was quite a contortion to twist sufficiently to grab the man's right sleeve and left lapel without being stabbed, but he succeeded. He bent his knees to get under his attacker's centre of gravity, and gave a terrific tug. The man somersaulted over his back and thumped the ground heavily. Not bad for an amateur. Diamond grabbed the knife, but there was no need because the man was out cold.

The shout must have come from the nurse they'd seen attending to one of the coma patients. Now she was running straight past Diamond to the car. He followed.

One of the rear doors opened and Leapman climbed out, scattering fragments of broken windscreen from his clothes. Seeing the knife in Diamond's hand, he raised his arms. He was not the sort to fight for himself. Diamond ordered him to lie face down on the verge.

Naomi got out next, making a whimpering sound, in some distress, but not visibly injured. Her mother followed and held her.

Yamagata's body was lacerated extensively, but to Diamond's immense relief, he began to move. He must have been stunned for a while, and no wonder. Slowly but without assistance he withdrew his bleeding torso from the front of the car. Astride the heavily dented bonnet he sat tidying his hair.

The nurse had been examining the man in the driver's seat, feeling for a pulse. Presently she stood back and shook her head. From the look of him, his neck must have been broken. He'd taken the full impact of Yamagata's head.

Hospital staff rapidly appeared from all sides, some just to watch or take pictures – for a Japanese is never far from his camera – and others ready to help.

Diamond stooped and picked up one of Yamagata's flip-flop sandals, or *bedi*, lost or discarded in the action. He looked for the other and found it. A doctor who spoke English made himself known to Diamond and arranged for the security staff to take charge of Leapman and the surviving henchman, who was regaining consciousness. The police were called.

The sightseers surrounded Yamagata until a nurse persuaded him to remove himself from the car bonnet and go for treatment. He was extensively marked, but the cuts were superficial. In a few days there would be no scars. Diamond eased a path through the admirers and handed the flip-flops to their owner. He would have liked to apologise for the way he'd ranted and tried to break free. Instead, he bowed. They both bowed. Then Yamagata made a generous gesture. First, he pointed to the henchman being helped to his feet by a security man and then he tapped Diamond's chest with his forefinger, nodding at the same time as if to express approval. He bowed again and with a sense of ceremony returned the flip-flops to Diamond. Words weren't required. There was actually a scattering of applause. Diamond was glad he didn't have to speak because he couldn't have trusted his voice at that moment.

Yamagata looked around. Something still troubled him. He spotted Dr Masuda standing a short way off, holding Naomi by the hand. He strode across to them, exchanged a bow and a few words and then stooped and lifted the little girl into his arms.

She looked comfortable. Even contented.

The cameras clicked.

33

'Look at these! Jesus, what do they think I'm going to do?' The handcuffs on Michael Leapman really weren't necessary, but as the Yokohama police had insisted on this formality when they allowed Diamond to interview him, it was respected. They sat facing each other in leather armchairs in an office belonging to the senior detective, who observed from behind his desk with an interpreter beside him.

Diamond waited indifferently. He was confident that the protest would pass. If he'd ever seen a man who was ready to talk, it was Leapman, desperately wanting to justify his actions to somebody.

And the switch to sweet reasonableness was not long in coming. 'You know, in a way I'm relieved. I wasn't in control of my life any more. Mind if I tell it my way?'

A nod from Diamond and he was away.

'I can scarcely believe what an idiot I've been. Less than a year ago, I had things pretty well sorted. I was Vice Chairman, on a good salary in a prosperous company, although I have to say I could see the clouds gathering. Manny – the Chairman – wouldn't admit that we were slipping back in the pharmaceuticals league. He was a great personality, a real nice guy, a terrific manager in his time, but frankly he wasn't in tune with modern business. It's a shark pool now and Manny shouldn't have been there any more. I know the drugs industry. I was ambitious for his job and I expected to get it soon.'

'Through a boardroom coup?'

'Right. I had a surefire plan to reverse the slide, but I knew he wouldn't back it. Unknown to Manny, I'd already given the green light to certain research projects that he wasn't even aware of. Nothing unethical, just things that I considered Manflex should support to stay competitive. I diverted some funds quite legitimately from other projects we were phasing out and when the accounting got a little complex I actually injected some cash from my own pocket. It was an investment, the way I saw it. There was this project in Indianapolis with terrific potential.'

'Churchward's?'

Leapman nodded. 'Every drugs company in the business was looking for a breakthrough with Alzheimer's. Alaric Churchward was getting some sensational test results with PDM3. I was damned sure we had an all-time winner, and I was aiming to torpedo Manny with it. I knew he wouldn't back it without all kinds of guarantees we weren't ready to supply. The Board were unhappy with Manny and I expected to make my bid for Chairman any time. When I became boss I could give the drug my backing and turn Manflex into a top company again.'

'You had support on the Board?'

'For sure. But they didn't know about PDM3 yet. That was the ace up my sleeve. I told nobody.'

'You told the mafia.'

'I needed money to fund the project. More money than I possessed.'

'But from the mafia?'

Leapman's cuffed hands moved apart in a parody of a

man gesturing that he'd acted in good faith. 'At the beginning I didn't know they were the mob. They crept up on me. I wanted large injections of cash without questions being asked and I approached one guy I knew from way back, who promised to talk to a venture capital person, and so on. One day a wad of money arrived. I didn't know it was mafia money until they followed up. Then I found myself talking to Massimo Gatti, who everyone knows is a mafioso.'

'Yet you didn't back out at that stage?'

He glared at Diamond. 'You should try backing out on a man like Gatti.'

'So you were in his pocket.'

'They saw ways of making big bucks on the stock market. It was crazy. They set fire to one of the Manflex plants in Italy. Reduced it to ashes. You know why? To depress the market price so they could buy in on favourable terms. I wasn't a party to that, believe me. I only heard about it later. That was when I realised I was way out of my depth.'

'Did you know at the time that PDM3 was dangerous?'

'At the time I borrowed the money? Christ, no. What kind of monster do you think I am?'

'You trusted Professor Churchward?'

'Sure. He's a great scientist. Believe me, he wasn't part of this mess. Okay, he knew there were some ADRs – adverse drug reactions – but he believed they could be kept to a minimum with the right dosage.'

'When did you find out the truth?'

'About Jantac? Six or seven months back. By that time, there was no going back.'

'How did it come to light?'

'Alaric called me one afternoon with some technical query. He said he was aware that a number of preliminary studies had been started with the compound and not proceeded with. That's quite usual. Testing new drugs for biological activity can be a long and frustrating process and on top of that you're sure to have plenty of failures trying to discover if they have any medical potential. He wanted to know if there was anything still on file. I promised to run a computer check. I keyed in the chemical formula—'

'And found the file on Jantac?'

Leapman remembered and winced. 'It was a real kick in the guts. The crucial decisions were taken back in 1985, a couple of years before I joined the company. Dr Masuda had done two years of testing here in Japan in her research into alcoholic comas, using the same compound as PDM3 under the proprietary name of Jantac. I learned that Manny had personally axed the research after Dr Masuda detected liver damage that was caused by Jantac. The name Jantac was deleted from our list of drugs under research. I was deeply shocked when I learned this. By this time I'd staked my career and my personal savings in the same lousy drug.'

'Didn't you inform Churchward?'

'No.' Leapman shook his head, and it was an expression of regret. 'I faxed him some of the other studies I found, but I kept quiet about this Jantac bombshell. I hoped it might not be the serious problem it first appeared to be. Sometimes Manny Flexner was too cautious for his own good. He took no risks whatsoever with drugs. Every drug has ADRs, and I argued to myself that alcoholism causes liver damage anyway, so maybe those Japanese results wouldn't show up to the same degree in patients who drank in moderation. Alaric Churchward's brilliant work on Alzheimer's didn't have to be jettisoned just because Manny was so ultra-careful.'

'All right, you rationalised,' said Diamond, becoming

impatient. 'What did you do about it? Altered the records, for a start.'

'That was no problem. I could do that sitting in my office, and I did.'

Diamond refrained from pointing out that he should also have gone down to the basement where the old file cards were kept.

'Computer records are simple to wipe,' Leapman was saying. 'But this had a human dimension.'

Diamond gave a nod. 'And you can't wipe humans so easily.'

Leapman glared in defiance.'I am not a killer. Sure, I could foresee problems with Dr Masuda. She was a real risk if she got to hear about PDM3. It was quite possible that she had a grudge against Manflex for what happened. I made some enquiries and learned that after her research was axed she stopped work altogether. She hadn't gone back since. So I flew to Yokohama to see her.'

'Independently – without telling the mafia?'

'Yes. My idea was to buy her good will. I'd get her back to work on coma research, using some safe drugs we'd developed recently. Then I would change her file to make it appear that we'd continued to sponsor her without a break. But there was a complication.'

'Naomi?'

'Excuse me?'

'The child. Naomi is what I call her.'

'Ah. I understand. Yes, discovering that the little girl existed was a real shock, and even more so when I found that she was autistic. She needed round-the-clock attention. The only way I could get Dr Masuda back to work was by finding a surrogate mother. Well, I discussed it with Dr Masuda. After seven years of caring for a kid who doesn't respond one bit, she was ready for a break if we could find someone. I agreed to meet the cost. She already knew a woman in the University who'd had a kid who died. She'd wanted to adopt, but she was a single parent and the adoption agencies wouldn't play ball.'

'Mrs Tanaka?'

'Right. There was no question of letting her adopt, but we were willing to let her care for the kid. In fact, she could take her on a vacation. It worked out quite neatly in theory. Mrs Tanaka knew the kid a bit. I put up the money for a trip to England, to get – what name did you give her?'

'Naomi.'

'. . . to get Naomi right away at the time I was planning to unseat Manny Flexner. PDM3 was going to be the resignation issue and it had to be watertight.'

'But why? Why go to so much trouble over a little girl?'

'Because she was the living proof that Dr Masuda quit researching in 1985. I could buy Dr Masuda's silence, but I couldn't explain away the child if someone did some digging.'

'Who did you fear? Manny?'

Leapman shook his head. 'He was unlikely to make the connection with Jantac, even though he dumped it himself. He wasn't really a scientist. No, the people I feared were outside the company. The medical press, the stock market analysts, our rivals in the drugs industry. They're damned quick in dredging up anything adverse they can find on a new drug. Nothing was published on Jantac, but somebody somewhere could have heard a whisper.'

'So you sent Mrs Tanaka to London with Naomi.'

'It seemed like a neat solution, but she fucked up everything. Everything. Maybe those adoption agencies knew something, because Mrs Tanaka couldn't cope. An autistic child was all too much, and one day she panicked and abandoned her in Harrods. The next thing it was all over the British press and on TV. It was a news story. There was even an item in the *New York Times*. Far from hushing up the child"s existence, we'd got it all over the media. Our billion-dollar project was about to blow up in our faces, all because of one small girl.'

'But nobody knew the child's identity,' Diamond reminded him.

Leapman erupted. 'For God's sake! Every tabloid in England and Japan wanted to know who the dumb kid in Harrods was. It was a great human interest story. Our papers carried it. The only question was which smart-ass pressman would be the first to trace her mother.'

'Through Mrs Tanaka? You're telling me that's why Mrs Tanaka had to be murdered?'

'Listen, I was facing annihilation myself. Soon as one of those guys got to Mrs Tanaka she would blow the whole project. She'd tell them about the arrangement with Dr Masuda. The connection with Manflex would be out in the open. All those wiseguys looking for some flaw in PDM3 would be alerted. I had to act fast, and I couldn't do it alone.'

'So you explained the problem to your mafia friends and they put out a contract on Mrs Tanaka.'

'Not my friends. And I was never a party to murder.'

'But you kept them informed. She must have got in touch with you before she flew to New York with Naomi.'

'Listen, you've got to understand that these people were breathing down my neck. When Manny committed suicide and nominated David to succeed him, my plans went—'

'Out of the window?' said Diamond with the suggestion

of a smile, but he could hardly have expected a laugh from Leapman at this point in his story and he didn't get one.

'I was horrified when I heard what they did to Mrs Tanaka. Appalled. And, you know, first of all, I thought the kid must be dead as well.'

'I never heard of the mafia killing a child.'

'Well, no.'

'But they didn't object to throwing me in the Hudson and leaving me for dead,' Diamond added.

'You were too close to the truth. When you fixed that meeting with David Flexner, they had to act.'

'Yes, how was that done? Am I right in thinking Flexner's room was bugged and you tipped off your mafia friends?'

'Listen, by that time, I was being threatened too. Those people don't forgive anything.'

'But that's how it was done?'

'Essentially, yes.' He hesitated. 'Should I apologize?'

Diamond shrugged. He could be magnanimous now. 'And what exactly was the purpose of coming here to Yokohama?'

'Quite simply, to liquidate Dr Masuda. I want to make it clear that I came under coercion. I was under constant threat of being murdered myself. Those two who travelled with me were mafia hitmen. I was to lead them to her and Naomi would be used as bait. They planned to drive into the country, kill Mrs Masuda and abandon Naomi.'

'Do you really think they would have let you live?'

Leapman pondered this for a moment. 'Maybe not. Like I said, I'm glad it's over. I don't mind giving evidence when all this comes to court. I've been a damned fool, Mr Diamond, but I was never a willing party to the violence.'

Diamond felt a twinge in his back as he got up to leave. He wasn't quite the fighting machine he'd appeared to be earlier. 'You say that, Mr Leapman, but you were blithely prepared to sentence untold numbers of Alzheimer's patients to serious liver damage and maybe death so that you could be rich and successful. In my book, that's on a par with murder.'

'Are you leaving?' Leapman asked, sidestepping the accusation.

'As soon as I can get a flight.'

'What will happen to me?'

'You'd better ask a lawyer. I dare say they'll extradite you in time to give evidence against Massimo Gatti and his hitmen.'

Leapman twitched.

'You'll be safe behind bars for a while,' Diamond reassured him. 'After that, there's always plastic surgery.'

On the way out, he was stopped by one of the clerical staff and invited into another office, where, unknown to him, Yuko Masuda and Naomi had been waiting. The interpreter followed him in.

Dr Masuda was standing hand in hand with Naomi. She bowed and delivered a little speech.

'She says that she has learned of all the trouble you took to help her daughter and the danger you faced. She says that you saved both their lives.'

'Mr Yamagata did that,' Diamond said.

'She insists that she owes her life to you. She would like to repay you in some way.'

'That isn't necessary.'

'Excuse me if I take the liberty of speaking myself,' the interpreter said. 'It is our way in Japan. If you can think of some small service she can perform, it will ease the burden of debt that she has to carry now. A token of gratitude. Small thing, but very important.'

He glanced towards Dr Masuda. 'In that case, what I would really like is to hold her daughter's hand for a moment.'

'I think that would satisfy decorum.'

After it was explained, Dr Masuda nodded.

Naomi was standing beside her, gazing at the wall.

Diamond took a step closer and offered his hand.

Dr Masuda said something in Japanese.

Naomi placed her hand in his. She didn't look up, or do anything else, but that was enough. It satisfied decorum for a Japanese lady and it brought a lump to the throat of an unsentimental Englishman.

The ceiling still wanted decorating in the basement flat in Addison Road.

'I'll get some more paint tomorrow,' he promised.

'A bit of a comedown after all your globetrotting,' Stephanie said.

'Not at all. Domestic life has its attractions.'

She smiled faintly. 'That doesn't sound like the man of action I read about in the paper this morning.'

'Man of action? With my figure?' He dismissed the idea with a laugh.

'You don't fancy yourself as a sumo wrestler, then?'

'No chance.'

'The paper says you tossed an armed man over your back. It says you're Britain's sumo champion.'

'Get away!'

'Really. Do you want to see.'

'No, it's rubbish, and we both know it. I'm just glad to be home with you.'

Her smile became more definite. 'Did you, by any chance, remember the sneakers?'

Big he may have been, but he felt himself shrinking. 'There just wasn't an opportunity. Sorry, my love.'

She said, 'I wouldn't have mentioned it, but you did phone me from New York to check the size.'

He got up abruptly to delve into the hold-all he'd brought back from Japan. He took out a shoe-box. 'But I got these for you yesterday afternoon in a Yokohama shoeshop. They don't look quite so comfortable as American sneakers, but I was told they're better for the feet. They call them *geta*.'

With anticipation she lifted the lid. Then she gave Diamond a frown. She lifted out a small pair of the traditional wood and leather flip-flops.

'No sneakers?'

He shook his head. He'd been tempted to call them Japanese sneakers, but there were limits.

She took off her shoes and tried on the *geta*.

'Do they fit?'

She tottered over and aimed a mock punch at him. 'You're the bloody limit. I suppose I can wear them around the house.'

'Good,' he said, removing Yamagata's *geta* from the bag. 'I was given this pair myself and I'd quite like to wear them sometimes.'

The Tooth Tattoo

Peter Lovesey

The Bath detective solves a perplexing case with an international reach.

Peter Diamond, head of Bath CID, takes a city break in Vienna, where his favourite film, *The Third Man*, was set, but everything goes wrong and his companion, Paloma, calls a halt to their relationship.

Meanwhile, strange things are happening to jobbing musician Mel Farran, who finds himself scouted by methods closer to the spy world than the concert platform. The chance of joining a once-famous string quartet in a residency at Bath Spa University is too tempting for Mel to refuse.

Then a body is found in the city canal, and the only clue to the dead woman's identity is the tattoo of a musical note on one of her teeth. For Diamond, who wouldn't know a Stradivarius from a French horn, the investigation is his most demanding ever. Three mysterious deaths need to be probed while his own personal life is in free fall . . .

Peter Lovesey has been hailed by the critics as 'superlative', 'a master of the genre', 'never puts a foot wrong' and the Peter Diamond series as 'one of the most enjoyable police series around'. This new case for the greatly loved detective will bring new praise and much satisfaction for his legions of fans.

Out now.

The Stone Wife

Peter Lovesey

The new Peter Diamond case has the eminent detective
in pursuit of a murderer after a theft at an auction house
goes wrong.

Just as the bidding gets exciting in a Bath auction house,
three armed men stage a hold-up and attempt to steal Lot
129, a medieval carving of the Wife of Bath. The highest
bidder, appalled to have the prize snatched away, tries to
stop them and is shot dead.

Peter Diamond, head of the murder squad, soon finds
himself sharing an office with the stone wife – until he
is ejected. To his extreme annoyance the lump of stone
appears to exert a malign influence over him and his
investigation. Refusing to be beaten, he rallies his team
and begins finding suspects and motives.

The case demands that someone goes undercover. The
dangerous mission falls to Sergeant Ingeborg Smith,
reverting to her journalist persona to get the confidence
of a wealthy local criminal through his pop star girlfriend.
And soon, murder makes a reappearance . . .

Out now.